# WHISPERS FROM THE COVE

SMOKY MOUNTAIN SECRETS SAGA, BOOK 1

JEANNE HARDT

James – I hope you'll enjoy this new series!
Jeanne Hardt

Cover design by Rae Monet, Inc.
Edited by Cindy Brannam
Book formatting by Jesse Gordon

# CHAPTER 1

"They're comin'!" Lucas yelled. His frantic green eyes told Lily everything she needed to know.

She threw aside the socks she'd been darning and sprang to her feet. Her little brother huffed and puffed, nearly out of breath.

"How close are they, Lucas?" their ma asked, frantically helping Violet, Lily's sixteen-year-old sister, push the chestnuts they'd been cracking into a bucket.

"Don't know." Lucas leaned over and braced his hands on his knees. "I ran fast as I could when I heard the horn." Their closest neighbors had grandkids who kept watch at the entrance to the valley. They blew on their grandpa's hunting horn at any sign of trouble.

Life in the cove changed when the war came. After coping with this for three years, they instinctively knew what to do.

Lily's ma yanked up one of the floorboards and stuffed their scant food underneath, then covered it with a large rug. They all helped her move the wood table and chairs atop it.

Violet grabbed their pa's rifle, and Horace, the seven-year-old, managed the small wood box filled with barely enough ammunition to matter. They raced out the door. They'd hide the weapon in a hollowed-out log, then return to the house to act as if nothing was amiss.

Early on, it had been Lily's responsibility to guide their milk cow to a cave. Sadly, the soldiers had found it months ago. It hadn't been easy to hide her, and not just because of her size. She'd made too much noise that day. Even so, Lily had a hard time forgiving herself for not saving her. The soldiers had feasted on their dear Gertie, and now their family had no milk.

Truthfully, they had next-to-nothing—two chickens and a small pig were all that remained.

"Catch your breath, Lucas," Lily said. "Then go after the hens."

"I know." He shook his head and huffed. "You talk like I ain't done this before. I'll go where I always take 'em."

Their ma jerked her head toward the front door. "You *both* need to get goin'."

"Yes'm," Lily said.

She and Lucas raced to the barn. The hens were a bit harder to nab than the pig, so Lily helped Lucas first. Once he got one tucked under each arm, he hurried off and took them up the mountainside.

No one in the family knew when it was safe to go home again, but the soldiers rarely stayed deep in the woods after the sun set. Lucas and Lily would have to hide till dark.

She took hold of Penny. The piglet squealed, flipping and flopping in Lily's arms. It was all she could do to wrap her hands around Penny's snout to keep her quiet.

Lily tightened her hold, then fled up the hillside into the thick brush. She purposefully went in the opposite direction as her brother. They never hid in the same place. If one of them got caught, at least the other might be spared.

Her littlest brother, Isaac, was only five, so he stayed behind with her folks. Her ma tended him, while her pa sat helpless in a rocking chair in the corner of their four-room cabin. The man could do a lot more to help, but self-pity kept him from even trying. Lily did her best not to fault him for it, however—at times like this, they needed him.

Her heart pounded. Not so much from the climb, or from wrestling Penny, but from anxious fear.

It could be Captain Ableman coming to check on them. Though despicable in his own right, at least he wasn't too hard on the family. Unlike the renegade soldiers who went so far as to take the shoes off her pa's feet. Captain Ableman respected the fact that her pa had fought with the confederacy. He might not be so kind if he knew it hadn't been her pa's choice.

Penny fought Lily more than usual. The pig had gotten almost too big to tote around. She'd become Isaac's pet after their dog went by the wayside.

The piglet had been snuck over to their house by their neighbor. The same one whose grandkids blew the horn. Bringing Penny was one of the kindest acts Mrs. Quincy had ever done. She'd said that splitting up the litter was the only way to save them. Too many in one place, and they'd all be goners.

"Shh," Lily hissed into the pig's ear. "Or you'll be bacon by nightfall."

Being late September, leaves had just begun to fall, yet few covered the ground. Numerous sticks and underbrush crunched under Lily's feet. She tried her best to tread lightly, keeping her ears attuned to everything around her, and praying she wouldn't hear any other footsteps, or be heard herself.

She shouldered a lot of responsibility for her family. At seventeen, she was the eldest child. Had she been a boy, she'd have been drug off to fight like her pa.

Being born a female might've been a blessing, but she had her own war to wage. Soldiers took a shining to most any girl they could get their hands on, but not to romance them. Lily's ma had warned her and Violet both that the men had only one thing in mind, and *love* had nothing to do with it.

Damp warmth soaked the front of Lily's dress.

"No," she mumbled and held Penny away from her. "You wet on me."

The pig grunted and squirmed. Lily's brief ease on her hold allowed the animal to twist free. She landed on the ground and raced away, squealing.

Lily lifted her long skirt and sprinted after her, rounding a mass of thick trees.

A heavy hand grabbed her by the waist. Another covered her mouth.

"Shh," the stranger breathed into her ear. "They're close."

Her heart raced. She struggled to break free, only to have him tighten his grasp. "Don't fight me. I'm tryin' to help." He kept his firm hold and wrestled her backward to the ground.

His musky male scent filled her nose. Each breath she took came harder and faster. Her eyes shifted down to the large filthy hand pressed securely to her mouth, and the long dirty coat sleeve with worn-out tattered cuffs.

*Union blue.*

Though a mess, his uniform was unmistakable.

He breathed heavily beneath her. He had her pinned atop him with one arm secured around her middle and both his legs wrapped around hers. She couldn't move if she wanted to. Which, of course, she did. No man had the right to hold her this way.

She lay helplessly and listened to Penny's far-off cry, followed by cackling laughter and the roar of victorious soldiers. "We got us our supper!"

She whimpered, unable to help herself. She'd failed again. How would she ever explain it to Isaac?

She could only hope that Lucas had gotten away with the chickens. Her family needed the eggs. Winter was coming and food would be even scarcer.

"They're leavin'," the man whispered. "Lay still. I ain't gonna hurt you." His thick whiskers rubbed roughly across her cheek.

She blew heavy breaths through her nose, not trusting him one bit. Soldiers were soldiers. No matter what color they wore, they all wanted the same thing. Something she wasn't about to give.

Aside from a breeze blowing through the branches above, silence surrounded them.

He relaxed his hold.

She'd learned a valuable lesson from Penny and flipped her body around. With as much force as she could, she smacked his shoulder, trying to break free.

He winced and groaned, but tightened the grip of his legs and grabbed her arm.

She glanced at her hand, now sticky and moist.

*Blood.*

"I said I'm tryin' to help you." He kept his voice barely above a whisper. "Them soldiers was almost on ya. No pig is worth that. You should have more sense than goin' off alone in the woods with the likes a them about."

She glared at him. If her mouth wasn't covered, she'd give him a piece of her mind.

"If I take my hand away, you gotta swear you won't scream. All right?" His eyes penetrated hers. "It wouldn't be smart." He cocked his head to the side. "Can I trust you?"

She nodded into his hand, and he slowly lowered it.

"I have more sense than you do," she harshly whispered. "You coulda had us both killed if they'd seen you."

"I took my chances. I figured if you was hidin' from them, maybe you was a Unionist."

She wriggled in his grasp. "Let go a me."

"You gonna yell for them an' turn me in?"

"Course not. I ain't ignorant."

He eased his grip on her legs and released her. She quickly scooted off him and sat on the cool soil. *He* remained flat on his back.

The bedraggled man looked as if he'd been in the wild for some time. Covered in filth, completely unkempt, and worse yet, he smelled wretched. His uniform was not only torn in places, it also had two bullet holes and blood stains. The instant she'd gotten off him, he covered the one on his shoulder.

Lily eyed the spot. "*They* shoot ya?"

"Yeah. But I got away." He cast a dour half-grin.

She shook her head. "Funny. Like I couldn't a figured that out myself. As I told you, I ain't ignorant. An' by the looks of that hole in your chest, you should be dead."

His face fell, the grin completely gone. He brushed his hand over the tattered material. "Supplies ain't easy to come by. Like uniforms. *That* hole was put in another soldier. I inherited the coat."

"Lucky for you." She peered closer at his shoulder. "You need tendin'. A wound like that could cost you your arm if it gets infected."

He closed his eyes and nodded. "I'm aware. But I don't rightly care. I ain't got nowhere to go, an' I don't wanna fight no more. I'm done with it."

"So . . ." Lily crossed her arms and narrowed her eyes. "You just gonna lay here an' die?"

"Reckon I will."

"I can't let that happen. You might a saved my life for all I know. Least my *chastity*."

His eyes widened and his cheeks turned a deeper shade of red.

"I'm only speakin' the truth," she went on, undaunted by his discomfort. "You know it yourself. An' so you'll understand me better, you should know I ain't shy 'bout sayin' what's on my mind."

"I already figured that out." Another grimace of pain covered his face. His eyes squinted shut.

"It wouldn't be safe for us to go now," she whispered. "Though they got our pig, there might be other soldiers at the cabin. We need to stay here till dark. Think you'll *survive*?" She probably shouldn't have said it with so much sarcasm.

"Maybe. Less I bleed to death."

She huffed, then bent over and tore a long strip from the base of her skirt. "Ma won't be happy I done that, but we need to stop the bleedin'." She shifted onto her knees and faced him. "Unbutton your coat, so I can get a better look."

He eyed her, then made an effort. He grimaced whenever he moved his arm. So, she took it upon herself to help him finish with the buttons. It might've been forward on her part. However, she didn't care. Not after he'd been so forthright manhandling *her*.

The lightweight cotton shirt underneath his coat had fresh red stains, from his mid-chest upward to his left shoulder.

She wasted no time and untied the shirt strings at his neck to loosen it, then lifted the fabric and peered beneath.

"Hmm . . ." She blew out a breath. "It ain't pretty." Though she tried to focus on the injury, she had difficulty keeping her eyes off the mass of dark hair on his chest. The man resembled a bear in more ways than one.

He sat partway up, twisting in an obvious attempt to see what she meant, then let his head fall back onto the ground. "Hurts like hell."

She pursed her lips. "Reckon so. But you'd best get all your cursin' done now. Ma don't take kindly to that kind a talk."

"Sorry."

"No need to apologize to *me*. I've heard worse." She offered him a smile. Not sure where it came from, still she did it nonetheless. "I'd cuss myself, if I had a hole that size in me."

She carefully folded the cloth from her dress, pressed it to the wound, then covered it again with his shirt and coat. "Hold your hand here as hard as you can. It'll slow the bleedin'. Once I get you home, Ma will doctor you up."

He did as told, and she refastened the buttons on his coat.

"Thank you," he said, expressionless.

Something lay behind his eyes. More hurt than that of a wound. But it made sense. The war scarred everyone in many ways.

She studied his face even closer. Under all that facial hair, the man *might* be handsome. He had thicker hair than hers. Dark, wavy, and decorated with bits of grass and leaves. And though his brown eyes held sadness, she could also see kindness. He'd proven it by the way he'd protected her. Nevertheless, she wouldn't let her guard down.

She moved a short distance and sat, leaning against a tree. His heavy stench had begun to wear on her. "What's your name?"

"Caleb Henry. Yours?"

"I'm Lily. Lily Larsen."

"Sounds like a songbird. It's a nice name."

"I *don't* sing." They kept their voices low, yet it felt odd conversing at all with danger potentially close.

She scooped up a fistful of leaves, then tossed them into the air. "You sure them soldiers left?"

"They got their meal. They'd been tracking me for miles. I reckon they figure I'll bleed out. Your pig was more important than a lone Yank."

"Poor Penny." Lily mindlessly flung another handful of leaves.

"You shouldn't name your livestock. I'd think a mountain girl like you would know that."

"She was my brother's pet. We had a dog, but the soldiers ate him, too."

"Sorry." Caleb eased upright, still clutching his shoulder. "So . . . where exactly am I? I've been on the run over these mountains so long, I'm a little disoriented."

"Cades Cove."

"Tennessee?"

"Yep. You ever heard of it before? Cades Cove, that is."

"No. Not too familiar with many small places in Tennessee. I headed into the Smokies from North Carolina. My home's in Waynesville. Ever heard a *that*?"

Lily jutted her chin upward. "Yep. Reckon I'm smarter than you. But why are you wearin' blue an' not gray?"

Caleb looked away. "Most a North Carolina supports the Union."

"Good."

His head snapped around, and he faced her again. "*Good*?"

"Yep. Lotsa folks in the cove do, too. Truth be told, one a the reasons the rebels are so hard on us is because one of our preachers spoke openly 'bout supportin' the Union. Soldiers came in an' run him outta town. We haven't had services in years. Reckon we won't till the war's over."

"An' that's why the rebels try an' take all you got?"

"Partly. The preacher got 'em riled up. But not everyone agreed with him. Loyalties are divided between the North and South. Most of us keep to ourselves now, an' simply do all we can to survive."

"What 'bout your ma?" Caleb moistened his cracked dry lips. "Will she take kindly to you bringin' me home?"

Lily hugged her knees to her chest and sighed. "She's a fine Christian woman who'd help most anyone. That bein' said, she an' Pa will both be glad you're wearin' blue. Though my pa did his duty and served the confederacy, he never wanted to fight. For either side. We just wanted to be left alone. We had a good thing here. Plenty a crops. Livestock—even cattle. Now we barely have enough to keep from starvin'."

"So, your pa's there, too? At your cabin? How'd he get outta fightin'?"

"He couldn't hold his weapon anymore. Hard to do with only one arm."

"Oh." Caleb's eyes shifted downward. "I'm sorry to hear it."

"Now you know why I understand how important it is to fix you up."

They sat in silence.

Lily closed her eyes and prayed her family was all right. As many times as they'd done this, she couldn't erase the fear of losing them all one day. Too many folks in the cove had already lost loved ones.

*If the world don't get right soon, I might as well just shrivel up an' die myself.*

She shook her head to dismiss the thought. She'd never been one to wallow in self-pity. Even so, her life shouldn't be like this. Her ma got married at sixteen—younger than her. Started having babies right away. That's what Lily wanted.

Not this.

# CHAPTER 2

Caleb trembled, suddenly chilled. He assumed it had more to do with his injury than the falling temperature.

He glanced over at Lily, who seemed to be engrossed with the leaves and dirt she kept picking up from the ground. Maybe it was her way of keeping her eyes and mind off him.

After he'd gotten beyond her sarcasm and ill-demeanor, he'd decided she was pretty. Even in a plain brown dress. Though she was too thin, she had a comely face. She kept her light blond hair loosely braided down her back. He could imagine the long locks set free—it would look might fine. Sadly, her fair skin bore rugged-looking lines. Deep insets of worry on her brow. Something no young woman should bear.

She had every right to be poor-tempered. He'd practically attacked her. He'd simply reacted on instinct and hadn't had time to think of another way to keep her quiet. He'd done it for her own good.

A part of him wished he'd not found her. But once he had, he couldn't let the rebels get their hands on her. He'd witnessed what wicked men do to helpless females. He already hated himself for letting things happen in his past that he could've stopped.

*Never again.*

He didn't want to be afraid anymore. Sure, it would've been easier ignoring her. He could've just let the men have her, then laid down and let the blood drain from his body. If he'd done that, he could've forgotten *everything* . . .

His head whirled. Or maybe the world spun around him. "Lily?"

"Yeah?"

"I don't feel quite right. Things are gettin' blurry."

She jumped to her feet and leaned over him. "You're sweatin' sumthin' fierce. You must be burnin' up."

"No. I'm cold."

"I best get you home. We'll just pray them soldiers ain't there." She knelt beside him. "Put your arm 'round my shoulder. I'll help you up."

Regardless of being thin, Lily had surprising strength. She lifted him onto his feet with ease. The second he took a breath, he inhaled something rank. "What's that awful smell?"

She gave him a sideways glance. "*You*. Sorry, but you stink. I reckon it's been a while since you've had a bath."

He took no offense. "I know my own stench, and that's not what I'm smellin'. It's more like . . . *urine*."

She gulped, then cleared her throat. "Oh. Well, it ain't *mine*. You can thank Penny for that. I reckon her nerves got the best of her. She wet on me."

If Caleb wasn't so broken, he'd laugh. He'd begun to like this outspoken girl.

Fearing he might stumble, he kept a tight hold on her as they made their way down the hillside. He did his best to take in his surroundings. He'd seen his share of trees over the past month, but this area was exceptionally beautiful. Beech and maples were prominent. In another month, the hillside would be ablaze with a multitude of colors.

Truthfully, he found it a bit odd he could appreciate *any* kind of beauty anymore.

The ground leveled off and they eased out of the woods. Lily abruptly stopped. Her head jerked from side to side. "Don't see no one," she whispered, "but we're takin' a big chance comin' out in the open."

He understood her fear, yet he felt a sense of calm. He'd always had a sixth sense about danger. "I have a feelin' they took the pig an' left."

"Hope you're right." She took a large breath, then started moving again.

They passed a crystal-like, trickling creek, then came to a large clearing. To the right was a small log cabin with smoke billowing from the chimney. Beyond it, a vast beautiful valley.

"Incredible," he mumbled.

"Cades Cove," she whispered. "Loveliest place ever there was. I pray we can keep it that way."

"I can see why." Even fuzzy, he could easily discern its magnificence.

He grunted when a jolt of pain made him stumble.

Lily tightened her hold. "Just a little further. I aim to set you in the woodshed till I go in an' make sure the soldiers ain't inside."

He gave a slight nod, then slowed his breathing to try and minimize the discomfort.

She guided him behind the cabin to a three-sided structure stacked with chopped wood. "Pa used to chop as we needed it. Said it burned longer if it wasn't all dried out. Nowadays, we chop when we can an' try to stay on top of it. Worst thing we could do is let it run out. 'Specially with the weather gettin' colder."

"I wish I could help," he mumbled. "But I ain't much good for no one no more."

"Stop feelin' sorry for yourself. You're alive. You should be grateful." She lowered him to the ground and propped him against the woodpile.

Her reprimand stung. He scarcely knew the girl, yet for some reason, her opinion of him mattered. He lowered his eyes and stared at the ground.

"I'm gonna go in," she said just as sternly. "If it's safe, I'll tell my folks you're out here, then come back for you. Don't go doin' nothin' silly, like runnin' off somewhere. All right?"

*I couldn't if I wanted to.*

He lifted his head to meet her gaze and found her standing in front of him with her hands on her hips. "*All right*?" she repeated, more forcefully this time.

Why she cared so much had him stumped.

He drew his legs up to his chest to help steady himself. "I won't go anywhere." He felt he might topple over at any moment.

"An' keep pressure on that wound, you hear?" She hurried away before he could respond.

* * *

Lily hesitated on the front porch to gather some courage. She'd need it. Even if there weren't soldiers inside, she had to figure out how to tell her folks about Caleb.

She hadn't lied about her ma tending anyone who needed it, but she wouldn't take kindly to Lily bringing home a rebel. Her ma blamed the confederacy for all their troubles. After all, a band of rebels had forced Lily's pa to go to war. And though her pa's arm was lost at the hand of a Yankee, for some strange reason, her ma didn't put the blame on the northerner.

Lily saw the bigger picture. The war was two-sided, and *both* were at fault.

She constantly prayed for peace.

Standing tall, she inched the door open and peered inside. The sound of Isaac crying greeted her. He lay cuddled against her ma in the rocking chair.

Her pa stood at the front window staring out the glass.

"Oh, Lily!" Violet rushed across the room and embraced her. "We've been so worried."

"I'm fine." She quickly scanned around her. "Where's Lucas?"

"He ain't back yet." Violet released her hold. "We keep hopin' they didn't find him. Or the hens. After we found out 'bout Penny—"

Isaac bawled harder.

"Shh," her ma whispered, presumably more for Violet than for Isaac. "It's all right now." She said *those* words to him.

Violet grabbed Lily's hand. "A soldier came in while others were ransackin' the house. He said they got them a pig, so they all left. Horace climbed up in one a the trees an' watched them wander away 'cross the valley. I doubt they'll come back anytime soon. They got ill when they couldn't find no food."

"Good. Let 'em get ill. Long as they didn't hurt no one."

Violet lowered her eyes. "They was lookin' at me, Lily. In a way that made me feel sick inside."

Lily hugged her. "We'll be fine. This war hasta end sometime soon. Then the good an' decent men will return to the cove, an' things will be normal again."

Their pa turned from the window and grunted. "Ain't never gonna happen."

Lily sealed her lips and thrust her chin in the air. She wouldn't cross her pa, but she aimed to keep hope alive. At least in her heart.

"What happened to you out there?" Violet asked. "How'd you lose Penny?"

Lily let go of Violet's hand and knelt beside her ma and Isaac. Her little brother needed the explanation more than anyone.

"Penny wiggled outta my arms. The silly pig wet on me, an' I'm afraid I let loose enough that she got free. I'm sorry, Isaac."

He merely sniffled in response.

She smoothed her hand over his head. "Someday, I'll get you another one. At least, cuz a Penny, they left. Maybe they won't come back ever again." She looked directly at her ma. "Was it Ableman an' his men?"

"No. These soldiers had no leader. They was rebels thinkin' they was entitled to whatever they please. Found no food, but took one a our best quilts." Her hateful tone softened into a tender smile. "I'm glad you're all right, Lily."

"I might not a been, if a man hadn't saved me." The words came out easily, but the gasps around the room caused her stomach to roil.

"Man?" her ma asked, no longer smiling. "What man?"

"The one wearing Union blue that I stuck in the woodshed till I knew them soldiers wasn't inside."

Her pa moved beside her. "You put a Yankee in the woodshed?"

"Yessir. He's injured. Even so, he stopped me from runnin' right into them rebels."

"Violet," her pa barked out. "Horace. Go with your sister an' bring the man in. Do it now 'fore someone else happens by."

"Yes, Pa," they said in unison.

Lily hurried them out the door.

* * *

Caleb closed his eyes. His arm had started to ache from the pressure he kept on his shoulder.

The bleeding had slowed—maybe even stopped, but the worst was yet to come. The bullet would have to be removed, and it was lodged deep in his flesh. He'd surely lose more blood.

The sound of footsteps reopened his eyes. To his relief, it was Lily, followed by a boy and a girl who looked slightly older than him.

The boy eyed him. "Lawdy, you wasn't foolin'."

"Course not," Lily said. "I'd never lie 'bout sumthin' so important."

Though Caleb didn't know Lily well, he had a feeling she wouldn't lie about much of anything.

The other girl, no doubt Lily's sister, cupped a hand over her mouth and nose. "He needs a bath," she whispered, but he easily heard her.

He found it hard to believe he reeked that bad. Maybe he'd just gotten used to the smell.

Lily knelt beside him, the same way she had in the forest. "We can take you inside now. Pa said to bring you right in."

The boy went to his other side, but the girl gently pushed him away. "I'll help him, Horace. I'm stronger than you."

Horace stuck out his lower lip. "Not for long. Pa says I'm growin' every day."

The girls lifted Caleb to his feet.

Lily jerked her head toward her sister. "That's Violet."

"Hey," Caleb managed to mumble. Not a very kind response to an introduction, yet he couldn't do more.

Violet's nose wrinkled, and it looked as if she tried to smile. His offensive odor obviously bothered her. More so than it had Lily.

They guided him slowly to the covered front porch. Horace opened the door and held it while they went inside.

An older woman—he assumed to be their ma—was bent over in front of the fireplace, examining the contents of a pot. The heavy cast iron vessel rested above the flames, suspended from a pot hanger.

She lifted her head as the girls led Caleb to a chair at a wood table. The small-framed woman wasn't *ugly*, but had hardened features. Her hair formed into a tight bun at the top of her head. Without any strands framing her face, she appeared even harsher. Not a woman he wanted to cross.

"I'm heatin' water," she said. "Figgered we'd need it for wound-cleanin'." She eyed him up and down, then shook her head. "We could be in for a heap a trouble havin' you here."

"Sorry," he muttered. He once again closed his eyes and shifted uncomfortably on the hard chair. The pain from his shoulder had worked its way upward. His head pounded.

"That's my ma," Lily said. "An' this here's Pa. They'll know how to fix you up."

"Get his coat off," her pa said. "I need to see the wound."

Caleb kept his eyes shut. He couldn't bear to look at the one-armed man right now. Not when he could very well lose his, too.

Lily worked the buttons on Caleb's coat, then Violet helped her pull it from his arms and off his body. He shivered. The fireplace held large flaming logs, but he couldn't shake the chill.

Lily removed the blood-soaked fabric that she'd placed over his wound. He could've sworn her ma grunted. Dresses weren't easy to come by, and though Lily's plain garment was by no means *new*, the girl had willingly damaged it. Something they couldn't afford.

When she peeled away the shirt from his shoulder, he winced. Some of the fabric had adhered to his skin.

"Sorry, Caleb," she said. "We gotta get *this* off, too."

He opened his eyes a sliver and met her gaze. The worry lines on her brow deepened.

Her two little brothers hovered close, watching every move she made. Wide-eyed, curious, and *cautious*.

"Horace. Isaac," their pa said. "Back away."

They immediately obeyed.

The stern man received respect from the entire household. Caleb wanted to show his own, so this time, he kept his eyes on him.

Mr. Larsen leaned close and examined the wound, then gently brought Caleb's body forward with his remaining hand and peered at his back. "No exit wound. Lead's still in there."

Caleb sluggishly bobbed his head.

Mr. Larsen dug into his pocket, pulled out a pocketknife, and flipped it open. "Heat this real good in the embers, Rose." He handed it to his wife.

Now that Caleb got a good look at the man, aside from his lack of a limb, he appeared hardy. He bore strong facial features, with deep-set lines like Lily's, and those same kind eyes. The salt and pepper coloring in his beard and hair showed his age. Caleb assumed him to be near forty. Slightly older than *Mrs.* Larsen.

"You gonna cut him, Pa?" Horace asked.

"Have to. Gotta get the bullet out."

Little Isaac buried his face against Violet's skirt. "C'mon, Isaac," she said. "We don't need to watch." She took his hand and led him to the rocker, where she sat and lifted him onto her lap.

"Go get my shine." Mr. Larsen pointed at Horace. "You know where I hide it."

"Yes, Pa." The boy ran off and headed out the front door.

Mr. Larsen faced Caleb again. "Rose'll clean the wound good, then I'll dig out the slug. Be glad I'm right-handed. If you'd like, you can have a swig a my moonshine 'fore I cut. Might help a tad. It's good corn liquor. We'll pour some on the wound to keep it from gettin' infected."

Caleb had never been one to indulge in alcohol of any sorts. Being in pain could very well change his mind.

Lily stood back with her hands folded in front herself and kept quiet. Odd to see her that way, when she'd been so verbal. However, since her folks had taken charge, it made sense.

Mrs. Larsen came to the table, toting the pot of water. She set it down, then dipped a rag into it. "It's hot, but not boilin'. Won't scald you." She twisted the cloth and wrung it out, then ran it over the wound.

Caleb squeezed his eyes tight.

"Once we take care a this," she said, "we'll bring in the tub from the shed an' heat more water for a bath. You need it."

So he'd been told. *Several* times.

She finished her task, then lay the rag down.

"When I start cuttin'," Mr. Larsen said to her. "I'll need you to hold his shoulder." She'd no doubt act as his other hand.

The man retrieved the knife from the flames, held it in a cloth with his one hand, and returned to the table. Using his leg, he scooted another chair close to Caleb, then sat and faced him squarely.

"I need more light," he said to Lily. "Bring the lantern close."

She lifted the lamp from a stand beside a small green upholstered sofa. The piece of furniture seemed out of place amidst all the wood furnishings. Though slightly worn, it was finer than the other items.

It helped Caleb to focus on something other than the coming pain. But when the light flickered in Lily's trembling hand, he knew that she, too, understood what he faced.

She grabbed hold of the lantern with *both* hands and steadied it.

Horace came back in holding a jug. He set it on the table.

"Want it?" Mr. Larsen asked Caleb.

"Yessir."

"Rose." Mr. Larsen tilted his head toward the jug. "Give the man a drink."

She took the container, held it to Caleb's lips, then tipped it up.

The liquid burned going down, and he struggled to keep from coughing it out again. A few swigs might not help at all, then again, he figured it couldn't hurt. He sputtered a bit, then drank a good amount.

"Pour some on the knife," Mr. Larsen said.

His wife did as instructed. A whispered sizzle came from the still-hot metal.

"Now, close your eyes," the man said, dryly. "Think 'bout sumthin' good."

Caleb's lids pinched together. His ma's face came to mind, soon replaced by Lily's. It was easier thinking about someone new, than someone he'd hurt.

His body jerked as moonshine trickled into the wound. He gritted his teeth and slowly drew air through his nose. He'd barely recovered from the shock, when the hot blade pierced into his flesh. Every breath he took grew more rapid, and sweat beaded on his brow. He bit down harder. Excruciating pain replaced every other thought.

The man cut deeper. "It knicked the bone, but it ain't shattered. You're lucky."

Air hissed from Caleb's nostrils. He tightened his fists, fighting the agony.

"No," the man said. "You gotta relax."

Caleb eased the fingers open on his left hand, while keeping the right firmly clenched.

"Just 'bout got it." Mr. Larsen twisted the knife deep inside Caleb's shoulder.

Fresh blood trickled down his chest. As far as the knife was buried, it'd surely come out his back.

He groaned. His heavy breaths intensified.

*Dyin' woulda been easier.*

"You're doin' fine," Lily whispered. "Hold on just a little longer."

Caleb's head spun fast, as if the chair he was on turned in circles.

"Got it," the man muttered and removed the knife.

Caleb let out a long breath. His shoulders relaxed and dropped.

The man released his own huff of air. "Be glad you wasn't hit with one a them mini balls. It woulda shattered your arm. I know from experience."

Caleb started to open his eyes when a jolt of pain pinched them shut again. "Ugh!" He clamped onto the seat of his chair. Mrs. Larsen had covered his mangled flesh with more moonshine.

"Don't move," Mr. Larsen grumbled. "I'm almost done with ya." He stood.

Caleb panted. His chest heaved every time he exhaled. "What now?"

The man returned to the fireplace and stuck the knife back into the embers. "Gotta seal the wound."

This time when he wielded the knife in front of Caleb, he didn't waste a second. He pressed the hot steel against Caleb's raw skin.

He screamed. The horrid smell of burnt flesh sickened him. A rush of pain swept from head to toe.

Everything went black.

# CHAPTER 3

Lily knelt beside Caleb. Her ma had laid out blankets for him on the floor, not far from the fireplace, and her pa had been generous enough to give him a shirt to wear. It wouldn't be an easy item for her pa to replace, but Caleb's blood-soaked garment had to be thrown away.

"I can't believe he passed out," Violet said over Lily's shoulder.

Lily felt an overwhelming need to defend him. "He was hurtin', an' I reckon he hadn't eaten in days. He was already lightheaded."

"Wish he woulda had a bath first." Violet waved her hand in front of her face, then wandered off to the kitchen and started helping their ma with supper.

She'd already been fussing about another mouth to feed. Maybe once Caleb got well, he could hunt. Make up for whatever they rationed out for him.

Lily agreed that a bath would do him good, but she'd never fault him for fainting. Uncomfortable as it might be, he looked right peaceful lying on their floor. Better for him to sleep than fight the pain.

"Lily," her ma fussed. "Leave him alone. Come help."

"Yes, Ma." She reluctantly left his side and crossed to her. "Shouldn't I go look for Lucas? It's almost dark. It ain't like you need my help with the food. There's barely enough to matter."

"Don't take that attitude." Her ma held up a single finger. "We hafta be thankful for every morsel. But you're right 'bout Lucas. He might not know them soldiers is gone. Go on an' fetch him, just don't go yellin'. We don't wanna risk a stray rebel hearin' ya."

"I won't." Lily glanced a final time at Caleb before walking out. He still hadn't stirred.

She headed up the hillside on the opposite end of the cabin. The side Lucas always went when they heard a warning. There was a cave-like burrow in the mountain about halfway up. She assumed he'd be there.

Regrettably, she found it empty.

Her heart pattered harder. She'd been so sure he was fine, but now . . .

"Ouch!" Something hard struck the top of her head, then bounced off into the underbrush.

She peered upward.

"Good aim, huh?" Lucas laughed. "Got you real good!"

"Why, you little—" She pinched her lips together to keep from saying what she shouldn't. "What are you doin' up in that tree?"

"Hidin'. Just what I's s'posed to do."

Now that she could see him clearer, she noticed a hen tucked under each of his arms. "How'd you get up there with them birds?"

"Weren't easy. Can you help me get 'em down?"

She huffed—not in the mood to climb trees—but did it regardless. She eased up onto the branches beneath him and held out her hands for one of the chickens. "This is the silliest thing you ever done. You coulda broke your neck."

"Might still." He grinned. Her red-headed brother was the most rambunctious of the three boys. A twelve-year-old, who'd do most anything. For attention, or just for the heck of it.

She never would've imagined a chicken could look scared, but the brown hen in Lily's arms had eyes as wide as the eggs it laid.

Lily carefully made her way back to the ground. Lucas practically shimmied down the tree, clutching his own bird.

"Ma's fixin' supper," she said and jerked her head toward the cabin. "Oh, an' we got a guest."

"Huh?" Lucas wrinkled his nose, crinkling the freckles on his face.

"A Yankee. Pa cut a bullet outta his shoulder."

"No foolin'?"

"He's sleepin' right now on the floor." She hurried down the hill. If Caleb had woken up, he might need her.

Lucas followed right on her heels. "Did he scream when Pa cut him?"

"*No.*" She wasn't about to tell him that Caleb yelled when their pa cauterized the wound. Why let her brother enjoy someone else's misery? "But I know he was hurtin'."

"Dang. I hate I missed it." He pushed past her and increased his pace.

"Watch your mouth, Lucas Larsen. Ma'd wash it with soap if she heard you cussin'."

"Pa says it all the time."

"He's a grownup. You ain't." She leered at him.

Unfortunately, he'd gotten too far ahead of her to see it. He kept going, unbothered by her reprimand. Sooner or later, his attitude would get him in trouble.

At least he'd saved the chickens.

They carried the hens inside the house for the time being.

Cleaning up after them would be an added chore, but they couldn't risk losing them. Tomorrow they'd scout the area and make sure no one else was about. Then, the birds could be put in their pen again.

One wandered a bit too close to Caleb, so Lily shooed it away as quietly as she could.

Caleb stirred, then moaned.

She bent down and eased her hand onto his forehead.

*He's burnin' up.*

Not good at all.

Her ma stood close by, carefully removing potatoes from the embers in the fireplace.

"Ma," she whispered. "He's feverish."

The woman peered his way, then returned her attention to their meager food. "Go tell your pa. He can take a look at 'im."

She didn't appear to be at all bothered by Lily's revelation. Though her ma was a good-hearted woman, Lily believed she'd prefer to have Caleb die. While he lived, they were obligated to feed him. Christian charity warranted it, which meant less for all of them. No ma wanted her babies to starve, however, strangers were another matter. She bore no love for Caleb.

Lily went outside to find her pa. Since he wasn't in the house, that meant he'd either gone to the outhouse or to the barn to check his stash of moonshine. He might've wanted to make sure Horace secured the hiding place. More than likely, the man was indulging again.

She wandered into the barn and went to the far end. Her pa had built a false wall behind one of the stalls. Unless you knew about it, you couldn't see the narrow storage area. It looked like the rest of the barn—old and worn out. It even had open crossbeams to make it seem like an unfinished wall.

Along with the liquor, the small space held a few family treasures: her ma's wedding ring, two gold necklaces that had belonged to Lily's grandma, and the deed to their property.

"Pa? You in there?" She entered the stall and noticed the small opening slightly ajar.

Her pa's face appeared in the crack. "Sumthin' wrong?"

She crossed to him. The unmistakable scent of alcohol wafted over her. He'd been tipping the jug again.

"Caleb's runnin' a fever."

The man's head disappeared. Moments later, he inched out, then quickly shut the makeshift-door. With a small tug, he made sure it was tight and secure.

"Fever don't surprise me none," the man finally said. His words sounded a bit slurred. His moonshine-scented breath would likely catch fire if she lit a match to it. "His body's fightin' to heal itself. Reckon he'll be fine. Get some cool . . ." He waved his hand in the air as if trying to catch the right word. ". . . cool *water.* Yeah. Some water. Put it on a cloth to wipe him down. That'll help a mite."

She decided not to draw attention to his obvious impairment. "What if the wound's infected deep inside?"

"Time'll tell." He staggered through the barn. "Your ma got supper ready?"

"What little there is. Taters, carrots, and nuts is all we got for t'night."

"Nuff to fill our bellies." He turned and faced her. "Lucas get back?"

"Yessir. I went after him. The hens are fine, too. Maybe we'll have a few eggs by mornin'." Lucky for them, the soldiers hadn't found their stash of feed corn. Starving chickens wouldn't do them much good at all.

Her pa stumbled toward her, then braced his hand on her shoulder. "Lily. You be careful a that stranger. Till we know more

’bout him, keep your distance. Hear me?” His head bobbled around, like it was barely attached to his neck. He’d probably consumed a *lot* of liquor.

Soon after he returned home from the war, he’d started drinking. Said it helped the pain. Now, she assumed he did it out of habit. Or more than likely, as a way to escape. Her ma hated it, but the man of the house made the rules. No one challenged him.

“I’ll be fine, Pa.” She took hold of his arm. “My gut tells me he’s a good man.”

His eyes narrowed. “Mind my words.”

“Yessir.”

She kept a firm grip on him all the way back to the cabin. He didn’t even try to refuse her help. Once inside, she guided him to the rocking chair.

Her ma glanced their way, then huffed. No doubt, she knew he’d been drinking.

“Wash up to eat.” The woman nodded at the wash basin.

Lily’s brothers were already in their places at the table.

Still lying on the floor, Caleb groaned, but his eyes remained closed.

“First I need to go to the creek for water to help with Caleb’s fever,” Lily said. “’Sides, I ain’t that hungry. Let the others have my share.”

Without waiting for permission, Lily grabbed a bucket and headed out the door. After all, she was old enough to be responsible. If things were different, she’d be the woman of her *own* house. No one would tell her what to do or question her decisions.

The mountain stream blessed them with never-ending water. She couldn’t recall a time when the bed had run dry. Comforts were scarce these days. At least they’d not go thirsty.

She rushed to the creek and dipped the bucket, then hastened back inside.

Her ma didn't look one bit happy and donned a deeper scowl than she usually wore. Lily chose to ignore her. Someone had to take responsibility for Caleb. Though her folks had removed the slug and tended the wound, they'd obviously decided they'd done enough. Lily knew better.

She tossed an old rag into the bucket to soak up the cold water, then sat on the floor beside Caleb.

"Can we eat now?" Horace muttered.

"Yep." Their ma's single word came out harshly, but Lily understood. The woman had plenty to be angry about. She had a drunk husband, a Yankee in her home, and almost no food. One of those things alone could make any sane person ill.

It had been a very long time since Lily had heard her ma laugh. Honestly, she couldn't remember her own laughter.

Her stomach rumbled at the simple thought of food, so she put her mind on Caleb. She hadn't been completely truthful about not being hungry.

She twisted the cloth to remove the excess water, then glided the worn-out rag over his head and across his face. His body trembled, and he moaned.

"Ma?" Lily looked over her shoulder. "Shouldn't we make a poultice?"

"You go on an' do it. You know what's needed."

It should make Lily happy that her ma trusted her to prepare the medicine. However, she *couldn't* be pleased when she believed the woman was simply indifferent. "It's just 'bout dark, Ma. I'll never find what I need outside t'night. We got anythin' I can use in the cabin?"

"No. Reckon you'll hafta wait till mornin'." Her ma pulled out a chair at the table and sat. "Come eat a tater. You need sumthin' in your belly."

Lily once again doused the rag with cold water, then wrung out the excess. This time she folded the cloth and placed it over Caleb's forehead.

She bent low and put her mouth to his ear. "Don't die on me," she whispered. "T'morra I'll gather some plants that'll help you heal."

His eyes inched open. "Lily?"

Her breath hitched. "Yep. I'm here." Not only surprised, she was *relieved* to hear him speak. Her heart pattered with renewed hope.

"I'm awful thirsty."

Her ma grunted. "There's water in the drinkin' pitcher." Her words were dry and unfeeling.

*She's mad he's pullin' through.*

Lily dismissed the unpleasant thought. She didn't like to think of her ma as being heartless.

Caleb's eyes drooped, and he slowly blinked.

Lily stood and poured a glass of water, then returned to him. She tucked one arm under his shoulder and helped him to a seated position, making certain the cloth on his forehead stayed right where it was.

She placed the glass to his lips, and he readily drank.

His eyes met hers. "Thank you."

"Welcome." With great care and a dim smile, she eased him back again.

The poor man hadn't even been given a pillow. Lying on the hard floor was bad enough, *without* an injury.

Though her pa cast a wary eye, Lily headed for the room she shared with Violet and brought out her own down pillow. She tucked it under Caleb's head. "This'll help some."

His lids completely shut.

"Lily." Her pa scowled. "Eat your supper."

"Yessir."

She recalled a time when her folks were kind to *everyone* who came to their door. Too much mistrust brought on by the war had put an end to their ways.

Even so, Caleb had helped *her*. She'd do all she could to return the favor.

# CHAPTER 4

Caleb opened his eyes. Had it not been for the flickering firelight, he'd be in total darkness. And aside from the occasional crackle and pop from the burning wood, the small cabin was silent.

He sat up, then carefully got to his feet. His shoulder throbbed, but the need to relieve himself pushed him.

After taking a few moments to get steady, he trudged to the front door and went outside.

The pleasant nighttime air had a comforting scent. A mixture of pine and leaves, tossed together with one of his favorite smells—wood smoke. He closed his eyes and breathed it in, then tipped his head and listened.

Crickets chirped. Some distance away an owl screeched. Slightly nearer, water trickled. The sound increased his need.

He'd never find the outhouse in the dark, so he carefully stepped off the front porch and wandered a short distance. He took care of business, then returned inside.

The pallet on the floor came nowhere close to the comfortable bed he'd had growing up. However, it surpassed the rocky ground and muddy holes he'd bedded down in with other soldiers.

He fluffed the pillow and smiled. Lily had been gracious. Regardless of the fact her folks had tended his shoulder, he got the feeling they didn't want him in their home. They'd not uttered a kind word to him.

*Why should they?*

He'd not eaten anything yet, but he soon would. He'd take food out of their children's mouths. And as Mrs. Larsen had said, they could be in for a lot of trouble if anyone found out they were helping him.

*Even Lily will want me gone if she finds out the truth 'bout me.*

He'd take it to the grave with him. In the meantime, he'd suffer alone in silence.

His ma always said life wasn't easy. Still, what he had to cope with went beyond *hard.* If *she* knew what he'd done, she'd never want him home again. The very reason he had nowhere to go. He couldn't face her, or anyone in his family. Especially Rebecca.

Sleep would help.

He closed his eyes and drifted.

* * *

Sunlight beamed through the small window in Lily's room. She lay flat on her back and didn't move. Days gone by, she would've already been up doing chores. With no cow to milk, no horses to clean up after and feed, and only two chickens to gather eggs from, why bother?

She jerked upright.

"Chickens," she muttered, then threw off her blankets and stood.

Violet grumbled something unrecognizable and rolled onto her side, facing away from Lily.

With no need to rouse her, Lily decided to let her sleep.

Lily grabbed her robe and quickly put it on, then crept quietly into the main room. Her folks' door was shut, and the boys hadn't begun to stir overhead.

Fortunately, she had the good sense to step carefully. Otherwise, she would've landed her bare foot in a fresh pile of chicken droppings.

A quick glance at Caleb confirmed he was still sleeping. She intended to go out and find what she needed for the poultice, just as soon as she cleaned up after the hens.

*Where are you, you silly birds?*

She searched high and low, and finally found them under the table on the rug. To her good fortune, each sat on an egg.

*Two eggs to feed eight people.*

Meager, but better than nothing.

They needed meat. While she was out, she'd check the rabbit traps and pray real hard.

She stoked the fire, then added water to the kettle and swung it over the flames to heat.

"Mornin', Lily."

*He's awake.*

She spun around and faced Caleb. "How you feelin'?"

He slowly sat, groaning all the while. "Like I've been beat with a mallet." His hair looked worse than it had when he'd tackled her. The mass on the top of his head stuck straight out on end. With that and his smell, there was nothing appealing about him whatsoever.

She decided not to draw attention to his downfalls. "You feel that good, huh?"

He turned away, frowning. Her jesting hadn't helped.

One of the hens strutted by, then paused and dropped another pile.

"Lawdy," Lily mumbled. "They're goin' outside today. I don't *care* if they get taken. Can't stand havin' their mess in the house."

"Don't say that. You *do* care. But I agree. It ain't pleasant cleanin' up droppin's."

She dampened a rag and set about finding every bit of what they'd left behind. Once she'd sufficiently cleaned the floor, she nabbed the brown hen and headed for the door. "I'll be back for the other one. Watch it for me an' let me know if it ... well, you know."

"Yep. I do." He gave a slight nod, and she scurried away.

*Too much to do.*

Had she been smart, she would've made Violet get up. The entire household had gotten lazy, and there was no call for it. How would they ever get their lives moving forward again if they gave up and quit trying?

She set the hen in its pen, then marched back inside and nabbed the white one. When she eyed Caleb, he shook his head.

*Good. No more messes.*

After putting the white bird with the brown, she grabbed a basket and went to the creek to forage around for some of the plants she needed for the poultice. She found the rest in the woods.

The balm of Gilead would surely help lessen his pain, and the boneset should lower his fever. Some of the other plants would speed his healing.

She passed one of the rabbit traps and sadly found it empty. Maybe the one deeper in the woods would have one, but she didn't have time to check it. There were more important things to do.

When she returned inside, everyone was up and about.

Her ma's wrist rapidly twitched as she beat the two eggs and mixed them with cornmeal and a bit of water. Seems she'd retrieved the precious meal from under the floorboards. Using it would stretch the food. Though the cornbread would be plain and almost tasteless, it would fill their bellies for another day.

"Mornin'." Lily addressed everyone in the room. Most everybody responded accordingly, with little enthusiasm. Her pa merely grunted.

Lily crossed to the table and set down the basket, then went to the fireplace and wet a rag in the water she'd heated.

"Lily?" Caleb whispered. He'd not moved from his spot on the floor.

She leaned close. "Yes?"

"Is your family always this miserable?" He spoke so low she could scarcely hear him.

*Probably a good thing.*

"No. You're just seein' them at their worst. Sorry 'bout that."

"It's my fault. Ain't it?"

She touched a finger to her lips to hush him. "You're gonna be fine," she said, loud enough for all to hear. "I'm makin' you a poultice."

"Is that what all them plants is for?" Horace asked, poking around in the basket.

She hastened to retrieve it. "Yes. Don't fool with them."

"Hurry up now," her ma said. "We hafta eat off this table."

"Yes'm." Lily smoothed the warm, damp rag on the tabletop, then broke off pieces of the plants and put them at its center. Once she folded it up into a square, she added a *bit* more hot water to help draw out the medicine. If it got *too* wet, it wouldn't work well at all.

She believed she'd done it just right.

She sat beside Caleb. "I know your arm's tender, but this'll help." Without his permission, she loosened his shirt strings and eased it away from the wound. The shirt was the only fresh item of clothing on the man's body and had already gotten stained with seepage from the injury.

His bright red skin looked terrible. Though cauterized and sealed, it was raw and ugly.

Without thinking, she scowled.

"That bad?" he mumbled.

She shook her head, sat upright, and forcibly softened her expression. "I've seen worse." A lie, but one she deemed necessary. "This'll help the pain." She gingerly set the poultice over the wound. When he didn't jerk away, she applied a little more pressure. "Can you lay down an' hold it there for 'bout thirty minutes? Then you can take it off an' let it breathe."

"Reckon so. How'd you learn what plants to use?" He slowly lay back onto his pillow.

"The Cherokee learned their ways to lotsa folks 'round here, who passed them on to us. Ma's the most knowledgeable. I've watched her all my life."

Lily smiled and stood. "By the time we get breakfast ready, you should be able to remove it. Then we'll bring in water for your bath." Once again, she bent low to whisper to him alone. "Gettin' you cleaned up might help everyone's ill mood."

He didn't say a word, but his brown eyes locked with hers. Oddly, her heart fluttered.

She quickly moved away.

* * *

Caleb liked Lily more and more. He found himself constantly watching her, impressed by her skill and knowledge. Exactly the kind of woman he could've seen himself married to, if things hadn't happened as they did. He'd always wanted someone strong, smart, and selfishly, *beautiful*.

Lily was all that plus some.

Her sister, Violet, was fine-looking in her own right, but the younger woman seemed shy and not nearly as personable or capable. He enjoyed being around a woman he could talk to, and who'd actually talk back and carry on a conversation.

The poultice Lily made had already helped. The warmth felt good, and it had a pleasing smell. His shoulder didn't throb as much either.

Lily had him utterly enthralled. He knew it was too soon to be looking at her the way he was. But he couldn't help himself.

When he'd gone off to fight in the war three years ago, he'd been too young to give women much consideration. Now, at nineteen, his thoughts were of little else. Still, he'd never take a woman just for pleasure. That remained in his dreams. He'd had one last night he'd never forget. Another reason why he couldn't keep his eyes off Lily. He kept wondering if she'd behave at all like she had in his sleep.

He gulped and shifted his gaze. His thoughts were far from appropriate.

The scent of cornbread made his mouth water, then guilt set in. How could he eat what rightly belonged to this family?

"That what I think it is?" An unfamiliar freckled face hovered over the table. No doubt another one of Lily's brothers.

"Yep," their ma said. "Apple butter."

Lily picked up the jar and examined it as if it was foreign. "Where'd it come from?"

"'Neath the floorboards." Mrs. Larsen took it from her. "If them soldiers ever find our stash, we're done for." She glanced Caleb's way, eyes narrow.

"Is there more?" Lily asked. Relief covered her face. A sight that almost made Caleb smile.

"Some. You children need to go find more apples. Every tree in the cove couldn't a been picked bare. 'Specially up high. We got us another mouth to feed. Best be doin' sumthin' 'bout it."

No, a smile wouldn't come anytime soon.

With his hand still pressing the poultice in place, Caleb rose slowly to his feet and eased toward the table. "I appreciate all you done for me. I'll help however I can."

The children backed away.

Caleb understood. His bath was overdue, and they wouldn't let him forget it. He returned to the fireplace.

Lily rushed to his side. "You really should lie down. Don't mind them. I can bring you sumthin' to eat over here."

"No. I don't feel like lyin' down. I can keep the poultice in place just as well upright. I'm gonna go outside an' sit on the porch till y'all finish. If you have anythin' left, I'll eat. All right?"

"Ma will split what we have eight ways. You'll get some food." Her eyes widened when she spoke, and she emphasized her final words. Then, she smiled. "I ain't gonna stop you from waitin' outside, long as you feel up to it. Just don't wander off. An' keep your ears open. If you hear anyone at all approachin', hurry back in."

He nodded, then went out and sat on the porch's edge. His legs dangled freely.

The poultice had completely cooled, but he still kept it in place.

Unlike last night in the dark, he could see the valley plainly. Beautiful and peaceful.

He heeded Lily's warning and listened to everything around him.

A turkey gobbled.

Caleb scrambled to his feet, opened the door, and peered inside. "I swear I heard a turkey. You got a gun?"

Mrs. Larsen's head snapped around, and she faced her husband.

"Sure we do!" Horace enthusiastically said.

His ma smacked his arm. "Hush."

*She don't trust me.*

"I'm a decent shot," Caleb said. "Even with my bad shoulder, I reckon I can manage with a little help."

Lily leaned across the table, wide-eyed. "Pa?"

"It ain't safe." The man's brow creased. "Not yet. You children go an' pick apples after breakfast like your ma said. You can scout the area for soldiers while you're out. If there's a turkey—which I highly doubt—it'll still be there when we get around to lookin' for it."

Defeated, Caleb shut the door and separated himself from the Larsens. They were more worried about him being discovered than having fresh meat. Mrs. Larsen didn't even want him to know they had a gun.

He hated their mistrust. Somehow, he had to gain their confidence.

# CHAPTER 5

*Finally . . .*

Caleb gripped the sides of the bathing tub, closed his eyes, and let the warmth of the water embrace his body.

It hadn't been easy to stand by silently and let the Larsens work out the details. Mrs. Larsen had fussed about the proper place for a stranger to bathe in their home, while the boys argued over who should haul the water.

In the end, they'd agreed to erect a makeshift room for Caleb in the corner of the cabin by the fireplace. Basically, the very spot he'd slept the night before. As for the water, the two older boys, as well as Lily and Violet had brought it all in. They'd dumped several cold bucketsful into the tub, then boiled more water, which they added to make the bath just the right temperature.

As for his *room*, they'd suspended rope from the wood beams and fastened blankets to it in order to give him privacy. The oldest boy, who he'd learned was *Lucas*, had brought in the metal bathing tub from the barn. Even this freckle-faced boy acted wary of him. He'd set the tub down without saying a word and run off.

The only member of the family who seemed to trust him—or *speak* to him—was Lily. Not even her pa paid him any mind. Ever since he'd cut the slug out of Caleb's shoulder, the man hadn't spoken directly to him. The entire family talked *around* him.

"Remember, Caleb . . ." Lily's voice came through from the other side of the cloth barrier. "Keep your wound outta the water. I'll put on another poultice when you get out."

"Don't fret, Lily. I aim to get clean, but I'll mind your *advice*."

He spoke teasingly and expected one of her abrupt replies, yet got none. However, he heard mumbling from multiple voices. He couldn't make out who it was or what they said.

No matter. He intended to enjoy every moment of his bath.

Not completely comfortable stripping bare, with only a blanket between him and Lily, he'd gotten into the water with his underwear on. A ridiculous thing to do, even though they needed washing, too.

He stood and peeled them down his legs and off his body entirely. The water had already turned dark and muddy-looking. He truly had been filthy. Lucky for him, they had a decent supply of lye soap. He scrubbed until his skin was almost as red as his injury, making sure every inch of his body was clean.

He needed to wash his hair, but found it difficult. Not when he had to keep his wound dry.

He carefully tipped sideways—away from the injured shoulder—and doused his head. Using only one hand, he couldn't efficiently scrub his hair. It needed to be cut, too. As for his whiskers, they'd have to stay scruffy.

He reached over the side of the tub and picked up his shirt and trousers from the floor, then plunged them into the water. After soaping them up good, he rinsed them out and wrung them as best he could.

When the water cooled, he carefully stepped out. Lily had given him a raggedy towel to dry off with. This poor family had little, but it was better than nothing.

Until his clothes were dry, he decided to stay wrapped in a blanket. He hung the garments on pegs sticking out from the wall. Presumably the Larsens' coat hooks, since they were so close to the front door. For now, they served *his* purpose.

Honestly, he needed a full new set of clothes. Mr. Larsen's shirt was appreciated, but Caleb had no other pants than his uniform trousers. Regardless, they'd have to do.

"You done?" Lily asked.

"Yep. Hope no one else wants to use the bathwater. It's almost black." He parted the hanging blankets enough to peer through. "I ain't got nothin' to wear till my clothes dry. I'm fully covered with a blanket, an' I smell a whole lot better. Reckon I can come sit on the sofa for a spell?"

Lily's head drew back, then she nervously scratched at her neck. "Reckon so."

He stepped through to the other side, only to be met by a leer from Mrs. Larsen.

If he had the gumption, he'd smile at her, but it took too much effort. "Sorry 'bout all the trouble. Truly, I am. Once I get on my feet good, I'll leave, an' you won't hafta worry over me."

"Lily's makin' you another poultice," the woman said matter-of-factly. "Go on an' sit down so she can apply it."

Maybe his apology helped. At least she'd spoken to him.

He glanced around the small cabin. "Where's everyone else?" He kept the blanket firmly secured and moved to the sofa. It faced the ever-burning fire.

"I sent the other children to hunt for apples. My husband . . ." The woman squared her jaw. "He's in the barn tendin' things."

Caleb wondered why she'd spoken so harshly, but he wouldn't press her for more information as to what *things* she meant. With no livestock to tend, he couldn't imagine what he might be doing. Still, it was none of his business.

Lily stood at the table putting together the poultice. She kept her head low, even when her ma had made the odd-sounding remark.

He'd just gotten comfortable, when Lily sat beside him, holding the folded cloth.

"You *do* smell better," she said, then worked her lower lip with her teeth. "Open your blanket, so I can put this on your wound."

He was quite sure her ma's eyes were on them. Careful not to expose too much of himself, he pushed aside enough of his covering to give Lily access.

"Hmm. Looks a mite better already." Her eyes lifted and met his. "Still hurt?"

"Yep. Not quite so bad though."

She eased the poultice atop the wound, then held it there.

He winced for only a second, then focused on the warmth and her closeness. It helped calm him, and he tried to dismiss the unwelcome atmosphere.

"Your skin's warm," Lily whispered, then pressed her other hand to his forehead. "But you don't seem to have a fever no more."

The door opened and her pa walked in, immediately shifting Caleb's mood back to something drearier.

Lily quickly withdrew her hand. "*You* hold the poultice in place."

*His* wasn't the only disposition that had changed with her pa now present.

The man grunted, then stumbled and nearly fell. Mrs. Larsen grabbed him by the arm before he went down. "C'mon, Buck. I'll get you to the rocker." She led him across the room and helped him sit.

*Buck?*

Likely a nickname.

She put her face close to her husband's and sniffed. "Your mind clear?"

"Huh?" the man's head bobbled.

"Is your mind right? We gotta talk." She looked over her shoulder at Lily, then rested her eyes on Caleb. "All of us. While the children is gone."

Mr. Larsen sat up tall in the chair. "Course my mind's right, woman. What you wanna say?"

She got one of the wooden chairs from its place at the table and set it beside the rocker. With a loud huff, she sat. "We need to decide what to do with him." She gestured at Caleb as if he was a senseless stump who couldn't hear her.

Lily glanced at him, then she jerked her head around and faced her folks. "What's that s'posed to mean? He needs to get better. He just told you he'd leave once he's well."

Caleb chose to be quiet. Once again, he'd let them work things out. After all, he was a stranger accepting charity. He had no say.

Mrs. Larsen braced her hands on her knees. "Every second he's here is dangerous. If them soldiers find out we helped a Yankee, they won't go easy on us. They'll tear our cabin to shreds and hunt up all our remainin' goods." She clutched the arm of the rocker. "You know it to be true. They've only gone easy on us cuz a you, Buck."

Mr. Larsen's eyes drooped, though he nodded his agreement. "You're right. But we can't make the man leave. Not yet. He'll have a long way to go and needs to get his strength back. If he tried to outrun anyone now, he'd be done for."

"So, what do we do?"

*Yep, I* am *invisible.*

Lily shifted on the sofa and put her back to him, making him feel *more* insignificant. "I have an idea." She looked over her shoulder, eyebrows weaving, then returned her attention to her folks. "It may sound kinda crazy."

*This should be interestin'.*

"Go on," her pa said.

"Well, if I'm not mistaken, the only reason Caleb's a problem is cuz he's a Yankee. *And*, he's a man." Lily's chin jutted upward. "No one would think anythin' of it, if we had another woman stayin' here. Right?"

"Lily." Her ma scowled. "You're makin' no sense."

Her pa reclined in the rocker, grinning. "Reckon *I* know what she has in mind."

Lily cleared her throat. "Aside from a shirt or two, there ain't no other men's clothes that'll fit Caleb. But Violet an' me have several extra dresses. We could alter them to fit him more proper."

*What?*

Caleb rapidly shook his head. He was done being quiet. "'Scuse me? Did you say you wanna put me in a *dress*?"

Mr. Larsen sniggered. "That's where I figgered she was headed."

Lily spun around to face Caleb. "Don't you see? If you go outside wearin' men's things, word'll get out a man's livin' here. That'll bring soldiers for sure. 'Specially if the ones chasin' you got wind of it. Even when we don't see 'em, they're spyin' on us with them scopes. They're used to seein' the boys an' us women. They know pa cuz he's missin' an arm. But if an able-bodied man starts showin' himself, they'll be on us like flies on dung."

"Lily," her ma scolded. "Ladies don't talk that way."

"Girl's right," her pa said, then pointed at Caleb. "Less you're ready to leave, you best consider Lily's idea. If rebels come after you, we can't protect you. Long as you're here, you'll need to dress like one a the women whenever you go outside. Even to use the outhouse. Otherwise, you put us all in danger."

Mrs. Larsen shot to her feet. "This ain't right. Dressin' a man like a woman is ungodly."

Lily stood straight as an arrow and faced her. "What's wrong with tryin' to protect him? He saved me, Ma. Or have you already forgotten that?"

"I ain't." Mrs. Larsen moved away from her and hovered above Caleb. "What do *you* say 'bout all this?"

The simple idea of it soured his stomach, but having Lily defend him gave him *some* comfort. "It's humiliatin'. Still, strange as it might be, it makes sense. I know if I left now, I'd die in the woods. 'Sides, I ain't got nowhere to go. If I return to Waynesville, they'll make me join up again, an' I can't fight no more." He swallowed hard and looked up into the woman's face. "Not just cuz a my injury, my *heart* don't want to. None of it feels right."

Mrs. Larsen's features softened. "Least we can agree on sumthin'."

Lily sat beside him again. "So," she boldly said. "Green or blue?"

"Huh?" Caleb stared at her, then her meaning sunk in. "Green. I've worn blue long enough."

"Good choice." She slapped her hands against her lap, then jumped from the sofa and headed to her room. In no time at all, she came out with a deep mossy green dress draped over her arm. "This one's never been my favorite, so I don't mind givin' it up."

He could see why. The color wasn't exactly feminine. In his case, he appreciated that fact. He covered his face with one hand and shook his head. "How will you explain this to your brothers an' sister?"

"*I'll* do it." Her pa's words came out solidly serious. "I'll sit 'em down soon as they come in an' tell 'em. They'll know better than to give you any grief over it. I'll see to it."

"Lucas won't be so easy," Lily said. "You know how he loves to tease."

"He won't." Her pa's eyes met Caleb's. "We'll help you, but I expect sumthin' in return. Soon as you're able, you're gonna pull your weight 'round here."

"Yessir." Caleb tried to dismiss the thought of putting on the garment in Lily's hands, but he knew he couldn't stay inside forever. "There's a turkey in the woods I aim to kill. An' if I hafta dress like a woman to do it, I will."

"There's a slight problem with that." The man's face became solemn. "We can't shoot. Not only do we have scant ammunition, if you go shootin' a gun, it'll draw attention. We're savin' the bullets in case sumthin' happens an' we hafta defend ourselves. You'll need to come up with another means to get that turkey. *If* it exists."

"It does. I swear I heard it." Not being able to shoot changed everything. Caleb could craft a bow, but even then, his injured shoulder would make drawing it nearly impossible.

"Well . . . we'll see 'bout that." Mr. Larsen looked away. His body deflated as if he was utterly defeated. It had to be horrid not being able to provide for his family. As unwelcome as Caleb felt, he still pitied the man.

Mrs. Larsen was anything but pleased. She grumbled and yanked the dress away from Lily. "I'll let the waist out, then you can try it on." She went into her bedroom and shut the door.

Not much could go on in this tiny house without everyone knowing it. Even with the door shut, he could still hear her fussing.

At least Caleb had his own little corner. He liked being close to the fire. And since it seemed he'd be staying a while, he intended to make a more comfortable bed. Maybe Lily would be willing to help him.

* * *

It had never been Lily's intention to humiliate Caleb, but when she'd come up with the brilliant idea to dress him like a woman, she had to share it.

And though he may not like what came next, he didn't have a choice.

He looked cozy sitting on their sofa wrapped up in a blanket. Still, she didn't want to waste any time. She waved her pa's razor. "It's gotta go, Caleb. I know some womenfolk have whiskers, but not like yours."

His head tilted upward. "I was never fond of this ratty old beard anyways. Reckon you can help me trim my hair, too?"

"Nope. Best leave it be. I can braid it when it gets a bit longer. For now, you'll need to wear a bonnet when you go out."

His eyes popped wide. "A bonnet? Or a *braid*?"

She crossed her arms and stood firm. "It's the only way. Even in a dress, your head still screams you're a man. Wanna get caught?"

"Course not. But never in my life thought I'd hafta stoop to sumthin' like this."

"It's only till the war ends. You best be prayin' for peace." She jerked her head toward the wash basin. "You can shave over there. I'll get you Pa's mirror."

"Got some scissors?"

She cast a leery eye. "Not for your hair, right?"

"No. My beard's so long, I need to cut it first."

"I knew that." She pursed her lips, then headed to her ma's room and got the scissors from her sewing basket. She'd finished the alterations on Caleb's dress and left it lying atop her bed, though he'd not come anywhere close to it. It would take some doing to get him to try it on.

Lily's curiosity piqued. Anticipation over seeing him without facial hair had her heart pumping hard. What kind of features lay beneath all those whiskers? She hoped she'd be able to focus on his face rather than what he looked like in her dress. If she laughed at all, it surely wouldn't set well with him.

The front door burst open, accompanied with laughter. The kind from her siblings she treasured.

"Look, Ma!" Isaac held up an apple. "Lucas climbed the trees an' got us a heap!"

Violet, Lucas, and Horace each set a full basket of apples on the table.

"There's more," Violet said. "This here's all we could carry."

Their ma folded her hands together and gazed upward. "Thank you, Lord."

Looks like they'd be making more apple butter.

Horace pointed at Caleb. "Why's he in a blanket?"

Their pa got up from the rocker. "I need you kids to come outside on the porch. We gotta have us a talk."

Violet's brows drew in with concern, and she looked Lily's way. Lily offered her an encouraging smile. Violet tentatively nodded, then followed her brothers back out the door, along with their pa.

"Once he's done talkin' to them," her ma said. "We got apples to tend." She crossed to the fireplace and stoked the fire.

Caleb stood by the wash basin, struggling to keep the blanket in place. He'd removed the poultice, and Lily planned to fix another one before he went to bed. Even if he had two *good* arms, she doubted he could manage the razor. Not while fumbling to keep from exposing himself.

She handed him the scissors. "Least you can shave in peace. I'll hold the mirror for you."

He sighed, long and hard, but said nothing.

"I was wonderin' . . ." She hoped she wouldn't come off as being too forward. "When you're feelin' better, an' they all know 'bout the dress an' all, you reckon you'd be up to goin' with me to check the rabbit traps?"

"Traipsin' 'round in a skirt, huh?"

"*I* do it all the time." She cocked her head and slowly blinked, then positioned the mirror in front of his face.

He clutched the blanket with his weak left hand and began snipping away some of the growth with his right. "The bonnet, too?"

"Yep. Can't take any chances."

His eyes narrowed. "*You* gonna wear one?"

"No. I don't like wearin' 'em. If I put anythin' at all on my head, I wear a scarf. Though sometimes in the summertime Ma *insists* I wear a bonnet to keep the sun off my face. You need to hide *yours* year-round."

"And you don't think I'll draw suspicion?" He kept snipping.

"Maybe. If someone comes snoopin', we'll just tell them you're shy. Good reason to hide behind a bonnet."

The wash basin had started to fill with globs of hair. He let out a frustrated-sounding sigh. "Ain't no way I can shave. I need both hands. If I let go a this . . ." Wide-eyed, he wiggled the blanket.

"You're right. Want *me* to shave you?"

His eyes shifted toward her ma, then came to rest on her again. "You ever done it before?"

"Yep. Ma used to shave Pa 'fore he went off to war." She leaned close to Caleb. "Ma fussed that his whiskers bothered her skin," she whispered, then stood tall again. "She learned me how to do it, cuz Isaac an' Horace was real little then, an' needed her more. They was underfoot all the time. It's been a while, but I promise not to cut you."

He eyed her closely, then nodded. "Don't see no other way. Even if I was fully dressed an' had both hands free, it still hurts to move my left arm."

She set the mirror aside, grabbed a chair, and positioned it close to the wood stand where the basin was. "Go on an' sit."

He sat without another question or remark. Seems he truly trusted her.

She poured some water from the pitcher and wet her hands, then worked up a lather with soap. Shaving her pa had never made her this nervous. Of course, it had been a long time since she'd done this, though she believed that was a very minor part of her unease.

Her stomach turned flips as she worked the lather into Caleb's beard and mustache.

At least her hands remained steady. She skillfully held the blade and drew it across his skin. After each stroke, she wiped it on a cloth to remove the hair.

He didn't budge. Every breath he took was slow and steady. Completely fearless.

Lily's breathing, however, quickened. She'd uncovered a handsome man. His big dark eyes blinked up at her—almost *twinkling*—as if he recognized her approval.

Clean-shaven, he looked younger than she'd thought him to be. Closer to her age.

"All finished," she mumbled and stepped away.

He rubbed a hand over his skin. "Smooth. You done good."

She held up the mirror. "See? Not one cut."

When he took the mirror from her hand, his fingers barely brushed against hers. Even so, her insides jumped, and her cheeks heated. She quickly turned her head. "I best be helpin' Ma."

"Thank you for the shave, Lily."

"Welcome." She took a quick glance over her shoulder.

He pulled the blanket close and stood. Much too handsome and totally bare beneath it.

*Oh, my.*

She gulped and put her attention elsewhere. Most of his whiskers had ended up in the wash basin, but some had landed on the floor. She took the bowl from its wooden stand and hurried out the door to dump it. Her feelings went every which way.

Part of her wished he'd turned out to be ugly and undesirable, the other part thanked the good Lord he wasn't.

Living with Caleb wouldn't be easy. All she could do was pray he'd make things better for her family. If he stayed till October, he could help her harvest their corn and plant some wheat for the following year. Though her folks might have given up hope that their lives could get back to normal, she'd never let it go.

# CHAPTER 6

The wonderful aroma of cooking apples filled the small cabin. Caleb's ma made the best apple butter he'd ever tasted, though he admitted Mrs. Larsen's rivaled it. It certainly added flavor to the bland cornbread.

His shoulder occasionally throbbed, but Lily's poultice was working wonders. He honestly believed his wound would heal without complications.

The tub hadn't been emptied and still sat in Caleb's *corner.* When the children had come back inside, their ma put them to work cleaning and cutting up apples. Even little Isaac helped with the washing, although his apples tended to have bite marks in them before they went into the pot.

Caleb decided to take it upon himself to empty the tub. That meant putting on the dress. Since everyone was ignoring him, he trudged to the Larsen's bedroom and grabbed the thing. When he returned to his place, he tried not to have eye contact with any of them. He adjusted the makeshift curtain, certain no one could see inside, and let his blanket fall to the floor.

Completely naked, he put the dress over his head and worked his way into it. His stiff left arm continued to give him trouble, but he wouldn't let it defeat him. He had to forget the pain and make himself useful.

To his surprise, the dress fit quite well.

*If Pa saw me like this . . .*

The man would never approve, even if the gown spared Caleb's life. Honestly, Caleb didn't know whether or not his pa had survived the war.

Glum as ever, Caleb tried to dismiss all thoughts of his family.

He looked down at himself. A sight that both repulsed and amused him. Even so, he wouldn't laugh. Not when everything was so dismal.

At least the dress wasn't frilly. Just plain green from the high neckline to the hem. The arms were a bit short and didn't quite come to his wrists, but he had plenty of shoulder room.

He moved every which way, and found it to be oddly comfortable. And though his underdrawers were a little damp, he tugged them on. He wasn't about to go outside bare-bottomed.

His old boots needed to be replaced, but they'd have to do. He'd neglected to wash his socks, which turned out to be a good thing. They might not be clean, but at least they were dry.

A bucket remained by the tub, so he scooped up some of the dirty water, took a large breath, and pushed through the curtain. He got out the door before he heard any reactions. No doubt, they were all laughing at him.

After tossing the contents of the bucket, he returned inside to empty more bathwater.

Lily blocked his way. "You forgot sumthin'." She held up a blue bonnet. "It don't match the dress, but I reckon no one will care."

Lucas chuckled and immediately got a smack on the head from his pa.

"Help him finish," the man coldly said.

"Yes, Pa." Lucas picked up another bucket.

Caleb took the bonnet from Lily, rolled his eyes, and put the thing on. It had the largest side flaps he'd ever seen on a hat like this. But it helped. It would hide a lot.

"Here," Lily said. "I'll tie it." She fastened the dangling bands of cloth into a large bow at his neck. "There. Nearly perfect. From a distance, you'll simply be another girl. Just hope an' pray no one gets too close."

Caleb grunted. "I'm glad this dress ain't cut low in the front. Otherwise, you'd a had to shave my chest, too."

Her cheeks glowed red. With a small sound resembling a whimper, she hurried away and rejoined her siblings in the kitchen.

Caleb inwardly grinned. He'd affected her.

*Not so outspoken anymore.*

With Lucas's help, they emptied the tub enough so they were able to lift it and carry it outside. They dumped the remaining water, then took the vessel to the barn.

Lucas wrinkled his nose. "You know you look strange."

Caleb stood tall, then fanned his skirt. "Don't you find me the least bit pretty?"

"That ain't funny." Lucas scowled and waved a hand. "Glad *I* don't hafta wear a dress. If I was older, I'd go fight in the war. You goin' back when your shoulder's healed?"

Caleb leaned against the wall of the barn. "No."

"Why? You 'fraid a dyin'?"

"Dyin's not the hard part. Livin's much worse. 'Specially when you gotta see folks you care 'bout bloody and beaten down. War's ugly. Mark my word."

"I hate them soldiers what keep takin' our things. I wouldn't bat an eye shootin' 'em. Maybe one day, I'll get my chance."

Caleb couldn't help but frown. The young boy had no idea how painful killing was. "I hope the war ends before you're old enough to fight."

Lucas kicked at the ground, then looked Caleb in the eye. "Ever kill anyone?"

His question pierced Caleb's heart. "Course I did." He choked out the words. "Lotsa men."

The boy smiled. A disturbing sight to see over something so horrible. "Will you tell me 'bout it?"

"No." *Never.*

Lucas eyed Caleb from head to toe. "How long you stayin' here?"

"Don't know. Long as your folks let me, I reckon." At least the boy dropped the subject of killing. A sign he had *some* sense.

"Hmm." Lucas crossed his arms. "You know Ma don't trust you. 'Specially 'round my sisters. You best not take a shine to them. Touch 'em, an' Pa will use his gun on ya. He threatened one a the officers once. Man named Captain Ableman wants Lily in a bad way."

Caleb's heart drummed hard and tightened in his chest. "How do you know that?"

"He cornered her in the barn. Tried kissin' on 'er. Pa walked in on 'em and made him leave. I ain't never seen the captain myself, cuz every time any soldiers come 'round, I have to hide with the chickens. But I heard Pa tellin' Ma."

"Does Lily care for him? The captain?"

"Lily don't like no men. 'Cept you. I ain't never seen her act the way she does when you're 'round. All goo-goo-eyed and girly."

Mr. Larsen appeared out of nowhere. "There a problem here?"

"No, sir," Caleb said.

Lucas crossed his arms. "We was just talkin'. I asked him 'bout the war."

"Go inside, Lucas." Mr. Larsen jerked his head in that direction. "Your ma has work for you."

The boy scurried away. Caleb started to follow him, till Mr. Larsen held up his hand and stopped him. "Don't go fillin' my boy's head glorifyin' the war."

"You don't hafta worry 'bout that. I ain't got nothin' decent to say 'bout it."

"Good." The man wore a stone-cold expression. "Even when I came home without an arm, Lucas still wanted to fight. Don't understand that boy. Not one bit."

Though grateful Mr. Larsen had opened up to him, Caleb didn't want to overstep his bounds. He chose his words carefully. "I reckon he just wants to grow up. Some boys think fightin' makes them men."

The man huffed. "That comin' from a man in a dress." His hard features transformed, and he chuckled. "Never thought I'd see the day."

"*You*?" Caleb smoothed his skirt. "*I'm* the one wearin' it." He tried to smile, but it wouldn't come.

"Least you got two arms. Be glad a that."

"I am. An' I have you to thank for it."

Mr. Larsen slowly bobbed his head. "Be grateful for Lily, too. Her poultice done a world a good." His mouth twisted from side to side, then he looked down and scratched at his neck. "I need to apologize for my wife. She ain't been the same since we've had to scrape to get by." He lifted his eyes. "She's a good woman. The war's made her bitter."

"No need to apologize." Yes, the man had most definitely opened up to him. Caleb glanced over at the cabin. "Lily asked me to go with her to check rabbit traps. Now that I'm properly dressed, do you mind? I'd like to help."

Mr. Larsen's eyes narrowed into slits. "Lily trusts you, an' as of yet, you ain't done nothin' to make me believe you'd harm her. As long as you're feelin' up to it, I won't object." He pointed a stern finger in Caleb's face. "But don't go gettin' *ideas* 'bout my girl.

You do, an' I'll turn you over to the rebels myself." His eyes pierced deep, his meaning as clear as fresh water.

"Yessir." Caleb swallowed the lump in his throat. Even with only one arm, he had no doubt Mr. Larsen could best him right now. Challenging him wouldn't be wise. For more than one reason.

* * *

Lily felt right proud of herself for staying stone-faced when Caleb came out wearing her dress. But she'd nearly crumbled when he referenced his chest hair. She had to stop picturing in her mind what he looked like beneath the ugly green fabric.

It bothered her that she gave it any consideration at all. She'd never had sinful thoughts about a man before. *Any* man.

*Lord forgive me.*

Violet tugged on her arm and guided her away from the others. "Caleb cleaned up good, didn't he?" she whispered, then giggled. "He sure smells better, an' he's handsome—aside from the dress." She smiled so broadly, her cheeks puffed up.

"Handsome?" Lily shrugged. "Reckon so." Her mind spun. "Don't go gettin' ideas 'bout him. Hear me?"

"Why? You an' I both should be married by now. The only men left in the cove are either old an' feeble or too young. An' now that we have someone of an appropriate age under our roof, it seems natural. His bein' good-lookin' sure doesn't hurt."

Lily couldn't argue the point. Maybe she didn't need forgiveness after all. Almost eighteen, she *should* be thinking about men in a grownup fashion. What could be more natural? However, it wouldn't be wise to rival her sister for him.

*I'm older, she'll hafta step aside.*

No. It pained her, but she needed to change her thoughts. Caleb Henry had to remain in her mind as simply a temporary addition to their living space. Besides, their folks wouldn't approve of her *or* Violet pursuing him. Not until they knew more about him. They might very well discover he was a heathen. That would never be suitable.

Lily had a lot to learn about their guest, and she intended to find out all she could. She prayed her shy sister would remain so and keep her distance.

# CHAPTER 7

Caleb trudged after Lily into an area of the forest thick with underbrush. He'd started feeling weak, but didn't want to let on that maybe he'd pushed himself a little too hard.

She pointed ahead of them. "It's right up here, where the path narrows."

The dress she'd put on today was prettier than her plain brown one. This one was a light peach color with tiny flowers dotted all over it. It seemed odd for her to traipse around in the woods wearing something more suitable for Sunday services.

*Maybe she wore it to impress me.*

She had no need to go above and beyond what she'd already done. He was already enthralled. "I'm glad I'm taller than you, or I'd be trippin' over the hem of this dress." He couldn't ease the feeling of foolishness, parading around in women's wear. "How do *you* manage?"

"Easily." She glanced over her shoulder, grinned, then giggled. "Sorry. I shouldn't laugh, but the expression on your face—"

"Don't say another word." He lifted the skirt a bit higher and kept going.

It wasn't so bad on flat ground, but climbing up the mountainside challenged him. And though it wasn't cold outside, his legs had gotten chilled from his damp underwear. Still, he wouldn't complain about being cold, or how much his shoulder ached. He liked having time alone with Lily.

She shrieked, startling him to his senses.

"What?" He moved to her side as fast as he could.

"We got us a fat one!" She bent over and lifted a hefty rabbit from the ground, clutching its long ears in her fist. "Ma's gonna be happy."

Caleb examined the snare. "You do that?" He gestured to the crossed sticks and twine.

"Yep."

"I'm impressed."

She primly pursed her lips and cocked her head. "Us mountain women know a thing or two. Don't women from Waynesville snare rabbits?"

Why his thoughts shifted immediately to Rebecca, he wasn't sure. She'd never step foot in the woods. "My ma left that up to us boys. She liked us to bring 'em home skinned and ready for fryin'."

"So, you have brothers? How many?"

His throat dried so fast, he feared he'd not be able to speak. He swallowed to try and ease it. "One. But he died."

"Oh. Sorry to hear it. Any sisters?"

"Yep. Two. They're older than me. They were already married an' gone when the war started. One's in Connecticut, the other Rhode Island."

Lily moved to a rock and sat, then pulled a knife from her skirt pocket. "What 'bout your folks?" She loosened the snare from the rabbit's neck, slipped it off, then set the dead animal on the ground.

"Ma lives alone right now—well *sorta*." His insides tumbled. He didn't want to talk about any of this. "Want me to skin it?" He nodded to the rabbit.

"No. I can do it." She leaned over and ran the knife around both of its ankles, then proficiently skinned the thing without flinching. As easily as removing a glove from her hand.

Once she freed the rabbit from its skin, she wasted no time and gutted it. "How can someone *sorta* live alone?"

He decided not to bring up his suspicions about Rebecca, so he told a half-truth. "Well, my pa's fightin' *somewhere*. I don't know if he's dead or alive. Hopefully, he's already come home to her, an' not in a box."

"Why don't *you* go home? Find out?" She rapidly shook her head. "Never mind. I know why. You said yourself they'd make you fight again. I don't blame you for not wantin' to." With a quick flick of her wrist, she tossed the guts into the brush. Except for the organs, which she held up like a prize. "Ma loves liver."

"Lily?"

Her eyes met his. "Yeah?"

"Why'd you want me to come with you? I can tell you know what you're doin'. You don't need my help."

Her cheeks reddened. "I wanted to find out more 'bout you."

"Oh." His stomach churned in a different sort of way. "Not much to tell."

"Don't say that. I learned you have kin. An' I know you understand what it feels like to lose someone. Your brother bein' dead an' all." She stood, still gripping the rabbit in one hand and its pelt in the other.

*I don't wanna talk 'bout him.* "Have *you* lost someone?"

She frowned and nodded. "Two sisters an' a brother. They was just babies when it happened. Don't know why *they* died an' the rest of us lived. It was hardest on Ma."

They headed back down the hill. As they neared the cabin, Lily pointed to a place on the other side of the creek, close to the homestead. "They're buried over yonder. Granny an' Grampa are in the cemetery by our church, but Ma wanted her babies close."

"How long since they died?"

"Daisy passed last year. Marigold died in 1862, an' Howard Junior the year before. He was named after my pa. They started callin' Pa *Buck*, when he hunted up the biggest buck deer you ever did see. Pa was right proud a that. I was only six when it happened, but I remember Pa's huge smile." Her face shadowed over and she stared straight ahead, as if lost in the memory.

Caleb rested a hand on her arm, and she jumped. "Sorry, Lily. For all of it."

She looked at his hand, then lifted her face and gazed into his eyes. "I want things to be right again. I wanna be happy. I know Pa can't get his arm back, but I wanna see him prideful. He stopped carin', an' he drinks too much. Ma hates that." Her hand shot to her mouth. "I shouldn't a said it."

"It's all right. I had a feelin' he'd been into the moonshine earlier." Caleb sighed, wishing he could make things better for Lily. Even if not for himself. "Let's go in. Make your Ma happy. At least for now."

Her lips twitched, yet she didn't smile. "Yep. For now." She headed toward the front door, but he stayed put. "Caleb? Ain't you comin'?"

He pointed at the outhouse. "I'll be in after."

This time, she *did* smile. "All right. Be sure to keep the skirt outta the way."

As humiliated as he felt in the dress, it was worth making her smile.

* * *

The hug Lily received when her ma saw the liver, warmed her to the core.

She helped her cut up the rabbit for stew. They'd all eat well tonight. And though they'd run out of salt some time ago, they had dried onion and some herbs to throw in. As hungry as they were, it'd be delicious.

Caleb seemed a bit lost as he wandered around the cabin and finally came to rest on the sofa. Lily believed he wasn't the kind of man accustomed to being idle.

He'd removed the bonnet the minute they came inside, but kept the dress on. Honestly, with so little to wear, he had no choice. She knew he was uncomfortable—to say the least.

Isaac cautiously approached him, and Lily watched and waited, trying her best to focus on the supper preparations. Violet hovered close. *Her* eyes also rested on Caleb.

"Mister?" Isaac poked Caleb in the leg. "Why you wearin' girls' clothes?"

Caleb glanced over his shoulder, questioning with his eyes, then faced Isaac again. "Didn't your pa tell you?"

"Sure he did." Horace answered for him and took a seat beside Caleb. "Didn't you listen, Isaac?"

Isaac shrugged "Uh-huh. But don't know what he meant. Boys don't wear dresses."

"You're right," Caleb said. "An' I can tell you, it ain't much fun. Still, your pa thinks it's a way to keep me safe."

Isaac's nose wrinkled. "You gonna wear it forever?"

"I hope not. When this war's over, I aim to get me a new pair a trousers."

Lily smiled at the gentle way Caleb spoke to her little brother. In almost no time at all, Isaac had wiggled himself between Caleb and Horace, and the three were talking about shooting marbles. One of her brothers' favorite games.

Their pa had made himself scarce again, and she assumed he was in the barn. Lucas was another matter. "Ma, where's Lucas?" The house seemed extra quiet with him nowhere in sight.

"He went scoutin'. Said he wanted to climb a few trees an' make sure no one was about."

"Pa go with him?"

"No." The abrupt word instantly soured her ma's face.

Nothing more needed to be said.

Once the meal was ready, Lily helped Violet set the table. Lily considered going to the barn to check on her pa, when the door opened and Lucas came in, dragging the man with him.

"Come help!" Lucas stumbled and their pa nearly fell to the floor.

They all rushed to him. Even Caleb, who put his good arm around him.

"Get him in the rocker," their ma said, her voice more panicked than usual.

They'd all gotten used to seeing him slightly inebriated, but his eyes had rolled up into his head, and he appeared near dead.

"I found him lyin' on the ground by the barn door," Lucas said. "I had a hard time gettin' him up."

"Buck." Their ma patted his face. *Hard.* "Buck. Open your eyes."

The man muttered gibberish.

Lucas frowned. "There was a jug on the ground beside him."

Caleb placed a hand on Lucas's shoulder. "Show it to me."

Her brother looked to their ma for approval. She nodded, then Lucas hurried out the door with Caleb following him. It didn't take long before they returned inside with the nearly empty jug.

"I thought it smelled rancid," Caleb said, talking faster than Lily had ever heard him. "I took a sip to be sure it wasn't just the moonshine I was smellin'. It was definitely foul, so I spit it out. Far as I know, moonshine don't go bad. Sumthin' else musta gotten into this container. He best be gettin' it outta his stomach." He faced her ma. "You got any ipecac?"

"A bit. Under the floorboards."

They shoved the table aside and moved the rug, then pried up several planks. Her ma had more things hidden there than Lily realized.

The woman pulled out a small box and produced a tiny bottle. "Get a bucket, Lucas, an' Lily, you hold your pa's head." She smacked his face once again. "Buck. You gotta drink this."

He groaned, head bobbing. Lily held it firm, then tipped it slightly backward. Her ma forced his mouth open and poured in a good amount of ipecac. She pinched his lips together, then rubbed his throat to make him swallow.

He almost choked, but the liquid went down. His body lurched and within seconds, he spewed. Fortunately, Lucas had the sense to hold the bucket in front of their pa's face, and everything he heaved went in it.

"Lawdy," Lily muttered. She gagged, seeing and smelling the vile vomit.

Their ma fluttered her hand, motioning toward the pitcher. "Get him some water, Violet."

"Yes'm." She hurried off and came back with a glassful. Before he had the chance to drink, he wretched again.

Caleb got a towel and dampened it, then pressed it to her pa's forehead. "He needs to get as much out of his stomach as he can. Good thing Lucas found him in time."

Lily's heart sank and tears formed. She'd gotten so used to the idea of her pa drinking, she never thought of checking on him. None of them did. They all just let him be whenever he went off to the barn.

She looked around the room and took in each member of her family. Yes, they'd lost hope, but they needed each other. They couldn't afford to lose another soul. Something had to change.

Her eyes met Caleb's, and she mouthed the words, *thank you.*

A slim smile lifted the corners of his mouth. Something she'd not yet seen. Then he put all of his attention once again on her pa. He rubbed the man's face with the cloth, then helped him drink from the glass Violet had brought over.

"He'll be fine, Mrs. Larsen," Caleb said. "Reckon now, he needs some sleep. When he wakes up, he can have some a that fine stew you're makin'."

Lily's ma wiped tears out of her eyes and nodded. "Makes no sense Buck couldn't taste that the moonshine was bad."

Caleb's brow drew in. "It wasn't his first jug. There was another not far from him that was completely empty. Reckon by the time he got to the bad one, he couldn't tell no difference."

His revelation didn't seem to surprise her ma at all, but she looked even sadder. "As you said, it was a blessin' Lucas found him." She kissed Lucas on the top of his head, then wandered into the kitchen and stirred the pot of stew simmering on the stove.

Violet got a blanket from their folks' bedroom and placed it over their pa. She carefully tucked it around his legs.

The man lay back in the rocker, already dozing. He breathed steady and strong. Caleb was right. He'd be fine. But that wasn't a guarantee forever.

They all gathered at the table, and after a brief prayer thanking God for the rabbit and good health, they ate in silence.

Lily noticed Caleb's eyes drooping. "You need some rest, too," she whispered across the table.

"Reckon I'll sleep good t'night. I'll have a full belly, an' I confess, I'm spent." He dipped his head to her ma. "Good stew, Mrs. Larsen."

"Thank you."

Lily placed a hand to her heart. Her ma had actually smiled at him. A sight she never thought she'd see. It brought out one of her own.

Amazing how a little food could change everyone's temperament. Even after a near-catastrophe.

* * *

While watching a game of marbles, Caleb nearly drifted off. He found the spot he'd taken on the sofa to be more comfortable than most anywhere in the house.

The three young boys skillfully rolled the colorful balls across the floor, using one as a shooter to push others out of a ring of string. Such a simple game, but something that had them all laughing and doing all they could to best each other.

Each boy had his own unique way of strutting with every victory. Caleb especially liked to watch Horace, who'd tuck his fists into his armpits, then flap his arms and crow like a rooster. Entertaining *and* comical.

Mrs. Larsen led her husband off to bed. Though she'd gotten him to eat a small amount of stew, she didn't push him. He'd complained of queasiness. By tomorrow, Caleb assumed he'd be much better. As long as he stayed away from the moonshine.

Once the Larsens left the room, Caleb caught Violet's eyes on him, accompanied with a smile. He'd noticed her looking at him several other times throughout the evening, yet whenever he returned her gaze, she quickly lowered her eyes. Definitely a shy girl.

Her interest in him had changed a great deal from their first encounter. A bath had accomplished more for him than cleanliness.

"Violet," Lily said. "You should get ready for bed. You boys, too."

"Can't we play another game?" Horace asked.

"You've been at it long enough." Lily folded her arms and looked at them as though *she* was their ma. "'Sides, you get too loud. You don't wanna keep Pa up."

Lucas picked up the string, and all three boys gathered the marbles, then put them into a leather pouch. They trudged up the stairs to their room.

Violet wandered close to the fireplace. "How's your shoulder, Caleb?" She had a softness about her that reminded him of Rebecca. Her voice and mannerisms were more feminine than Lily's, but he found Lily much more interesting.

"It's gettin' better."

"I'm glad. Don't like seein' you hurtin'." She fidgeted with her lavender skirt as she spoke and kept her eyes focused downward.

"Violet." Lily laid a hand on her arm. "Time for bed. Caleb needs sleep."

Violet's head lifted, and she faced her sister. "You comin', too?"

"In a little while. After I make another poultice for Caleb."

"Need my help? I'd be glad to."

"No. I can manage just fine." Again, Lily stood firm.

Violet's eyes shifted toward him. She moistened her lips, then let out a breath. "Sleep well, Caleb."

"Thank you." He looked from sister to sister.

*I'm in a heap a trouble.*

Personal experience afforded him an understanding of this kind of rivalry. Maybe he was misreading them, but his gut told him otherwise.

Before Violet went into her bedroom, she glanced over her shoulder a final time. Her eyes blinked ever-so-slowly. Almost mesmerizing.

Caleb shook his head. He didn't need this.

Lily went to the kitchen table and laid out the items for the poultice. "Oh, my," she mumbled, then came to his side. "I can't doctor you while you're in that dress. Why don't you take it off an' wrap yourself up in the blanket again? Then come back out an' sit on the sofa."

"All right. I'm ready to be outta this dress anyways."

He pushed through the curtain and wiggled out of the garment. It hurt to bend his arm, but he had the warmth of the poultice to look forward to. Not to mention, Lily's company *alone* for a short while.

He'd gone through a world of emotions over the past few days, and maybe he didn't deserve the fine treatment these good folks had given him. However, since he hadn't died, he wanted to get well so he could repay them for their kindness. A small act of penance might ease his soul. Though what he *truly* craved was forgiveness. And the person he needed it from the most could never give it.

He tightened the blanket around his body and went out into the living area. Lily had returned to the table and was preparing the cloth.

She glanced up, then immediately went back to her work.

He sat and gazed into the fire. Overhead, footsteps from her brothers soon quieted. The floorboards creaked from the girls' room as Violet prepared for bed. No sound whatsoever came from their folks' bedroom.

Memories of when his entire family had lived under one roof popped into his mind. The wonderful days before his sisters left home to marry, and when Abraham was still alive. Laughter. Singing. An abundance of happiness. He ached for all of it.

"Caleb?" Lily patted the cushion. "Where are you right now?"

"Huh?" He pivoted on the sofa and faced her, not even aware she'd sat beside him. "Oh. I was thinkin' 'bout my family."

"*Good* thoughts?" She gestured to his blanket and held out the poultice.

He pushed the material off his shoulder, exposing more of his chest than he'd intended. "Yeah. Real good." He fumbled a bit with the blanket, and she smiled.

"You're fine. I ain't seein' nothin' I haven't seen before." She placed the cloth over his wound. "It's healin' well. I don't reckon I'll need to do this again."

Her hand remained atop the warm cloth, making it even warmer. His heart thumped, and he closed his eyes, relishing her tenderness. "Lily. Violet. Rose." He opened his eyes a sliver. "All flowers. I assume that was on purpose."

"Yep." She worked her lower lip with her teeth. "Ma was the first *flower*. My folks told me that when I was born, Ma made it clear she wanted all her girls to have pretty, flowery names. She named Daisy an' Marigold, too." Her head turned, then she looked at him again, grinning. "When Howard Junior came," she whispered. "Ma wanted to call him Sweet Pea an' Pa had a fit. He said no boy of his would have a sissy name." Her smile completely faded. "Then he died, an' it didn't matter none. Pa's heart broke just as bad as Ma's over losin' him."

"I'm sorry, Lily. At least they have y'all. Your pa has three fine boys." He stared into her eyes. "An' two beautiful girls."

She gulped so hard, he heard it. "Pa wants another boy." The words squeaked out of her mouth. "Course, Ma says she's tired a birthin' babies. But the way I see it, if the good Lord sees fit to give 'em another one, then so be it." Her hand eased off his shoulder. Since he'd reclined back into the sofa far enough, the poultice stayed in place.

Lily's eyes remained locked with his. "Do you believe in God, Caleb?"

"Yes, I do. 'Fore the war, I was a regular church-goer. I still pray, but I don't reckon God's happy with me anymore." He leaned his head against the cushions and let his entire body relax.

"Why?"

He rotated his neck just enough to see her. "*Thou shalt not kill*. I done my share."

"It's *war*. Even in the Bible, God sent his people to fight an' kill."

"I'm well aware. But what *I* done wasn't holy. It'll never be forgiven."

Her eyes searched his.

If she wanted a better explanation, he wouldn't give it. He looked away, hoping she'd understand his gesture and let it drop.

She stood. "I best get to bed. If you'd be more comfortable, why don't you sleep right here?" She patted the cushions. "T'morra, I'll gather some straw to make you a decent mattress. Sound good?"

"Thank you. I'd like that. Not easy to stretch out on this sofa."

She backed away and inched toward her bedroom door. "I'm glad you're here, Caleb." Without another word, she disappeared into her room.

*I'm glad, too.*

He shifted sideways and brought his feet up onto the cushions. His full body didn't fit on the short sofa, so he kept his knees bent. Still uneasy, he lay back and tried to get comfortable. No matter which way he turned, he couldn't make it happen. It would be impossible to sleep here.

He pressed one hand against the poultice and stood, struggling to hold the blanket in place. At least if it dropped now, no one would see him.

The hard spot on the floor of his little corner of the cabin would suit him fine for one more night.

With his eyes closed, he dismissed every bad thought and put his mind right. He wanted to drift into a world of pleasant dreams.

# CHAPTER 8

Lily fully believed God would forgive any sin, as long as the person who committed the act confessed and asked for absolution. Caleb was being much too hard on himself, but she could tell he didn't want to talk about it anymore. Maybe in time he'd feel he knew her well enough to speak of it again. After all, telling someone your troubles started the healing process.

When she'd come into the room and settled herself in bed, the rate of Violet's breathing affirmed she wasn't asleep. Lily considered talking to her, then quickly dismissed the idea. Her sister had her sights on Caleb. If conversation led in that direction, Lily would never be able to sleep.

*I can't sleep regardless.*

Her troubled heart ached. The man had only been in their house a few days, and he'd disrupted everything. She and Violet hadn't argued in many years. As of yet, Caleb's presence hadn't brought one on. Lily wanted to keep it that way.

*Maybe* I'm *the one who should step aside.*

She loved her sister wholeheartedly. If Caleb could make her happy, wouldn't that be a good thing?

Lily rolled onto her side and faced the wall. At times like this, she wished she had her own bed. Of course, once winter came, she'd appreciate her sister's warmth. She couldn't recall a night that Violet hadn't been beside her. They were used to each other.

*But I'm old enough to have a* man *in my bed.*

She closed her eyes and pictured Caleb. Whenever she'd touched him, his body radiated far more heat than Violet's. He'd most definitely keep her warm at night.

A pleasant sigh escaped her, and Violet stirred.

Lily faked a soft snore, praying her sister wouldn't speak.

*Lord, what am I doin'?*

If she could figure *that* out, she might get some rest.

* * *

It had been well past midnight by the time Lily had finally fallen asleep. She couldn't recall dreaming.

*Doggone it.*

She *wanted* to dream.

The bed felt unusually cold. She turned over and found Violet's side empty.

Lily flung the blankets off and jumped up.

*Violet's never up before me.*

She jerked the bedroom door open and peered out. Her heart sunk into her bare feet. Her sweet sister was sitting on the sofa talking to Caleb. Though Violet was fully dressed, Caleb sat casually in his usual blanket attire.

The man needed sleepwear.

Lily understood why he hadn't yet put on his dress, but still . . .

Grabbing her robe, she walked out and headed straight for the fireplace. "Mornin'." She put her back to the fire and faced them.

"Mornin', Lily." Violet covered her mouth and giggled.

Caleb simply lowered his eyes.

Unsure why they were behaving so strangely, Lily lifted her chin high in the air. "What's so funny?"

"Your hair." Violet pointed, then pinched her lips tight, smirking.

Lily hadn't considered checking the mirror before coming out. It never mattered before now. No one in the family ever cared about her appearance.

She raced back to their bedroom, shut the door, then sat at their small vanity. Aside from the bed and wardrobe, it was the only piece of furniture in their little room. Something their ma claimed to be a *luxury*.

Lily's eyes popped wide at the reflection.

She always braided her hair before bed, and it usually stayed in place. All her flopping about in the night had loosened it. Hair stuck out wildly from every criss-cross.

She rapidly undid it and brushed it smooth. Without thought, her hands began another braid, then she stopped and loosened it again.

Her pa had told her many times that her hair was lovely. Caleb should be allowed to appreciate it. Besides, she had to do *something* to erase the vision she'd just gifted him with.

Because it had been braided for so long, her hair had appealing waves. Its length reached the middle of her back. She brushed it until it shined, then put on a two-toned blue dress and paraded out again.

To her delight, Caleb immediately looked her way. His smile nearly melted her into the floor. Bigger and brighter than the last one she'd seen. She gladly returned it.

"Lily." Her ma's brisk tone ruined the mood. "Go check for eggs." The woman eyed her up and down, then shook her head.

"Why do *I* hafta get the eggs?" Lily gestured to Violet. "She was up first."

"It's *your* chore. Get goin'."

"Yes'm." Lily headed out the door, grumbling to herself.

Her ma wasn't a fool. She, too, understood how things in the cabin had changed.

Lily hoped she wouldn't try and interfere with nature's natural progression. It was bad enough having to compete with her sister.

"I bring in the eggs," she muttered under her breath. "I set the rabbit traps. I chop the wood. I make the poultice." Her fists tightened. "I fix the meat an' tan the hides. Violet does little more than set the table an' look pretty. It ain't fair."

Even when Violet went with her brothers to fetch apples, Lucas was the one who climbed the trees and picked them. Violet would just stand below, catch them in her skirt, then put them in a basket.

None of this had bothered Lily before; now it blared at her just like the Quincy's hunting horn. Loud and crystal clear. "Everyone has time to *play* but me."

She stomped her way past the barn to the chicken pen. Only the white had laid. Lily scowled at the brown. "You gettin' lazy, too?" She lightly poked its feathery breast. It clucked, flapped its wings, then strutted to the far side of the pen.

Lily stared at the single egg in her hand, then sat down hard on her rump. She didn't like herself at the moment.

When she gazed around their property, something even uglier struck hard. They'd let it go. Everything was a mess. Her ma's flowerbeds overflowed with weeds, so much so that the pansies and fall wildflowers couldn't be seen. Buckets and tools lay here and there. Every one of them used to have its own place on shelves in the barn. Her pa had tended every implement and kept them clean and sharp. He simply didn't care anymore.

*I want everythin' beautiful again. My life. Our home. Everythin'.*

Tears threatened.

She blinked hard several times, then looked past the ugliness and took in her blessed cove. Crying would be silly on such a glorious morning.

The sun beamed down and glistened on the dew in the fields. It sparkled like gemstones. The brilliant blue sky held billowing white clouds that drifted slowly past her range of sight. Nature didn't know Lily's troubles—or those of the country. It kept on being the beautiful portrait God painted each and every day.

She needed to appreciate it. *Cherish* it.

Starting with the corn crop. She needed to see how much of it remained.

*Breakfast first.*

She returned inside with the egg and managed a smile when she noticed her pa sitting in the rocker. A nice rosy color lay in his cheeks.

Giggling came from overhead, followed by a loud thump. Her brothers liked to wrestle when they first woke up.

And though Violet remained at Caleb's side, Lily decided to disregard it. If Caleb chose her, then so be it.

Lily held up the egg. "Only one."

Her ma reached for it. "Better than none." She cracked it into a bowl and beat it together with the contents. Presumably corn-meal. They'd have corncakes and apple butter once again.

"Violet," their ma said. "Come set the table."

"Yes'm." She stood, but not before looking at Caleb and briefly touching his arm.

A tinge of jealousy flooded over Lily. Instantly, her chest hurt. To get her mind off it, she went to her pa. "How you feelin' this mornin'?"

He kept his eyes down, as if ashamed. "Better."

She bent over and kissed his cheek. "I'm glad." *No time like the present.* Maybe she could help restore his pride. "Pa? How'd you like to help me put up some a your tools outside? With winter comin' an' all, I thought you'd want them outta the weather."

"Don't feel up to it right now. Some other time."

"*I'll* help." Caleb's unexpected words startled her, but slightly eased the pain in her heart.

She spun around to face him. "You sure *you're* up to it?"

He lightly patted his shoulder. "Thanks to you. Whatever you put in that cloth did a world a good."

"I'll help, too," Violet called out from the table.

"Wonderful." Lily tried to hide her disappointment. "With three of us, we should get it done right fast."

When Lily glanced at their ma, the woman simply shook her head. Sooner or later, Lily had a feeling, she'd speak her mind.

* * *

Caleb begrudgingly put on the green dress *and* the silly bonnet, then headed outside.

He admitted he enjoyed the attention Violet paid him. He'd learned she was sixteen. Plenty old enough for courting. Still, he had no business pursuing anyone.

Setting his mind on hard work would help.

It didn't take long to understand Lily's concern over the many implements laying about. Some were half-buried in the dirt. They'd probably been out during a number of rainstorms. He gathered up small dowels and spades, as well as larger hoes and pitchforks.

Lily came to him with her arms loaded down with buckets and jars. "C'mon with me." She jerked her head toward the barn.

They lay everything on the dirt floor, then rearranged items on a large three-tiered shelf on one side of the structure. They had plenty of room for the smaller items they'd brought in. Once those things were set in place, they neatly lined up the larger tools along the wall.

Lily beamed. "Much better."

They returned outside to look for more.

A dilapidated plow lay propped against a corner of the barn. It had been there so long that grass had grown around it.

Caleb yanked it free, then brushed away mud from the metal.

Lily stood over him. "Reckon we can use it?"

"This old thing?" He examined it closely. "Maybe. If I fix it up some. But . . . what you gonna get to pull it?" He hadn't seen a horse or even a mule *anywhere*. Not since the soldiers left.

Her face fell. "We used to have the finest team a horses you ever did see . . ." She touched the wood handle on the plow. "We'll figure sumthin' out."

He had a horrid vision of himself in a dress pulling the plow, and Lily maneuvering it through the dirt.

He'd succumbed to female attire out of necessity, but some things were too far-fetched.

"Caleb?" Her softened voice brought him from his ridiculous thoughts. "You ever farm?"

"Yep. I know farmin' better than most anythin'. Lived on one most a my life. We grew mainly wheat an' corn." He rose up tall. "What you plannin' on plowin'?"

She pointed far off. "We got corn in a field over there that'll need harvestin' soon. Then, we got wheat to sow." She squared her jaw. "I ain't ready to give up, just cuz folks tend to take what we got. I'll plant the crops, even if I hafta put the wheat in the ground with a spade an' shovel. Someday, I know it's gonna get better again. Why not do what I can to start now?"

Violet wandered close. Caleb hadn't seen her lift a finger. She'd just been roaming around watching them. "Start what, Lily?"

"Workin' the farm. Each an' every one of us needs to help. Includin' Isaac. He can pull weeds."

"But why?" Violet splayed her hands wide. Unlike Lily's, they were completely clean. "Why work on sumthin' that'll be ripped from our fingers?"

"You don't know it for certain." Lily huffed out a breath. "Don't you care 'bout our land, Violet?"

"Course I do. But I don't aim to stay here for the rest a my life." She peered into Caleb's eyes. The girl had become braver since they'd gotten better acquainted. "I'd like to move away an' start a family of my own."

Her meaning couldn't have been plainer. He averted her gaze and nodded at Lily. "I'll help however I can. But we shouldn't sow the wheat till late October. Reckon that means I'll need to stay a while. Not sure that'll set well with your folks."

"If you help with the farm, they won't mind. Like Pa said, he wants you to pull your weight. We best get sumthin' better for you to sleep on, or your bones will ache so much you won't be able to move."

"You mentioned straw. You got some hidden somewhere?"

She jerked her head backward toward the barn and pointed over her shoulder. "Up in the loft. Hay's all gone, but there should be enough straw for a bed tick."

Violet sighed. "I'm gonna go in an' see if Ma needs me. You two don't." Caleb sensed her displeasure with his disregard for her advances. She left before either of them said a word.

Lily watched her go, then faced him, frowning. "You know she's fond a you, right?"

"I ain't blind."

"Good. Don't hurt her. She's never had a beau. An' you just happen to be the only eligible man for miles."

He leaned against the side of the barn and crossed his arms. "So that's all that matters? Me bein' eligible? An' *male*?"

Lily's cheeks rose high from a broad grin. She covered her mouth and stifled a giggle. "Sorry. But havin' you say that in my ugly old dress tickles me. An' that bonnet framin' your whiskers makes it hard *not* to laugh. They sure do grow quick." She continued to struggle controlling her laughter. "Lucky for you, you have *other* redeemin' qualities."

He'd gotten so used to the garments, he'd forgotten he was wearing them. He couldn't blame her for laughing. "What might those be?" He peered deeply into her eyes.

Her mood instantly changed, and every bit of humor vanished. She drew a strand of her loose hair forward and casually ran her fingers through it. He liked that she'd left it out of the braid. However, watching the sensual act dried his throat.

*Nothing* Violet did affected him this way.

"To *our* good fortune," Lily said, then licked her lips. "Aside from the dress, you're fine to look at. Course, havin' you help with the farm makes all the difference in the world to me."

His skin heated and his palms started to sweat. "What *you* think matters to *me*."

They stared at each other, unmoving. He wanted desperately to touch her.

Again, she moistened her lips. "Follow me." She walked away, and he gladly obliged.

# CHAPTER 9

Having Violet's feelings hurt in any way would never suit Lily. Still, she couldn't deny being happy that Caleb had followed her instead of her sister.

*He made me laugh.*

It felt incredible.

Another belief she'd kept close to her heart was that things happened for a reason. Caleb may have been lost in the woods, but no doubt he was meant to find her. How else could she explain the good fortune of having a willing man to help with the farm? One who understood what needed to be done.

Granted, most men could farm. Not all were *eager.* Especially when wounded.

She crossed a large expanse of open grassy fields, then stopped when she reached the corn. Years past, they had much more, but at least this acre yielded some decent stalks.

Caleb moved beside her. "It should be cut soon." He grabbed a cob and peeled back a portion of the husk. "Yep. It's ready. Why ain't ya been eatin' some a this?"

"Pa always says we should wait till the first frost. Hasn't happened yet."

"I understand his reasonin' for the field corn, but you can still pick some of it now to eat."

How could she make him understand? "Pa sets the rules in our house."

Caleb tried to object, so she put up her hand to stop him. "He feels it's best we let it dry, so we can make meal. It lasts longer."

"Yes, but—"

"I know you see him as a drunk. The man *I* know is smart an' able. The war ruined him. We try all we can to build him up an' respect his wishes."

"You're a loyal daughter." He reached for her hand, but she stepped away.

*It's too soon.*

He hadn't fully convinced her that he wasn't like every other man she'd encountered since she'd *blossomed into a woman.* As her ma had called it. "We've already lost a great deal of corn. Just look at the stalks. Others have taken advantage of it."

"Everyone's hungry." His head shifted side to side. "How did you get all this planted? I doubt your sister was any help." His half-smile quickly faded, when Lily faced him, expressionless.

It would be painful to answer his question, but she wouldn't lie. "I had help. There's a captain in the army who'd frequently been comin' by. I asked him if he could spare a few of his men an' horses to help me get the crop in. After all, the soldiers helped themselves to most of our livestock. I told him it was the least they could do." She stared at the ground. "Course, I'm sure they'll be comin' back to collect it."

"Lily?" Caleb moved closer. "The way you're actin' makes me think there's more to it."

She slowly lifted her head and met his gaze. "Captain Ableman wants to collect *me*, too."

Caleb's eyes didn't waver from hers. "Lucas told me. Sumthin' 'bout him kissin' you in the barn."

"Well, I swanee." She stomped her foot. "Nothin's sacred in our house. He had no business tellin' you."

"Don't be mad at him. He's only tryin' to protect you. He warned me to keep my distance. Said your pa wouldn't hesitate pullin' a gun on me if I tried to touch you. Like he done Ableman."

*My goodness.*

Even her little brother looked out for her chastity. "The captain deserved it. I didn't want him comin' near me. If Pa hadn't shown up when he did—"

"Don't think 'bout it." He brushed her cheek with his hand, then drew his fingers through a strand of her hair. Seemed Caleb wasn't paying any mind to Lucas's warning.

The sensation Caleb created by his simple touch sent tingles throughout her body. Like nothing she'd ever felt before. "Caleb, I . . ." She stopped, not sure what to say.

"Lily." He whispered her name like a prayer. "I won't touch you, less you want me to. But I've been drawn to you since the first time I saw you."

She focused on his dark eyes and tried to dismiss the way the feminine blue bonnet outlined his strong masculine features. "Like I told you before, I'm glad you're here."

*Breathe, Lily.*

Even reminding herself didn't help. Excitement and fear had her heart racing. She whipped around, lifted her skirt, and sped home.

* * *

Caleb leaned over and braced his hands against his knees. Lily had taken every bit of his breath. If she'd stayed another moment, he'd surely have kissed her, and he could've sworn she wanted him to.

What a sight that would've been for anyone watching from afar. Two *women* coming together passionately in a field of corn.

Cades Cove would be gossiping for years.

Why she ran off had him stumped. Even so, maybe it was for the best. A fine woman like her shouldn't be with a man like him. The loyalty she showed her pa proved her quality. Her family allegiance ran deep, and Caleb respected that.

*I'll help her with the crops, then leave.*

He could go to another state far away and start a new life. Somewhere the war hadn't tainted. Then maybe in time, he could forget it all.

He trudged toward the cabin, despising himself once again.

A bugle blared and he gasped. He whipped his head around to determine where it had come from. If soldiers were near . . .

Lucas raced out the front door.

Caleb rushed to him and grabbed him by the arm. "Where you goin'? The bugle—"

"It's a mail call. I gotta go see if we got any."

Caleb's heart calmed. He stood tall, releasing the boy. "Mail? Where?"

"The Quincy's house. Mr. Quincy's the postmaster. Someone brings the mail once a week. We gotta collect it there." He studied Caleb's face. "You best get inside. Your whiskers are showin' again." Smirking, he ran off.

Caleb took his advice and went in. Lily's beautiful brown eyes looked his way, then immediately turned.

He pointed over his shoulder. "Lucas said you might have mail?"

"Maybe." Mrs. Larsen lifted her head. She sat at the table, sewing on the dress Lily had worn the day he'd tackled her in the woods. "Even if we don't get any, they'll have news to share. Lucas is right good at relayin' all he hears."

Yes, Caleb had already experienced the boy's ability at eavesdropping and tattling.

Caleb rubbed his scruffy face. "Lily? Would you mind so much shavin' me again?"

She eased across the room and stood beside him. The air thickened simply from her closeness. "I should've realized I'd need to do it daily. Your hair's so dark—you can't hide it."

He glanced at the sofa, where Violet was sitting. She kept her eyes forward, gazing at the fire, seemingly ignoring them. Maybe he'd *already* hurt her.

"Once I can move my arm better," he said, "I can try to do it myself. But I confess, I ain't never been too good with a razor."

"I don't mind." Lily scooted a chair from the table and set it beside the wash basin. Just like before. "I'll be right back."

Caleb sat and waited.

Mrs. Larsen turned all her attention to the dress. It looked like she was adding on a strip of material to the place Lily had torn. Sadly, it didn't match very well, though he doubted Lily would care.

Mr. Larsen dozed in the rocker. The other two boys sat on the floor close to the fireplace, not too far from Violet's feet.

They both had slates and were screeching slate pencils over the surface. Caleb winced at the unpleasant sound, but after a short time, he grew accustomed to it. Obviously, Mr. Larsen had, too.

"What are they workin' on?" Caleb asked Lily, when she returned with the razor.

"Letters of the alphabet. We all help them, but Violet has the best penmanship."

Her words turned Violet's head. She donned a brief smile, then faced forward again.

The sight relieved him, though he probably worried too much. He wasn't a great catch. The girl shouldn't *want* to trouble herself with him.

He closed his eyes and enjoyed the feel of the lather Lily spread across his face. Something in her touch felt more intimate than before.

*Stop thinkin' that way.*

The peace in the cabin ended when Lucas returned. "No mail." He plopped into a chair at the table. "But Mrs. Quincy's nose has been in our business."

"What?" Mrs. Larsen stopped sewing, and Lily stilled the razor.

"Her grandson, Billy, was spyin' on us. He saw Caleb outside with Lily. Course, he thought she was a girl, an' he knew she was too big to be Violet or you, Ma."

Lily moved closer to Lucas. "What did they say 'bout him—*her*?"

Lucas laughed. "He don't look like a *her* right now."

Caleb's face was only half-shaved. One side remained covered in lather.

"Lucas Larsen," Lily fussed. "Tell us what they said."

"Mrs. Quincy wanted to know who she was, an' when she got here."

Wide-eyed, Mrs. Larsen grabbed his hand. "What did you tell her?" Her eyes narrowed, and her face hardened.

Lucas puffed up tall and pulled his hand to himself. "I said she's my cousin. Come from St. Louis."

"Oh, my dear Lord." His poor ma rapidly fanned her face. "A lie that can't be undone. I know she'll come by wantin' every last detail. How could you say such a thing, Lucas?"

"What was I s'posed to say?" His lips screwed together, then he leaned across the table. "If I'd a told the truth, it woulda spread for miles. We'd a likely seen Captain Ableman at our door to take Caleb away."

"Boy's right."

Every head in the room snapped around, facing Mr. Larsen. The man wasn't sleeping as soundly as Caleb had thought.

"But Buck." Mrs. Larsen scooted her chair back, went to him, and knelt down. "Harriet Quincy knows I have a sister in St. Louis, but I've never before mentioned children. Helen's barren.

How do I explain a cousin? Worse yet, why would Helen ever send a girl to the cove at a time like this?"

Mr. Larsen ran his hand over his wife's head in the most loving gesture Caleb had seen him display. "We'll work through it. Figger out sumthin' to make sense. Then we'll all tell the same story." He looked from face to face. "Hear me?"

"Yes, Pa," all the children said at the same time.

With the exception of Lily. She took her place beside Caleb and once again drew the blade across his skin. "What kinda tale would *ever* make sense?"

Her ma returned to the table and sat. "Well . . . let's talk it through." Her hands shook as she picked up the fabric and needle. "First, since she's barren, we'll say the girl was orphaned, an' they adopted her." She swallowed hard and began to sew.

"Good, Rose," Mr. Larsen said, slowly rocking.

"But why come *here*?" Lily asked. "Ain't like we have sumthin' to offer her."

Her ma's breathing grew more rapid, as did the rate at which she pulled the needle through the cloth. "Helen knew we needed help on the farm, so she sent her."

"Makes sense to me," Lucas mumbled.

"But how did I . . . I mean, *she* get here?" Caleb asked. Everything else seemed to be falling nicely into place.

Mrs. Larsen huffed out a breath. "My sister an' her husband, Stuart, have plenty a money. If not for this horrid war, they'd have sent her by rail to Knoxville. Yet from all we've heard, many of the rail lines have been destroyed or taken over by the army. So, the only way they could've gotten her here would be by hirin' someone to bring her." She slammed the dress onto the table, then clutched her chest. "A trip that would've taken *weeks*. They'll *never* believe us."

"Why not?" Caleb took the towel Lily handed him and wiped the remaining soap from his fully shaved face. "If your sister is generous an' caring, an' she believed sendin' you some help would be the right thing to do, I'm sure she could've found someone willin' to bring me. Especially if the price was right."

He looked over at Mr. Larsen, who grinned and nodded.

Mrs. Larsen shifted her eyes between him and Caleb. "An' then, the hired man would simply go on his way. Possibly without bein' seen. Right?"

"Yep." Mr. Larsen rocked quite a bit faster. "Reckon we got us our story. You children been listenin'?" He pointed at the boys on the floor.

"Yes, Pa," Horace said.

Isaac's face scrunched together, then he stuck his nose in the air. "Caleb's a girl from St. Louis where Auntie Helen lives." His words came out like gospel.

"Good nuff," their pa said.

Mrs. Larsen's cheeks lost all their color. "Lord, forgive us for lyin'," she mumbled, then bent her head low and kept sewing.

"But what do we call Caleb?" Horace asked. "That ain't no girl's name."

"You're right." Mr. Larsen gazed upward as if looking for inspiration. "Her name's Callie. Close enough, ain't it, Caleb?"

"Yessir." He sighed and smoothed his skirt.

Seems he'd be wearing it for quite some time.

# CHAPTER 10

*Callie?*

Every thought spinning through Lily's mind revolved around Caleb, as she mindlessly stuffed straw into the bed tick. Yes, it had been her idea to dress him like a woman, but she'd never considered giving him a girl's name.

Lies always had a way of coming around and causing more trouble than good. Though she deemed these particular false-hoods *necessary*, she couldn't help but worry. Now that Mrs. Quincy knew they had a guest, she'd surely come by to meet *her*.

Unfortunately—thanks to a set of spectacles she'd gotten from a doctor in Knoxville—the old busy-body had perfect eyesight. If the woman got within ten feet of Caleb, she'd know he was any-thing other than female.

"How you doin' up there?" Caleb hollered from below, star-tling Lily from her thoughts.

As ever-present as he'd been on her mind, she'd momentarily forgotten he was so close. Silly thing to do when she cared so much about him.

"Lily?" The concern in his voice warmed her. "You all right?"

"I'm fine." Since his shoulder hadn't healed completely, she'd insisted he not climb into the loft. "I've almost got enough. I'll toss the tick down, but *don't* try catchin' it." She peered over the edge.

He grinned and held out his arms.

*He loves to tease.*

Whether insinuating he'd disregard her warning about catching the bed tick or perhaps lifting his arms for her, she wasn't completely sure. But he'd definitely been smiling a lot more lately. Every time he did, it sent her heart pattering as fast as a spooked rabbit.

She poked a handful of straw into the casing, attempting to distract her over-working heart. "Be glad we had this old tick. It's a mite worse for the wear, but it's clean. With a few blankets, you should sleep just fine."

"Thank you, Lily. I appreciate all you've done for me. The pillow was more than kind. I'll return it soon as we get in the cabin."

She scooted close to the edge. "You keep it. I have another that suits me." Not nearly as soft and comfortable as the one she was letting him use, yet she wouldn't dream of taking it away from him. "Now then . . ." She waved her hand to the side. "Step outta the way."

He obliged without gest this time.

With a gentle shove, the tick fell to the barn floor. Some of the straw fell out, and Caleb bent down and started stuffing it back inside.

She moved to the ladder and climbed down. "I'll sew up the openin' when we get it in the cabin." She gathered up bits of wayward straw to help him.

"Thank you."

"You say that all the time." She laughed when their hands bumped together as they simultaneously tried cramming in straw. "Your folks taught you manners. *Thank you. Yessir. Yes'm.* I appreciate you showin' my family so much respect."

"They didn't hafta help me. I'll never be able to repay all you done for me."

They both clutched onto the bed tick. Caleb stood motionless and simply looked at her. No smile this time, but the hunger in his eyes said something else.

*He wants to kiss me.*

She'd seen the same intent gaze from Captain Ableman.

Instinct told her to bolt, or at least look away. She chose to ignore it. Her eyes remained affixed to his. "Helpin' with the farm is all we need," she whispered, then gulped. His fingers rubbed over hers in a tender caress.

Their faces inched closer. His warm breath dusted her cheek.

"Hey!" Lucas ran in, and Lily quickly stepped back. "You two best get your tails in the cabin. I just seen Mrs. Quincy comin' up the road."

Exactly what Lily had feared. "We gotta hide you, Caleb."

His eyes met hers again. "But she knows I'm here. Well, she's expectin' *Callie*."

"An' if she sees *her* up close, she'll know we've been lyin'." Lily took a firm hold on the tick and hurried from the barn.

She considered telling Caleb to run off and hide in the woods, but how would they explain Callie's absence? It would be out of character for her family to allow the girl to wander alone in a strange place.

Caleb ran up beside Lily, grabbed the other side of the mattress, and kept pace with her.

"I'll keep a watch on Mrs. Quincy," Lucas said and took off the other direction.

With Caleb's help, Lily dragged the tick into the house. They placed it in his corner, all-the-while being watched by her ma. The poor woman looked scared to death, pacing and mumbling.

Lily gestured to Caleb's bed. "Lay down. I'll close the curtain an' tell Mrs. Quincy you ain't feelin' well. That should do for now."

He nodded and did as she said, then she tugged on the curtain until she was certain it wouldn't gape open.

Horace giggled. "You all right, Ma?"

The woman stopped pacing, yanked out a chair at the table, and sat. "Right as rain." Her damp face said otherwise. She was sweating something fierce.

Violet took the chair beside her, then grasped her hand. "We'll be fine, Ma. We all know the story."

"Yep!" Isaac proudly chimed. "Caleb's Callie from St. Louis."

*Oh, my.*

If he repeated the same thing when Mrs. Quincy arrived, they'd be done for.

Lily rubbed her temples. "That's right, Isaac, but you best keep quiet while Mrs. Quincy's here."

Their pa stood from the rocker. "Come with me, son." He took Isaac's hand. "You an' me is goin' for a walk."

The boy's eyes widened like saucers, then he beamed. He happily followed the man out the door. No sooner had it closed, and it opened again.

Lucas walked in followed by Mrs. Quincy.

Lily's ma stood. "Hello, Harriet. Right kind of you to come by." Her lips twitched a mite when she smiled, but Lily doubted Mrs. Quincy noticed.

The large round woman crossed the room and stood beside the table. "Nice to see you, Rose. I've come to meet your niece." She held her spectacles tight to her face with her right hand and peered around the room. "Where is she?"

It truly amazed Lily that at a time when folks struggled for food, Mrs. Quincy somehow retained her more-than-full-bodied size. Worse yet, the woman loved to gossip and frequently instigated disputes amongst residents of the cove. Her behavior made it nearly impossible to like her. Especially now. She could ruin everything.

Lily's ma lifted her chin and pointed at the curtain. "Callie's restin'. I'm afraid she's . . . *ill.*"

"*Oh.*" Mrs. Quincy clutched her chest and waddled backward toward the door. "Your boy shoulda told me." She nervously cleared her throat. "Hope you feel better soon," she called out, addressing the curtain.

"Thank you."

Lily almost burst out laughing at Caleb's high-pitched squeaky attempt at sounding like a sick female. Needing to compose herself, she spun around and faced away from their neighbor.

"Oh, my," the woman muttered. "She sounds simply awful."

"Yes," Lily's ma said. "Came on her quite sudden-like."

Lily eased herself into a position to watch the interchange, but kept her lips pinched tight.

Mrs. Quincy's rump pressed against the shut door. "I won't trouble you anymore today." She turned on her heels and fumbled with the doorknob. Without saying another word, she opened it and fled.

Lily's ma slumped down into her chair and sighed. "Thank heavens."

Lily let out her own relieved exhalation, then crossed to her and rested a hand on her shoulder. "Illness is always a good deterrent." After giving her ma a pat, Lily moved to the curtain, parted it with one hand, and peered inside. "You coulda pretended to be asleep."

"Why?" He used the same horrible, grating voice. "I thought I done quite well. She believed I was sick."

Lily rolled her eyes and stepped away. The man certainly amused her. Whether or not they could keep up the charade long enough to manage the crops was another story.

Their near-kiss added an even greater complexity to their ordeal.

She wanted Caleb in a way she'd never experienced before.

Oddly, it felt incredibly good.

* * *

Caleb chuckled silently to himself, but in mere moments, he completely sobered.

He shouldn't be happy. He'd brought Lily into his life in a way he never should have. Their flirtation had to stop before things got carried away.

He lay still on the comfortable tick and shut his eyes.

*I'll make a mess of everythin' if I keep goin' on like this.*

If Lucas hadn't interrupted, Caleb would've kissed Lily. He wanted to hold her, and he was as certain as the sun would rise tomorrow, she would've let him.

"Callie, *dear*," Lily teasingly called out in a manner that affirmed everything he'd thought. "You can come out now."

His heart thumped. "I'm kinda tired." He no longer altered his voice and removed every trace of playfulness. "Reckon I'll take me a nap if that's all right with you."

"Maybe she *is* sick," Horace said. He used the feminine reference as if he believed it to be true.

Footsteps neared the curtain. "You all right?" Lily's sweet voice wrenched his confused heart.

"I need some rest. My shoulder an' all." Another lie. It didn't bother him one bit.

"Oh." She sounded suspicious. "Well, maybe I should have a look at it. It might need another poultice."

"The man's tired," her ma harshly said. "Leave 'im be."

"Yes'm." As Lily's steps took her further away, Caleb's heart sank.

He'd not come here to hurt more people, yet everywhere he went, he ruined lives.

*I shoulda bled to death.*

Self-pity wasn't an attractive trait, but he didn't want to impress *anyone*.

Even long before he fully appreciated them, he used to gloat over the way girls looked at him and ignored Abraham. Their ma had always fawned over Caleb, calling him her *handsome boy.* Oftentimes, she completely ignored his brother.

Rebecca had changed everything.

Maybe Caleb had been trying to prove to himself that he'd retained the charisma to attract females, so he'd been toying with Lily and Violet.

He tightened his fists.

*No.*

He didn't want to believe he was still that kind of man. His feelings for Lily went deeper. It wasn't a game, which scared him even more.

# CHAPTER 11

After losing numerous nights of sleep fretting over his situation, Caleb came to a firm decision. He'd help with whatever needed to be done on the farm, which included staying until the wheat could be sown. Even if they had to plant it with shovels and spades.

*A dismal prospect.*

October had arrived, but as of yet, no frost. Since he wouldn't cross Mr. Larsen, he abided by the man's wishes and didn't push to harvest the corn. Hopefully, they could do it soon.

In addition to helping around the farm, he internally struggled with a much harder decision. He stopped his flirtatious pursuit of Lily. However, whenever he got anywhere near her, the urge to reach out and grab her overwhelmed him. To make it easier, he paid most of his attention to her little brothers.

Caleb had become quite good at marbles. Enough time had passed that his shoulder moved with ease. Not only did it make shooting marbles simpler, but when the time came to plant, it would be a lot less painful. He hoped they could somehow acquire a horse or mule to pull the plow. If they had to do everything by hand, his wound could be reinjured.

"Time to get in bed, *boys*." Lily's tone had grown increasingly harsher. She'd started to sound like her ma. "Put the marbles away."

Caleb glanced up at her from his seated position on the floor, but she immediately turned her head.

Lucas snickered. "Best do as she says, *boy*." He poked Caleb in the leg.

Violet's demeanor had also changed. She kept her distance from him and rarely spoke. To anyone.

*The sooner I leave, the better.*

Caleb hunted down marbles that had rolled out of reach, then dropped them into the leather pouch in Horace's grasp. Before the boy took off to the loft, Caleb ran a hand over his hair. "You played a good game."

"But I lost." His head tipped to the side, and he frowned.

"Don't matter. What's important is how you play. You did your best. Maybe next time you'll beat me."

"*I'd* like to beat you," Lily mumbled under her breath, then bustled off to her bedroom and shut the door.

Violet had retired over an hour ago, along with her folks.

Horace looked up into Caleb's face, still frowning. "Why don't my sister like you no more?"

How should he answer? No words came to mind, so Caleb shrugged.

Lucas took the pouch of marbles from his brother and motioned to the stairs. "Lily's a woman, Horace. Someday you'll understand their minds don't work right. Not like ours."

"Oh." Seemingly satisfied, Horace followed his brother to the loft.

Isaac shuffled after them. Before climbing the steps, he turned, smiled, and waved his little hand. At least not everyone in the house wished he'd leave.

*The boys are safe.*

Their sisters were another matter.

One day they'd come to understand he'd done them a favor.

* * *

If Lily didn't need Caleb's help, she'd kick him from their home tomorrow. Once they'd sown the wheat, she'd make him leave.

She'd done all she could to piece together the change in his behavior. She'd believed with every part of her that she'd broken through to him. He'd smiled and laughed, then just like a snuffed-out fire, he'd changed in an instant.

It had started the day of Mrs. Quincy's visit and had grown steadily worse. Now, he paid her little-to-no attention. He went by himself to the rabbit traps and prepared the meat, he pulled weeds with Isaac, and he even took off scouting with Lucas.

The man faithfully wore his dress and bonnet whenever he went outside and let her shave him daily. Otherwise, he'd become a stranger.

She crawled into bed beside Violet and cuddled close. It was getting colder every day.

Violet sniffled.

*She's cryin'.*

"Violet?" Lily whispered. "What's wrong?"

"Nothin'." Her shoulders jerked, and she sobbed harder.

"Tell me the truth."

Ever-so-slowly, Violet shifted onto her back. "We're destined to be old maids."

"Oh, sweetie. Don't say that." Lily propped herself up on one elbow. "This war will end soon, an' you'll find a wonderful man." She drew her fingers through her sister's hair, attempting to calm her.

Tears trickled down Violet's cheeks. "We both thought *Caleb* was wonderful. An' we were wrong. There ain't no decent men no more."

Lily agreed with her regarding Caleb, but she wouldn't give up on every man in the country. She let out a long sigh, then dabbed at Violet's tears with the sleeve of her nightgown. "Have faith. God won't have us growin' old alone. He loves us too much."

"If He's so lovin', why's He allowin' this war?"

"There's a lotta hate in the world that God didn't put there. That don't mean He don't care. I reckon He's up in heaven cryin' every time a soldier dies. Fact is, He's probably weepin' for *you* right now, cuz He feels your broken heart."

"Yours, too?"

Her words brought tears to *Lily's* eyes. She quickly wiped them away. "Mine ain't broke. I thought Caleb cared 'bout me, but he only cares for himself. I'm glad I came to realize it 'fore he took a stronger hold on my heart."

Her insides ached simply saying the words. She hurt whenever she got near him. Admittedly, he had a tighter hold than she was willing to confess.

Violet took her hand and squeezed. "Lily, he'll be gone soon. In time, I doubt either of us will remember what he looks like."

Lily lay flat on her back, still holding onto her sister. "I hope you're right."

For some time, they were silent. If not for Violet's occasional sigh, Lily thought she might be going to sleep.

The girl released a longer, *louder* sigh. "I feel better now." Violet let go of her, then tugged the blankets high up to their necks. "Talkin' helped. I'll try to do better an' be more optimistic like you." She rolled onto her side, facing away from Lily.

*Optimistic?*

Though she'd always tried to see the bright side of things, right now, her life seemed darker than the bedroom. After all, she was older than Violet. The time necessary for Lily to find a husband was rapidly running out.

* * *

"They're comin'!" Lucas yelled from the loft overhead.

Lily sat bolt upright in bed.

The hunting horn blared, and the entire household sprang to life. Violet and Lily threw on their clothes and rushed from their room.

"Soldiers?" Caleb asked, looking right at Lily. He, too, had put on his dress and stood firmly in the middle of the floor with his arms crossed over his chest.

Lucas flew to the front door. "I'm goin' for the chickens." Without another word, he was gone.

Like a well-rehearsed dance, Lily and her ma moved the kitchen table. Caleb and the children grabbed the chairs, then they shoved the rug aside.

Her ma dropped to her knees, jerked up one of the planks, and started tossing in anything of value. "Buck. Give me your boots."

The boots were in their regular spot by the fireplace. He nabbed them and pitched them to her.

Fortunately, since they'd not yet started breakfast, no food had been set out. All the cornmeal remained hidden.

Her ma put the board back in place, and they shoved everything where it belonged.

"Pa," Violet said, "is your gun in your room?"

"Yep. Behind the chest a drawers."

She headed that direction.

"What do we do 'bout *him*?" Their ma pointed at Caleb, looking as if she might cry.

"He needs to hide," Lily said. "Anywhere but here."

"She's right." Her pa gestured to the door. "Get on outta here an' find a place to lay low till sunset."

"Yessir." Caleb reached for the doorknob, then froze.

Heavy boots stomped onto the front porch.

Violet whimpered, standing in the doorway of their folks' bedroom, rifle in hand.

"Put it back," their pa barked.

She whipped around, then returned empty-handed.

Lily's ma fluttered her hands wildly at Caleb. "You're sick. Get behind the curtain."

Caleb had the blankets secured before Lily could take a breath. Sickness might have worked before, but this time she feared he'd be caught.

Isaac watched every move with wide eyes. If the boy said anything at all . . .

Lily held a hand to her wildly beating heart. She cared more for Caleb than she wanted to admit. If discovered, they'd likely kill him and not bother taking him back to camp. They'd probably see it as a waste of their energy.

Never before had her family been given such late warning, yet the soldiers had never come so early in the day. The Quincy's grandson must've been caught off guard, and the soldiers found them all sleeping. The boy would've waited to blow the horn till the men left their house.

Lily could only pray Lucas hadn't been seen, and that no one would look behind the curtain or search through her folks' room and find the gun.

A heavy fist pounded on the door. It vibrated so hard, the noise reverberated through the cabin.

Violet rushed to Lily's side and grasped her hand.

"Open up!" Another firm knock.

From the sound of the footsteps, there was more than one soldier.

Lily's pa stood tall and paraded to the door. Stone-faced, he opened it.

"Good morning, *Buck*." There was no mistaking *that* voice.

Lily swallowed the huge lump in her throat. Captain Ableman had returned. No other soldier called her pa by that name. She saw it as his way of taunting him. After her pa had pulled the gun on him, the captain had become bolder. Likely to prove he wouldn't be bested.

"Ableman?" Her pa spoke coldly. "Why you here?"

The captain pushed past him, followed by two others Lily had never seen before. All of them wore fine gray uniforms. Neat. Tidy. Perfect. As if they did little more than wander the valley and terrorize common folk.

Violet tightened her grasp.

Captain Ableman removed his hat and smoothed his hand over his thick blond hair, then nodded at their ma. "Good morning, ma'am."

Her faced paled completely white, and she didn't utter a sound.

The captain chuckled and roamed through the room. He curiously eyed the blanket curtain, but didn't touch it.

The first time Lily had seen him, she'd thought he was handsome. Though her pa's age, he was taller and broad-shouldered. And he had unusual gray eyes, brought out by the color of his uniform.

Nothing about him appealed to her any longer.

He fanned his arm above the table. "Shall I assume you have no breakfast for us?"

Lily's pa moved beside him. "I asked why you was here. We ain't got nothin' to feed ya."

"That's not exactly true." The captain's prim and proper speech infuriated Lily.

*You think you're so much better than us.*

"B-but . . ." Her ma found her voice, yet it sure wasn't coming out well. "We d-*don't* have any food."

A sly smile formed on the man's face. He looked directly at Lily. "I saw the corn crop. We'll be taking what's ours."

Lily let go of Violet and marched over to the disgusting man. "It ain't yours."

He licked his lips and studied her from head to toe. Sweat trickled down her back. The other two men smirked.

*What did he tell you 'bout me?*

Captain Ableman inhaled deeply. His broad chest rose high. "That which you sow, so shall you reap." Another grin. "We sowed, we're here to *reap*."

If only she'd listened to Caleb, they would've already harvested the corn. They could've hidden it.

Her ma hissed out a breath, then shook a single finger. "Don't go quotin' scripture in my house, when I know you're usin' it for devil's work." She didn't stutter once.

"Sweet woman," Ableman said, unfazed. "I'm a Godly man. Haven't we been gracious to you in the past? We won't take *all* of it. Only our fair share."

One of the other soldiers wandered close to Violet, smiling at her like he'd never seen a female before. She stood frozen to the floor, but her body shook.

"Our fair share," the man repeated Ableman's words, then touched Violet's cheek.

She gasped.

"Get your hands off my girl!" Their pa stepped between the pair and scowled at the man. His eyes shot fire.

Ableman laughed. "No gun this time, Buck? I'd say you're at a disadvantage."

A loud cough erupted from behind the curtain.

Ableman's head snapped to the side. "Who's back there?"

"My niece." Lily's pa glared at him. "She's sick. We been prayin' we don't *all* catch it. Already lost more than one child."

The three soldiers exchanged glances, then briskly walked to the door.

"We'll take the corn and go," Ableman snarled. "But mark my words, we'll be back. You have plenty more that we want. Sooner or later, we'll take it." His eyes rested on Lily.

She shuddered. It felt as if his gaze had penetrated beneath the fabric of her dress. Instinctively, she covered her bosom.

Ableman's brows lifted. With a sickening smile and nod, he left, followed by his two despicable lap dogs.

Violet burst into tears.

"They ain't worth cryin'," Lily said. She took her sister into her arms and held her. "Shh. They're gone. No need to cry."

Caleb's head eased out from the curtained space. Air hissed from his nostrils. "If they lay a hand on your girls . . ." His anger-filled eyes pinched into slits. "Next time, let me shoot 'em."

"Reckon I'd let ya." Lily's pa clenched his single fist, then beat it on the table. "Damn them!"

Violet jumped, then sped off to the bedroom, closing the door behind her.

"Buck," their ma fussed. "You know better than to talk that way."

"Woman." He pounded again. "Now's not the time."

She pinched her lips together, then turned her back to him.

Still breathing heavily, Caleb inched into the room and stood beside the sofa. Lily could swear he wanted to bolt after the men. His wild expression reminded her of an animal ready to chase its prey—wanting to kill.

Lily hadn't been able to take her eyes off him, and when he looked her direction, their gaze locked. Something that hadn't happened in almost a month.

Her belly fluttered, and her heart raced. An utterly different feeling than she had being scrutinized by Captain Ableman.

The fury in Caleb's eyes turned to worry. Then his concern became something resembling longing. She couldn't look away. Somehow, she had to find a way to confront him.

*I know you care.*

She blinked, and in that instant, broke their contact.

He sat on the sofa and faced the fire, which barely flamed. The large, slow-burning back log had nearly died.

"Can you stoke the fire, Caleb?" Lily said as kindly as she could. "Don't want it to go out."

He nodded, but didn't look at her, then got up, poked around at the embers, and added another log.

Lily took a seat at the kitchen table. "What should I do 'bout the corn?"

"Nothin' right now," her pa said. "Till we know them soldiers is gone, keep yourself inside. Violet, too. I don't trust them. Not one bit."

"Reckon Lucas is all right?"

"We'll know come nightfall."

Lily's worry over her *littlest* brother had been unwarranted. Poor Isaac still looked scared to death. He huddled in the corner with Horace.

She almost went to them, when Caleb motioned for them to join him on the sofa. The boys wasted no time. Isaac climbed into Caleb's lap and laid his head on his shoulder. Caleb tenderly stroked the boy's head.

A bad man would never do something so loving.

There had to be a reason why he'd shunned her, and she aimed to find out.

# CHAPTER 12

Having Isaac close, calmed Caleb. He'd grown especially fond of the little boy. More so than his older brothers, though Caleb cared about them, too.

Truthfully, the entire family had worked their way into his heart. They were good folks who didn't deserve this kind of horrid treatment.

When Ableman had spoken to Lily as he had, it was all Caleb could do to stay hidden. He'd wanted to pummel the man.

Caleb knew other soldiers who believed it was their right to take any woman they desired. He'd heard many a man boast about the spoils of war. As if a woman's body was just an object—no different from food or animals they'd helped themselves to.

*Lily and Violet ain't safe.*

After hearing the lust in Ableman's voice, Caleb realized he had a far more important reason to stay. He'd protect the women, or die trying.

Isaac tapped Caleb's arm. "Wanna play marbles?"

"Not right now. Maybe later." He smiled at the boy and got one in return, then Isaac rested his head down once again.

Caleb sensed Lily's eyes on him. He moved his head one slow inch at a time, till he'd turned it just enough to see her from the corner of his sight. She and her folks sat at the kitchen table, unmoving and silent, as if they were afraid to do a thing.

He couldn't blame them. If her ma gathered provisions for breakfast, she'd risk being discovered. And since Lily's pa had told her to stay in the cabin, she, too, seemed unsure what to do. Such a strong woman, yet suddenly so frail.

*If only I could hold her.*

He scolded himself for the thought. He'd done well distancing himself from her. Just because he cared didn't give him the right to upset her life by bringing himself back into it.

"I'm gonna check on Violet," Lily whispered, then scooted her chair from the table and went into their bedroom.

*Good.*

Caleb breathed a bit easier, but the day drug on.

Mrs. Larsen brought out her Bible and read scriptures aloud. Horace and Isaac played marbles for a while, then got their slates and worked on their letters.

At one point, Violet and Lily returned to the table. They sewed and listened to their ma read.

Caleb felt utterly useless.

He dozed on the sofa, as did Mr. Larsen, close by in the rocker. It helped time pass, but it didn't ease the rumblings of every stomach in the room.

"This is silly!" Mrs. Larsen slammed the Bible shut. "I'm fixin' some food. They ain't comin' back. Not with someone sick inside." She stood. "Help me move the table."

The girls did as she asked, and soon the woman was on her knees digging through items under the floorboards. "Wish I had some eggs."

They'd be fortunate if they still had *chickens*. Caleb's gut told him Lucas was fine, but he wouldn't fully relax until the boy came home.

As dusk set in, they nibbled on cornmeal mush mixed with apple butter. Surprisingly tasty. Then again, hunger made Caleb appreciate anything.

Another hour passed and full-on darkness set in. Along with the glow from the fire, two lanterns provided light for the room.

Mrs. Larsen paced. "Lucas should be home by now." She nibbled her fingernails. "Buck? Reckon it's safe to send Lily after him?"

"No," Caleb firmly said. "Ableman could be outside waitin' for her."

Mr. Larsen sluggishly nodded. "He's right."

"But what are we s'posed to do?" His wife fisted her hands on her hips. "It's gettin' right cold. Lucas can't be out all night, an' Lily's the only one who knows where to look for 'im."

"I'll be fine." Lily looked directly at Caleb. "I doubt the captain will be watchin' us after dark."

Caleb folded his arms over his chest. "Don't be so sure of yourself. Men'll lie in wait for sumthin' they want." He kept his eyes affixed to hers. This was too serious to back down.

When Lily lowered her eyes, Caleb moved his attention to her pa. "If you let me take your gun, I'll go with Lily to look for Lucas. An' you can be sure, I won't hesitate shootin' any of them soldiers if they come close."

"Shootin' in the dark ain't too bright." Mr. Larsen leaned back in his chair and let out a long breath. "I don't see no other way. Take a lantern. If them men is out there, it'll draw them to ya, but it'll also give enough light to see your way, an' to shoot if you hafta." He jerked his head toward his bedroom. "Violet, fetch my gun. Horace. Go get the ammo box."

"Yes, Pa," they both replied and hurried off.

Caleb found it unusual that the bullets were kept in a different location than the gun. Not a wise thing to do if they needed to quickly load it.

Horace brought the box down from the loft and handed it to his pa. The man drew out three bullets, then extended them to Caleb. "One for each man. Hope you're as good a shot as you claim."

"I don't miss." Caleb tucked the ammunition into the pocket of his skirt. "They won't be expectin' a *woman* to know how to handle a gun."

Lily huffed. "I hope you don't hafta shoot at all." She put on a coat, then handed him another. "This is Violet's, but I reckon it'll fit you."

With the lantern in her grasp, she headed for the door. Caleb tied his bonnet, slipped on the coat, then followed her, clutching the rifle.

The crisp night air crept up Caleb's dress, and he shivered. "Don't know how you women tolerate these clothes."

"Shh." She leered at him, then faced forward and plodded across the grass toward the mountainside.

He increased his pace to keep up with her. "There's no one about. I'm sure of it." His intuitions gave him *some* comfort.

"You can't be certain. If you was, why bother with Pa's gun?" She moved further up the hill.

He grabbed her by the arm. "Lily. Stop a minute."

She faced him, scowling. "My brother left this mornin' without a coat. I know he's cold, an' I wanna find him."

"So do I. But . . ." *I might not get another chance.* "Lily, I don't want nothin' bad to happen to you. That's why I brung the rifle." He stepped closer. "I care 'bout you."

"Coulda fooled me. You ain't even *looked* at me for weeks. I thought we had sumthin', but I ain't gonna put up with no man playin' me like a fiddle. I don't want no on-again-off-again man. Hear me?" She whipped around and took a step. His hold kept her from moving farther. "Let go!"

"Not yet." Gently, he brought her nearer. "There's reasons I kept my distance, but I can't fight my feelin's for you no more. When Ableman—"

"Hush." She pressed her fingers to his mouth. "Don't talk." Her chest heaved and she inched even closer.

The glow from the dim lantern eerily lit up her face, yet she'd never looked so beautiful. She caressed his cheek with a trembling hand. "Caleb," she whispered, then kissed him.

He nearly dropped the rifle. His heart beat so hard, it thumped in his ears. He eagerly returned her kiss. Her warm lips tasted as sweet as the apple butter.

When they parted, he wanted more. He'd given in to his craving, relieved she'd initiated the act. It left no doubt that she wanted him.

"I love you, Lily." He buried his face in her hair. "I have for some time now. Forgive me for bein' distant. There's things 'bout me—"

"Shh . . ." Her lips glided over his face, brushing his skin with soft pecks. "You can tell me everythin' later. But I know there ain't nothin' you can say that'll change how I feel 'bout you. Cuz I love *you*, too." Her mouth covered his again. As their kiss deepened, she softly moaned.

The sensual sound brought out a much stronger desire. One he'd be a fool to satisfy.

*I hafta control myself.*

He took a large breath and glided his fingers into her thick hair. "We best find Lucas."

She rapidly nodded, then took hold of Caleb's hand and led him up the hillside.

Could she truly be so forgiving? Maybe love *would* overcome all. One thing was certain, he wanted to try. Fighting his feelings had made both of them miserable.

Loving Lily felt right. Whether he deserved her or not.

* * *

*He loves me.*

The thought kept Lily moving forward with a smile on her freshly kissed lips. She'd dreamed about kissing him many times. The actual contact surpassed the finest of dreams.

Still, she wasn't foolish. For now, she and Caleb needed to keep their feelings between them. Her folks had too much to worry about without fretting over what she and Caleb might be doing any time they were alone.

Just the idea of being with Caleb somewhere by themselves and undisturbed, warmed her to the core. In stark contrast, a foreign prickly sensation brought chill bumps to her skin. Her heart fluttered, but she'd never felt so wonderful.

*Love's amazin'.*

Her mind spun in fantastic ways. Finally, she could envision a future that included a husband, and someday, children.

She squeezed his hand, saying nothing. Words weren't necessary. The caress of Caleb's thumb across the back of her hand perfectly answered her.

They neared the small cave, where she hoped to find Lucas. She let go of Caleb and held the lantern high. "See that burrow in the side a the mountain?"

"Nope."

She led him closer. "There's an overhang and bushes that hide it right well. Lucas oftentimes goes there. Last time he hid up in the trees, but with so few leaves now, it'd be easier to see him an' not such a good idea."

"Let's hope he's in the hollow. That enclosure might keep him warm."

Lily sighed with relief when they reached the opening. Lucas's silhouette showed in the glowing lamplight. He lay on his side, facing inward.

*He ain't movin'.*

"Lucas?" Heart pounding, she poked him in the back.

The boy inhaled deeply, then sat up and rubbed his eyes. He let out a loud yawn.

"You was sleepin'?" Lily shook her head. "You had us all worried sick!"

"Shh!" He waved his hands. "Wanna bring them soldiers back?"

"No." She should've had more sense than to yell, but frustration had gotten the best of her. "Where's the hens?"

He scooted to the side of the opening. "I put 'em far back as I could. I was gettin' tired a holdin' 'em."

The white strutted out, and Caleb grabbed her. Lucas latched onto the brown.

"I'm glad you're okay, Lucas," Caleb said. He peered into the burrow. "Right warm in there, an' not easy to see. I'll hafta remember this place."

Lily almost held his hand again, but fortunately wised up before she did. It wouldn't be smart to give Lucas any indication of her affection for Caleb. "Think you could find it 'thout me?"

He looked from side to side. "Not sure. You might hafta show it to me again in the daylight."

"*I* can bring you up here," Lucas said, then shivered. "Dang it's cold."

Lily lightly thumped him on the side of his head. "Watch your mouth." She glanced at Caleb, who quickly turned away.

*Was he smirkin'?*

Lucas made no remark and headed down the hill. She and Caleb stayed right behind him. They all moved slower than normal, treading carefully in the dark. The lantern helped, yet the shadows it cast created difficult and uncertain steps.

At one point, she came close to stumbling, but caught herself in time. Caleb nearly dropped the hen, ready to catch her, and she nervously waved him away.

Lucas looked over his shoulder. "Want *me* to hold the lantern?"

"No. I'm fine."

He shrugged and kept going.

"You sure?" Caleb whispered. He kept the hen tucked under one arm, and placed his other hand at the small of her back. When he lightly rubbed, her breath hitched. Even through her thick coat, he created feelings she couldn't ignore.

"*Don't,*" she whispered, then widened her eyes and gestured toward Lucas.

Caleb brought his hand to himself, nodding.

"What you two whisperin' about?" Lucas said, glancing back.

Caleb caught up with him. "I was just tellin' your sister not to fall."

"Oh." Lucas didn't press the matter further. A very good thing.

Their ma covered him in kisses the minute they walked through the door. They let the hens loose in the cabin, which meant messes in the morning, but Lily didn't care. Her brother and the birds were safe, and her heart hadn't stopped dancing.

Life definitely showed promise.

# CHAPTER 13

After a pleasant night's sleep, Caleb woke scolding himself. Until he told Lily everything he'd done, he wouldn't be comfortable moving forward with her. She might've said nothing would change her feelings for him, but she could very well alter her opinion once she knew all the facts.

Not only that, she might ask him to leave immediately—not even care about having him help with the crops.

Thinking she may never want to see him again kept his stomach churning.

"Silly chickens," Lily fussed from the other side of his enclosure. "Messiest birds ever there was." She continued to mumble, all the while grunting and groaning.

The sound of sloshing water, followed by a brisk scrubbing noise, affirmed she was cleaning the floor.

He found himself smiling. She had a way about her that made even the most disgusting chores humorous.

"I'll help," Violet said, her soft voice drastically different from her sister's. Sweet and feminine, but his interest in her stopped there. Someday, he hoped to be able to call her, *sister*, himself.

"Least we got us two eggs this mornin'," their ma said.

He'd grown accustomed to the harshness in her words. It was her way of communicating. Underneath her tough exterior, she *had* to be a gentle woman. Otherwise, her children wouldn't be so kind.

*The war has changed her, too.*

Caleb linked his fingers behind his head and just lay there, taking it all in. The boys stirred overhead, and the tiny cabin came to life. He felt more a part of it now than ever before. However, he couldn't be overly kind to Lily or they'd know something had changed. He'd have to act somewhere between standoffish and affectionate.

He'd behave as a friend and nothing more . . . till they were alone.

Or, he could go to her pa and ask permission to court her.

*Dumb thing to do.*

Until he knew for sure she'd accept his truths, he needed to wait. Even then, if he was lucky enough to have her approval, her folks wouldn't agree to a courtship while trying to keep him hidden. In order to live under the same roof, Caleb would have to marry her immediately. Until the war ended, their open relationship would be much too risky.

Secrecy had to be kept.

In many ways, it made loving her more exciting. Only Lily would know what his true thoughts were behind every nonchalant glance. And he'd enjoy imagining what might be going on inside *her* mind. Her passionate kisses had him anticipating extraordinary intimacy.

Simply thinking about what they'd *already* done aroused him. For now, he could overcome the feeling by getting up and putting on the green dress. That alone would squelch his desires.

He tugged on his underwear, then yanked the gown over his head. When he looked down at his pathetic self, his manly needs vanished.

"Mornin'," he said as he pushed through the curtain.

Lily was on her knees scrubbing the wood floor. She lifted her big brown eyes and smiled. "Mornin'. Sleep well?"

"Yep." He nodded to the other women in turn. "Mornin', Violet. Mrs. Larsen."

The older woman grunted, busily stirring something in a pot.

Violet donned a slim smile, but didn't speak. A behavior that had become common for the girl.

The boys thundered down the stairs into the main room, and Lucas flew to Caleb's side. "After breakfast, want me to take you to my hidin' place, so you can see where it is in the light? Then, we can scout around an' see if there's any sign a them soldiers."

"Well, I—"

"I need Caleb to come with *me* to the cornfield," Lily jumped in, then stood. "We gotta see if any's left."

Lucas's head moved back and forth, and he studied both Caleb *and* Lily. "I'll go with you. Then after, Caleb an' me can scout. All right?"

Though Caleb wasn't being tugged in different directions by two females, he was still being pulled apart. He needed some time alone with Lily, yet after spending nearly a month paying attention to the *boys*, it wouldn't be easy. They'd be horribly suspicious if he suddenly ignored them.

"Sounds fine with me," Caleb finally said.

"Lucas." His ma jerked her head toward the front door. "Go to the barn an' check on your pa. He got up right early, an' hasn't come back inside."

"Yes'm." He raced away.

Lily went to her ma and set a hand on her arm. "He hasn't had a drink since he got so sick. You don't reckon—?"

"Hope not. But he was hurtin' last night. Talked foolishness, sayin' he could feel his hand. The one what ain't there." She stirred faster than ever.

Lily's eyebrows wove, her face covered with concern. "Want me to go after him, too?"

"*No.*" Her ma's head snapped to the side. "Wait to go out till we know for certain them men is gone. Hear me?"

"Yes'm."

Lucas returned, frowning. "He's fine, Ma. But he won't come in."

"Tell me more." She set aside the pot.

Lucas ground his foot into the floor and kept his head low, staring downward. "He's been tippin' the jug. He's sittin' in the stall, leanin' against the wall with the thing in his lap, mumblin' 'bout how worthless he is."

Caleb's chest tightened, aching for the man. "Ma'am, let me go an' talk to him. All right?"

Her brows dipped low. "I don't know." Though the woman always gave the impression she was tough as nails, tears welled in her eyes. "Lucas? You see any sign a them soldiers?"

His head popped right up. "No'm. Reckon they went off. You know they never stay long. What with *illness* in our house, they'll probably keep away. Least for a while."

Caleb moved closer to Mrs. Larsen. "I ain't worried 'bout them men. I'll be fine." He grabbed his bonnet and put it on. "I think I can help your husband."

She wiped away her tears and sniffled. "All right."

Before leaving, Caleb glanced Lily's way. Her soft smile carried him out the door.

He trudged to the barn, wondering just how drunk Mr. Larsen really was. More than anything, Caleb hoped he'd say the right thing to the man, and not make matters worse.

The barn door stood wide open, so he went in and walked slowly up the middle. As he passed each stall, he peered in. The emptiness of the building saddened him. At one time, no doubt the place had been full of life.

When he reached the stall at the very back, he found Mr. Larsen, just as Lucas had described him.

Caleb carefully held onto his skirt and tucked it beneath his rear, then sat beside the man. The scent of alcohol hung heavy.

Mr. Larsen's head bobbled and his eyes squinted nearly shut. "Caleb?"

"Yessir. It's me."

"Thought you was *Rose* for a minute there." He chuckled, then took another swig from the jug. "You ain't as purty."

Caleb reached for the large bottle.

"No!" Mr. Larsen sneered and hugged it to his chest. "It's mine!"

"Ain't you had enough?"

The man lifted a finger in the air and waved it around. "You aim to preach at me?" Though slurred, every word came out clearly.

"No, sir. But your wife's worried 'bout you. Your children, too." Caleb feared Mr. Larsen might not remember any of this conversation. Regardless, he decided to press on and try to get through to him. "Drinkin' yourself to death won't help them. They *need* you."

"I ain't good for no one." He blubbered into tears and sobbed. "Can't do nothin' no more. Can't even protect my girls. Only a matter a time, an' them men'll come an' take 'em. Have their way with 'em, then cast 'em aside like *whores*." He downed another swallow, then wiped his mouth and nose with the back of his hand.

The disgusting word emboldened Caleb. He yanked the jug from the man's grasp and set it far out of reach. "You should be ashamed a yourself!"

Mr. Larsen's head jerked back. "What?" He stretched out his arm, reaching into empty air. "Give it back, damn you!"

"*No.*" He took the man's chin in his hand and peered into his bloodshot eyes. "Just because you ain't got an arm, don't give you the right to let your family suffer for it! They respect you. Look to you for guidance. They still see you as the man a the house, but you're actin' like a weak fool! You was doin' fine for nearly a month. You don't need no moonshine! If you wanna protect your family, you gotta keep your mind clear!"

"But . . . Ableman . . ." His chin quivered. "He said he'd be back. He wants my Lily."

"So, you're gonna stay drunk an' let him have 'er?"

Mr. Larsen's face puckered up and he cried harder. A painful sight to see. Though drunk, the man obviously cared. The liquor magnified his reactions and broke down all his restraint.

"Listen . . ." Caleb put a hand on his shoulder. "I can help protect your daughters, but I can't do it alone. It'll take both of us. Understand?"

The man's head slowly bobbed. "I don't want my girls defiled. Them soldiers had their way with a fourteen-year-old on the east end a the cove. Shamed her . . ."

A knot formed in Caleb's belly. "Is she all right?"

"She's dead. Died birthin' one a them bastard's babies."

Caleb placed a hand to his mouth, speechless.

*The poor girl.*

Since everyone in the cove knew each other's business, Lily and Violet had likely heard about her. They had to be well aware of the risks they faced.

Lily acted much bolder than Violet, and Caleb believed she'd never let on how scared she was of Ableman and his men. Deep down, he was certain *both* girls were terrified. Neither would be able to defend themselves against such strong soldiers.

The thought of those men's hands on the girls boiled Caleb's blood, but just like he'd asked of Mr. Larsen, he had to keep his senses.

Mr. Larsen pushed against the floor with his hand and tried to stand. He wobbled side-to-side. Caleb jumped to his feet and helped him straighten, then kept an arm around him to keep him from falling over.

"I need to sleep this off," the man mumbled, then twisted his head sideways and looked in Caleb's face. "I'm glad to see my girls lost interest in you. You ain't a bad man, but I don't want no foolin' around in my house." He poked a finger into Caleb's chest. "Understand my meanin'?"

"Yessir. You don't hafta worry none 'bout me. I care 'bout your daughters like a brother would."

"You best keep it that way." After tapping Caleb's chest several additional times, the man tried walking from the barn. He staggered horribly, but Caleb kept him upright and moving forward.

Even inebriated, Mr. Larsen got his message across. Now more than ever, Caleb and Lily would have to be careful and keep their feelings hidden. Her pa needed to heal. Caleb wasn't about to hurt him further.

When they entered the cabin, Mrs. Larsen looked their way, then quickly turned her attention to the stove. Lily's sad eyes stayed on them, but everyone remained silent.

Caleb guided Mr. Larsen to his bedroom and helped him lie down.

The man blinked up at him, trickling tears down his cheeks. "Thank you, son."

The term froze Caleb where he stood. "Welcome," he muttered, then covered him with a quilt.

He walked from the room and shut the door, wondering how much Mr. Larsen would remember. Hopefully, he'd retain all of it, but no matter what came out of their encounter, Caleb intended to give him a lot more attention. He'd get him on his feet working the farm, and help him recall how to properly lead the family.

* * *

Lily ate very little breakfast. She wasn't overly hungry and preferred having the food go to her siblings.

She found it almost impossible to keep her eyes off Caleb. Still, she forced herself. She could tell he'd been doing the same.

When she gave him his morning shave, she felt something entirely new. Electricity flowed from his skin into her fingertips. She had to remind herself to breathe and steady her hands. Cutting him wouldn't be wise.

Once she finished, she tossed him a towel. "That'll do for now." She made a point to keep her words as unfeeling as they'd been the past few weeks.

"Thank you," he muttered, just as impassionate.

She grabbed her coat. "We best be checkin' the corn. You ready?"

"*I* am." Lucas yanked on Caleb's arm. "Let's go see what they left for us. If there ain't none, we can go lookin' for them turkeys again."

Lily wished her brother hadn't decided Caleb was his new best friend. He'd make it difficult to find any time alone with him.

"I'm sure there'll be *some* corn," Caleb said. "If there is, we'll leave it be till after it frosts and kills the plants. Like your pa said, the dried corn will go farther. Once the stalks are dead, we can cut 'em an' pull the fodder. Maybe we can find someone in the cove who needs the feed. Work out trade for the use of a horse or mule."

Lily nodded, appreciating Caleb's respect for her pa's wishes. "Mr. Quincy has an old mule. Less the soldiers got it. I hate to talk to Mrs. Quincy, but she might be willin' to barter. We just hafta figure out how to keep her away when we're ready to plant the wheat."

Lucas's demeanor perked up and he donned a huge smile. "So, we're only gonna *look* at the corn? That means we'll have lotsa time to scout."

Caleb headed toward the door and jerked his head for Lucas to follow. "First, let's see what we find in the field."

Lucas wrinkled his nose. "Don't you wanna scout? Hunt up turkeys and make sure them men is long gone?"

"Course I do." Caleb glanced at Lily, then disappeared behind his curtain. He came out putting on Violet's coat. Lucas bundled up in his own.

"You mind, Violet?" Caleb asked. "Can't wear a *man's* coat."

"*I* ain't goin' out," she whispered. "I'm gonna stay an' help Ma."

"Thank you." He grasped the doorknob.

Horace bustled across the room. "Can I go with 'em?"

"Me, too?" Isaac asked.

Their ma's head bobbed. "Put your coats on, an' mind your sister." She eyeballed Lily, but Lily didn't need the unspoken reminder. Her ma always expected her to look after the other children.

But why in heaven's name did every one of her brothers want to tag along when she wanted to be alone with Caleb?

Lily shuffled them out the door.

*God must be tryin' to teach me a lesson in patience.*

She breathed in the crisp morning air. Though they needed rain, she appreciated the pleasant clear weather. Traipsing about in the fields and getting soaked and cold didn't sound so appealing.

She kept in pace with her siblings, but Isaac was having difficulty keeping up with them. She almost scooped him into her arms, when he ran to Caleb and tugged on his skirt.

Caleb stopped and bent to the boy's level. "Yes?"

"Can I ride piggyback?"

"Reckon so." He grinned, squatted down, and Isaac climbed on. "For now."

Isaac clung to him, giggling. While keeping one hand around Caleb's neck, he patted the side of Caleb's bonnet with the other. Lily could scarcely keep herself from laughing.

"I want a turn, too," Horace said.

Lily shook her head. "You're too big. 'Sides, *Callie* might get tired. We can't be wearin' the poor girl down before she even gets to the field."

Caleb lifted his head high and pushed back the bonnet flap. He peered over his shoulder, around Isaac's small frame, and winked.

Lily prayed no one had seen the gesture. Especially Lucas.

Grinning inwardly, she looked away. Her heart fluttered, but not just from Caleb's flirtatious action. Even with him and the boys close, she couldn't wash away a tinge of nervousness. She kept expecting Captain Ableman to appear in the cornfield at any moment.

They reached the field, and Caleb eased Isaac onto the ground.

Lily clutched a hand to her heart, taking in the disappointing sight. "There had to be more than the three a them what done this." She moved deeper into the rows of stalks. "Looks like they took all of it."

"Uh-uh." Isaac pointed. "I see one down here."

Lily bent low to look where he'd indicated and found a small ear. One that hadn't fully matured. She yanked it from the stalk. "Course they left this one. It ain't worth squat."

Caleb took it from her hand. "The field's large. There's gotta be more."

"They had all day to pick it. While we was holed up in the cabin, they were out here takin' our food. I hate 'em." She didn't want to cry, but her tears formed regardless.

Isaac extended his arms, and she picked him up.

"Don't cry, Sissy." He burrowed into her shoulder.

Lucas kicked one of the stalks. "I'll shoot 'em all dead. Every man what took sumthin' from us, I'll put a bullet in his head."

"Stop talkin' that way, Lucas Larsen," Lily fussed. "It's killin' what got us into this predicament."

Isaac's face scrunched together. "What's a dicament? I thought we was in a *cornfield*."

She hugged him close and kissed his cheek. Even in the direst of times, he warmed her heart.

"Lily," Caleb said. "I know there's gotta be more corn. Let's go on back to the cabin. The way the weather's turnin' it'll freeze soon enough, then we'll have plenty a work to keep us busy. We'll salvage all we can."

"Even the little ears?" Isaac asked, pointing to the small excuse of an ear of corn in Caleb's hand.

"Yep. Even that tiny bit a corn can provide food. You found the first one, an' I'm right proud a you." Caleb ruffled Isaac's hair and prompted more giggles.

Lily didn't think it possible, but Caleb's actions brought even greater love into her heart. She'd kiss all over his face right now if they were alone.

*Not a chance.*

# CHAPTER 14

When they returned to the cabin, Caleb wanted to share their findings with Mr. Larsen, but the man was still asleep. Likely for the best. He'd undoubtedly wake up with an awful headache and irritable disposition. Dealing with his ill mood could wait.

However, Lucas couldn't.

They'd scarcely set a foot inside, when the boy tugged on Caleb's arm. "C'mon. Let's go."

"Give him time to rest," Lily fussed.

Lucas leered at her. "Why do *you* care all of a sudden?"

Caleb swallowed hard and waited, hoping she'd say the right thing.

Lily jutted her chin in the air. "I only care 'bout you wearin' him down. We may not have fieldwork to do yet, but there's plenty else to do. Like laundry."

"Laundry?" Lucas grunted. "That's women's work. He may be dressed like one, but he ain't. We're gonna go hunt us up some meat." He moved to their ma. "Reckon we can take Pa's gun?"

"Gracious sakes, no." Mrs. Larsen took his face in her hands. "You know full well what your pa says 'bout shootin'. It draws curiosity. Don't want no one comin' by snoopin'."

"*I* do." Lucas stepped away from her. "I want them soldiers to come back so we can kill 'em."

As much as Caleb shared his feelings, the boy's infatuation with killing troubled him.

Mrs. Larsen threw her hands in the air. "Lord, help us."

"Let's go, Lucas," Caleb said. "An' don't you worry, ma'am, we'll be as quiet as field mice."

"Can I go, too?" Horace asked, and true to form, Isaac stood right by his side, begging with wide eyes.

"Not this time," their ma said. "You boys stay in an' work your letters."

They pouted and wandered away.

Caleb headed for the door.

"Your dress needs washin'," Lily dryly said.

"It's all I got to wear." He stared straight at her. Though her words came out *harsh*, her eyes told him otherwise. "I'll wash it myself t'night 'fore bed."

"Good." She pursed her lips. "None of us want you stinkin' again."

Lucas gave him a little shove. "C'mon. She's bein' her ugly self. Don't wanna stay here an' listen to her naggin'."

Nodding, Caleb opened the door.

They'd efficiently fooled her family.

* * *

Lily hauled the washtub inside and placed it in the corner of the kitchen. Violet was already heating water in the fireplace kettle, as well as more on the woodstove. Had the weather been warmer, Lily would've rather done the laundry outdoors.

Their ma had shut herself up in the bedroom with their pa, and the boys were sitting in front of the fire, drawing pictures on their slates. Not the alphabet they were supposed to be working on, but Lily wouldn't chide them for it.

Violet brought out the washboard and leaned it against the wall. "I'm glad you said sumthin' to Caleb 'bout washin' that old dress." She spoke just above a whisper. "He was far from smellin' as poorly as he did when you brought him home. Even so, I didn't like gettin' anywhere near him."

"Why should you?" Lily also kept her voice low. Not only to keep from disturbing her folks, but the little ears in the living room liked to repeat conversations. "Didn't we agree he's not worth pursuin'?"

"Course we did. I feel badly you hafta work at *all* with that man." She sat on one of the kitchen chairs and gestured for Lily to take her own seat.

Lily obliged. "Sumthin' wrong?"

"Don't you think Caleb's gettin' too big for his britches?"

A snicker came out of Lily before she could stop it. "Sorry. Since he don't *wear* britches, it tickled me." She sobered and sat tall. "Why do you say that?"

"He's gettin' bossy. Takin' over an' tellin' Pa what to do."

"I don't see it that way. He helped Pa by bringin' him in from the barn." Lily didn't care for the direction of thier conversation.

"Well, what 'bout Lucas? The boy thinks Caleb hung the moon. You an' I both know it ain't so."

Lily had gotten into another *dicament*—as Isaac had called it. If she agreed with her sister, it could create trouble for Caleb somewhere along the line, and if she *dis*agreed, Violet might see into her feelings for him.

Lily nervously scratched the back of her neck, contemplating what to say. Things were too complicated to draw her sister into their ploy.

*Maybe in time . . .* "Right now, I don't reckon he's hurtin' no one. But . . ." She took Violet's hand and leaned close. "We best keep our eyes on him an' make sure he don't step outta line."

Her sister jerked her head into a firm single nod, then sighed. The sternness she'd displayed vanished, replaced by deep worry lines on her forehead. "Lily? Do you think Captain Ableman will come back with them other soldiers?"

Though she hated to say it, Lily couldn't lie about this particular matter. "*Eventually.*" She grabbed Violet's other hand and held both tight. "We'll be ready for 'em. As much as we dislike Caleb, I believe him when he says he won't let 'em hurt us."

"I wish they'd *all* leave us alone. I've decided I'd rather be an old maid than have the likes of *any* of them touch me."

Lily let go of her, then gently stroked her sister's cheek. "Someday, you might change your mind."

"What's an old maid?" Horace hollered.

"Shh!" Lily shook a finger at him, then pointed at the closed door.

Horace huffed and slumped down over his slate.

Isaac giggled.

She cherished her little brothers, but wished they all lived in a bigger house. One that offered more privacy.

A private conversation with Caleb was becoming increasingly necessary. They'd likely have to have it in the middle of the night, while everyone else slept.

* * *

Caleb settled against the soft bed tick, utterly content. His freshly washed dress hung near the fireplace and should be dry by morning.

He'd appeased Lucas by spending the entire afternoon with him, then pleased his ma when they gifted her with two rabbits. They all ate their fill.

As for Mr. Larsen, the man had been wide awake when they'd arrived home, rocking casually in front of the fire. He'd said little, but for today, Caleb was satisfied with that. He planned to get him talking tomorrow and if all went well, he'd eventually have the man outside working. The very thing he needed.

The only regret Caleb had was not getting the chance to speak privately with Lily. Somehow, he had to find a way. Much needed to be said.

He shut his eyes and let his head sink into the pillow. The fire crackled and popped—the only sound in the cabin.

He'd almost drifted off, when the creak of a board startled him wide awake. Whoever was crossing the floor treaded lightly.

These kinds of footsteps weren't unusual. Occasionally, someone would get up in the night to use the outhouse. Caleb had always done his best to ignore them.

His heavy lids shut again, and though his ears stayed attuned to the noise around him, his heart rested. He sensed no danger.

He gasped when his curtain parted and someone stepped through.

"Shh . . ." The hushed whisper could barely be heard, but he had no doubt . . .

*Lily.*

Calm left him, replaced by a fierce raging energy that coursed through his blood. His formerly still heart pounded, fueled by danger and excitement.

Without another sound, she lay beside him and draped an arm over his chest. Regardless of her being on top of the blankets, her nearness overwhelmed him and dried his throat.

She moved so close, her lips tickled his earlobe. "All day I've wanted to be near you," she breathed into his ear. "I don't know what we're gonna do. I can't keep pretendin' I don't care."

He rolled onto his side and faced her. Their heavy breaths mingled.

"Lily. If we're caught, your pa will make me leave."

She grabbed onto him and kissed him, obviously ignoring his warning. He couldn't resist her advances. Ever since their first kiss, he'd wanted more.

He circled her with his arms and drew her so close that the only things separating their bodies were the blankets and her nightgown. They kissed over and over again, until they were almost breathless.

When she pushed him onto his back and lay atop him, he held up his hands. "Lily, don't."

She didn't move aside. Instead, she dropped her head against his shoulder. Her long loose hair fell across his body like silk, and he happily drew his fingers through it.

She pushed down the blankets and exposed the wound she'd doctored.

*What's she gonna do* now?

Heart pounding, he closed his eyes and sank deeper into the bedding as her lips glided over his scar.

The chaste girl couldn't possibly realize how she was affecting him. Could she?

Her mouth skimmed up his neck until her lips were once again beside his ear. "I love you."

"I love *you*." He rolled her over and devoured her with a stimulated, hungering kiss.

Her hands glided along his bare back, but stopped before reaching his underwear.

*Thank God.*

He'd never bedded a woman, though every part of him wanted to. If he allowed it to happen, *he'd* be the man on the other end of her pa's rifle. And deservedly so.

She raked her nails lightly up his back toward his neck. A much safer direction. He shivered and a soft moan escaped him. This forward girl would surely be the death of him.

Even in the dark, he swore her eyes sparkled. She radiated happiness.

He placed his lips to her ear. "Lily, there's things you need to know."

"Are you married?"

"Course not." He prayed they were speaking softly enough. He lifted his head and listened for a moment to make certain no one stirred.

She yanked him close again. "Then there ain't nothin' I'm worried 'bout."

"But—"

Her mouth covered his and stopped him from speaking.

He loved kissing her and could carry on like this all night, but he had to tell her . . . "I lied to you."

Her body went rigid.

"Lily?"

"Wrap up in that blanket an' meet me by the outhouse." Her words held no feeling.

Their fire had been doused, snuffed out by truth. She stood and disappeared through the curtain.

He tugged on his boots, tied the bonnet in place, then wrapped up tight in the heaviest blanket. He, too, had often made nighttime trips to relieve himself, so he shouldn't be so nervous. But he couldn't overcome the fear of being discovered with her.

The half-moon gave off little light—an even greater inconvenience than the awkward blanket. He stepped slowly and carefully.

When he neared the outhouse, Lily took hold of his arm and guided him away from it, deeper into the trees.

He was glad to see she'd put on her coat, in addition to her nightgown and robe. If she got sick from the cold, he'd never forgive himself.

"You lied?" She still whispered, but her tone had hardened. "What 'bout?"

The next few minutes could change his life forever. For better, or for worse, the time had come to tell her. "I wasn't fightin' for the union. I was a rebel."

She smacked his chest. "How could you lie 'bout that? If my folks knew—"

"They woulda doctored me an' shoved me out the door. Right?"

"In a heartbeat. Ma *hates* rebels. They've made our life hell." Heavy breaths hissed from her nose. "Where'd you get the uniform? Kill some Union soldier and strip him bare?" She slapped him again—harder this time—then took a step back. "That bullet hole in the center of your coat. The one you said wasn't yours. It belonged to the man you killed. Didn't it?"

"Yes." He choked out the word. Visions of that day flashed into his mind as if it'd just happened. Tears pooled in his eyes. "He was . . . my brother." He dropped to the ground and hugged his knees to his chest. The one thing he swore he'd never tell a soul had spilled from his mouth.

He covered his face and rocked back and forth, wishing away the painful memory. Uncontrollable sobs erupted. He cried for the very first time over his loss.

Lily stood without moving, saying nothing. Her silence worsened his suffering.

He assumed she'd eventually leave him there. Disgusted with his revelations. Instead, she eased onto the ground beside him, put an arm around his body, and drew him to her. "Tell me what happened."

Caleb sniffed and stared at the ground. "We fought 'bout politics. Which side was right, an' which was wrong. We were young an' foolish. Boys who barely understood what life was all about, let alone how a country should be governed." He wiped his eyes with the corner of the blanket. "Pa joined the Union army. Left us boys to work the farm till *we* was old enough to enlist. Abe said he was gonna be like Pa an' wear blue. I told him he was crazy. That the South had to fight for its land an' freedom. Told him we'd lose everythin' if we sided with the North."

"Do you still believe that?"

He glanced up at her. Darkness kept him from reading her expression. "I don't know what to believe anymore. I just want it all to end." He covered his face again, but he'd never be able to hide his shame.

"But . . ." Lily sounded so defeated. Like he'd broken her heart. *Betrayed* her. "Why'd you shoot him?"

"I didn't know it was Abraham when I pulled the trigger." He let out several sobs, then quickly stifled them. He had to compose himself and act like a man. "We were battlin' near Asheville. Like every other encounter, I watched men get bloody and mutilated. Fightin' for my own life, I shot at anyone wearin' blue." He pinched his eyes shut and clenched his fists. "I got separated from my company. 'Fore I knew it, I was surrounded by Union soldiers. I hid in the underbrush, prayin' they'd not see me. Then a lone soldier got close. His bayonet pointed right at me. I'd seen men bludgeoned to death by them blades. Not how *I* wanted to go."

"So, you shot him." Her matter-of-fact tone increased his pain.

His chin quivered and more tears threatened. He sucked breath in through his nose, then blew it out again in staggered bursts. "I pulled the trigger when he was less than three feet from me. In that brief second before the shot took him down, he said my name."

He shifted his body and faced Lily. "He recognized me." Tears streamed down his face. "He'd come close to talk to me. That's why *he* hadn't shot."

Caleb scrambled to his feet and stood with his back to her. He knew she'd never look at him the same way again. A decent man wouldn't kill his own brother. "I knew others were near, so I drug his body into the bushes and switched clothes. I left Abraham in the gray uniform he hated. Only God knows what happened to his body. Wearing blue, I got away. I distanced myself from the Union army and fled into the Smokies. That's where the rebels saw me and chased me till I ran into you."

A wolf howled somewhere far away, but Lily's distant breathing bothered him more.

He couldn't look at her. Maybe she'd walk away and leave him in the woods. Then he could wander off and die somewhere from exposure to cold. At least he could leave the earth having confessed his sins.

"It's *war,* Caleb," her gravelly pain-filled words spun him around. "You didn't mean to kill your brother. You was savin' yourself from the enemy."

"The enemy . . ." He took a step closer to her. "I *loved* him."

She moved nearer. "I know. That's why you've been so broken. For a time, I thought you'd never smile. Then one day, I seen it. I wanna help you keep it there." Her hand slowly moved upward. Her fingertips touched his lips. "This is the real reason why you don't wanna go home, ain't it?"

He shut his eyes and nodded, pushing more tears onto his face. "How can I tell my ma *I'm* the one who killed Abraham? How can I face Rebecca?" Her name slipped out unintentionally, but he feared her the most.

"Who's Rebecca?"

He lifted his lids and looked straight at Lily. "Abraham's wife. We knew her since we was kids. They snuck off an' married a few months before that ugly battle. I got word from my ma tellin' be 'bout it, an' how happy she was. She said Abe's company had been camped near Waynesville, an' that's how he got away to marry her. She told me he finally had a decent reason to get done with the war an' come back home." His tears flowed faster. "I made Rebecca a widow."

Lily smoothed her hand across his face, wiping away the evidence of his pain. "My poor, Caleb." She dotted his cheeks with light kisses. "I'm so sorry."

"I hate myself for what I done. I can't make none of it right."

She wrapped her arms around him and laid her head against his shoulder. "I'll help you through it."

He kissed the top of her head and let his tears flow. They stayed silently locked in an embrace.

They both gasped at the sound of snapping twigs.

"Lily?" Violet called out. "Where are you?"

Lily flattened her hand on his chest. "Stay here," she whispered. "Wait to come inside till you've given us enough time to get back in an' settled." She gave him a quick kiss on the lips. "I love you."

Without saying another thing, she hurried away. It didn't matter, because the words she'd left him with were all he needed to hear.

He'd bared his soul, and she still loved him. And though he'd not told her everything about Rebecca, it didn't matter. His history with her was in the distant past, and no longer relevant.

Maybe Lily truly could help him overcome his pain. Some of the heaviness in his heart had already lifted.

He waited until he heard the front door shut, then trudged to the outhouse, took care of business, and quietly returned to his place in the cabin.

Lily wouldn't come to him anymore tonight, but he had a feeling that one day she'd lay with him again.

*I need to marry her . . .*

# CHAPTER 15

"It's a shame your stomach is givin' you grief," Violet whispered to Lily as soon as they lay down in bed.

It was the only excuse Lily could come up with for *taking such a long time in the outhouse*. Truthfully, she'd not stepped foot in there, but Violet would remain none-the-wiser. Most nights, her sister wouldn't even wake up when Lily crept out of bed. The girl slept soundly.

If only tonight hadn't been an exception.

"I feel much better now," Lily said and sighed. "Sorry I made you fret."

She'd wanted to stay with Caleb. Comfort him. Let him know she'd not turn her back on him for what he'd done. Killing his brother had been a dreadful mistake, brought on by a despicable war.

She honestly couldn't blame him for not wanting to go home.

Violet cuddled against her. "I worried them soldiers nabbed you an' took you away."

"A greater reason to have stayed inside, silly girl." Lily stroked her sister's hair. "If they'd a taken me, they'd have grabbed you, too." She kissed her on the forehead. "Next time, keep your tail in the cabin. All right?"

"Fine. Just try not to go out in the middle a the night. It ain't safe."

"I can't control my digestion. Hopefully, it won't trouble me again anytime soon."

Lily closed her eyes and listened to every breath Violet took. Her chest rose and fell slower and slower, and conversation ended.

It gave Lily the chance to delve into her own thoughts, which of course, revolved around Caleb. The man she intended to marry.

She'd not fully grasped why she'd been so forward with him. Perhaps an underlying fear that her sister might once again recognize his redeeming qualities and pursue him herself.

*That's plum silly.*

He'd professed his love to *her*. Violet was no longer a threat.

Lily had to admit Caleb brought out her deepest desires. He'd set something free.

She'd guarded her purity from Captain Ableman. The man disgusted her.

Unlike the captain, Caleb had a heart. In *her* mind, his confessions didn't condemn him. They proved how intensely he could love.

She'd give him all the time he needed to grieve and overcome all that would keep them from having a happy life together. But she'd be right by his side, helping him through it. Just as she'd promised.

Though she hated the idea, she knew she had to ease up on her affections. Not only could they get them in trouble with her folks, but she could tell she'd made Caleb nervous by being with him in his bed.

*Oh, my goodness. I was in a man's bed.*

Her heart thumped harder.

At the time, it had felt right. *He'd* felt right.

Physical closeness was supposed to be part of loving a man. However, as her ma frequently read to them from the Bible, it was something to be done in the marriage bed. A way to make babies and populate the earth.

*Be fruitful an' multiply.*

She almost giggled, but stopped herself. When she'd climbed atop Caleb, she could tell he was ready to be fruitful.

*I shouldn't torment the poor man.*

One day soon, she hoped they'd have another opportunity to talk. Until then, she'd treat him as a friend and hope no one in the family suspected anything. As much as her folks had come to like him, if they discovered he was a rebel, they'd never trust him again.

* * *

Caleb had slept dreamlessly through the night. His mind had been eased by telling Lily everything, and it had been simple to sleep once he'd returned to his bed.

He shivered and sat up. The house felt colder than usual.

When he pushed through the curtain with his blanket covering him, he found Mr. Larsen already in the rocker in front of the fireplace. The fire barely flamed. The man simply stared at it as if it would right itself, then his head lifted and he pointed to the dying embers. "Fires goin' out."

Caleb scolded himself for not bringing in wood before going to bed. "I'll fetch some logs." He'd left his dress draped over the sofa to dry. He fingered it, glad to find no remaining dampness, then moved into his enclosure and put it on.

Once his bonnet and boots were in place, he headed outside.

Frigid, frost-covered ground greeted him.

*I shoulda worn Violet's coat.*

He hastened to the woodshed and loaded his arms down with cut logs, then bustled back inside. He'd need to chop more later.

"Our first frost," he said to Mr. Larsen as he stoked the fire and added wood. "We'll be able to cut the corn soon."

"Yep." The man kept the rocker moving. "Reckon you'll need my help."

Caleb's head snapped to the side. "That I will."

Mr. Larsen chuckled. "Can't chop wood with one arm, but I can swing a mighty blade."

"I'm sure you can." Caleb grinned, then returned his attention to the fire.

Doors opened and the house came to life.

The boys almost tripped over each other coming down the stairs. They raced to the fire and put their backsides to it.

"Pa?" Isaac said. "Lucas told me it was gonna snow last night an' bury us. It didn't, but *could* it?"

"Lucas." Their pa shook his head. "I told you not to mess with your brother."

"I ain't done it!" Lucas rolled his eyes. "I told him the truth. Last year it drifted through cracks in the walls. I woke up with a *snow* blanket."

It brought to Caleb's mind that the same thing had happened to Abraham and him when they were boys. A *happy* memory. The kind he wanted to keep close. "It'll be a while 'fore we get snow, but I can help your pa patch the house to keep the drifts out."

"Good," Lucas said. "Nearly froze my tail off last night."

Caleb glanced toward the kitchen, only to catch a leery eye from Violet. Though glad she'd lost interest in him, he believed her disinterest had turned to dis*like*. That didn't set well. Maybe Lily could help somehow, though he didn't know what she could do or say without raising questions.

Lily looked even more beautiful this morning. He gave her a slight nod, but otherwise remained expressionless.

She jutted her chin in the air. A gesture he'd grown accustomed to seeing. If he didn't know her heart, he'd swear she despised him, too.

She strutted to the door. "I'm goin' out to check for eggs."

"Wear a coat," Caleb said, only to get a grunt from Violet. "It's right cold outside," he added, but it did no good. Violet still glared at him.

The shy, quiet girl had become a mite hateful.

Lily put her coat on. "I ain't ignorant." She marched out the door.

Lucas snickered.

If Caleb could survive living in these conditions until the war ended, it'd be a miracle. "I best go chop more wood 'fore breakfast." He didn't wait for anyone's approval, and he didn't bother asking Violet if he could wear her coat. Chopping wood would keep him plenty warm without it.

He knew none of the boys would ask to join him. They were too busy heating their tails. This might be the only chance he'd have today to get Lily alone.

He hurried to where they kept the hens. Lily looked up as he approached the pen and smiled. That alone warmed him to the bone.

"Any eggs?" He pointed at the birds.

"Nope." She frowned. "Reckon we best be puttin' them in the barn with it gettin' so cold. I'll need to fix 'em up a nestin' area, or we won't get much a anythin' from them."

They had very little time before her family would wonder where she was. He nodded toward the woodshed. "I gotta chop some wood."

A knowing expression covered her face.

They both practically sprinted to the lean-to. Behind it, no one from the house could see them. Granted, they risked being discovered by a nosy neighbor, but it was unlikely anyone would be out in the cold so early. And if they *did* happen to spy, they'd see more than they bargained for.

He yanked her close and kissed her. The first one *he'd* initiated. The intensity she displayed kissing him back nearly put him on the ground.

"Violet hates me," he muttered, when they came up for air.

"She thinks you're vile." Lily's lips moved over his face. "I'll try to find a way to help."

"Good." He kissed her even deeper, then nuzzled into her neck and breathed her in. "You best get inside."

She stepped away and held a hand to her breast. "Good mornin'." With a smile and a curt nod, she left.

"Whew . . ." Caleb wiped his damp brow, then grabbed the axe.

Her affections overwhelmed him, though they happily carried him through the day.

He was thrilled when her pa offered to help fix a place for the hens in the barn. With no other animals about, the chickens had free range. Once the barn doors were closed, they'd have a much better chance of staying warm and maybe produce an egg or two.

Since Caleb's shoulder had healed, he climbed into the hayloft and pushed the remaining straw over the side. Lily and Lucas raked it into one of the stalls.

Caleb climbed down the ladder and smiled at their pa, who disregarded his disability and proficiently formed the straw into a nesting area. "Too bad we ain't got a rooster."

"So we could get more chickens, right Pa?" Lucas said, puffing up tall.

"Yep. That's how it works." He patted the boy on the back.

Lily kept her eyes on the barn floor.

*Yep, that's how it works.*

Caleb shook his head, needing to remove the thoughts that came to mind. But he couldn't help himself. He was a grown man who loved a woman and wanted her in every possible way.

*To have and to hold till the day I die.*

Hard work.

Hard work.

Hard work.

The only thing that kept his mind and body busy and off Lily.

That afternoon, he went with Mr. Larsen and Lucas to check the cornfield. To Caleb's relief, Lily stayed behind in the cabin.

The frost had done a world of good. If they were lucky to have some rain-free days to dry out the dead plants, they could cut it next week.

Lucas huffed and pulled on one of the stalks. "We done out here?"

"For now," his pa said. "You got somewhere else you'd ruther be?" He ruffled the boy's hair.

"I wanna hunt with Caleb."

Caleb smiled. "Fine with me. Let's go check the rabbit traps. Then, I think it's high time you an' me make a bow an' some arrows. By Thanksgivin' we might have us a deer, or even a bear."

Lucas's eyes widened. "You know how to do that? Make arrows an' such?"

"Course I do. Without a gun, we ain't got much choice. If there's game to be had, we best be shootin' it."

"Pa?" Lucas grabbed his arm. "Don't let Horace an' Isaac come with us. They're too little to be messin' with arrows."

"You can be sure your ma will keep 'em home." Mr. Larsen got a far-off look in his eyes. "I'm goin' back. You two go on an' see what you can hunt us up for supper."

Caleb set a hand on his shoulder. "You all right?"

"I'm a mite thirsty." He gulped and clutched his chest.

"Plenty a *water* at the cabin." Caleb had no doubt the man understood him. Because he certainly knew what *Mr. Larsen* had in mind.

Lucas stood in front of his pa and tipped his head back, staring up at the man. "Don't do it, Pa."

Without a word, Mr. Larsen smoothed his hand over the boy's red hair, smiled, and walked away.

Lucas's shoulders dropped along with his enthusiasm.

"He'll be fine," Caleb said. "Just say a little prayer he won't stop by the barn to check on the chickens."

"I gave up prayin' years ago." Lucas walked off, and Caleb followed.

* * *

New excitement pushed Lily on a daily basis.

Every day she woke, wondering if she and Caleb could sneak a kiss, or at the very least a penetrating gaze accompanied with mysterious underlying thoughts and desires.

Sometimes, she felt selfish wanting him so badly. She eased her self-interest by sharing him with her family.

She'd been proud of the way he'd been spending so much time with her pa. She'd noticed more color in the man's face as well as the return of a twinkle in his eyes that had disappeared along with his arm. He'd not tipped a jug since the day Caleb had brought him in from the barn.

They'd harvested the corn, and to their good fortune, they'd found enough ears to make meal that would get them through the winter.

Better still, her pa worked a deal with Mr. Quincy. They traded the fodder for the use of his mule as well as enough seed that allowed them to plant a decent crop of wheat.

Mrs. Quincy had yet to return and nose around, but Lucas had informed them after a mail-run, that she'd asked about

Callie's size. Seems her grandsons had remarked they'd seen Callie in the cornfield and claimed she was well over six-feet tall. An unusual height for a young woman. Luckily, the boys had kept their distance, or they'd have noticed other unusual features.

Lily knew why they didn't come any nearer. If they got close, they risked being asked to help. The boys were known to be lazy. At least they had the good sense to blow the hunting horn when necessary.

All of that suited Lily just fine. They could all breathe easier if every member of the Quincy family stayed home.

Thanksgiving was only a few days away, and Lily had a lot to be thankful for.

"Be careful with that!" her ma fussed at Lucas, who was waving an arrow in the air.

"Oh, Ma. I ain't gonna hurt no one."

"You could poke your brothers' eyes out if you ain't careful. Them points is sharp."

"She's right," Lily said. "Stop wavin' it about. You an' Caleb goin' huntin'?"

"Yep. The bucks are ruttin'." He grinned. "Know what that means?"

"Yes, I do." Lily had understood animal ways for some time. Since her brother had approached thirteen, he'd become overly interested in how they reproduced. His face showed it. First the chickens, now the deer.

Their ma grumbled and flipped to the next page of her Bible.

Caleb walked in, briskly rubbing his hands together. "I swear it feels like it's gonna snow."

"I hope not," Violet whispered. She kept her eyes down, focused on her embroidery.

It had taken time, but Lily was relieved her sister had started speaking to Caleb without sounding hateful. Even so, the two rarely communicated.

"Ready to go shoot us a big buck?" Lucas, on the other hand, wouldn't leave him alone.

"Reckon so."

Her ma lifted her head. "Wear your scarves. Can't have you catchin' your death."

"Yes'm," Caleb said. He glanced at Lily and smiled, then picked up a scarf from a basket by the door and circled it around his neck a few times. "Wanna go with us?"

Lily almost laughed at the way Lucas's face scrunched up, but it also emboldened her. "I'd like that. Ain't never killed no buck before. Only small game."

"Why's *she* gotta go?" Lucas whined.

"To learn," Caleb said.

Lucas kicked at the floor.

Their ma shook a finger. "Listen young man. That attitude a yours is gonna get you in trouble someday. Mind your manners, *and* your sister. Hear me?"

"Yes'm."

"Bet you can't shoot a buck bigger than the one I got," their pa called out from his rocker. "I'd go with you myself if I wasn't so tired."

Her little brothers sat at his feet. They'd not bothered asking if they could go, but Lily knew they wanted to. They'd been told more than once that hunting with bows and arrows wasn't something they could do till they were older.

"Next time, Mr. Larsen," Caleb said and nodded to the door.

Lily bundled up in her coat and scarf, as well as mittens and a hat.

Lucas grumbled all the way up the mountainside.

"We ain't gonna see nothin' if you keep makin' so much noise," she said to him.

He looked over his shoulder and glared at her. "*You're* the one talkin'." He increased his pace and soon was some distance ahead.

*Brothers.*

Caleb eased up beside her. "He doesn't like to share his time with me," he whispered.

She leaned close. "I know the feelin'."

Caleb clutched his bow with one hand and put his other on her back. "I'm glad you came with us."

"Where are you hidin' your arrows?" She looked him up and down, grinning.

Though the cold warranted rosy cheeks, she could swear his face instantly reddened. "Lucas has 'em."

"Oh. So, he has the arrows, an' you have the bow. Who's gonna shoot?"

"We hafta find sumthin' to aim at first."

Lucas came running toward them. "I heard sumthin'. Sounded like two bucks fightin'. You know—antlers smackin' together an' all."

Caleb held up a hand. "*Hush*. If that's what you truly heard, we gotta be quiet. We don't wanna spook 'em."

All of Lucas's anger vanished. Excitement widened his eyes. "Maybe we can get us *two* bucks," he whispered.

They crept further up the hill, then stopped and listened.

Sure enough, Lily heard what sounded like antlers banging together, along with snorting and heavy breathing.

"They can get right mean in rut," Caleb whispered. "We don't wanna get too close."

"But I wanna *see*." Lucas's excitement grew with every word. He nearly danced in his boots.

"Fine. But we best go slow."

Without thinking, Lily took Caleb's arm.

Lucas rolled his eyes. "You're such a big chicken. So scared you gotta hang onto someone."

*Good. Let him think that.* "You're right. Reckon huntin' bucks ain't meant for us girls."

She casually squeezed Caleb's arm and prompted a grin.

They moved into a thicket of trees, then they saw it. Not two bucks, but one.

"Oh, my." Lily held a hand to her heart. "The poor thing."

"Poor thing?" Lucas waved an arrow. "We couldn't get any luckier."

Somehow, the buck had entwined its antlers in the crook of a tree and couldn't get loose. He jerked and pulled, snorted and huffed, unable to break free. Saliva dripped from the sides of his mouth, and he sounded as if he was in pain.

"Hard to say how long he's been there," Caleb said. "I'm sure he's thirsty *and* hungry."

"So am *I*." Lucas patted his belly. "What are we waitin' for?"

Lily tightened her grip on Caleb's arm. "Put him outta his misery."

Lucas rapidly nodded, then handed Caleb an arrow.

The buck sniffed and pawed at the ground. His head thrashed harder.

"He smelled us." Caleb stepped away from Lily and positioned the arrow on his bow.

Lily held her breath.

Caleb's stance alone showed skill and experience. He held the weapon perfectly still, then drew back his arm. His eyes closed for a mere moment, then he reopened them and blew out a long breath.

*Thwap!*

The arrow sped through the air and plunged into the animal's chest. The buck's head reared, his legs frantically kicked, then his body went limp, draped against the tree.

"Yes!" Lucas yelled. He strutted around as if *he'd* taken the fatal shot. "We got us a buck!"

"That was horrid," Lily mumbled.

Caleb strode to the animal and pulled out the arrow. "Dyin' is never pretty, but he'd a been worse off if we hadn't found him an' stopped his sufferin'."

Lucas shook his head at Lily, then rolled his eyes and joined Caleb. "She shoulda stayed home." He looked over his shoulder. "We gotta cut it up now. Reckon you better leave. You bein' so *sensitive* an' all."

"I ain't leavin'." She stomped across the forest floor, no longer caring how much noise she made. "I've skinned more animals than *you* have, Lucas."

He grunted and nudged Caleb.

"Lucas." Caleb turned from the deer and faced him. "Your sister's one a the most capable women I ever met. *I* understand why it bothered her watchin' the buck die. Didn't it upset you at all?"

"Uh-uh. Why should it?"

Caleb dropped to one knee and looked him in the eye. "You should feel it in *here*." He pressed a hand to Lucas's chest. "Seein' sumthin' suffer should make your heart ache."

"It's just a dumb ol' deer."

Caleb stood tall, then took Lucas by the arm and led him around to the other side of the tree. The two faced the buck head-on. "Look at his eyes. Ain't he beautiful?"

Lucas curled his lip and glanced up at Caleb like he'd lost his mind.

"Don't you see?" Caleb persisted. "He was strong an' majestic. His antlers are incredible." He touched a finger to each one. His lips moved as he silently counted. "Twelve points." Smiling, he ran his hand over the animal's head.

"If he's so amazin', why'd he get stuck in this tree?"

Lily let out a long sigh. Though she appreciated Caleb's determination, her little brother would never understand. She worried about the boy's heart.

She drew her knife from her pocket and crossed to them. "Let's gut it here, then drag it close to home to butcher it. We'll have plenty a meat to share with the neighbors. Can't have Mrs. Quincy starvin'." She met Caleb's gaze, and they both grinned.

"We gotta take the horns to Pa," Lucas said. "See if they're as big as the ones he got."

It seemed Caleb's efforts at bringing out some kind of emotional sentiment from Lucas hadn't worked. The boy had a one-track mind, and it veered nowhere close to his heart.

# Chapter 16

The scent of venison lingered in the small cabin. In addition to the wonderful meat, Caleb had enjoyed roasted potatoes, carrots, and stewed apples. A Thanksgiving he'd never forget. After a lengthy, but appropriate prayer of thanks given by Mr. Larsen, they'd all eaten heartily, laughed, and enjoyed each other's company.

Mr. Larsen had taken half the deer to Mr. Quincy. The man had a smokehouse and offered to smoke the meat and return part of it. They hung the remaining un-smoked venison in a secret room in the barn, that Mr. Larsen had revealed to Caleb. Numerous jugs of untouched moonshine sat on shelves there. The man had said he'd keep it only to treat wounds. Hopefully, he'd stay true to his word.

Once it snowed, they'd pack the meat in barrels, and surround it with fresh snow. The frozen venison would last through the winter without spoiling. Even without salt. Living in a cold climate had its advantages.

Lucas asked over and over again to hunt for another deer, but Caleb had told him they didn't need the meat, and unless something changed, hunting was unnecessary.

The boy's hunger to kill troubled Caleb, and he knew it bothered Lily, too.

Before crawling into bed, Caleb had put a large back log on the fire and also stacked plenty of wood beside the fireplace. It was their lifeblood. Without heat, they'd all perish.

With the wheat sown, meat secured, and cracks in the chinking filled, they were ready to survive the coming winter.

Being snowed in with the Larsens could prove to be interesting. He expected many nights of listening to Mrs. Larsen read, games of marbles, and charades. A new favorite of the entire family. Of course, Horace always acted the most animated.

And with every day that passed, Caleb's love for Lily grew.

He chuckled.

*Like the flower itself.*

For some reason, he couldn't sleep. He stared upward into darkness. The holiday brought memories of those gone by. Years ago, on the day before Thanksgiving, Rebecca had come to their house with a pie she'd baked. Though he was only fifteen at the time, he'd flirted with her. Simply because she'd paid more attention to Abraham and had handed the pie directly to him.

Caleb had gone so far as to tell her he *cared* for her, when all he'd wanted was to prove he was still the brother every girl wanted most. His ma knew that his claims of affection were false and cautioned him not to toy with Rebecca's feelings.

His dear mother had always been able to see through him. She knew him better than anyone.

*I was horrid.*

He pinched his eyes tight and tried to wash away the memory.

Horrible as it was, killing Abraham made Caleb want to be a better man. To become fully good and decent like Abe had been his entire life.

A familiar creak turned his head.

The firelight cast shadows on the ceiling above his curtained barrier. The large flames also gave off enough light that enabled him to dimly see everything around him.

*Please, be Lily.*

She'd not come to his bed since that one special night, but he kept hoping. Just to be near her.

The curtain parted, and his heart thumped. The very person he hoped for stepped through.

As she'd done before, she lay down and draped an arm over him. Her lips tickled his ear. "Happy Thanksgivin'."

Without speaking, he turned on his side and kissed her.

The icy chill in the air disappeared. His heart burst with love. He swore he didn't merit this incredible woman, but he'd grown tired of fighting himself and chose to cherish her.

"Marry me, Lily," he whispered.

She stroked his cheek. "You proposin'?"

"Reckon so."

"I want to, but we can't. Not yet. There ain't a preacher 'round for miles. Remember? I told you ours was run outta town."

"I gotta marry you soon. I'm achin' for you."

She placed a peck on the tip of his nose. "We hafta wait, but maybe not for long. Mr. Quincy told Lucas the other day, there's rumors the war may be endin'. Once spring comes, maybe we can get you outta that silly dress an' into some proper trousers. Then we can find us a preacher. Just don't tell my folks what you told me. All right? It'd ruin everythin'. Let them keep believin' you are who you claimed to be."

His breath hitched. He could've sworn he heard someone in the other room. Though he and Lily had been whispering, and he doubted anyone could discern what they'd said, whoever was out there would know he wasn't alone.

He placed a hand over her mouth and craned his neck.

The fire crackled.

Lily lowered his hand, and once again put her lips to his ear. "They all have full bellies. Nothin's gonna wake 'em." She sat up, lifted his blankets, and climbed in beside him.

"What are you doin'?"

"I wanna be close." She rested her head on his bare chest. Her fingers twirled through the thick patch of hair at its center.

When she turned and kissed his skin, he lost his breath. "Oh, Lily . . ."

He rolled her onto her back and glided his hand down her side. Even through her flannel nightgown, he felt the curve of her form.

They kissed like lovers, and his body pushed him to go further.

*I can't . . .*

He flopped onto his back and linked his hands behind his head. The only way to keep them off her. "We gotta stop."

"Why?" She burrowed into him. "I don't want no one else, an' you just asked me to marry you. So, I reckon that means you feel the same. I wanna love you."

"We hafta wait. Don't you see?"

She whimpered and resumed tormenting him by fingering his chest hair.

He grabbed her hand and stopped her. "Your folks are so close that if I *belched*, they'd hear it."

She lightly giggled.

"I'm serious, Lily. Your pa would shoot me if he walked in on us. I ain't even lovin' on you right now, but if he found you in my bed, I'd be a dead man."

"Want me to go?"

"Yes. I mean . . . *no*. But you hafta."

A door opened, and they froze.

Caleb's heart thumped in his ears. So loud, he feared whoever had come into the living area would hear it.

Lily trembled.

Footsteps crossed the floor and a breeze from the opened front door swept under the curtain and made it billow.

"Ate too much," Mr. Larsen grumbled and the door shut again.

"Pa's goin' to the outhouse," Lily whispered. "Should I hurry to my room?"

"No. It's too risky. What if he turns 'round an' comes right back in? We can't chance him seein' you come out from here. Wait till he returns an' goes to bed."

"All right."

She clutched onto him. Her rapidly beating heart throbbed against his chest.

Two souls in love, and both scared to death.

"I won't do this again." She barely breathed the words.

He softly rubbed her back to calm her, but touching her certainly didn't help *him*. If he ever had her this close again, he doubted he could resist her.

After what seemed like an eternity, the front door opened. Mr. Larsen walked across the floor.

To Caleb's horror, the rocking chair squeaked and kept on creaking in a steady rhythm.

Even in the dim light, he could tell Lily's eyes were wide as wagon wheels. Though she said nothing, her body shook.

For some unknown reason, the man had decided to sit in the rocker, rather than return to bed.

He groaned as if in pain, mumbling something indiscernible.

*Digestive issues.*

He'd eaten at least three large portions of venison. None of them had had so much meat in a great while. No wonder the man wasn't feeling well.

Caleb tightened his hold on Lily, then placed a soft kiss on the top of her head. She cuddled close and tenderly stroked his arm. Eventually, she stopped quivering.

As much as he loved holding her, knowing her pa sat less than ten feet away put a damper on his joy.

Loud snoring soon replaced the squeaking of the rocker.

* * *

*Why'd I do this to myself?*

Lily should've had more sense and stayed in bed with Violet.

Now that her pa was asleep, she had to make a move. He'd been known to doze in the rocker all night long. If tonight happened to be one of those nights, he'd still be there in the morning, and she'd definitely be discovered.

She rose and kissed Caleb's cheek. Speaking wouldn't be wise. Not even a whisper with her pa so close.

As quietly as she could, she lifted the blankets and scooted onto the floor.

Caleb reached for her, shaking his head.

She touched a single finger to her lips, then crawled on her hands and knees under the curtain. If she stayed low, maybe her pa wouldn't notice her. *If* he happened to stir.

Heart pounding, she eased onto her feet, but remained hunched down as she made her way through the living area.

The floorboards creaked loudly beneath her.

"What's that?" Her pa jerked to his feet and whipped around.

Lily's insides tumbled. She slowly stood fully erect.

"Lily?" he whispered. "What are you doin'?"

She pointed at the water pitcher on the countertop. "I got thirsty. I was tryin' to be quiet so I wouldn't wake you. Sorry." She, too, kept her voice to a hushed whisper.

He motioned her over. "Don't apologize." With a low groan, he placed a hand over his belly and rubbed it in slow circles. "I ain't feelin' too well. Ate too much."

"We all did." She bent down and kissed his cheek. Never had she felt so relieved. "I'm gonna get me some water and get back to bed. Hope you feel better soon, Pa."

He gave her hand a loving pat. "I'll be fine. Learned me a thing or two. Next time, I'll go easy on the meat."

She giggled, then covered her mouth and gestured to the curtain. "Don't wanna wake Caleb."

Her pa nodded. "I best get to bed myself. Gotta keep your ma warm." He smiled, trudged to his room, and shut the door.

Lily stepped close to the blanketed enclosure. "Night, Caleb," she whispered.

"Night." Her heart danced at the sound of his light raspy word.

They'd escaped what could've been a drastic discovery. She was sure Caleb had heard everything that had been said in the conversation with her pa. And no doubt, it had calmed his worries, just as it had hers.

Temptation to join him again lasted a mere second, then she hurried off to bed.

Violet hadn't budged and lay there, peacefully asleep, so Lily eased in beside her and pulled the covers up high. She smiled uncontrollably.

*I'm an engaged woman.*

He'd asked. She'd accepted. What more needed to be said?

Granted, they had a great deal of *planning* to do. Not only did they need to decide when to tell her folks, they had to determine where they'd live. Leaving the roost wasn't wise. Not with her pa's limitations. He needed as much help with the farm as he could get.

Besides, most newlyweds in the cove stayed close to their families. Since Caleb had grown to care for hers, she believed he'd be agreeable to the idea. And when the grandbabies started to come, she knew her ma would want them near.

*Babies . . .*

Lily smiled for the rest of the night.

# CHAPTER 17

Secrecy had many downfalls. Lily nearly burst wanting to share her news. As happy as she was, her good sense prevailed. She and Caleb would keep quiet about their intentions until the war ended and he could become a *man* again.

Not only that, selfishly, she wanted to continue their ability to sneak away from time to time for a bit of affection. If the truth came out, her pa would never trust them to be alone, till they said their vows.

She enjoyed watching Caleb from a distance. Her husband-to-be had incredible strength. The way he swung the axe when he chopped wood set *her* on fire.

What warmed her the most, however, was the way he treated Isaac. She'd seen it many times. Caleb acted gentle and loving, and he'd carry on conversations with the boy that showed he cared about what her little brother had to say, regardless of his young age.

Every night, Lily would go to bed and dream about her life with Caleb and what a wonderful pa he'd be.

Time passed, but not fast enough for her liking. If only they'd get the news that the war had ended.

December brought even colder temperatures. On mornings like this, she hated to get up and leave the warmth of her covers.

Isaac raced into the room and stood at the foot of the bed. He slapped his hands against the quilt, hitting her legs. "Sissy, it snowed! Come see!"

Lily glanced sideways at Violet and grinned. They simultaneously flipped their covers back. Every year, they looked forward to seeing the beauty of the first snowfall.

Laughing, they grabbed their robes and headed to the living room.

To keep the cold out, heavy blankets had been hung over every window. Lily went to the one beside the front door and pushed it aside enough to see out. Violet pressed against her and peered over her shoulder.

Everything in sight had been covered by a blanket of clean white snow. It sparkled in the sunshine. Lovely and pure. Tiny flakes continued to fall, adding to the groundcover.

"Lily," her ma said. "Bundle up an' check for eggs. An' let go a that blanket 'fore the cold gets in."

"Yes'm." Lily let the quilt drop freely.

Violet sighed. "It's so beautiful, Ma. I like lookin' at it."

"Then *you* go get the eggs."

"In the cold?" Violet's eyes widened. "It's Lily's chore. I'll let her do it." Smiling, she meandered to the sofa and sat beside Horace and Isaac.

Lily moved away from the window and glanced into her folks' bedroom. The bed had already been properly made.

Her pa was nowhere in sight, nor was Lucas. She couldn't hear Caleb rustling around behind the curtain either. He certainly couldn't be sleeping. Not with all the ruckus in the house.

"Where are the men?" she asked her ma.

"Got up early." Her ma gestured to Caleb's sleeping area. "*He* woke your pa. Said his gut told him sumthin' ain't right. Lucas heard 'em stirrin' and came down. They all went scoutin' to see if Caleb's feelin's amounted to anythin'."

"How long they been gone?"

Her ma's chin lifted high. "Little over an hour."

Lily hurried to her room and got dressed, then bundled up for the weather. She put on her thickest socks and shoved her feet into boots.

With her scarf wrapped around her face, she headed for the door.

Her ma stopped her. "Where you goin'?"

"For eggs. Remember?"

"Lily." She peered into her eyes. "Don't get no ideas 'bout lookin' for them. Hear me?"

"Yes'm." Her ma released her, and Lily headed out the door.

She paused on the front porch, attempting to comprehend the silent hush over the valley. Snow mysteriously muted everything.

In order to better focus, she shut her eyes and listened. The partially frozen stream trickled. Aside from that . . . *nothing.*

When she stepped onto the ground, she noticed snow-filled footprints. Three sets. They headed toward the main road that passed by their cabin.

She'd hoped to hear the men talking, or at least the sound of their return. Maybe some heavy footfalls and breathing. No such luck.

*They must be somewhere far from here.*

Worry roiled her stomach.

She opened the barn door and went in. A small amount of snow had drifted inside, but overall the place was much warmer than the open air.

The chickens had left their mark throughout the building. She had to dodge piles of droppings. At least she could scoop them up with a shovel and toss them out, rather than have to scrub them with a rag and hot water.

She found the hens nestled in their bedding. To her good fortune, the white had laid. She patted her head. "Good girl."

Instead of cleaning the messes, she rushed back with the egg.

She stomped the snow off her boots before going into the cabin, then handed the prize over to her ma. "The hens like bein' in the barn. But I'll hafta go later an' clean up after them."

"Glad you got an egg." Her ma took it and set it aside. "I'm gonna wait to fix breakfast till the men come home. Don't want it to get cold."

Lily hung up her coat, unwound the scarf, and dropped it along with her mittens into the basket by the door. Since her ma didn't need help with the meal just yet, Lily happily scooted the rocking chair close to the fireplace and sat.

She'd always loved to rock, yet the chair had become her pa's favorite place to sit, so she rarely got the chance.

"Don't fret 'bout Pa, Lily," Isaac said. "He's with Caleb. Nothin' bad'll happen."

Violet shook her head and frowned, but kept silent. Though recently she'd been acting less ugly to Caleb, Lily knew she still had her doubts about him. Violet had vowed never to trust *any* man.

Lily looked over her shoulder at her ma, who sat at the kitchen table reading her Bible. "Ma? Did Pa take his gun?"

The woman kept her eyes on the Good Book. "Yep."

The idea of the men carrying a weapon both helped *and* troubled Lily. If they encountered soldiers, they'd be more likely to be fired upon. On the other hand, having a gun meant they had *some* protection.

Lily rocked faster, said a quick prayer that they'd hurry home, then stared blankly ahead.

A single item rested on the fireplace mantel. A clock, given to her folks as a wedding gift. They'd considered storing it in the secret room in the barn, but decided no one would want the old thing. Lily doubted it had much value, yet she affixed her eyes to it.

Minutes ticked by slower than ever.

The boys giggled over drawings on their slates. Violet had initiated a game, where she'd draw a simple line or swirl, and they'd add to it and make strange animals or nonsensical objects. Lily couldn't manage a laugh. Her heavy heart wouldn't allow it.

Boots stomping on the front porch brought her out of her gloom. She hopped to her feet, raced to the door, and swung it wide.

The three dear men stood there, brushing snow off their clothes.

Caleb met her gaze. His brows drew close together, and he didn't cast even a *slim* smile.

Lily remained in the open doorway, unable to wait for answers. "What happened?"

Her pa pointed into the cabin. "Get inside. You're lettin' in cold air."

"But—"

"Lily." He jerked his head and pointed again.

"Yessir." Disheartened, she pushed the door almost shut and returned to the fireplace, but didn't sit in the rocker. She leaned against the wall and waited.

The men came right in and removed their coats. Caleb took his bonnet off and flakes of snow fell to the floor.

Lily's ma took hold of her pa's arm. "You look a sight." She stroked his bright red cheeks. "What'd you find out there?"

"Rebel soldiers." His hard expression was as cold as the ice he'd left outside. "Hundreds of 'em."

Lily clutched her chest. "*Hundreds*? But . . . no one blew a horn. Why?"

"They couldn't. Them soldiers is camped everywhere. Small groups huddled together 'round fires. One a them is camped beside the Quincy's cabin. 'Bout fifty men. Even a handful a horses. I reckon them rebels have everyone in that house scared to do much a anythin'." He trudged to his rocker, sat, and hissed out a long breath. "We stayed hid, but sooner or later, they'll likely come traipsin' 'round here." He shook a finger. "You girls keep yourselves inside."

"Yes, Pa," Lily said, but Violet didn't utter a sound. Her face had gone ashen.

Caleb grabbed a chair and carried it close to the fire. He sat and held his hands to the flames. "Your pa's right. Best you stay in. An' I reckon, I'll hafta stay with you."

Her ma cracked the egg into a bowl and started whipping it to death. At least she'd found a way to take out *her* frustration.

Lily felt like a caged animal. She slapped a hand against the wall. "It's silly stayin' inside. We done it before, an' lost most of our corn."

Caleb looked directly into her eyes. "It's important."

"How are we s'posed to use the outhouse?" She thrust her chin into the air and crossed her arms.

"A pot will hafta do for now," her ma mumbled from the kitchen.

*So much for bein' outside an' enjoyin' the snow.*

Lily immediately scolded herself for being selfish. She'd been told to stay indoors for her own protection. She couldn't fault them for that. However, she now had another reason to despise the soldiers. They were ruining her winter.

"Why do you reckon they're here?" she asked her pa.

"Hard to say. If I coulda talked to Russel Quincy, he mighta shed some light. If the rumors are true 'bout the war nearin' its end, I 'spect the rebels came here to hide. Word is the North is winnin'."

"It ain't fair." Lily wanted to scream the words, but kept her composure. "Just cuz our beautiful cove is in the middle a nowhere, they decide to use it as an escape. Why can't they take their tails home where they belong?"

Caleb's face softened into a dim smile. "They will. In time. Maybe sooner than later. There ain't much food to be had here. Hopefully, they'll rest up and be on their way."

"That's right," her pa added. "An' Rose, don't be cookin' no venison till they're gone. If they come anywhere close an' smell it cookin', they'll hunt it up. We don't want them to find our hidin' place."

"All right." Her ma dumped the contents of the bowl into a pan. "You'll hafta make do with corncakes an' apple butter for a while."

Just when things had started looking brighter, everything darkened around Lily. She wanted to go to Caleb and hold on tight, simply to feel reassured. But even that was impossible.

* * *

Caleb tossed and turned. He couldn't sleep. Every little sound brought him instantly alert.

Fifty soldiers close by meant fifty threats. Mr. Larsen only had fifteen bullets left. And even if Caleb used his bow and arrows for defense, they'd easily be overcome.

*Far too outnumbered.*

The best possible outcome would be that the men truly were on their way home and had no intentions of disrupting the families in the cove.

*Lord, make 'em leave.*

Even prayer didn't bring rest, but it comforted his spirit.

Lily's unease made matters worse. He *had* to protect her.

His hope lay in the rumors. If the war ended, he and Lily could move forward with their lives together. Everything would take a turn for the better.

A heavy fist pounded on the front door.

Caleb jerked upright. *He* certainly couldn't answer it.

He sat there, breathing hard. Helpless.

*BAM! BAM!*

A knock much louder than the first time.

Everyone in the house stirred, but only one interior door opened. Lantern light lit up the room.

"Stay put," Mr. Larsen mumbled as he passed the curtain. His footsteps neared the front door. "Who's there?" He yelled the word with challenging anger.

"It's Jeremy! Jeremy Quincy! Please open up!"

*Mr. Quincy's oldest grandson.*

Caleb's heart thumped as hard as the young boy's fist.

*This ain't good.*

Mr. Larsen brought the boy inside, then shut and relocked the door. "What's wrong?"

The boy burst out crying. "They . . . they shot Grampa!"

The entire household sprung to life. Footsteps pounded down the stairs, and Lily's bedroom door opened. It sounded as if every member of the family had gathered around the boy, but Caleb had to remain hidden.

"C'mere, Jeremy," Mrs. Larsen softly said.

Caleb parted his curtain enough to peer out. The troubled boy clung to her.

"Shh," she whispered, then guided him to the sofa. "Take a big breath, then tell us what happened. Violet, get the boy some water."

"Yes'm."

The child sniffled and cried, then sipped from the glass Violet brought him. "Grampa's dead." His chin quivered, then he wiped his face with the back of his hand. "They shouldn't a done it."

"Tell us everythin'." Mr. Larsen said.

After drinking more water, the boy handed the glass to Violet. "Grampa went out to get our pig. Gramma wanted him to bring it inside. But them soldiers was roastin' it." He puffed out a few breaths. "Grampa came back an' told Gramma. Said he was gonna make 'em pay for the meat. That it was only right. So he grabbed his gun and went out to talk to 'em."

"That's what I woulda done," Lucas said, standing up tall.

"Hush, boy," his pa fussed, and Lucas pinched his lips together, scowling.

Caleb shut his eyes and shook his head. Lucas didn't understand the bigger picture. Mr. Quincy didn't have a chance against so many soldiers.

Jeremy blinked several times, causing newly formed tears to stream. "Gramma heard a shot an' ran out. I followed her, thinkin' I might could help. Before we got far, we ran into a soldier draggin' Grampa's body to the cabin. He said they shot 'im, cuz he was aimin' to shoot *them*." He covered his face and bent his head low. "The man told Gramma he was keepin' Grampa's gun, an' that we best stay away."

"Damn them!" Mr. Larsen pounded his fist on the arm of the rocker.

Mrs. Larsen covered the boy's ears and pulled him against her. "Hush, Buck. The child's upset enough as it is."

Jeremy looked up into Mrs. Larsen's face. "Gramma's talkin' nonsense. Say's she'll poison 'em all. But I'm scared. If she's does anythin', they'll kill her, too. Then me an' Billy won't have no one."

"Your gramma won't do nothin'." Mrs. Larsen spoke soft and gentle. Highly unlike her usual self. "She's rightfully angry right now. Hurtin', too." She smoothed her hand along his hair, then turned to her husband. "What can *we* do, Buck?"

Caleb already knew the answer. *Absolutely nothing.* At least where the soldiers were concerned.

Mr. Larsen stood and bent down in front of the boy. "You go home an' tell your gramma I'll come by when the sun comes up. We'll help take care a your grampa's body. I ain't gonna risk goin' now. Sneakin' around in the dark would get me shot if any rebel happened to see me. Can *you* make it back home again?"

"Yessir."

Mr. Larsen rose and brought the boy to his feet. "We'll figger sumthin' out, so try not to cry no more. 'Specially in front a your gramma. She'll need you to be strong. All right?"

Jeremy frowned, but nodded. "Reckon I'm the man a the house now. Best be actin' like it." He followed Mr. Larsen to the front door.

Caleb assumed Jeremy to be around eleven. Not even as old as Lucas. Too young for so much responsibility.

No longer crying, the boy left. Caleb eased out from his enclosure. "Mr. Quincy shoulda known not to come at them carryin' a gun."

"True," Mr. Larsen said. "But he's a proud man."

"A proud *dead* man," Lily said with a great deal of spite. "I want the war over so we can get back to livin'. I *hate* what's happened to our cove."

"An' country," Violet whispered.

"Amen," their ma mumbled. "Only thing what's gonna help us is faith." She crossed to her husband and took hold of his arm. "Let's get some sleep. We won't be no good to no one if we can't keep our eyes open."

The man wrapped his arm around her. "You're right, Rose. You children get on back to bed, too. T'morra I'll do what I can to find out more 'bout them men. Y'all say some prayers they'll high-tail it outta here."

"*Exactly,*" Lily said. "An' good riddance."

Everyone dispersed, but Lily lingered. She cautiously looked around the room, then locked eyes with Caleb and mouthed, *I love you*.

He merely blinked, and she'd already joined her sister in their bedroom. His heart weighed heavy from her absence.

*Love.*

The world needed an abundance of it.

Caleb returned to his mattress and pulled the blankets up to his neck.

The dangerous rebels had killed an innocent man without giving it a second thought. He hated the fact he'd fought alongside them. It might've been months ago, but memories of all the killing haunted him. For all he knew these very soldiers could be a part of his former company.

Sleep wouldn't come anytime soon.

# CHAPTER 18

Lily defiantly crossed her arms. "I'll be fine, Pa."

"No. You ain't comin'. If them soldiers is still camped outside the Quincy's cabin, God only knows what they'd do at the sight a someone purty as you."

"He's right, Lily," Caleb said. "Stay here with us. Lucas can go with your pa."

"Yep." Lucas strutted, puffed up and proud. "I'm a man now. Pa told me so." He grabbed the gun from the corner of the room, where it had been left leaning against the wall. "I'll shoot 'em if I hafta."

Their pa yanked it out of his hand. "Ain't no one gonna be shootin'." He scowled and returned it to its place. "The gun stays here with Caleb. He might need it more than us."

Lucas kicked at the floor. "I wanna shoot someone."

Their pa cuffed him upside the head. "Hush, or I might change my mind an' leave you here."

Lily smiled, glad to see her brother reprimanded. She'd been tempted to do it herself.

The pair bundled up in their winterwear and headed for the door. Lucas grumbled under his breath, but didn't openly speak.

Their ma hurried across the room and wrapped her arms around their pa. It wrenched Lily's heart watching her folks hug so earnestly.

"Take care a yourself an' our boy," her ma said. "An' be sure to tell Harriet how sorry I am."

"I will." They kissed on the lips. Something Lily hadn't seen in a long while.

*They're both scared.*

Her pa and Lucas walked out, and a gust of icy wind swept through the cabin.

Lily quickly moved to the rocking chair and gradually got it moving. Caleb took a seat on the sofa. Within seconds, Horace and Isaac joined him. They all appreciated the warmth from the fire, but Lily knew Caleb gave them more comfort than the flames. His secure presence had drawn them there.

Violet and their ma sat silently at the kitchen table, while once again, Lily watched the hands of the clock on the mantel.

Minutes turned into hours.

Her ma slammed her Bible shut. "I hate this confounded waitin'!"

Caleb patted the top of Isaac's head, then stood and took the seat beside her. "Mrs. Larsen, they'll be all right. I feel it in here." He tapped his hand to the center of his chest. "Don't know why I get these kinda feelin's, but I've had 'em all my life. I reckon I'd know if sumthin' bad had happened to your husband an' boy."

She tenderly stroked the Bible. "Lord help me, I can't go on like this. Livin' every day in fear. Buck can't dig no grave. It was senseless him goin' over there."

Lily got up from the rocker and joined them at the table. "Them three boys can dig. The ground ain't frozen solid. Pa will tell 'em what to do, an' they'll manage just fine."

Her ma looked upward as if searching for something. She continued to caress the Good Book. "I don't wanna bury *my* husband. Or another child. If that happens, you might as well put me in the ground with 'em."

Lily grasped her hand. "Stop talkin' that way. Hear me?"

"Can't help it." She reopened the Bible and stared at the pages.

Another hour went by. Lily paced, then rocked some more. Caleb and Violet wrangled the boys into a game of charades, but Lily didn't feel like participating. Not today.

She wandered to the window and lifted the corner of the quilt. Large snowflakes fell from the sky and accumulated on the already covered ground. If they came down any heavier, her pa would have trouble finding the way home again.

Her breath caught. "I see 'em!"

Her pa and Lucas walked sluggishly side by side, with their arms around each other. It looked as if Lucas was holding the man up.

"Pa looks tired," Lily said over her shoulder.

She faced them again, and the truth hit hard.

*He wouldn't . . .*

She opened the door to let them in, along with the scent she dreaded. "Pa?"

He stumbled and nearly fell. Caleb jumped to his feet and helped him to the rocker. Lily's ma muttered something utterly unladylike, but Lily didn't fault her for it. She'd thought the same things.

"Mrs. Quincy was tippin' the jug," Lucas said. "Pa claimed it was only right to join in her grief."

Lily's ma shot to her feet and stomped across the floor. "That's where you been all this time?" Fury spewed from her lips. "Shame on you, Buck!"

His lip curled into a grin. "She was bein' hopsitable." His smirk grew larger. "Hopsmitamal."

"Hush!" Her ma shook a finger in his face. "You're drunk as a skunk. God forgive you."

His head teetered back and forth.

"He won't be no good for no one anytime soon." Her ma turned her attention to Lucas and grasped him by the arm. "You shoulda stopped 'im."

"Me? I ain't gonna cross Pa."

She sat on the sofa and jerked Lucas down with her. "Tell me everythin'. Them soldiers trouble you?"

"Uh-uh. They was gone. Mrs. Quincy said they left long 'fore we got there." He grinned up at Caleb. "You shoulda seen all them tracks goin' every which way. They got into some kinda scuffle 'fore they left."

"How do you know that?" Caleb asked, but her pa's loud chuckle kept Lucas from answering.

They all gaped at the man.

Her ma slapped his leg. "You're a mess, Buck."

"Not as bad as them *rebels*." He snorted, laughed harder, then belched. "Harriet gave 'em some *nasty* shoonmine. *Moon*mine." He waved a hand and wheezed. "You know what I mean."

Lily rolled her eyes, then looked away. She hated seeing him like this and couldn't remember the last time he'd gotten so drunk he couldn't properly form words.

"Least they left," Caleb said. "Once the snow eases up, Lucas an' me can go scout. Make sure they've *all* gone."

*Wonderful*. Lily would have to start worrying all over again.

Lucas grinned from ear to ear. "Can we take the gun this time?"

Caleb glanced at Lily's pa, then turned toward her. His eyes searched hers as if asking for permission. "Reckon we can. We might need it, an' your pa can't use it in his condition."

Lily clutched Caleb's arm. "Just promise you won't let Lucas touch it."

"Why?" the boy whined.

She leered at him. "Cuz you're too eager, that's why. You'd probably shoot a neighbor by mistake."

Her pa's head dropped to his chest, and he loudly snored.

Lucas stood and faced Lily with his hands tightened into fists. "You ain't the boss a me."

Their ma cuffed the back of his head. "*I* am. You ain't touchin' no gun. Hear me?"

"Yes'm." Grumbling, he strode away and stomped up the stairs to his room.

"That boy's gonna cause us some trouble." Their ma covered her face with her hands. "Tainted by the war."

"He'll be fine, ma'am," Caleb said. "Come spring, I reckon we'll see big changes here. We'll have us a good crop a wheat, an' hopefully peace. Lucas is growin' up. He's only tryin' to find himself. But you've given him a strong foundation. He won't stray."

Lily appreciated Caleb's confidence. However, she had a lot of doubts about her brother. He'd shown signs of being a troublemaker, even *before* the war.

* * *

The snow had fallen steadily for days.

Caleb had been the one to make every decision about venturing outside, while Mr. Larsen returned to sobriety. Even after the alcohol left his system, he suffered for a full day with a horrible headache. Worst of all, his wife had been hard on him. Fussed every chance she got.

Caleb understood. The poor woman simply wanted to keep the man who'd finally gotten his life in order. If he slipped once, he could easily slip again.

He'd said, *I'm sorry,* so many times that Caleb had lost count. He had yet to hear Mrs. Larsen forgive him.

Lily had gone much easier on him. Caleb had seen her pat him on the back a time or two. Mostly after her ma had relentlessly badgered the man.

Lily sauntered up beside Caleb. "We'll never be like them," she whispered in his ear.

He smiled, but when he caught Violet's eye, his heart sank. She looked knowingly between the two of them.

Caleb put his back to her and leaned close to Lily. "Your sister knows 'bout us. I can tell."

Honestly, it surprised him nothing had ever been said. He and Lily had relaxed their communication and never shied away from interacting. Being in such close proximity in the tiny cabin hadn't helped.

"I'll talk to her tonight," Lily whispered. "It'll be okay."

Caleb walked away, wanting more than anything to touch her. It'd been weeks since they'd snuck a kiss.

He lifted the quilt on the window and peered outside. The sun glimmered against the snow, and none currently fell.

He went to the stairwell and craned his neck upward. "Lucas! Wanna go scout?"

The boy had been spending a great deal of time in his room, yet the instant Caleb called out to him, he came bounding down the steps.

"Course I do!" He lit up like the sun.

"I'll go, too." Mr. Larsen came out of his bedroom and headed for the door. "Rose. I'm goin' with 'em."

"I heard." She spoke without feeling.

They had more ice between them than what hung as sickles from the roof. Caleb hoped her heart would melt long before spring.

He put three bullets in his skirt pocket. Strange how his garments had become ordinary. He tied on the bonnet and put his arms through the sleeves of Violet's coat, then bundled up completely by adding a scarf. Fully ready, he grabbed the gun.

At least no one would question a woman toting a rifle. Not in these troubled times.

"Be careful!" Lily called out as they went outside.

Caleb looked back and smiled.

*A goodbye kiss sure woulda been nice.*

* * *

It felt like a part of Lily walked out the door whenever Caleb left. She wanted to go with him, but her ma wouldn't approve of *her* scouting.

*It's gonna be a very long winter.*

Violet tugged on her arm. "Come to our room. I wanna talk to you."

Their ma glanced up from her needlework, huffed a breath, and kept sewing.

Lily's mind spun. She had no doubt what Violet wanted to discuss, but followed her regardless. Violet shut the door behind them and they sat atop the bed. The chilly room offered privacy, but little comfort.

Lily decided to approach her sister as nonchalantly as possible. "What's on your mind? Sumthin' you don't want Ma to hear?" She took hold of Violet's hand, then leaned close and whispered. "Don't you think it's awful the way she's been treatin' Pa? Her Christian heart should've forgiven him right away. After all, he was only tryin' to appease Mrs. Quincy. An'—"

"Hush, Lily. For heaven's sake. I wanted to talk to you, not be talked at *by* you."

"Sorry." She sat up straight. "Go on, then."

Violet released her, then folded her arms over her chest. "You've changed your mind 'bout Caleb, haven't you?"

"*Shh.*" Lily pressed a finger to her lips. Truthfully, she *wanted* to tell Violet her feelings, but definitely didn't want their ma to know. "Yes, my feelin's have changed. Caleb's been good to Pa, an' he's helped with the farm in more ways than one. Without him, I reckon we'd be starvin'."

"So, you don't believe anymore that he's a *bad* man?"

"Not at all." She mindlessly ran her finger over the quilt, glanced over her shoulder at the shut door, then leaned close to her sister again. "Truth be told, I *love* 'im."

Violet's eyes popped wide. "*Love*?"

Lily silently nodded. Her heart beat rapidly simply saying the word.

"Does he feel that way 'bout you?"

"Well . . ." She swallowed hard, worried she might say too much. Still, she pressed on. "He said so, an' if askin' me to marry him is any indication, then I'd say he's a mite taken with me." She grinned, then covered her mouth with one hand, trying not to giggle.

"Marry you?" Violet flopped back onto the bed. "Ma an' Pa would have a fit if they knew." She jerked upright again, grabbed Lily's shoulders, and brought her close. "Has he kissed you?"

Lily's cheeks heated, no doubt red as a beet.

Violet gasped. "He *has*, hasn't he?"

"Yes. An' it was wonderful." This time she took both of Violet's hands and squeezed. "I've been dyin' to tell you, but I've been so scared. I don't want our folks to lock me up an' throw away the key."

"They'd do it, too. If they found out he's had his lips on you . . . oh, *my*. Pa'd never trust him again."

"That's right. An' Ma would boot him out the door." Lily shut her eyes and pictured the horrid scene. She could never tell Caleb's secrets, especially with the way her ma had recently decided to be so unforgiving. If she couldn't forgive her own husband, she'd never show mercy to Caleb.

Violet cupped her hand to Lily's cheek and she gasped, startled from her thoughts.

"Sorry, Lily. Didn't mean to scare you. If it makes you feel any better, I've come to notice Caleb's goodness. He'll make you a fine husband."

Lily grabbed onto her sister and gave her the biggest hug of their lives. "Thank you." When they separated, she kissed her cheek. "You can keep this a secret, right?"

"Course I can. I've been doin' it for some time now. Still, *you* best be careful. I seen how you two whisper to each other. Sure as shootin' Ma has, too. You don't want her confrontin' you an' hafta lie 'bout it. Hidin' things ain't so bad. But I don't need to remind you how Ma despises liars."

"You're right. We'll hafta do better." She stroked Violet's hair. "Want me to brush it for you? I know you like that."

Her sweet sister smiled brighter than she'd seen in a great while. Sharing this secret had done a world of good. Not only did it strengthen their bond, Lily finally had someone she entrusted with her feelings for Caleb. Her heart nearly burst with joy.

Winter wouldn't be quite so cold anymore.

# CHAPTER 19

Lily paced. Life wasn't one bit fair.

Things *had* been looking up. For months, no sign remained of a single soldier anywhere in the cove, her family had plenty of food to last the rest of the winter, and they'd survived snow and temperatures well below freezing. But being trapped with nowhere to go for help had set them in the middle of a horrific nightmare. Roads from the cove wouldn't be passable again until spring, and they had no way of reaching a doctor.

Lily grabbed onto Caleb and lay her head on his shoulder. After she'd told Violet about her feelings for him, Lily had been cautious about their interactions. She'd also managed to make him aware of the conversation she'd had with Violet, so he'd understand why she'd been more distant.

None of that mattered anymore.

"She's gonna be fine," he whispered. "Your ma's takin' good care a her. She knows what to do."

Tears pooled in Lily's eyes. "But Violet's burnin' up." She lifted her head and looked directly at him. Her chin quivered out of control, yet she couldn't stop it. "What if she dies?"

He stroked her hair and pulled her to him. "She won't."

The fever had come out of nowhere. Lily had woken in the night, drenched from Violet's perspiration. Though her sister had complained of being cold, her skin had been on fire. Two days had already passed, and the fever remained.

They assumed she'd gotten the illness from Jeremy Quincy. He'd come by to fetch some cornmeal for his gramma, and Violet had given it to him. The boy had seemed as if he'd run the entire way—sweaty and out of breath. When Violet got sick, Lily and Lucas had gone to check in with Mrs. Quincy to see if Jeremy was well. The woman wouldn't even open the door. She'd yelled for them to leave due to fever.

Lily's ma had moved Violet into her bedroom to tend her. Her pa had been sent upstairs with the boys. He'd mumbled something about finally getting some peace, which didn't help matters with her ma.

Everyone had been firmly told to stay as far away from Violet as possible. Of course, their ma *had* to be close to her, which meant she had the greatest risk of being overcome by the illness.

Lily sniffled and sighed, clutching Caleb harder. "I'm horrid."

He tenderly lifted her chin and peered into her eyes. A sight that warmed her, but made her feel worse. She didn't deserve an inkling of happiness right now, and he studied her with deep, loving thoughtfulness. "Why'd you say that?"

"Cuz all I should be thinkin' 'bout is Violet, an' prayin' for her return to health. I'm selfishly frustrated."

His head drew back. "I don't understand."

"T'morra's my birthday. The twenty-third a February. I wanted to celebrate—sumthin' much better than how we spent Christmas. I'll be eighteen, an' by all accounts a full-fledged woman. But I can't be happy 'bout it with Violet in there strug-glin' for every breath."

"Eighteen?" He stroked her cheek. "An' so beautiful."

*Oh, my.*

Her heart pitter-pattered, adding to her guilt. She needed to concentrate on the dire situation and not Caleb's gorgeous eyes. "So." She cleared her throat. "When's *your* birthday?"

He grinned. "It was in August. The fourteenth."

"An' just how old are you, Caleb Henry?" She jutted her chin high. Maybe he wouldn't see through her longing and retain some respect for her. After all, what man would want a woman who only thought of herself when her sister could be dying?

"I'm nineteen." He glanced around the room, then faced her again and moistened his lips.

The two of them were essentially alone. Aside from her ma and Violet, everyone else was upstairs. Lily knew what Caleb wanted. She also craved it.

It was risky, but she tipped her head back and obliged him. The first kiss in months.

It warmed her to the tips of her toes and took away every tear.

"I've missed you," he whispered against her cheek. "So much."

"You, too." Though tempted to kiss him again, she stopped when Violet loudly moaned, then stepped away from him. "One day, I hope we can openly love each other."

"We will."

Her ma's bedroom door creaked, and the woman peered out. "Bring me more water."

"Yes'm." *If she'd looked out mere seconds before . . .*

Lily hurried to the kitchen and poured water into a pan, then took it to her.

Her ma's sweat-covered face looked haggard. Her gray hair hadn't been cared for in days and lay tangled around her shoulders. Her hands shot into the air when Lily got a bit too close. "Hold it by the end of the handle an' stretch it out to me. Don't come any nearer."

"Yes'm."

Her ma grabbed the pan and disappeared into the room, shutting the door behind her.

No one else had yet shown signs of illness. Lily had been the most vulnerable, having slept with Violet the night she'd become feverish.

Fortunately, Lily felt strong and healthy. She prayed she'd stay that way.

* * *

Lily couldn't get comfortable. No matter which way she turned in bed. Though tired, every time she closed her eyes, she heard Violet whimpering from the adjoining room. The pitiful sound broke her heart.

Hours drug on. It was well past midnight and Lily could do nothing more than rhythmically blink into the darkness.

*I'm eighteen.*

She smiled at the thought, then had another. One that didn't belong in her mind, but she couldn't overcome it.

In order to listen keenly, she held her breath. No one stirred overhead.

*Reckon I'm crazy . . .*

Her aching heart pounded at the simple notion of what she wanted to do. Her mouth and tongue instantly dried—the perfect excuse to get out of bed for a drink. And if she got *that* far . . .

She pushed her blankets aside and eased onto the floor. Her wildly thumping heart nearly burst from her chest as she removed her undergarments and tucked them under her pillow. Her long nightgown kept her plenty warm, especially with excitement coursing through her veins.

*I want this.*

She'd not shut her door tight, so it opened without making too much noise. Every inch across the floor marked a success.

She poured a small amount of water into a cup and drank.

Still, no one stirred.

Her selfishness bothered her even more, but she pushed on. Because of her sister's illness, Lily had the freedom to leave her bed undiscovered.

There was no risk of Violet and their ma coming out of *their* bedroom. Everyone stayed perfectly in their assigned places. Lily would never get this opportunity again.

She crept silently to the curtained enclosure, barely able to breathe.

She most definitely wanted this. More importantly, she wanted *him*. Maybe the need to be near him had become greater since so much grief and uncertainty surrounded her. She longed for closeness and *love*.

She knelt low and pushed her hand through the opening.

Caleb shifted, then rose on one elbow. The dim firelight revealed the concern on his face. He questioned her presence without saying a word.

She wouldn't risk *speaking* to answer him. As quietly as she could, she lifted the blankets and lay down. A reply he'd surely understand.

Though Christmas gifts had been almost nonexistent, her ma had scrounged enough material to make Caleb a long sleepshirt. Yes, it kept him warmer, yet Lily wished she'd found him barechested. She wanted to feel his skin.

They stared at each other in near darkness. Their heavy breaths mingled and heated the air.

She pressed her body into his, then put her lips to his ear. "Love me . . ." Her raspy words barely made a sound.

His chest heaved, and he shuddered, but he didn't hesitate. He rolled her onto her back and kissed her like never before. She grasped his shoulders, then slid her hands down his muscular arms. The feel of him elevated her need. Like the water had satisfied her thirst, she yearned for him to take away another kind of emptiness.

She found it almost impossible to control her staggered breaths. Their love intoxicated her and constricted her chest. How could something feel both terrifying and wonderful at the same time?

He lay partially atop her, and his firmness pressed against her thigh. His need seemed as great as hers, yet she sensed hesitancy.

She'd never been afraid to pursue what she wanted, so why should this be any different?

She pressed her cheek to his. "I love you," she whispered, then fearlessly moved her hands down his back.

When she reached the edge of his nightshirt, she tugged it upward, finding him bare beneath. Her trembling fingers roamed across his skin. He wouldn't question her intentions now.

Her hands tingled as they traveled his perfectly formed body.

He shuddered and softly moaned, then burrowed his face into her neck and glided his lips over her skin. "My Lily," he murmured and placed soft kisses in the hollow of her throat.

She shut her eyes and focused on the feel of his hands. Just as she'd done to him, he yanked at her gown until he reached bare flesh. "Are you sure?" His voice quivered, but she'd never heard any words spoken softer or more sincere.

She rapidly nodded, and he brought himself fully atop her. Their kisses grew in fervency.

They might not be legally wed, but they'd pledged themselves to each other. She had no hesitation allowing him to go further. Though she couldn't keep her legs from shaking, somehow, she managed to ease them apart.

Caleb kissed her long and deep. They tasted and hungered for something neither of them had experienced before. Their hearts had joined months ago, and now . . .

She gasped, then held her breath.

Her more-than-ready body easily accommodated him. Even so, she felt a brief bit of discomfort.

He froze, hovering above her. He panted out quick breaths, eyeing her in the dark . . . questioning.

Her ever-present boldness took control. She eagerly grasped his bottom and encouraged him to continue. He went slowly at first, and soon she grew comfortable in their joining and moved with him.

She'd always understood how men and women came together, but couldn't comprehend how it would feel. Love connected them in a physical bond that would never be broken. They'd become part of each other. Something beautiful and private only the two of them shared.

Love overwhelmed her and almost brought tears to her eyes, but crying wouldn't be wise. It might give him the wrong impression, and she wouldn't dream of ruining this moment.

She'd crossed a boundary and arrived fully into womanhood.

It endeared her the way he struggled to keep quiet. He pinched his lips tight and squinted his eyes shut. Had they been completely alone, she imagined they'd make animalistic sounds like wild beasts. Ravenous and eager. But this silent hunger held its own beauty.

She, too, had to control the tiny whimpers that wanted to escape her. The pain had lasted mere seconds, replaced by joy. She gazed up into the face of the man loving her. Her heart pounded steadily harder as he increased his pace.

They had the good fortune of secure floorboards on this particular part of the floor. Otherwise, their act would've woken the entire cabin.

Excitement coursed through her veins like hot water. Heat built at the point of their union until she swore she'd scream. She clamped onto Caleb and thrust her hips high, stifling every sound that wanted to burst out of her.

He arched his back and thrust a final time, then shuddered. With a heavy sigh, he folded down, gently rolled off her, and fell onto his back, breaking their bond.

Lily draped herself over his chest and cuddled close, then placed her hand to his heart. It thumped hard—just like hers.

Their love had been sealed forever.

* * *

Caleb threaded his fingers through Lily's long blonde hair.

He'd craved her for months. Truthfully, he'd wanted her when he'd tackled her in the forest. Then, it had been lust for a beautiful woman. Tonight, he'd made love to the one he wanted to share the rest of his life with.

*My Lily.*

He gave her a little squeeze, and she lifted her head and smiled.

It bothered him that they didn't have more time. An experience like this needed to be savored, yet she'd have to get back to her room before anyone woke up.

There was a great deal he wanted to say to her. He was afraid he'd hurt her, but in the end, he swore she'd enjoyed their lovemaking as much as he had.

The only downfall? He wanted more of her. He'd never been more thankful that he'd not given in to the women who'd come to the encampments. The soiled doves who followed the soldiers and stripped them of their pay.

Even though he'd hungered for affection, it had been easy to resist them. Most were dirty. Some even toothless. Men in the camp were desperate and took what they could get. Caleb knew of several soldiers who'd paid for the act with their lives, thanks to the nasty diseases some of the women carried. Another good reason to stay away from them.

He moved his arm and placed his hand on Lily's waist, then tenderly caressed her. His perfect Lily. Beautiful, amorous, smart, and wonderfully bold. Well-worth waiting for.

She hugged him tighter. "I don't wanna go," she whispered.

He kissed the top her head. "I don't want you to."

With a sigh, she rose and braced herself against his chest. "Are you happy?"

*How could she question it?*

Even whispering was risky, but he doubted the soft sound would carry far. "Course I am. I ain't never been happier." He put his hand behind her head, drew her close, and kissed her. "I love you."

"Forever?"

"An' ever." He kissed her again, prompting his body to want more.

He ran his hand along her side, then brushed it across her breast. Granted, her gown covered it, but his heart raced again from the feel of it. Firm, full, and well-rounded. The core of her femininity. He jerked his hand away.

*Not a good idea.*

Playing with fire led to burns.

"It's all right," she whispered, then took his hand and returned it to her breast. "I'm yours. *All* a me."

He blew out a slow, steady breath, trying all he could to rein in his desire. "We'll have more times together. You need to go to your room."

She sadly nodded. "I love you." With a quick peck to his lips, she inched out of their bed.

He ached the moment she vanished through the curtain.

Lily Larsen would hold his heart till the day he died.

# CHAPTER 20

"Violet's fever broke!"

Lily jumped out of bed at the wonderful words her ma yelled for everyone in the cabin to hear. She raced from her room and sped over to the woman, who stood in the doorway of her bedroom, bedraggled as ever.

Her ma held up a hand. "Best stay back for the time bein'. Just bring me a drink. Violet's thirsty. An' once you're dressed, fetch me the bathin' tub an' heat some water. We're both filthy. A bath'll do us good."

"Yes'm." Lily hurried to the water pitcher and poured a full glass.

While taking it to her ma, her pa nearly took a tumble on the stairs. He caught himself before going down. "Rose? She's gonna be all right?"

"That she is." Her ma bobbed her head in a single nod. "*You* okay, Buck?"

He meandered across the floor and stopped within several feet of her. "Been a mite lonely."

"Well, then . . ." The dear woman crossed her arms and looked him up and down. "Once I know for certain Violet's fully recovered, an' I wash the beddin', you're welcome in my bed."

"*Your* bed?" He chuckled, then waved his hand. "I'd be right happy 'bout that."

Her ma squared her jaw. "Then mind your manners an' help Lily with the tub."

"Yes, *ma'am.*" He winked at her.

Lily viewed her folks' playfulness through different eyes. Before, she'd seen it as innocent jesting. After spending a night in Caleb's arms, she saw an underlying meaning in their actions. Though they'd been married almost twenty years, she believed they still enjoyed intimacy. Lily and her siblings were proof of their many unions.

Lily found it sweet, but disturbing. She didn't care to envision them that way.

Her brothers bounded down the stairs, then raced to the sofa and the warmth of the fire.

Lily's thoughts turned to Caleb, and she glanced at the curtain. Why hadn't *he* come out when her ma yelled?

She moved close to his space and tingled from head to toe, simply recalling the feel of their passion. When she carefully listened, she heard nothing behind the draped quilts.

She bolstered her bravery. "Caleb? Did you hear? Violet's gonna be fine."

No answer.

Every head in the room faced the curtain.

"Caleb?" Lily carefully parted the drape and peered inside, only to find an empty bed.

She gasped. "He's gone."

"What's wrong with *you*?" Lucas grumbled. "You shouldn't be stickin' your nose in there. If he ain't on his mattress, he's probably usin' the outhouse."

"Boy's right," their pa said. "You ain't got no business lookin'. What if you'd found that man standin' there bare-naked?"

Her little brothers tittered.

She boldly faced them, never to admit it would be a sight she'd welcome. "You're right. I wasn't thinkin'. I best get dressed an' fetch that water for Ma."

"I'll get the tub from the barn." Her pa smiled. "Time to put everyone in their proper place."

Lily hurriedly got her clothes on. She shouldn't be worried in the slightest that Caleb had left her for good. It had to be as Lucas suggested. She'd surely find Caleb in the outhouse.

With a bucket in each hand, she headed out, bundled up for the weather. The instant she stepped off the front porch, she noticed large footprints in the snow and followed them.

The white frozen ground crunched beneath her boots. She passed the outhouse and continued up the hillside. When she saw Caleb in the distance, her heart rested.

She increased her pace, and he turned at her approach. Though she expected him to smile, he cast a painful frown.

"Caleb?" She set the pails on the ground and went to him. "What's wrong?"

He cupped his hand to her cheek. "I shouldn't a done it. We shoulda waited."

*No.*

She didn't want him to have even *one* small regret. "You feel bad 'bout last night?"

"Course I do. We ain't married yet. I took advantage of—"

"Hush." She pressed her fingers to his lips. "No one took advantage of anythin'. *I* came to *you*, remember?"

He grabbed her hand and cuddled it against his chest. "Yes. But you was hurtin' over Violet. I let myself get carried away, an' took sumthin' from you, you can't never get back. An' if I hurt you—"

"Stop." She wrapped her arms around his waist. His sweet face looked so cute framed by her silly bonnet. "I'm fine. I wanted what we done. If times was different, I'd already be your wife. We only did what was natural for two people in love."

"Oh, Lily."

They kissed and melted away the icy air.

"You see," she whispered. "Nothin's gonna harm our love. It'll keep gettin' stronger."

"You swear I didn't hurt you? In *any* way?"

"Not last night. The only thing that pained me was findin' your bed empty this mornin'." She let out a soft laugh. "I thought you'd left me."

"Never." They kissed again, then he backed away. "We shouldn't be so foolish out here in the open. But I'm countin' the days till we can lay together every night."

She bit her lower lip and nodded.

He pointed at the buckets. "Need help gettin' water?"

"I'd like that." Thinking of her sister, she broadly smiled. "Violet's fever broke. Ma needs water for a bath. Reckon things is gonna get back to normal now."

He, too, lit up with a bright smile. "That's wonderful. Though *normal* means I can't touch you again for heaven only knows how long."

"Spring's comin'. We'll find ways to sneak off. An' when the news comes that the war's over, we'll tell everyone 'bout us an' put you in some proper trousers."

He laughed and flared his skirt. "I'm gettin' kinda used to this. Still, there's other things I'd rather have every day. Wearin' pants will suit me just fine."

His meaning fluttered her heart. She handed him a pail to get her mind right. "C'mon. Let's get that water, an' if anyone asks, I ran into you when you was comin' outta the outhouse."

He grinned "Already been there."

* * *

Caleb finally breathed easy.

He'd fallen blissfully asleep last night, but woke feeling horribly guilty. He'd taken Lily's chastity, and as he'd told her, she could never get it back again.

That fact aside, he'd never seen her happier, so he decided to allow himself some joy. He whistled as they dipped the buckets into the frigid creek water. Lily giggled and grinned at him.

He loved her even more for accepting all his faults as well as his body. They had no secrets between them, only private confidences they wouldn't share until the time was right. But he'd abide by her wishes and keep *his* lies from her folks. He'd do anything to keep peace in her family.

They hauled many buckets full of water into the cabin and heated it on the stove and over the fire.

Mr. Larsen had brought in the tub from the barn and placed it in his bedroom. Mrs. Larsen stripped the bed and tossed the bedding onto the floor of the living room. And while she and Violet took turns bathing, Lily fetched a smaller washtub that she used to scrub the sheets.

Caleb helped her hang another line of rope from the beams on the ceiling, and they pinned up the wrung-out sheets to dry.

Though weak, Violet sat cuddled on the sofa. No fever remained and her face had regained its color.

She smiled at Caleb as he fastened the final clothespin. A sight that warmed him. Since Lily had told her about their affections for each other, Violet's sweet expression acknowledged her approval.

"I'm glad you're well." He offered his own smile. "We were all prayin' for you."

"I'm happy to know you pray." She cuddled into the blankets that surrounded her. "Can you get some wood for the fire?" She grinned, pointing at the near-empty stack of logs.

"Yep." He put his coat back on. Well, truthfully, it was *her* coat, but he'd worn it more than she ever did. He might as well claim it as his own.

He glanced at Lily before walking out.

*So beautiful an' good.*

No, he'd never leave her.

Not for anything or anyone.

* * *

Two days had passed since Violet's fever broke. She looked better and had regained most of her strength. Lily was glad to see her eating more. Their ma made a big pot of venison stew with carrots and potatoes, and Violet had eaten a full bowl.

After the meal, their ma insisted she lay down and rest. Just to be sure she'd fully recovered.

Lily helped clean up the kitchen. "Ma? Reckon I should go check in on Mrs. Quincy? Make sure they're okay?"

"That would be right kind a you." Her ma scooped some left-over stew into a large bowl. "Take this with you. They might could use it."

Lily folded a towel around the container to keep it warm.

"Bundle *yourself* up just as good," Caleb said. "It's cold outside."

"I'm well aware." She acted curt for her ma's benefit.

"Lily." The woman fussed. "There's no need to be rude. Caleb's concerned for your welfare."

"Maybe so." She flashed him an unconcerned glance. "But he acts like he's the only one in this cabin familiar with the weather."

"Mind your manners," her pa said.

"I am. I'm *bundlin' up* like he told me to." She briskly put on her coat and twisted the scarf around her neck, then grabbed the bowl of stew and headed out the door.

Once she'd gotten clear of the cabin, she giggled.

*I shoulda been a stage actress.*

She trudged over the frozen ground. Only a few inches of snow remained. Soon, it would all melt and everything would come to life again. She loved how the world brightened in the springtime. It was easy to imagine the colorful flowers, green grass, and budding trees. Aside from all of those beautiful things, hope for a happy future lifted her heart the most.

She knocked on the Quincy's door.

"Who is it?" Mrs. Quincy hollered from the other side.

"Lily, ma'am. I've come to make sure y'all are well. Ma sent along some stew."

The door inched open.

Mrs. Quincy looked worse than Lily's ma had the entire time Violet had been sick. The woman's gray hair stuck straight out on end, her spectacles were missing, and her face had paled an ugly grayish color.

Lily took two steps back. "You ain't well, are you?"

"Why'd you say that? I'm fine. The boys been sick, but I ain't."

"Oh." *Coulda fooled me.* "You hungry? Ma made plenty." She held up the towel-covered bowl.

"Mighty kind a her." Mrs. Quincy took it, then bent close and sniffed. "Smells decent. Reckon it's edible."

Lily pinched her lips tight. She forced a smile and kept quiet.

"How's that cousin a yours? Callie, right?"

"Yes'm. She's doin' well. Violet got sick from your grandson, but she's better now, an' the rest of us didn't get ill. Are your grandsons over it?"

"Yep. An' now that Russell's gone, they've been drivin' me up the wall. Won't mind me one bit. Jeremy has it in his head he's the man a the house now. He struts around like he owns the place, but come spring I aim to show him what responsibility is. If he don't work, he ain't gonna eat. If he knows what's good for him, he'll help me. 'Specially when we start gettin' mail again."

She shook her head and grunted. "That reminds me . . . I was diggin' 'round in some a Russell's papers an' found a letter for your ma. He musta missed it." She scratched her large belly, glanced over her shoulder, then faced Lily again. "Don't feel right invitin' you in. Place is a mess. Wait here an' I'll fetch the letter."

She went inside before Lily had a chance to respond.

Lily sighed and waited, wondering who'd written and how old the letter might be.

She casually looked about, taking in the property. The Quincy's cabin was much larger than Lily's home. Mr. Quincy had always been proud of the place and kept it up well. It appeared his wife didn't have the same exuberance for it.

Honestly, Lily was relieved Mrs. Quincy hadn't asked her in. The foul odor that had come out when she'd opened the door had nearly taken Lily's breath. It smelled as if something had died inside.

Possibly, the place just needed to be aired out from the boys' illness. More than likely, as little care as Mrs. Quincy had taken fixing *herself* up, she'd probably applied the same poor effort to her house.

The woman returned and extended an envelope. "Here you are. Seems it's from your aunt in St. Louis. Reckon she wrote inquirin' 'bout her daughter."

Lily carefully examined the envelope. Thank goodness it hadn't been opened. Her ma had once remarked that she believed Harriet Quincy's busy-body nature inclined her to read other people's mail. Something not only rude, but also unlawful.

"Thank you," Lily said, smiling. "Hope you enjoy the stew. No rush returnin' the bowl."

She couldn't leave fast enough. Not only did she want to hurry home with the mysterious letter, the foul stench had upset her stomach.

She walked briskly, and soon the crisp air refreshed her.

"Ma!" Lily burst through the door. "You got a letter."

"Shh." Her ma put a finger to her lips. "Violet's sleepin'."

"Sorry." Lily handed her the envelope and everyone gathered around. "It's from Aunt Helen."

Her ma sat at the kitchen table and stared at the letter. "I didn't think mail had been comin'."

"Mrs. Quincy said she found it in her husband's papers. She don't know how long it's been there." Lily took a chair beside her. "Ma, her house was nasty, an' I don't reckon she's had a bath in a dog's age."

Her ma patted her hand. "Be kind. She lost her husband. We can't judge her grief."

"Yes'm."

They all watched as her ma turned the envelope over and over again in her hands. Her fret lines deepened.

"Ain't you gonna open that thing?" Lily's pa pointed at it. "We'd all like to hear it read."

"Yeah, Ma," Lucas said. "Maybe there's money in there."

"I doubt it." She swallowed hard, then carefully opened the letter. "It's dated the tenth of June. Russell Quincy had this for *months*. Why didn't he give it to us?"

Lily's pa placed his hand on her ma's shoulder. "Don't know, Rose. But it don't matter none. We got it now. So, go on an' read it."

She smoothed the two sheets of paper on the table, then lifted the first one close to her face. "My dearest Rose." She cleared her throat and slammed the paper down. "Don't know why she wrote *dearest*. Helen's never been that fond a me."

"Just keep readin', Ma," Lucas said. He grabbed the empty envelope, shook it, then grumbled.

Lily knew there wouldn't be any money inside. From all the stories she'd heard of her Aunt Helen, the woman was a miser.

Her ma lifted the letter again. "My *dearest* Rose." She rolled her eyes, then kept reading. "I pray my letter finds you an' your family well. Stuart an' I are prosperin'. His shippin' business has grown durin' this horrid war. It saddens me knowin' we're bene-fittin' from the sufferin' of others, but we're acceptin' our wealth as a blessed gift from God." Her ma shook her head and huffed.

"Keep readin', Rose." Lily's pa pulled out a chair and sat on the other side of her ma.

"It ain't easy." Her fist tightened and nearly crumpled the paper. "She's so conceited. Barely says hello 'fore she starts in on how rich they are."

Lily held out her hand. "Want *me* to finish readin' it?"

Her ma handed over the letter without batting an eye.

Lily quickly scanned it and found where she'd left off. *Blessed gift from God.* "I'll never understand why you chose to stay in the mountains. Life there is never easy. An' now that your husband has been maimed, I assume you're havin' an even more difficult time. You'll be happy to know I pray for you an' your children every day.

"Stuart an' I have come to terms with the loneliness brought on by the lack of offspring." Lily lifted her head and looked at her ma. "She talks awful fancy. Why can't she just say, we wish we coulda had babies?"

"That's her way. She went through some uppity schoolin'."

"Reckon you're glad *you* didn't hafta go."

Lily's pa chuckled. He took her ma's hand and kissed it. "She got *me* instead. Helen was swept away by Stuart Clark. *Uppity* in his own right. She ain't never been normal since."

"Oh, Buck." Her ma covered her mouth and giggled. A sound that hadn't come from her in years. "Be kind."

Lily smiled and met Caleb's eyes. They twinkled just as her pa's had.

"Reckon I best finish this." She cleared her throat and once again found her place. ". . . lack of offspring . . . Truthfully, in these uncertain times, we're thankful we didn't bring new life into this frightenin' world. Children should never have to experience the horrors of war."

She set the page down and picked up the next. "Our country is blessed to have the leadership of President Lincoln. Such a fine man, an' one whom my dear husband had the pleasure to personally acquaint himself with." Lily peered over the top of the page. "Lawdy. Does she ever stop braggin'?"

"No." Her folks said in unison.

Lily giggled. "Your husband did a disservice to our country by fightin' with the rebels." She slowed with each word that left her lips, taking them in like a punch to the stomach. Every bit of humor faded. Lily's belly churned, but she forced herself to keep her eyes on the page and continue reading. If she looked at her pa, she couldn't go on. "We pray he's seen the error of his ways. He paid a wretched price for challengin' the Union.

"From everythin' I have been told, soon the rebels will be defeated an' our country can be whole again. A divided nation cannot stand. God willin', the rebels will lay aside their brutal weapons an' swear their allegiance once again.

"I have felt for a very long time that it was important for me to share my feelin's regardin' the state of our country. After you wrote an' told me how Howard lost his arm, I struggled with how I should respond. After many months of deliberation, I decided to be truthful and believe with all my heart God is guiding my words. Although your husband strayed from that which is right an' proper, I will not hold it against you or your children.

"I would love to hear from you again, dear sister, so my mind can rest knowin' you are properly cared for. If you should need my help, don't hesitate to ask. However, Stuart has the final say in any decisions I make. So, please, don't request money. He is a generous man, though not where his finances are concerned. I am sure you understand.

"I must close for now. We are hostin' an affair I must prepare for. We have invited many important people, includin' the governor of our fine state. Even in times of war, we who are civilized know how to entertain. I wish you well. With love, Helen."

Lily slapped the letter onto the table. "I don't reckon I like her much."

Her ma took the pages and tucked them back into the envelope. "She used to be kinder. Marriage changed her. That an' movin' outta Tennessee."

Lily wiggled a finger at the envelope. "She was hateful to Pa. She don't know he didn't *wanna* fight for the rebels. You should reply an' set her straight!" Anger heated Lily's face. "An' what else would we want from her 'sides money? Reckon she means more *prayers*?"

Her ma stroked the top of her hand. "Prayers are *always* welcome. There ain't no need to get all riled up. We know what's true." She smiled at Caleb. "Least you was Union. Her hateful words can't bother *you* none. Nevertheless, what Helen says don't matter. 'Sides, I think it makes her feel better offerin' to help. Though she ain't puttin' forth much a anythin'."

Caleb's lips twitched. "My ma used to tell me words can't hurt you."

"Smart woman."

Lily swallowed hard and kept her eyes on Caleb until he looked at her. She could only imagine what he must be thinking. Their gaze met for a brief second, and he turned his head.

Her pa stood and wandered to his rocking chair. "We don't need nothin'. From that woman or no one else." He sat and slowly got it moving. "Least I can say I *know* someone with money. Whether they wanna share it with family or not."

"Uncle Stuart knows Abe Lincoln," Horace said. "You ever met anyone like *that*, Pa?"

"Nope. But it don't matter none. I got all a you. Them other folks don't amount to a hill a beans."

Lily scooted her chair back, walked over to her pa, and wrapped her arms around him. "I like how you think. An' I'm sure glad I live here an' not with Aunt Helen." She kissed his cheek. "I love you, Pa. You didn't deserve her ugliness."

He smiled and patted her arm. "I've known that woman long as I've known your ma. I pay 'er no mind."

Lily kissed him again, then stood tall. "Anyone up for a game a charades?" They all needed to do something fun and get their minds off the contents of that letter.

Horace and Isaac raced to the sofa, wildly nodding.

Her heart eased when Caleb laughed and joined them, followed by Lucas, who grumbled unenthusiastically.

"Y'all go on," her ma said. "Just keep it down. Violet needs her rest."

They did as she asked and played the quietest game of charades in Larsen family history.

Lily often exchanged knowing glances with Caleb. Their intimate time together remained fresh in her mind and overpowered all the hate her aunt had written. Lily hoped *Caleb's* thoughts were only on the good things, and since his smile no longer seemed forced, she believed they were.

She prayed they'd soon have another opportunity to be alone. For now, they'd simply enjoy being part of a loving family. A true blessing in its own right.

# CHAPTER 21

*Sweet, blessed April.*

Lily hugged herself and lifted her face to the sunshine. The wheat crop was coming in beautifully and would soon be mature enough to harvest.

The spring also brought fresh greens in the fields. After a winter of canned vegetables, potatoes, and venison, something crisp and fresh would taste wonderful.

She gathered wild cresses, then went to the stream bank for toothwort. Here and there, early wildflowers had begun to blossom. By May, the fields would be ablaze with an abundance of colors.

She couldn't be happier. Something even more glorious awaited her.

She'd woken with a queasy stomach. Though it had quickly subsided, it gave her a good excuse to stay behind. She expected her flow any day. She and her ma often endured their woman's time on the same dates each month. Violet right after. It never seemed fair that women had to bear such inconvenient discomfort. Not to mention, a great deal of laundry.

*Long as it don't come today.*

Her ma's had arrived yesterday. While *inconvenienced*, the woman kept to her room.

Her pa had taken her siblings to the ramp patch on the northern hillside some distance away. Ramp only grew in the upper elevations, so they'd have to climb high to find it. It would be an all-day trip.

Violet had completely recovered from her illness and for a change, *wanted* to get out of the cabin. She'd grinned at Lily as she walked away. Maybe Violet had read her thoughts and knew what she planned to do, and left so she could accomplish it.

*They'll be gone all day.*

Lily nearly sang the thought.

She loved the taste of ramp, but doubted she'd eat much. It left behind a heavy odor. One that lingered on the breath for days. She wouldn't do anything to dampen Caleb's desire to sneak away somewhere to kiss her.

Today's *sneaking* would go beyond that.

It had been more than a month since they'd coupled, but she'd thought of little else. Her heart *and* body ached for Caleb. Like before, opportunities such as this had to be taken advantage of.

She returned to the cabin with the greens and placed them in a bucket of water to keep them fresh.

"Lily?" Her ma called out from her room. "Is that you?"

"Yes'm." She moved to the bedroom door, but didn't open it. "You all right?"

"Good as I can be. Don't hafta tell *you* how it feels." She moaned and the bed creaked. "Wish I was done with this. Every time, your pa sees it as hope for another child. He'd think otherwise if *he* had to bear it."

Lily glanced at the clock. She needed to go. "Ma, I'm goin' back out for more greens. We'll have us a nice supper t'night."

"Caleb goin' with you?"

"No. Don't reckon so. He's in the wheat field. Hopefully, no one will bother him."

"You feelin' well enough to be out?" Again, her ma groaned. After all these years, why hadn't she grown accustomed to the pain? Lily didn't mind it near as much and would never moan and carry on like someone dying.

"It hasn't come yet. I'm fine." *An' soon I'll be wonderful.* "Get better, Ma."

Lily hurried from the cabin.

* * *

Caleb's heart beat faster with each step up the mountainside. He and Lily had made plans that morning while he'd chopped wood. Everyone in the family had gone to gather ramp. Something he'd never acquired a taste for.

Though there was some risk in what they were about to do, his love for Lily drove him and pushed aside the danger. Besides, his gut told him they'd not be discovered.

He found the burrow in the mountainside empty. So, he spent his time waiting for Lily by gathering brush to make bedding. At this point, if someone spotted him in the woods, he'd be seen as a woman likely foraging for food. But the dress and bonnet were the only things feminine about him. His need was that of a driven male.

Twigs snapped and footsteps neared.

*Lily . . .*

She quickened her pace and flung her arms around him. They kissed with urgency.

"Inside," he said, coming up for air. "Just to be safe."

She bent low, went in, and he followed. Immediately, the small space warmed.

She'd brought along a blanket that she placed over the bed of brush. "You've been busy." Grinning, she lay back and stretched out her arms, then her smile became something more enticing that set him on fire.

"All for you." He enthusiastically lay upon her.

They kissed over and over again. His hands took on a life of their own and wandered her body, only to elevate his need.

They tugged their skirts up to their waists, both bare beneath. He wasted no time and joined with her.

He'd ached for this connection. To be a part of her again.

She raked her hands into his hair, which now touched his shoulders. Her fervent kisses drove him to near madness. "You feel so good, Lily."

"Tell me you love me." She arched into him, then pulled back her hips, over and over again like their bodies had forever been accustomed to this kind of movement.

"I do." He thrust harder.

She yanked him to her and kissed him deeper, then pushed against his chest and stared into his eyes. "Once we're married, we'll do this every night." She panted hard, smiling with so much joy it brightened their enclosure.

He never questioned his own pleasure, but it pleased him greater knowing she enjoyed having him. They kept moving like one perfectly attuned body, and he left his eyes open so he could see the sparkle in hers.

Her smile broadened, and she caressed his chest, sending shivers throughout his body. The way she moved was drawing his seed. He couldn't contain it any longer and burst inside her. "Yes!" He dropped down and let out a loud moan.

She giggled and wiggled beneath him. "That yell mighta brought the bears outta hibernation."

"Let 'em come." He lay against her, still joined. "As good as you make me feel, I reckon I could *wrestle* one."

Her hands caressed his bottom. "Reckon you could." She sighed and calmed, yet kept her fingers sliding back and forth across his skin. "In all seriousness, you make me feel like anythin' is possible. 'Fore you came, my family was slidin' downhill. No one cared 'bout nothin'. 'Specially Pa. But now, he's smilin' again, an' I swear he's gained his pride back."

Caleb eased onto his side and faced her. Though he hated separating, he certainly didn't want to crush her small frame by staying atop it. He lifted her skirt higher and caressed her bare belly. "What your aunt said 'bout rebels—"

"What brought that up? 'Specially now?" Her brow dipped with worry. Something he never wanted to put there. "This is for us. Precious time we can't waste worryin' 'bout Aunt Helen."

"I ain't. It's just . . . what she wrote only burned into my mind that your whole family would hate me if they knew I was a rebel."

"Didn't we already decide we won't tell? They'll never know." She worked her lower lip with her teeth and ran her fingers through his hair. "I see no faults in you whatsoever. I love you Caleb Henry. So let all them other things go."

"I wanna tell your folks 'bout *us*. It's high time. I reckon they'll accept it. But we best be prepared to be separated for a spell."

She moistened her lips, then smiled. "I'm ready to tell. An' since you're right 'bout the possibility of separation, let's stop talkin' an' enjoy what time we have." Her eyes searched his. "Is it wrong a me to crave havin' you this way?"

"Wrong?" He tenderly kissed her. "There ain't nothin' wrong 'bout our love."

They stared at each so intently, her deep gaze reached his soul.

With a sensuous smile he'd never forget, she urged him atop her once again.

He happily accommodated her.

* * *

Lily cautiously exited the little love nest she'd created with Caleb. She straightened her clothes and stood tall. Never before had she felt like such a complete woman.

She'd taken a lover. One who'd soon be her husband.

After looking every which way, she faced the burrow and bent low. "Ain't no one out here," she whispered, "but wait a bit 'fore you leave."

"Yes, ma'am." She nearly dove back inside from the enticing way he'd said the words.

She floated light as air down the mountainside. Soon, everyone would know about their love for each other. They'd decided to wait until her ma felt better to tell *both* her folks at the same time. Caleb had understood why her ma locked herself away a few days each month.

Her sweet husband-to-be knew a lot about females. He'd remarked that *his* ma acted the same during her time. And when his sisters had started their flow, they'd used it to their advantage to get out of doing chores.

Lily wasn't afforded that luxury.

She'd never imagined she could openly discuss such things with any man. Caleb changed her mind. She could talk to him about anything at all and not feel ashamed.

*Husbands an' wives* should *be that way.*

She stepped onto the front porch, then remembered the greens. In her ma's mind, the sole reason she'd left again.

Lily raced to the stream and found an ample supply of bear lettuce. Something she'd overlooked before, but a kind redemption. She hurriedly picked it, then returned home.

To her horror, her ma had gotten out of bed. She sat at the kitchen table reading her Bible.

At least *someone* wasn't sinning.

"Hey, Ma." Lily hoped the woman hadn't noticed the short-lived shock on her face. "You must be feelin' better." She took the lettuce to the counter and started washing it.

"I am." She lifted her eyes from the Good Book. "You've been gone quite a spell for so little lettuce."

"Sorry 'bout that. It's such a glorious day. I got all caught up in the beauty of it. Daffodils is bloomin' everywhere."

"Reckon you shoulda gone with your pa." Her eyes returned to the Bible.

The door opened and Caleb walked in with a load of wood in his arms. His sweat-covered face gleamed. "Feelin' better, Mrs. Larsen?"

"That I am." She didn't look up. "How's the wheat?"

"Growin' fine. Ready for harvest soon."

"Good." She kept reading.

Lily met his gaze. The feel of his hands on her skin was too fresh. She wanted more. "Caleb? Reckon you could help me some? I ain't had the chance to give the barn a good cleanin' since we put them hens back outside."

"Reckon I can. Less your ma has sumthin' she'd ruther I do. Do you, ma'am?"

She shook her head. "You two go on. Just mind yourselves. Now that the roads is clear, I reckon we'll be seein' more soldiers again."

"We'll be careful." Lily kissed her ma's cheek, then left with Caleb.

She nearly took hold of his hand as they walked to the barn. It probably wouldn't have mattered. They'd look like two cousins strolling hand-in-hand. What could be misperceived?

"You know Ma won't let us go off like this once we tell," Lily said. "But I kinda like gettin' her blessin's right now."

He turned his head and grinned. "Blessin's to *work*, not play."

They opened the barn door and the stale stench took Lily's breath. "I shoulda done this weeks ago."

Though tempted to shut the door, Lily left it open to air out the interior. She grabbed a broom. Before she could sweep, Caleb pulled her into his arms.

"I know I can't love on you here," he whispered and nuzzled her neck. "But I had to hold you. I love touchin' you, Lily."

She kissed him, then backed away. "With them doors open wide, anyone could walk in."

"You're right." He folded his arms. "Since your ma seems better, wanna tell them t'night?"

"No. She ain't all that well. Didn't you notice how short she was? Wouldn't even look at you."

His brows dipped low. "She's always been that way."

"Trust me, Caleb. She needs another day or two."

"Hmm. Sure you ain't changin' your mind 'bout tellin'?" He rubbed his chin, which definitely needed to be shaved. She should've already done it today.

"No. I *wanna* tell. But we gotta be certain Ma's in her best mood."

"All right." He took the broom from her hand. "Let's do a little cleanin', then I wanna show you the wheat."

"I already seen it." She carefully eyed him. "What's *really* on your mind?"

"Aside from *you*, not much." He inched closer again. "If we clean the barn completely, we won't have a reason to come back out t'morra. Way I see it, if them doors is shut, we can at least sneak a kiss or two." He wiggled his brows. "'Specially if we ain't told your folks 'bout us yet."

"Well then . . ." She adjusted the large bow at his neck. "Callie, my dear, let's go take a peek at that wheat. Leave the cleanin' for t'morra."

They left the barn door fully open while they checked the field. When they returned to the cabin, Lily's ma had locked herself up in her bedroom again.

Lily took the opportunity to sit beside Caleb on the sofa. They enjoyed watching the fire dance in the fireplace while holding hands, unseen.

She didn't know what might be going on in *his* mind, but *she* relived their time in the burrow. Kiss by sweet kiss and every tender touch. The fresh memories were strengthened by the feel of his fingers rubbing across hers.

Love consumed her.

# CHAPTER 22

"I can't believe this actually worked." Lily wrapped her arms around Caleb and drew him closer. "I knew Ma felt worse yesterday than she let on. She didn't even recall we'd mentioned cleanin' the barn."

"I'm glad. Otherwise, she mighta asked why we wanted to do it again." Caleb's mouth moved along her neck. He dotted it with kisses, then gently sucked, all the while tenderly caressing her breast.

She loved how he'd become comfortable touching her without apology. Her heart belonged to him, along with her body.

She'd given him a good shave that morning, more for her benefit than his. Not only did his rough whiskers bother her tender skin, they had to keep up his feminine appearance. Her ma's warning of the soldiers' possible return warranted it.

She closed her eyes and savored every second. His mouth returned to hers and devoured her with passion and need.

"I wish we could . . ." He panted bursts of air. "You know . . ."

She giggled. "Course I do. I was thinkin' it, too. I love bein' close to you that way."

"Like a husband an' wife are s'posed to." He grinned and kissed her again. "We gotta get married soon."

"Yes," she rasped, moving her mouth over every inch of his face, till their lips joined again. She'd never tire of his kisses. They wrapped up in each other, arms grasping tight. Reaching. Needing . . .

"Well, what've we got here?" The unwelcome voice thundered through the barn.

Lily and Caleb froze, locked in an embrace. She peered over his shoulder to find her worst nightmare walking toward them.

She shifted her eyes to Caleb's, mere inches from her own. "Ableman," she whispered.

Caleb swallowed so hard, she heard it. And if she could hear such a simple sound, why hadn't she been aware that the barn door had opened?

They were utterly defenseless.

*What do we do?*

The man smirked and kept coming closer. "Hello, Lily. I assume, this is your cousin, Callie?"

Any moment now, the captain would be close enough to see Caleb's face. He'd know they'd been hiding a man.

She held Caleb firmer and kept his back to Ableman. "Yes, she's my cousin. She's visitin' from St. Louis."

"So, I heard. I was told she's a large girl. I can see that now." He licked his lips in a provocative way. "I'm afraid I bring *tragic* news. President Lincoln was assassinated."

Lily gasped and Caleb's body tensed.

The captain grinned. "As I'm sure you understand, I see it as a *good* thing. However, we're losing this war. I'm on my way home to Knoxville, but since I was passing through, I decided to share the news and specifically pay *you* a visit. You owe me something."

Lily glared at him. "I don't owe you nothin'."

"You're mistaken. I kept your family from starving. I deserve more than the shriveled-up corn we took." Again, he moistened his lips. His chest rose and fell faster every time he inhaled. "I'm a *giving* man, and one who knows how to be tight-lipped. I won't tell a soul about your *tendencies*, but I expect something in return." He reached out and ran his fingers along the back of Caleb's hair. It hung loosely below his bonnet. "I can see we both enjoy women. Why don't all *three* of us have some fun? After all, I can offer something neither of you can. Trust me, it'll make the experience much more enjoyable." He took off his coat and tossed it aside.

Caleb breathed harder and faster.

"Don't," Lily whispered, terrified Caleb wouldn't listen.

Fire filled his eyes.

He whipped around and planted his fist into Ableman's jaw. "Bastard!"

The man stumbled backward, but didn't fall. His eyes popped wide, then he chuckled. "Oh, my, my. Quite a punch for a *girl*." He rubbed his jaw and eyed Lily. "I always knew you'd be the kind of young woman who likes to play. Perhaps *I* should've worn a dress. Maybe then you'd have welcomed my advances." He smirked and laughed harder.

Lily held tightly to Caleb's arm, praying he wouldn't lash out again. His fists were no match for the captain's gun.

Ableman fingered the pistol at his waist and kept his eyes on Lily. "Are your parents aware of what you're doing with *him*? I doubt they'd approve." His attention moved to Caleb. "So, who are you really? A deserter? A fugitive runaway?"

*BANG!*

Lily's breath hitched and her body jerked.

Captain Ableman groaned, clutched his chest, then dropped to his knees. Lily nearly buckled herself, the second she saw Lucas standing behind him with her pa's rifle.

The boy triumphantly smiled. "I got me one!"

"Lucas, no!" She clasped onto Caleb. "He shot 'im in the back!"

Ableman fell to his face, gurgling. Blood seeped from his body and pooled on the barn floor.

Caleb stormed past him and grabbed the gun from Lucas. "What were you thinkin'?"

"I stopped him!" Lucas snarled. "What was *you* gonna do? Your fist didn't even knock 'im down."

"Captain Ableman!" The shout came from somewhere close. Sounds of running footsteps neared the barn.

Lily's heart raced. Her eyes darted back and forth between Caleb and Ableman's twitching body.

Caleb wrenched hold of Lucas's arm. "How many are there?"

"Two more. Same one's what was here before, oglin' Lily an' Violet. Reckon they want *you*, too. *Callie*." He smirked as if it was something to jest about, fueling Lily's anger and elevating her fear.

She smacked his face. "You're gonna get us all killed, Lucas!"

They had no way out, except through the front barn door. The soldiers would surely see them, but they had to try.

She took Caleb's face in her hands. "You gotta run. Get far from here. Come back for me when the war's over."

"But—"

She kissed him hard, right in front of her brother. "I love you. Don't ever forget it."

Lucas's lip curled. "*Yuck*."

"Hold it right there!" A tall soldier appeared. The same man who'd come onto Violet. His eyes moved quickly around the barn, taking everything in. He lifted his rifle and aimed it at Caleb, then jerked his head beyond them. "Johnson, get the gun from that big girl. Looks like she shot the captain."

Caleb kept his head turned to the side. His bonnet shielded them from seeing his face.

Lily searched his eyes, unsure what he might do. Her heart pounded harder. Nothing could stop this from getting uglier.

Johnson cautiously eased into the barn and inched toward Caleb. "Just hand it over nice an' slow, missy. Do anythin' outta line, an' Sergeant Douglas will hafta shoot you."

Out of nowhere, a shovel swung through the air and smacked the sergeant across the head. He fell to the floor with a thump. Fast as lightning, Caleb hit Johnson with the butt of her pa's gun and put *him* on the ground.

Lily shook her head in confusion. Everything had happened so fast.

Her pa stormed in, breathing hard.

"Good hit, Pa!" Lucas chimed. "I ain't never seen you swing a shovel like that! Want me to shoot 'em now so they won't talk?"

"You ain't shootin' no one. Don't know how you got outta that cabin with my gun, but I aim to tan your hide!"

"Why? I shot *him*!" Lucas pointed at Ableman. "He was goin' after Lily and Callie. He woulda found out Callie ain't no girl! Them other men think *she* shot 'im."

Caleb walked back to Ableman and knelt beside his body. He studied him intensely. The pool of blood had grown larger by the second. "He's dead." He looked directly at her pa. "Your boy had perfect aim. Straight through the heart."

"Well, we ain't gonna shoot no more. Hear me, Lucas?" Her pa moved close to Caleb. "You gotta leave. I only seen these three, but there's likely more in the woods. Get yourself inside an' put on some a my clothes, then hightail it outta here. It's the only way to keep you safe."

"What 'bout *you*? They ain't gonna let the captain's murder go unpunished."

"They think a girl done it. I'll tell 'em you got scared an' ran off. We'll figger sumthin' out. Now, go!" Her pa shooed Caleb out the door, then followed him.

Lily burst into tears.

Lucas rolled his eyes and poked her in the arm. "You best thank me for savin' you. If you do, I won't tell Pa 'bout you an' Caleb. You know how he feels 'bout men kissin' on you."

"Caleb's different. We love each other."

"Don't matter none. You was sneakin' 'round. Ma an' Pa won't take kindly to that." He leered at her. "Say thank you."

"Thank you, Lucas." She muttered the words without feeling. Numbness had set in.

He smirked and walked away.

Lily stood in the middle of the floor amid three bodies. One dead. Two living and breathing, but out cold.

*Caleb.*

She lifted her skirt and ran to the cabin.

* * *

The house stirred with commotion. Caleb's head pounded, trying to take it all in.

Mrs. Larsen mumbled to herself and paced, while Violet openly cried. Seemed the soldier he'd knocked unconscious had made advances to her again, but had stopped when the shot rang out.

Caleb had tried on several pairs of Mr. Larsen's pants. None of them fit, so he put on the Union blue trousers he'd stripped from his brother. He'd sworn never to wear them again, yet with everything falling apart around him, he had no choice.

At least he didn't have to wear the hole-filled coat. Mr. Larsen's shirt fit him well.

When he came out from his curtained enclosure, Lily stayed near, crying as hard as her sister. He wanted to hold her, but couldn't. Truthfully, he had no idea when he'd be able to touch her again.

She sucked in air. "You reckon Lincoln's really dead?"

"Don't know why Ableman would lie 'bout sumthin' like that."

Her ma stopped in the middle of the floor. "Them other soldiers told us Lincoln was shot at some stage actin' affair. Them men was all sociable till they tried grabbin' Violet. When Buck went for his gun, it wasn't there. Then we heard the shot." She threw up her hands and paced again. "Lord, help us."

Lily stuffed some food into a pillow casing. "This should get you by till you get home."

*Home?*

"I can't go there."

She handed him the bag. "Yes, you can. If Lincoln's dead, an' the war's done for, then go home an' make things right with your ma." She sniffled and wiped her eyes. "Mas never stop lovin' their children. I know she'll take you in."

He looked from face to face. Horace had an arm around him, and Isaac clung to his legs, staring up at him with slowly blinking eyes. The sight tugged at Caleb's heart, so he shifted his attention to the boys' pa. "I appreciate all you done for me. I promise, I'll come back soon as I can."

"Ain't no time for sweet goodbyes," Mr. Larsen said. "Get goin' 'fore them men wake up."

"Yessir." Caleb headed for the door. His heart ached so much, it weighted his body down. It was all he could do to turn the knob and step outside.

Lily followed him onto the porch. "Caleb?" Her chin quivered and tears streamed down her face. "Remember what I told you."

"I do." He mouthed *I love you*, then sprinted away.

# CHAPTER 23

Lily trudged into the cabin, her heart wrenched from her chest. She felt vacant. Completely empty.

If only she and Caleb hadn't snuck away. If they'd discovered the soldiers were near, they could've pretended Callie was sick again. It had worked before. That's what they should've done.

*If.*

*Coulda.*

*Shoulda.*

No amount of thinking how it might've been would change a thing.

No one had blown the hunting horn, so they'd been caught, defenseless. And now, Captain Ableman was dead, and the other soldiers believed Callie had killed him.

Lily tried to imagine how it all would've played out if Lucas hadn't come in.

*Sumthin' much worse.*

Ableman had a gun. He'd likely have shot Caleb.

At least now, she knew without a doubt, she'd see him again. He could easily survive the mountains and find his way home. After all, he was healthy and strong. Unlike before.

Maybe she shouldn't be so hard on Lucas. As wrong as it had been to shoot Ableman in the back, he'd saved Caleb's life.

"Wipe your eyes, Lily." Her pa handed her a handkerchief. "We gotta tend to them men."

"But Buck . . ." Her ma's eyebrows wove up and down. "What'll we tell 'em?"

Everyone gathered around him. "Well . . ." He huffed out a large breath, then puffed up tall. "Let 'em go on thinkin' Callie done it, an' she run off."

"They've been told she's my *niece*. Harriet Quincy loves to give details. If they question her, she'll tell them 'bout Helen livin' in St. Louis. What if they send soldiers to talk to Helen? We'll *all* be found out."

Her pa stroked her ma's cheek. "Then, we tell 'em we lied 'bout her."

"What?" Lily nearly choked. "You ain't gonna tell 'em 'bout Caleb, are you?"

"No." He gazed upward. His head bobbled around like it did when he was drunk. But he was stone sober. "We tell 'em, we lied 'bout her bein' a niece, an' that we took Callie in outta Christian kindness. That she was a runaway 'thout a home. Showed up on our doorstep from only God knows where. An' we knew if folks here learned the truth, they'd be scared a her. 'Specially when they found out 'bout her *mental* disorder."

"Oh, dear Lord," her ma mumbled. "This gets worse by the minute." She clutched her breast and dropped into a chair.

"No, Ma." Lily sat beside her, no longer crying. "This is really good. *I'm* startin' to believe it. See . . . if her mind ain't right, it'd make sense for her to shoot someone. An' if we don't know where she came from, they can't go lookin' for her." Lily grinned at her pa. "I like it. It's a perfect lie."

Her ma groaned, but her pa stood even taller, then strutted across the floor. "God gave me a fine dose a common sense when I's born."

"I can't 'member all that," Isaac said.

Lily eyed him. "So, don't talk."

"I'll remember it," Lucas said. "Makes sense to me, too. Just don't forget, *I* was the one who killed him. He had it comin'."

Her ma's eyes shot fire. "I ain't never gonna forget. An' you best be sayin' your prayers an' ask God forgiveness for shootin' a man in the back."

"I *had* to, Ma!" He frowned and crossed his arms. "I ain't askin' forgiveness for nothin'."

"Ma?" Though Lily hated to cross her, she needed to speak her mind. "He saved me. Caleb, too. I'm glad he shot the man."

Her ma's lips pinched together. She opened her Bible and stared at the pages.

"C'mon," her pa said. "Lily. Lucas. You two help me. The rest a you stay here with your ma." He headed for the door. "Rose?"

She lifted her eyes, expressionless.

"Take down Caleb's blankets, but leave the mattress. I'm gonna bring them in here. They'll need to rest, an' might need some doctorin', but I wanna watch every move they make. Don't need 'em hidin' behind no curtain."

Her head silently bobbed.

When they got to the barn, the man called Johnson was sitting upright, holding his head in his hands. He still appeared dazed.

Lucas passed by him and went to Ableman, then knelt down and poked him in the back. "Yep. He's dead."

Their pa jerked his head toward the side of the barn. "Get over there, boy. Don't move till I tell you to."

"Yessir."

Johnson teetered, but caught himself before tipping over. "What happened?" He squinted at Lily as if trying to bring her into focus. "You ain't the girl what hit me, are you?"

"No, sir." Her throat dried. She turned to her pa for help.

He dropped down on one knee beside the man. "The woman what done it is long gone. She ain't right in the head. Killed your captain, then took off for the hills. Damn woman took my gun with 'er. Reckon we won't see her again."

Lily glanced at Lucas, who smirked and kicked at the floor.

Johnson rubbed his head. "We was goin' home. Cap'n had a wife. Three kids. All this time fightin' a war, an' he gets put in the ground by a crazed female. Ain't right."

*A wife an' three kids?*

Lily had to bite her tongue. His poor family would be better off without him.

"No, it ain't right," her pa said. "Reckon you can stand?"

"I can try." The man allowed him to help him up.

"I'll get you to my cabin, then come back for your *friend*. But mind my words, if he touches my Violet again, I'll finish what Callie started."

Lily gaped at her pa, then snapped her mouth shut. He'd obviously concocted another lie. What he meant had her stumped.

"I don't understand," Johnson mumbled.

*That makes two of us.*

"You know full well that friend a yours wanted my daughter, Violet." Her pa looked Johnson in the eyes. "She hit him with the shovel the minute she had the chance. I can't blame my girl for protectin' her innocence. You got children?"

"Yessir." Johnson stared at the ground.

"Then I ain't gotta say no more, do I?"

"No, sir."

Her pa guided him out of the barn, then stopped and looked back. "Lily. Stay here with your brother, an' I'll be right back. Watch him so he don't do nothin' stupid."

"Yes, Pa." She had greater respect for the man. He'd tied up every loose end and kept himself out of trouble, too.

They walked slowly away.

"What's he think I'm gonna do?" Lucas said. "I ain't got a gun no more."

"If you did, would you shoot that man lyin' there." She pointed at the sergeant.

"Maybe. It'd be more fun if he was awake."

"Shame on you!"

He slyly grinned, then wandered closer. "Shame on *me*? You best never talk to me like that again, or I'll tell our folks what you done. I seen how you an' Caleb eyed each other when you thought no one was lookin'. What else did you do with him? Hmm? More than kissin'?"

She slapped his face, then quickly pulled her hand to herself. "Sorry. I had no right. But you shouldn't talk that way."

"I'll let you get by with it this time. Just don't never do it again, or I'll tell."

The sergeant moaned.

Lily turned her attention to him and tried to disregard her brother's warning. She leaned over the man's body. He had a horrible gash on the back of his head, seeping blood. He needed stitches. *Badly.* It was a miracle he was alive.

"Sergeant?" The word barely squeaked out of her. "Sergeant Douglas? Can you hear me?"

"Ugh . . ." He grumbled something else, but Lily couldn't understand him. However, he wasn't one bit happy.

"My pa will be back soon, an' we're gonna get you inside. We'll fix you right up."

The man seemed to be trying to open his eyes. They fluttered and spasmed, otherwise, he didn't budge.

"He's gonna die," Lucas nonchalantly said, then moved beside him and leaned close. "Looks like he's hurtin' bad. Suits me just fine."

"Your mind ain't right, Lucas. You shouldn't find pleasure watchin' someone suffer."

He stood fully upright with his nose in the air. "I like hurtin' them 'fore they do sumthin' to me."

She shook her head in disbelief. "Ain't nothin' Ma taught you from the Bible sunk in? We're supposed to love our enemies."

"That don't make no sense. Do you *love* that dead man?" He pointed behind him. "I know what he wanted to do to you. I stopped 'im, cuz I care more 'bout you than him." His expression softened into something more human and sympathetic.

It gave her hope for his soul. "I appreciate what you done. But I don't like how you enjoyed doin' it. Killin' should never be *fun*."

"You're a girl. You don't understand how men think. Pa told me that once 'bout Ma. God made men an' women different for a good reason. Men ain't afraid to defend what's theirs."

"Everythin' all right here?" Their pa appeared in the doorway of the barn.

"Yep." Lucas nudged the sergeant's leg with his foot. "He ain't woken up. Reckon he's dyin'."

Their pa bent over the man. "Let's get 'im up. We'll take him inside so your ma can stitch 'im."

"What 'bout Ableman?" Lily asked.

"Once we settle this man, we'll come back an bury 'im. He'd start to rot if we wait for the men in his company to do it. Hard to say whether or not they'll come by here, an' his buddies ain't in no condition to do it, or to fetch them for that matter."

Their situation couldn't get much more dismal.

"Lily, you get the man's shoulders." Her pa handed her a towel. "Put this around his head first. Lucas, you get his legs. I'll do what I can to hold up his middle. Good thing he ain't fat."

"Pa?" Lily carefully wrapped the towel. "Did you tell Violet what you told us?"

"Course I did. An' she feels just awful 'bout hurtin' this man." Her pa flashed a grin.

*Good.*

Every lie was in place.

# CHAPTER 24

Caleb raced up the hillside. He'd caught sight of at least ten additional soldiers not far from the Larsens' cabin. As of yet, they'd not seen *him.*

He darted in and out of trees, unease pushing his blood hard and fast.

If he didn't put aside thoughts of what might be happening at the cabin, he'd likely turn around and go back. That would only lead to more trouble.

He prayed the Larsens would be fine and focused on Lily's words. *Go home an' come back to me when the war's over.*

His gut told him that time would come soon, and it gave him the will to keep moving. However, his internal instincts had let him down in the barn, overshadowed by desires for Lily.

*We was careless an' foolish.*

What they'd done couldn't be changed. For now, he had to place all his energy on getting home.

If he traveled straight east, he'd eventually reach North Carolina. Then he'd simply veer a little south to get to Waynesville.

What he'd find there was another matter entirely.

If his ma didn't want him near her, he'd have nowhere else to go.

*I hope you're right 'bout mas, Lily.*

Beautiful, passionate Lily. Thinking of her, he smiled and kept running.

* * *

Lily's stomach churned. She'd watched many burials, but had never been so actively involved. Knowing her brother had murdered the man didn't help. As bad as Ableman was, the act had been sinful.

It didn't take long to get him in the ground. It had sufficiently softened from spring rains. They'd easily agreed not to put him anywhere close to the graves of their other family members. Instead, they planted him on the opposite side of the creek, a short distance up the hill.

"We'll let his men know where we put his body." Her pa nodded at the mound of dirt. "If they're inclined to unearth him an' move him elsewhere, they're welcome to do what they please."

"Pa?" Lily had been waiting for the right time to ask. "What *really* happened to your gun? Caleb didn't take it with 'im."

Lucas perked right up and moved in closer. "Yeah, Pa. Where is it?"

The man narrowed his eyes. "Someplace safe."

That was good enough for Lily. She glanced at the fresh grave and sighed. "I hate what happened."

Her pa wrapped an arm over her shoulder. "Put it outta your mind. What's done is done."

"Yes, Pa."

They returned to the house, where her ma sat at the table doctoring Sergeant Douglas. Horace and Isaac watched every move she made. The woman skillfully pushed the needle in and out of the sergeant's skin. It amazed Lily that their ma could get *anything* done with the boys' bodies pressed against her.

When they'd brought the unconscious man in from the barn, they'd placed him in a chair at the kitchen table. He'd immediately slumped over with his head resting on the surface. His position had given her ma the access she needed to sew. She'd trimmed away all of his hair surrounding the wound, then went to work.

She'd been cleaning it, when they'd left her to bury Ableman. Lily wished she'd already finished doctoring him. Watching that needle pierce the man's skin kept her stomach uneasy.

Lucas moved in close and peered at the wound. "Reckon he feels it?"

Their ma's eyes didn't shift from her task. "If he does, he don't show it. Best he's not awake."

Lucas poked the sergeant's arm. "I *want* him to feel it."

Their ma's head popped right up. "Buck. Get this boy away from me this instant." Her eyes flashed fire.

Their pa grabbed Lucas by the ear. "Get on up to your room. We'll have a talk 'fore this is all over."

Lucas stomped up the stairs.

"Sometimes . . ." Their ma huffed out an exasperated breath. "I swear he ain't ours. I worry over that boy's soul."

"He'll be fine, Rose." With a sigh of his own, her pa walked over to the rocking chair. He'd positioned it close to the mattress on the floor, where Johnson lay sleeping.

Lily felt a mite sorry for the man. From all she could tell, he was a follower who did whatever Captain Ableman and Sergeant Douglas told him to do. He seemed meek, and Lily didn't want him harmed.

Truthfully, she hated to see anyone hurt.

*I'm nothin' like my brother.*

"Will he die, Ma?" Horace asked and pointed at the sergeant's head. "That's the biggest cut I ever seen."

"Mine was bigger," their pa boldly said.

"That is was, Buck." Their ma tugged on the thread, wound it into a knot, pulled it tight, and snipped off the end. "As for whether or not he'll live, only time will tell. I done all I can." She glanced toward the rocker, then took Horace's hand. "Go to the barn an' get me a jug a moonshine." She whispered the words, but Lily assumed her pa had heard. Even though he kept rocking without acknowledging them.

Horace hurried away.

"Lily, I need your help movin' this man to the mattress." Her ma scooted her chair back and stood. "You, too, Buck."

They carefully lifted him off the chair and carried him to the bed tick. His eyes still hadn't opened.

Horace returned with the jug and handed it to their ma. She squatted down beside the sergeant, opened the container, and poured a small amount on the wound. "Will it be a problem if I keep this in the cabin for the time bein'?" She posed the question to Lily's pa.

"Nope."

"Good. Lily, help me move the table. I aim to put it under the floorboards."

"Horace?" Their pa waved him close. "Did you shut the room up proper after you got my shine?"

"Yessir."

He patted Horace's blond head. "Good boy. Now, help your ma."

Her little brother lit up with a smile. He had such a tender heart. If only Lucas had the same.

Lily helped with the table and once the moonshine was secure beneath the floorboards, they set everything back in place. The two men on the mattress were none-the-wiser.

"Ma?" Lily asked. "I'd like to check on Violet. She's bein' awful quiet." She'd shut herself up in their bedroom.

"You go on. Your pa an' me can keep an eye on them soldiers."

Lily went into the room and closed the door behind her. Her sweet sister stood silently at the window peering out. She barely batted a lash. The girl looked mesmerized by something outside.

Lily sat on the edge of the bed. "You all right?"

"Did he die?" She kept staring straight ahead without moving a muscle.

"No. He might could, but it'll be a while 'fore we know."

Violet wiped at her eyes. "I *want* him to die. It'd make things easier for us." She slowly turned and faced Lily. "Pa's silly stories. Now *I'm* the one who hurt that man. No matter what he done to me, I'd a never been so brutal."

Lily stood beside her. "You don't know that for certain. If he'd a touched you the way he wanted to, you might see it different."

"He *did* touch me. Here." She placed a hand to her breast. "He didn't even care Horace an' Isaac saw. That's when Pa went for his gun an' everythin' fell to pieces."

"Violet." Lily took hold of her arms and looked in her eyes. "He had no right to touch you. No matter how highfalutin he thinks he is."

Tears dripped onto Violet's cheeks. "The other man laughed when he done it. I was so embarrassed. If the gunshot hadn't gone off, I know they woulda tried more. They see us all as ignorant helpless fools."

"Oh, sweetie." Lily pulled her sister close and let her cry. "An' here I thought that other man was meek." She stroked Violet's hair. "That's what I get for thinkin'."

"You've misjudged men before." Violet sniffled and lifted her head. "You reckon Caleb will be all right?"

"I do." She guided her sister to the bed, and they both sat. "We was gonna tell our folks how we feel 'bout each other, but we didn't get the chance."

"It's best." Violet smiled and grasped her hands. "Now you can look ahead to a future with him, without Ma an' Pa fussin'. I know he loves you. He'll surely come back an' marry you." She grinned and let out a soft giggle. A sound far better than her painful tears. "Most importantly, he'll be wearin' trousers again."

Lily dried Violet's damp cheek with her sleeve. "I certainly do hope so. I fear he kinda liked my old dress."

They laughed and hugged each other.

"I'm glad you're my sister," Lily said. "I love you."

"You, too." Violet's eyes shifted downward. "Someday, I hope a decent man comes for *me*."

Lily kissed her on the forehead. "He will. Just be patient. Good men are worth waitin' for."

She closed her eyes and pictured Caleb. There was no telling how long she'd have to wait for him. In the meantime, she'd hold onto their precious memories and relive each one in her mind. One day, they'd make more.

Of that, she had no doubt.

* * *

"Stop!"

The loud scream jerked Lily upright in bed. It had come from the living room, likely from one of the soldiers.

Violet's arms flailed. "What's goin' on?"

"I aim to find out." Lily got up and put on her robe, then carefully opened the door.

Flickering light from a lantern lit up the room. Her pa knelt on one knee beside the sergeant. "You gotta calm, or you'll bust your stitches."

Johnson sat up and rubbed his eyes. "He's right, Vincent. You got beaned real good."

*Vincent?*

Seemed like a fancy name for a despicable man.

*Vincent* moaned in an anything-but-fancy way, then reached for the top of his head.

Her pa grabbed his hand before he could touch the wound. "Leave it be."

Lily turned to the sound of footsteps on the stairway.

Lucas crept down, but stopped halfway. "Need my help, Pa?"

The man waved his hand. "Get back in bed."

With a grunt, her brother turned around and did as he was told.

Her pa probably would've welcomed his help, yet they all knew the reason Lucas offered. Now that the sergeant had woken up, the boy could witness suffering.

The man moaned fiercely. "Just shoot me. I can't take the pain."

Lily eased out her door. "Pa? Can *I* help?"

"Get my moonshine. This man needs it."

"But—"

"Go on, Lily. Do as I say."

Getting it meant exposing their hiding place. Her pa had to realize it, so why take the risk?

Her feet wouldn't budge.

"*Now*, Lily."

Her pa's stern voice pushed her to act, but her belly twisted with every step she took.

She moved the kitchen chairs, scooted the table over, and slid the rug off the loose slats. Johnson had his eyes on her the entire time.

If only her ma had left the moonshine on the counter. Lily knew why she'd made it harder to reach. No matter how long it had been since her pa had tipped the jug, her ma always feared he'd do it again. So why give him easy access?

Lily pulled up the long floorboard, then reached inside and brought out the moonshine.

"Pour some in a cup an' bring it here," her pa said.

She did as he asked, leaving the hole open in the floor.

Her eyes met her pa's when she handed him the cup. She tried to read into his thoughts, but couldn't understand why he'd let her expose them this way.

His brows dipped low. "Leave the shine on the counter. Once you get the table in place, get back to bed."

"Yes, Pa."

She sluggishly went through the motions, with a confused, aching heart.

When she crawled into bed, she felt numb, sickened by the ordeal.

"What happened, Lily?" Violet whispered.

"I got moonshine for the sergeant." She let her head sink into the precious pillow she'd loaned to Caleb. It still smelled like him. The only comfort she'd have tonight.

# Chapter 25

Lily hesitated before opening her bedroom door, fearing what she might find on the other side.

The sun had been up for more than an hour, and so had she. She'd laid in bed, waiting for something horrid to happen.

Violet gave her a little nudge. "Go on out, Lily."

When she opened the door, the first thing that came into her line of sight was the bottle of moonshine on the kitchen table. It lay on its side, open and obviously empty.

*No.*

Loud snoring came from several sources.

Lily tiptoed into the main room, followed by her sister. Their pa sat slumped over in the rocking chair, clutching a cup. The two soldiers lay flat on their backs, sprawled out partially atop the mattress.

Though the floorboards above her creaked, none of her brothers came down the stairs. They, too, were likely scared. Aside from Lucas, who was probably sulking.

The snoring grew in volume, sounding like a large herd of congested bucks.

"Oh, my." Lily sighed and walked slowly to her pa.

*That's odd.*

The cup in his hand was nearly full. Quite a miracle it hadn't spilled all over his trousers. She knelt beside him and carefully took it from his hand.

He startled and his eyes popped wide. "Lily?" There wasn't even a *trace* of liquor on his breath.

"What happened here, Pa?" she whispered.

The kitchen floor creaked and drew Lily's attention. Violet crept slowly toward the front door, most likely headed for the outhouse.

Lily returned her focus to her pa. "Are they drunk?" She gestured to the men on the floor.

"Yep. Got 'em both liquored up real good. Got tired a listenin' to that sergeant whimper. For a military man, he ain't got no backbone."

She gazed at the content of the cup in her hand. "Did *you* have anythin' to drink?"

"I pertended to." He chuckled, then instantly sobered. "Right hard resistin', but I wouldn't let my guard down. Not with my family to fend for."

She perched on the edge of the sofa, glanced over her shoulder at the soldiers, then faced her pa again. "Why'd you have me get the moonshine when Johnson was watchin'? I bet my *teeth* he'll go diggin' 'round in our hidin' place." She purposefully kept her voice down. The men still snored, but she didn't want to take any chances.

Her pa patted her face, then stood. "Come with me."

He led her onto the front porch. "Didn't wanna risk them hearin' what I have to say."

"I'm listenin'."

"Lily, I'm glad you trusted me last night an' did as you was told. I *wanted* 'em to see where we hid the liquor. Since I planned to get 'em drunk, I needed 'em to think all our supply is under our floor. Don't want 'em snoopin' elsewhere. Even if they take what's left 'neath our floorboards, we got plenty more in the barn."

"They might not be happy when they can't find no more moonshine."

"We'll tell 'em they drank it all." He snickered. "If they want more, I'll send 'em over to Harriet Quincy. She might put rat poison in their drinks, but it won't be my concern."

Violet stepped onto the porch. She clutched her belly with one hand and hurried inside.

"I feel sorry for you women," their pa said. "Reckon her time's come."

In such small living space, none of them could hide a thing. Lily's brothers didn't understand about a woman's flow, but her pa was well aware. Men had to cope with it almost as much as women. Though they didn't have the pain and inconvenience, they had to put up with female irritability for a time.

Lily touched her own stomach. A disturbing revelation made it flutter. Why hadn't *her* time come? Come to think of it, she hadn't had a flow since before her birthday.

Her mouth dried.

*Oh, lawdy . . .*

*Caleb.*

* * *

Even in April, nighttime in the mountains got bitterly cold.

Caleb had managed to find dense brush each night to burrow in and sleep, but he got little rest.

He thanked God to have finally gotten out of the mountains. His feet hurt, his bones ached, and he was horribly hungry. Being alive made up for it.

He'd found some greens to nibble on, as well as bits of left-over smoked venison Lily had stuffed into the pillow casing she'd given him. He'd eaten the corncakes the first day. Horribly, he'd succumbed to munching on some ramp. He could still taste it after more than twenty-four hours.

Each step got him closer to home.

His whiskers reminded him of Lily and their daily shaving ritual. Even his long hair brought her into his thoughts. She'd tried braiding it, but he wouldn't have it.

He chuckled and kept walking.

His chest tightened at the sight of his old homestead. Fond memories rushed in, though it didn't look quite right.

Small articles of clothing had been hung to dry on the line that extended between two trees behind the house. No children that small had been living there in years.

The fields had been partially planted, and the vegetable garden had few sprouts. The once *thriving* place seemed foreign.

He mustered his courage and headed for the front door. It felt appropriate to knock, regardless of having been his home for most of his life.

A small woman holding a toddler opened the door barely enough to see out. She cautiously eyed him up and down. Of course, he knew he must look a sight.

She shifted the child to her other hip, further away from him. "Can I help ya?"

"Um . . ." He swallowed hard, then cleared his throat. "Is Mrs. Henry home?"

"Who?"

"Alice Henry. She lives here. Least she did last year."

Another child appeared at the woman's feet. A little dirty-faced boy who clung to her legs. "Go on to your grampa," she said to him, then her eyes lifted to Caleb's. "We bought this place in November, just 'fore the snow came. Me an' my grampa. He's helpin' me with my children. My man died fightin'."

"I'm sorry to hear it. Do you know what happened to the folks what lived here?"

She nodded. "Them women moved into Iverson's hotel in town."

"Hotel?"

"Well, he runs it like a boardin' house. Folks often stay there a long spell. Sorry I didn't recall that name you said. The older woman was right kind. Gave us a fair deal on this here property." Again, she studied him from head to toe. "You might should go there. Looks like you could use a good meal. Maybe a bath." She wiped at her nose. "Mr. Iverson's known to be charitable."

"Thank you." He turned to leave.

"Know where it is?"

He nodded, saying nothing. He had to assume his pa hadn't survived the war. Otherwise, his ma would've stayed here. It pained him knowing he'd never see the man again, but hurt even more picturing his ma at a hotel. Most women who tarried in those places for any length of time did so to sell themselves. It gave him some comfort recalling that Mr. Iverson was a decent Norwegian immigrant. Not a man who'd run a house of ill repute.

Being told his ma wasn't alone troubled him more than anything. He assumed the other woman with her must be Rebecca.

Caleb had no choice but to face his greatest fear.

* * *

Days passed and Lily still had no flow.

She'd attributed her queasiness to all the stress of her situation, till the truth slapped her upside the head.

She'd have to hide her condition and pray Caleb returned sooner rather than later. Once she grew larger, she couldn't pass herself off as simply fat. There wasn't enough food in the county to warrant a belly the size of a watermelon.

Fortunately, because of the commotion in their cabin with the soldiers underfoot, her ma had paid no mind to her condition.

Or lack thereof. She hadn't even questioned Lily's scant amount of laundry. Nor had Violet. Violet had been spending her time avoiding Sergeant Douglas and washing her own things.

To their relief, Johnson left to find the rest of their company and returned with a handful of men, who dug up Ableman's grave. A nasty task. They placed him in a pine box and asked a lot of questions, but since Johnson and Douglas both confirmed they'd seen a *tall mountain woman* with the gun, the soldiers accepted it as fact. They called it a sad loss, yet one that came with war.

They all seemed more concerned with going home than looking for a crazed female with a rifle.

As for Sergeant Douglas, he never said a word about Violet whacking him with the shovel. Maybe he was grateful her ma had the decency to sew him up, and that her pa hadn't shot him for trying to have his way with his daughter. Sergeant Douglas likely had a wife and children at home, just like Captain Ableman.

*The dirty dog.*

Lily stood on the stoop and watched the men march away. "Good riddance to every last one a them."

"Amen," her ma muttered.

The soldiers had rummaged through the storage under the floorboards, as Lily suspected they would. They left with several bags of cornmeal, half a dozen jars of apple butter, and sadly, both hens. But as her pa had reminded her, they had plenty more supplies in the barn. Their hidden room had remained a secret.

If all went well, they'd bring in a fine crop of wheat that would allow them to buy more hens, a rooster, a cow, and maybe even a horse. And if the war ended as Lily hoped, they could all rest easy and not fear having it all taken away again.

She clutched her belly and sighed. She wouldn't be completely at peace till Caleb walked through the front door.

* * *

Caleb recalled coming into town many times as a boy. It had bustled with activity and now lay dormant.

He walked along Main Street and passed Doc Garrison's office, wondering if he still lived. He'd been too old to fight in the war, but *because* of his age he could very well be dead.

Caleb glanced down at his Union blue trousers. He hoped no one would recognize them as uniform pants. Even so, he hated wearing them. They did nothing but remind him of what he'd done to Abraham, and being here magnified his guilt.

Like the cove and his own family, Waynesville had been divided in loyalty. Regardless of whether someone fought for the North or the South, too many good folks had died. But no matter how many families here had lost loved ones, the only one truly troubling him was the one he'd killed.

Guilt and pain rushed over him like a turbulent river churning everything in its wake. His time in the cove with Lily felt more like a dream than reality. He'd been allowed to love her, and she'd given her heart to him. Nothing here was that rosy.

Truth stung.

He couldn't hide it under a skirt any longer.

His heart thumped as he looked up at the two-story hotel. He'd been inside once before. Six years prior. He'd been thirteen, and they'd come here to celebrate his sister Clara's engagement. Her wealthy fiancé had brought them here for supper. Then he'd taken her to Rhode Island and Caleb hadn't seen her since.

No wonder Mr. Iverson took in steady boarders. Caleb doubted many people traveled to Waynesville anymore with the need for a room.

He had to make his feet take the steps to the front door. His heart resided in his throat as he walked in and made his way to the front desk clerk.

The middle-aged woman remained on her rump behind the desk, with her nose in a book. She lifted her eyes when he approached. Her hair had been pulled so tightly atop her head, it drew the skin on her face taut. "Here for a room?"

"No . . . that is . . . *maybe*." He scratched the back of his head. "I'm here to see a woman."

The clerk slammed her book down, stood, and crossed her arms. "This ain't that kind a hotel."

His cheeks instantly heated. If he could, he'd bury his head somewhere. Instead, he waved his hands. "No. That came out all wrong. I'm lookin' for Alice Henry. I was told she's here."

The clerk leaned across the desk and peered at him. Top to bottom. "What's your business with *Mrs*. Henry?"

"None of *yours*." He harshly bit off the words, then regretted it. With bolstered courage, he splayed his arms wide. "I know I look a sight, but I'm her son."

The woman stumbled backward and landed in the chair. "You can't be. I attended the graveside service. If you're her son, who'd we bury?"

"Likely Abraham. I'm Caleb. Her *other* son."

"Oh, my." The befuddled woman fanned herself, then stood again and leaned against the desk. "You wait here. I'll get Mrs. Henry." She lifted her skirt with one hand and bustled away.

Caleb took a seat in a chair close to the door, tempted to bolt. But he couldn't. Not now. He'd made himself known and there was no turning back.

It felt as if he'd already been defeated, before he'd gotten the chance to make amends. Sighing, he leaned forward and put his head in his hands.

*God help me.*

He had no idea how much he'd tell her. All he had to do was bide his time, till he could go back to Lily.

# CHAPTER 26

As each minute ticked by, Caleb found the idea to flee more appealing.

He could leave, and his ma would just wonder why he'd bothered to come at all.

Having nowhere else to go kept him in the chair.

He got a good whiff of himself. Though not as ripe as he'd been when he'd ran into Lily, he didn't smell pretty by any means. A warm bath, fresh clothes, and a good haircut and shave would solve a few of his problems. Forgiveness was the only thing that would overcome the rest.

Rapid footsteps approached. Practically running.

"Caleb?"

His heart wrenched. He jumped to his feet, and his ma nearly put him on the floor. As dirty and nasty smelling as he was, she covered him in kisses.

He held onto her and his sobs came out of nowhere. Deep, heavy, and filled with remorse along with streaming tears. "Oh, Ma." Her comforting arms hadn't changed in all these years. A place he'd always felt safe.

She rocked him back and forth. "I thought I'd lost you, too." With her own tears falling, she took his face in her hands and peered deeply into his eyes. "My boy."

He couldn't find a single word to say.

The clerk came up behind them, and though his ma kept her arms around him, she turned to her. "This is my son, Caleb."

"I'm right happy for you, Mrs. Henry."

"I'm takin' him to my room. We have some catchin' up to do."

The woman nodded, and Caleb walked with his ma down the long hallway as if trudging through dense fog. As beautiful as ever, *she* stood tall and proud. Her waist-length hair held more gray than before, but it looked just as fine. She still wore it in a single tight braid that fell across the front of her dress and tied with a red ribbon at the bottom. The same image he'd carried with him to war. His lovely, warm-hearted ma.

They rounded a corner and continued on to the very last room in the corridor. She pulled a key from her pocket and inserted it in the keyhole.

In a daze, Caleb stepped into the room.

Dotted here and there were furnishings he recognized. His folks' silver candlesticks on the fireplace mantel, his ma's rocking chair that had been carved by his grandpa, and the quilts on the beds made from material taken from his and his siblings' old clothes. It felt strangely like home.

His ma guided him to a chair in front of the fireplace. "We've done best we could."

"It's might fine," he managed to say, clutching the seat of the chair. Light-headed, he feared he might fall to the floor.

"It has a *bathin'* room." Her smile broadened, and she gestured to a door on the far end.

"A room just for that?"

"Yes." She stood taller. "Aside from the Iverson's large suite, ours is the only room in the hotel with this luxury. It allows a bit more privacy. I'll have the porter fetch some water so you can have a good soak an' get cleaned up. Wouldn't that be nice?"

"Yes'm." He rubbed his dry throat. "Do you have any *drinkin'* water?"

"Course I do." She crossed the room to a wood stand that held a bowl and pitcher, then opened a small cabinet underneath, withdrew a glass, and poured it full of water. "Here." After handing it to him, she sat in the rocker and studied him. "I apologize for bein' outta sorts, but havin' you here . . ." She fidgeted with her skirt. "Are you a deserter? Your pants . . ." Her brow creased in confusion. Others he'd encountered may not have seen them as uniform trousers, but his ma certainly had. And though soldiers in the confederacy sometimes wore blue pants, they were never this dark of a shade.

"I know. Union blue. Not my color." He drank down nearly everything in his glass. "I stole them from a dyin' soldier. I was surrounded an' woulda been shot. Changin' uniforms allowed me to escape."

"Well, then. You did what you had to in order to survive. We all have." She frowned and looked away, then faced him again. "What 'bout your shirt? It ain't no uniform."

"I met some kind folks who took me in an' patched me up. Got shot in the shoulder, but I'm fine now. Once I got well, I decided to come home. I was scared you wouldn't want me here. An' Ma . . . I don't aim to fight again. I just hope they don't find me an' try to *make* me."

"Oh, sweetheart." She scooted her rocker closer and took his hand. "I prayed every day you'd be spared. I know the war's 'bout to end. I don't reckon *anyone* will come lookin' for you. Like you, all them soldiers wanna get home." Tears welled in her eyes. "I've lost too much already. I *won't* lose you again."

How could he tell her he didn't intend to stay? He'd have to find the right time. "I'm here, Ma. Less they *drag* me outta here, I won't go."

"Good." She tenderly caressed his hand. "Last August, I got word that your pa had been killed, then . . ." Her gentle touch turned into a firm grasp. "I know this'll be hard for you to hear, but Abraham was shot. He died back in September. Not long after your pa."

Caleb released her and took another long drink, emptying the glass. "The clerk said you'd buried a son, so I had a feelin' . . ."

She stroked his cheek and looked at him with so much sympathy it only magnified his guilt. He couldn't talk about this right now, so he chose to swallow the pain and push on. "I already knew *Pa* must be dead. I went to the old house first. They told me where to find you. Why'd you hafta come to a hotel? Why not go north to Clara or Mary?"

"Your sisters have their own lives to live. But they've been kind enough to send money. It allows me to stay here. 'Sides, I didn't wanna leave Waynesville. It's always been my home."

She tipped her head to one side and gazed at him with her pity-filled eyes. Something he didn't earn or deserve. "My dear, sweet boy. Now that you've come back, I have hope again. An' maybe you can help Rebecca, too."

At the mention of her name, his throat closed up. He lifted the empty glass, begging with his eyes for more water.

His ma stood and hurriedly refilled it. "You must've had a horrid time gettin' here."

"Yes'm." He guzzled the cool liquid, but it didn't help. He had to ask. "Does Rebecca live with you?" He gestured to the two beds.

His ma sadly nodded. "She had nowhere else to go. Her folks are gone, an' she has no siblin's. Did you get my letter 'bout her an' Abraham gettin' married?"

"Yes'm. I was happy for them. Just hate how everythin' ended up." *An' it's all my fault.*

"She an' I are a little like Ruth an' Naomi." She sighed. "Whither thou goest, I will go, an' where thou lodgest, I will lodge." His ma frequently quoted scripture throughout his upbringing. Seemed that hadn't changed.

She shook her head, then softly laughed. "The poor girl is saddled with her mother-in-law."

"I'm sure she don't see it that way. She's always loved you. But . . . how's she copin' with Abraham's death?"

"Not well. You know how tender she is." Her slim smile turned to a frown, and her sad eyes searched his. "She's with child."

The words sliced into his heart like a blade. Not only had he killed his brother, but Abraham's offspring would grow up without a pa. He stared at his ma, unable to speak.

She stood and extended a hand. "C'mon. There's a cloth over there by the bowl an' pitcher. You can wash your face. I'll send for hot water so you can bathe. I can tell none a this is settlin' well, an' I understand why. You loved your brother. No matter your differences, you were blood." She lifted him to his feet and grasped his shoulders. "I know you're tryin' to be strong, but there ain't nothin' wrong with lettin' your feelin's out."

He numbly let her lead him through the room.

* * *

Caleb closed his eyes and let the warm bathwater soothe him.

His ma had promised a haircut and shave. One of the hotel porters also worked as a barber for the guests. He had a chair set up for that purpose on the main floor of the hotel, close to the lobby. Once Caleb was clean, he'd go to be groomed.

"You all right in there?" his ma called out from the other side of the door.

"Yes'm."

"I managed to wrangle up some clothes for you. Mr. Iverson is 'bout your size an' happily gave them."

"Thank you, Ma."

"I had him burn them trousers you was wearin'. I thought you wouldn't wanna see 'em again. I'll set these here by the door."

She was right about the pants. "I appreciate it. I'm 'bout done in here."

"You should know . . ." His ma's voice cracked. "I haven't told Rebecca 'bout you yet. She's workin' in the kitchen, an' I didn't wanna upset her. I reckon I need to ease her into your bein' here an' all."

He let his body sink below the surface of the water. How could he face her?

"Caleb?"

Even underwater he could still hear his ma. He jerked upright. "Yes'm?"

Silence.

"Ma?"

"I'm here. I just feel a mite odd askin' you this."

"Go on."

More silence, yet this time he didn't push her.

"Years ago," she finally said. "You claimed to have feelin's for Rebecca. In the beginnin', I assumed you was tryin' to best your brother. But after a time, I saw sumthin' more than that. I think you actually cared for her, an' I hope you might still."

He sat up straight, hardly able to breathe. Her implications hit hard. His lies had already come back to haunt him.

"Caleb?"

"Yes'm?"

"She's a lovely girl, an' her baby needs a pa. Your comin' here is the blessin' I prayed for. I've always believed God has perfect timin', an' I reckon He sent you home to help her an' the child."

*No.*

"Tell you what . . ." The pleading in her voice took a softer, less-desperate tone. "You think on it. I *know* you cared once. Maybe when you see her, it'll all come back to you."

He gripped the sides of the tub so hard his hands started to shake.

*Is this my retribution?*

Maybe it was the sacrifice he'd have to make for killing his brother. One that meant letting go of Lily.

He shook his fists in the air, then grabbed hold of his thick hair and cinched his grasp.

*I love her!*

No. He couldn't do it. He *wouldn't* do it. He'd help with Rebecca's child as best he could, but he'd never let go of Lily.

*God help me . . .*

* * *

The sleeves of Mr. Iverson's shirt were a bit too short, as were the legs of his trousers. Even so, Caleb made do. The clothes were clean and otherwise comfortable.

The barber held up a mirror. "Are you satisfied?"

Caleb turned his face from side to side, then lifted the mirror to look at his hair. "Yep. Much better."

"Your mother will be pleased." The man spoke with refinement and stood tall, drawing his shoulders back.

"Where are you from?"

"Maine." He removed the towel he'd draped around Caleb.

"What brought you *here*?"

The man smiled. "Change." Curt and simple.

Caleb decided not to press him further and got up from the chair. "Thank you."

The barber nodded, grabbing a broom. While he swept up the large pile of hair, Caleb walked away.

He rubbed his smooth face, and of course, thought of Lily. But the time had come to see Rebecca.

He returned to the room and knocked. His ma had promised to get him his own key, but he was uncertain where he'd sleep. The suite held only two beds and no sofa. It seemed he was destined to lie on the floor once again.

The door inched open.

He gulped.

Rebecca's ebony eyes peered into his.

He quickly looked down, only to regret it. Her enormous belly bulged beneath her yellow, floral-print dress. So dainty and feminine, and heavy with child.

She stepped back. "Come on in."

The air around them thickened, nearly suffocating him. He loosened the button at his neck, then stepped into the room and closed the door. His ma was nowhere to be seen, likely on purpose.

Rebecca reached out both hands, and he took them. Her soft skin felt nothing like Lily's. Of course, Rebecca had never butchered a rabbit or plowed a field.

"You look exactly how I remember you," she said and lightly squeezed. "Always so handsome." She shyly turned her head.

"So do you." His cheeks warmed. Something they'd done a lot lately. "Well . . . 'cept for . . ."

*I'm a bumblin' fool.*

"My belly?" She released him and cupped her hands over the bulge. "It's all right, Caleb. Don't be embarrassed."

"I ain't. I just . . ." Nothing was coming out right. Rebecca's beauty didn't help matters. Regardless of her belly, he was sure her perfectly formed face still turned heads. She'd kept her shining black hair braided down her back. Her flawless dark skin reflected her scant amount of Cherokee blood from generations past.

She silently stood in front of him as if waiting for *something*.

So, he decided to say the only thing that mattered. "I'm sorry 'bout Abraham."

"Thank you." She motioned to the chairs by the fireplace. "Let's sit, so we can comfortably talk."

His legs weakened and he feared his knees might buckle. Though far from *comfortable*, he willingly obliged.

She sat in the rocking chair and folded her hands once again atop the unseen child. It only emphasized what lay beneath and bolstered Caleb's guilt.

"When's the baby comin'?" he asked.

"In 'bout two weeks." She gazed downward. Her shoulders slumped, and she frowned. "Abraham's company had camped near here, an' he got leave to marry me. We had two wonderful nights together. Least I'll have his child to remember him by."

Caleb's stomach knotted. "You have other memories. We knew you a long time 'fore the war." *Why'd I say* we*?*

Her head lifted. "You liked my pies." He could tell she tried to smile. Too much pain obviously kept it from coming.

"I liked *you*." The words slipped out without thought.

Was it his guilt trying to make her feel better?

Her hand moved in slow circles around her stomach. "I still enjoy makin' pies." Her eyes met his.

This time, he didn't look away, but gulped hard. "I like *eatin'* 'em." He pushed out a smile. One that probably appeared as idiotic as he felt.

Her cheeks reddened, and her eyes lowered. "I bake desserts for the hotel. Have been for quite some time. When we had to leave the farm, Mr. Iverson graciously offered us a room. Your sisters' generosity has paid for it. What little I make from the pies wouldn't give us a night's rest."

"What 'bout government money? Ain't you entitled to some kind a widow's benefits?"

"Those things take time. There are women here in Waynesville who lost their men early on. They're still waitin'."

Rebecca spoke so beautifully. Refined like the barber, but fluid like a song. Soft and melodious. Almost mesmerizing.

*Stop!*

He scolded himself, having no right to enjoy being with her.

She shifted in the chair. "*Oh*." The word squeaked from her lips, mouse-like. She genuinely smiled for the first time and sat upright. "The baby kicked."

"Did it hurt?"

"No, silly. It's too tiny to hurt me. But it's strong, an' wants to be born."

The door opened and drew Caleb's attention. A welcome interruption.

His ma paraded in. "I see you two are gettin' reacquainted. You hungry?"

Caleb shot up from his chair. "Yes'm. That I am."

"I'm *always* hungry." Rebecca scooted to the edge of the rocker and struggled to push herself up onto her feet.

Caleb carefully grabbed her arm and helped her.

"Thank you." She coyly looked away. "I'll do better once the baby comes."

He glanced at his ma and found her beaming. "The cook has roasted chicken for supper. An' for dessert, we have Rebecca's apple pie to enjoy." She turned around and reopened the door. "Caleb, do you mind helpin' her to the dinin' room?"

"Course not." He couldn't refuse his ma's request. Still, why all of a sudden did Rebecca need help? Hadn't she been doing fine without him? He assumed she'd eventually have gotten out of the rocker by herself, but he wanted to act gentlemanly, so he assisted her.

*Ma's pushin' us together.*

He extended his arm, and Rebecca tucked her dainty hand into the crook of his elbow.

They followed his ma down the hall.

Lily would be crushed if she saw him this way.

*What am I doin'?*

He'd unintentionally landed in a mess and was rapidly losing control.

He doubted he could eat a bite.

# CHAPTER 27

Caleb managed to eat more than he thought he could. He devoured the apple pie. Yes, Rebecca certainly knew how to bake to a man's liking.

The small dining room held eight tables. Each accommodated eight guests, but only a dozen chairs held diners. Aside from the three of them, as well as Mr. Iverson and his wife—who happened to be the front desk clerk, a woman young enough to be his daughter—there were seven other folks staying at the hotel. How they kept it operational was a mystery.

No doubt Mr. Iverson appreciated the money Caleb's ma contributed.

Rebecca laid her cloth napkin on the table. "I'm goin' back to the room to rest for a spell."

Caleb stood and helped her from her chair. "Want me to go with you? I mean . . . help you get there?" It'd be a miracle if he ever talked to her without stumbling over his words.

"No need to bother. Why don't you stay here with your ma an' talk a while? I'm sure you have plenty to say to each other." She dipped her head and walked away.

Caleb remained on his feet till she was out of sight, then sat down again.

His ma reached across the table and took his hand. "Your eyes sparkle when you talk to her. Did you know that?" She squeezed, then released him.

If his eyes had glimmered in the slightest, he thought even less of himself. How much further could he betray Lily?

He sipped from his water glass. "Rebecca's a kind girl." His fork gleamed, bouncing rays of sunlight from the large dining room window. He moved it back and forth, almost entranced by the flickers of light.

"You're fidgetin', Caleb. I've made you uneasy. Or maybe, it's Rebecca that's brought out your nervous behavior." She tapped on the table, and he lifted his gaze. "You *do* have feelin's for her, don't you?"

"Course I do. Every time I look at her, I think a Abraham. Ma, I . . ." He struggled with how much to say. "Don't you understand? I was a rebel. I fought against my brother. I—"

"Caleb." Her tone sounded harsher than anything she'd previously said. She leaned across the table. "Yes, you fought with the confederacy," she whispered, "but you can't blame yourself for Abraham's death. For heaven's sake, *you* didn't fire the shot that killed him."

"But—"

"Let. It. Go. Hear me?" She dabbed her mouth with a napkin. "I know you're heartbroken. But you came home at the right time. Rebecca needs you, an' by the longing on your face whenever you glance her way, I reckon you need her, too." Her eyes shifted around the room. "Let's take a stroll. All right?"

"Yes'm." He helped her up, then gave her his arm.

They walked along the well-manicured path surrounding the hotel. Spring flowers lined each side, as well as finely trimmed shrubbery. The air could be a little warmer for his liking, but he didn't mind it so much. His heart troubled him more than the temperature.

He'd come close to telling his ma what he'd done to Abraham. Never again. No one would know but Lily.

His ma leaned into him as they casually walked. "I've asked the porter to bring a cot for you. I understand it'll be a bit uncomfortable sharin' a small room with two women, but it's only temporary. I'm expectin' money from Clara any day now. Once it comes, I'll see 'bout gettin' another room."

"Ma, I don't want you spendin' *your* money on *me*."

"It's only to get you started. And *comfortable*." She let out a small laugh and patted his arm. "An' since you're uneasy 'bout takin' some a the funds from your sister, if you're willin' to work, there's some to be had. Maybe even at our old farm. They're strugglin' to keep up the crops. Once you have money comin' in, you can pay me back. Then in time, perhaps you can buy a house. One large enough for a family."

*Family . . .*

His ma stopped walking and faced him. "Rebecca's child will be born soon. Though I hate to put pressure on you, I'd like you to come to a decision 'bout your feelin's for her as soon as you can."

"Ma, there's sumthin' I gotta tell you."

"What?" She let out a little laugh. "You're not hidin' a wife somewhere, are you?"

"No, but—"

"Then, what's troublin' you?"

He took a long, deep breath. "There's a girl. The daughter a the folks what helped me get well. A mountain girl."

"A *mountain* girl? An' you're fond a her?"

"Yes."

She folded her arms over her chest. "How long have you known her?"

"A few months." Truthfully, it had been *eight*, but he didn't want his ma to know how long he'd been there. It would complicate things.

"An' how long have you known Rebecca?"

"Most all my life."

His ma brushed her hand along his face. "If she hadn't chosen Abraham, I reckon you'd a married her. You'd best be searchin' deep into your soul. That mountain girl don't need you the way Rebecca does. An' there certainly ain't no child to consider with that other girl."

"What 'bout how *I* feel? I *love* Lily. I made a promise to go to her when the war ends."

"Lily. A pretty name." Her face lost all its color, and she frowned. "I was certain God brought you home for Rebecca."

"How do know she'd even want me? She loved *Abraham*."

"She an' I have had many a talk 'bout you boys. She struggled just as much decidin' who to marry as the two of you wrestled over who'd win her heart."

"She did?"

"Yes. She cared for both a you. An' from what I can tell, that hasn't changed. I saw plainly how she looked at you durin' supper."

"I ain't so sure, but I'll help how I can."

"Not if you leave." She turned away and stared toward the sky. "The Bible tells of more than one instance of a man dyin' and leavin' behind a widow." Her eyes slowly blinked, then she grasped onto his arm. "It's God's will that if there's an eligible brother, he take the grievin' widow to himself, marry her, an' raise her children."

"I don't recall them stories."

"They're there. Believe me." She gestured to the path, then linked her arm through his and started walking again. "I want you to be happy—sumthin' that ain't easy these days. If you promised Lily you'd see her when the war ends, then take the time now to decide if it's what you're truly meant to do. But give Rebecca a chance. Get to know her again. Your heart might lead you in another direction."

"I doubt it. There ain't no one like Lily."

His ma sighed and stopped once more in the middle of the path. She let go of him and looked him in the eye. "It's your life, Caleb. I love you, an' I'm here simply to offer advice. I won't make *your* decisions." She placed her hand flat against his chest. "But know this . . . Sometimes, *hungerin'* for a woman feels like love. It ain't. Real love is gentle an' givin'. It grows over *time*. I understand it's hard to have desirable feelin's for Rebecca right now. Not in her condition. But try to remember what she was like when you knew her before. Eventually, she'll be ready to give herself again. If you choose her, you'll hafta be patient, but think how happy you'd make your brother knowin' his wife an' child would be cared for in a lovin' manner."

Why did her words have to make so much sense?

"All right, Ma. I'll think on it."

"That's my good, handsome boy." She rose up on her tiptoes and kissed his cheek. "Now then, let's go see 'bout gettin' you settled in our room."

A new kind of guilt weighed him down. He begrudgingly followed her.

Maybe time *would* solve everything.

But he couldn't make *everyone* happy. Someone would be hurt, no matter his decision.

*My sweet Lily.*

No, he'd never hurt *her*.

***

Lily fell back onto her mattress, utterly exhausted. They'd been in the wheat field all day. If only Caleb had been there to help.

They needed him now more than ever. *She* needed him in more ways than one.

They'd borrowed an extra scythe from the Quincy's, so they had two to cut the field. Even her ma had gotten out and helped. With only one arm, her pa couldn't manage the scythe with a cradle. It took two steady hands on the tool and a lot of endurance. Cut after cut. The cradle kept the stems from falling to the ground, and her pa and the boys grabbed and bundled them.

Tomorrow they'd start again until they finished all five acres. Then the threshing would start. Separating the wheat from the chaff would be even more difficult and time consuming.

"Violet . . ." Lily could scarcely keep her eyes open. "I ain't never been so tired before. I'm plum tuckered out." They'd finished their supper, but it wasn't even *close* to bed time. Even so, Lily wanted to sleep.

Violet sat beside her on the bed and sipped a glass of water. "I'm tired, too, but you look plain awful. Reckon you done too much?"

"Maybe." She rolled onto her side, facing away from her sister. "Can you close the door? There's sumthin' I gotta tell you."

"Course." Violet did as she asked, then returned to the bed.

Lily didn't want to carry her burden alone anymore. She slowly eased onto her back again and placed her hands over her stomach. "You know how much I love Caleb, right?" Though she wanted to shout the words from the highest peak, she kept her voice low.

"Yes. An' he loves you." She smiled and rubbed Lily's arm. "Don't worry, he'll come back."

"I know. I'm just worried it might not be soon enough." Lily shut her eyes, building up her bravery. "Sumthin' happened 'fore he left." This shouldn't be so hard, but she feared her sister might think poorly of them. "Violet, I laid with him. More than once." She inched her lids open to witness her sister's reaction.

Violet's eyes grew as large and bright as a full moon. "You mean, you two . . ." She swallowed hard. "*Coupled*?"

"Yes." Lily sat up and took her hand. "Only cuz we love each other. It felt right an' *good*. I mean . . . in the proper sense of the word. You know, *appropriate*. Like we was already married."

"You *ain't*. Pa'd *shoot* him if he knew."

"But *I* initiated it. I went to him an' asked him to love me. Reckon Pa would be right in shootin' *me* instead." Lily drew invisible patterns on the quilt with her fingertip. "I think I'm with child. Truthfully, I *know* I am."

Violet gasped and her face turned an odd shade of pale white. "Oh, lawdy. No wonder you want him back this minute."

"I can't hide it forever. I only hope he gets here'fore I get too big. I know he'll marry me, but I don't wanna shame the family. The longer he's away . . ."

"Reckon you could write him? Tell him 'bout the baby?"

"No. This is sumthin' I gotta do in person. He's got enough to worry 'bout. Trust me on that."

"All right." Violet pulled Lily into her arms. "It'll be our secret. But you gotta take care a yourself. Swingin' that scythe can't be good for the baby."

"I've worked hard all my life. I'm strong. The baby'll be fine." She separated from her sister, then pulled her dress taut against her stomach. No bulge yet, but it wouldn't be much longer till she'd start to show. "I reckon it happened on my birthday. If I'm right, it'll come in November. I'm sure Caleb will be here long 'fore then."

"Your *birthday's* when you done it? When I was *sick*?"

Lily worked her lower lip with her teeth, then jutted her chin high. "I was hurtin'. Worried you was gonna die. I needed comfort."

"An' Caleb gave it to you." Concern filled Violet's eyes. "You was vulnerable."

"Yes, but that ain't why it happened. We did it outta love."

Violet stared downward. "He best come back. I didn't like him once, an' I swear, if he hurts you, I'll *hate* him forever."

Lily took Violet's chin in her hand and lifted her head, then stared into her eyes. "He *won't* hurt me. He's gonna be your brother-in-law, so you'd best not hate 'im."

Violet smiled again and nodded. "A baby . . . I'm a mite jealous."

"Don't be. Truth be told, *I'm* scared to death."

"I'm gonna get you some water. You look like you could use a drink." Violet stood and walked out of the room.

Lily lay back and shut her eyes. Yes, she was scared. She didn't rightly know what to expect, even though she'd seen her ma through more than one pregnancy. She had so many questions, but couldn't ask.

Time had become her new best friend. She needed it to slow down, so she could gather her wits and give Caleb the opportunity to return to her.

*He won't let me down.*

It was the only thought that kept her from crumbling.

# CHAPTER 28

Caleb woke with a wrench in his back. The cot came nowhere close to being as comfortable as the bed tick he'd slept on at Lily's.

He shut his eyes, recalling the dream he'd had. He and Lily had been tangled in a lover's knot in the burrow on the hillside. He had to wash away the recollection, which brought out something even more *uncomfortable*. Having had her, his body craved gratification.

The sun hadn't risen, but *he* had.

He climbed from the cot and tiptoed to the door. A trip to the outhouse would help. Hopefully, by the time he got there, his mind and body would be set right again.

A scant amount of moonlight filtered into the room from a slit in the drapery. Scarcely enough to see by. He bumped into a chair and stubbed his toe. "Ugh . . ." He had to clamp his mouth shut to keep from crying out. His toe throbbed for several seconds, then subsided.

He glanced at the sleeping women, faintly breathing. Rebecca lay flat on her back, her mounded stomach pushing up the blankets.

Caleb already felt love for the child. How could he not? The baby carried his family's blood. Whether boy or girl, he'd cherish it.

He hurried out the door as quietly as he could.

Lanterns were left constantly burning by the outhouses. A courtesy to guests who used them both day *and* night. The facilities sat far back from the hotel for good reason. No perfume could cover up the smell.

Caleb took care of business as fast as he could and returned to the room.

He perched on the cot and didn't lie down. Though he'd been covered with a quilt his grandma had made, he wasn't *home*.

Tears formed. Ridiculous for a man, yet he ached for what he had at Lily's.

Of course, he missed *her*, but he smiled thinking of Horace and how he comically played charades. And how little Isaac liked to cuddle on his lap and laugh at the simplest things.

He even missed Mrs. Larsen. The abrupt woman had worked her way into his heart. Though cold, she was only concerned with the welfare of her family. An admirable trait.

Rebecca whimpered and jolted him from his thoughts.

He stood and crossed to her, then eased down onto the edge of her bed.

Even in the dim light, he could tell she was crying. She sniffled and whimpered again, obviously not asleep.

Stifling his own tears, he glanced at the other bed. His ma lay faced in the opposite direction. He hoped she was sleeping.

He leaned close to Rebecca. "Shh. It's all right." As gently as he could, he dabbed at her tears with the corner of the blanket.

She slowly lifted her hand and took his, then cuddled it against her cheek. "I'm afraid," she whispered.

"Is it the baby?"

"No. That is, well . . . in a way." She sucked in air. "Would you mind so much stayin' here beside me till mornin'?"

*What?*

He had to admit, her bed was softer than the cot and large enough for both of them, but what would his ma say?

He grunted.

*She'll grin ear-to-ear if she finds us together.*

"I'm sorry, Caleb." Rebecca let go of his hand. "I shouldn't have asked."

"No. Don't apologize. It's fine." He brushed her cheek with the tips of his fingers. "I understand how scared you must be, worried 'bout your baby's future. If my bein' here helps, I'll get my blanket an' lay atop yours."

"Well, I didn't mean for you to crawl in beside me. Your ma wouldn't take kindly to that."

Thank goodness the room was dark. His cheeks got so warm they heated all the way to his neck.

He got the quilt and returned to her. She'd scooted over to the far side of the bed. An enormous lump had formed in his throat and no matter how many times he swallowed, he couldn't dislodge it.

He recalled sharing a bed with his sisters now and then growing up. This was no different.

And if he believed that, he truly was a fool. If he thought of Rebecca merely as a sister, his heart wouldn't be beating so hard.

He let his head sink into the feather pillow. Within seconds, Rebecca had *her* head on his shoulder.

*Oh, dear Lord.*

If only he wasn't drawn to crying women. This particular woman smelled like roses.

*I'm in a heap a trouble.*

He shut his eyes and let his body drift. Hopefully, the soft bed would put him right to sleep.

* * *

The room door shut and Caleb's eyes popped wide. The scent of bacon and fresh bread made him even more alert.

"I'm glad you're awake," his ma said, grinning like she'd won a prize. "I brought breakfast. The two of you looked so sweet lyin' there, I didn't wanna wake you to go with me to the dinin' room."

*Damn.*

He'd never curse aloud in front of his ma, but now seemed an appropriate time to swear to himself. He should've stayed on the cot.

"It ain't like it looks, Ma." He pushed the quilt aside and stood. Luckily, he'd slept fully dressed, or he'd have given her more wrong impressions. Ones that would be silly for her to contemplate with Rebecca so near to birthing her child.

He scratched his neck. "She was cryin'. I offered comfort."

"A beautiful thing."

Rebecca groaned, sat partially upright, and yawned. "Mornin' Mrs. Henry. Caleb." She slid off the bed and onto her feet, then trudged to the bathing room and shut the door.

His ma smiled and set the tray of food on a small table beside the bed.

Caleb rubbed his chin. "Rebecca didn't hafta go off to get dressed just to eat. The food might get cold."

"She's probably usin' the chamber pot," his ma whispered. "The poor girl has difficulty gettin' to the outhouse."

"You mean she does her business in *there*?"

His ma covered her mouth and softly laughed. "It's not uncommon. But don't you worry, I'll empty it for her." She gestured to the food. "I've already eaten. This is for the two of you. I've got some *business* of my own to tend. Will you look after Rebecca for now?"

"Awful convenient for you to suddenly have so much to do."

"I *always* have things to do." She headed for the door. "You should remember that 'bout me."

"Ma?" He'd thought about this a lot last night. "Don't you miss Pa at all? You act so self-assured. Like all's right with the world."

She returned to his side. "I miss him every day, but he's been gone a long time. Though he may a died just last August, he left home when the war started. Four long years ago. I'd grown to accept livin' 'thout him." She lovingly ran her hand over his hair. "All *is* right with my world. You came home."

She walked away.

When their room door clicked shut, Rebecca came out of the bathing room. She went to the wash basin and cleaned her hands, then pointed at the tray of food. "It smells wonderful. Let's eat 'fore it gets cold."

Maybe she'd heard him.

He scooted the chairs close to the small table, then helped her sit.

He couldn't recall the last time he'd had bacon and crammed a full piece into his mouth.

Rebecca giggled. A sound more like a melody than laughter. "Slow down. No one's gonna take it away from you."

"Sorry. Reckon I lost my manners. But it sure tastes good."

"Good as my pie?" She said it so sweetly. Almost *too* sweet.

He couldn't look at her and piled food onto his plate as a helpful distraction. "Nothin's good as that."

"Caleb?"

Now he *had* to look at her. "Yes?"

"Can I be honest with you?" She held a piece of buttered bread in her small hand, poised like a picture. How could anyone be so pretty this early in the morning?

"Course you can."

"Last night, you commented how we all had shared memories. It always was the *three* of us. You, Abraham, an' me." She quickly took a bite of bread, then dabbed at her mouth with a napkin. "Do you know why I chose *him*?"

Caleb's chest tightened. "Reckon cuz you loved him."

"I loved you *both*."

*Why'd she hafta say* that?

He shot straight up from his chair and filled a glass full of water, then swallowed it down, making a point to keep his back to her. "Why are you tellin' me this *now*?"

"Please . . . sit down again." Her voice sounded so pained. How could he *not* do what she asked?

He sat and stared at the eggs and meat on his plate. His appetite had vanished.

"Abraham an' I never got the chance to know what it was like to be a married couple. Yes, we made a baby, but there's more to life with a man than that." She let out the saddest sigh. "Look at me, Caleb."

He obliged her, but doing so brought greater hurt. Her dark eyes had filled with tears.

"I chose him because I thought you were arrogant. A man too handsome for his own good, an' one who I didn't fully trust. But I see sumthin' different in you now. Sumthin' tender an' warm. I believe with all my heart, I was wrong 'bout you."

*No, you weren't.*

He couldn't say a thing. The need to run overwhelmed him, though he knew he had to stay.

She blinked and a tear dropped onto her cheek. "Do you remember the night you tried to kiss me, an' I turned my head?"

He silently nodded.

"I wish now I would've let you." Her tears streamed.

*Cryin' women . . .*

He got up from his chair and knelt beside her. "Please, don't cry. I reckon you've shed more tears than any woman ever should. Ma told me your folks is gone. I assume they died. When did it happen?"

"After I married Abraham. They'd been wantin' to go north. Ma had a sister in New Hampshire. So once I moved in with *your* ma, they left. They got the fever while travelin' an' didn't reach their destination." Her tears flowed faster.

"I shouldn't a asked. Here I tell you not to cry, then I make everythin' worse."

She shifted sideways in her chair and faced him. "You're wrong. Seein' you again has made everythin' better." She tentatively touched his cheek.

He breathed hard and fast. Her lovely face begged to be kissed, but he couldn't kiss her lips. He stood tall, bent down, and placed a small peck on her forehead.

"Becca . . ." The pet name he'd used for her came out of its own will. "I got some thinkin' to do. I hope you understand."

He couldn't leave fast enough and didn't wait for her to respond.

# CHAPTER 29

Lily stopped Violet from taking another swing at the wheat. "Show me your hands."

Violet set the scythe on the ground and turned her palms face up. They were covered with blisters—one open and bleeding.

"You ain't cuttin' no more." Lily grabbed the tool. "You're done. Go inside an' get some a Ma's ointment."

"*You* shouldn't be swingin' that thing 'round neither."

Their pa stepped between them. "What's the problem here?"

Lily lifted her chin. "Violet's hands is all torn up. She ain't used to doin' this kind a work."

"Then *you* do it. You did fine yesterday."

"Yes, Pa." Lily glanced sideways at her sister. "Go on to the cabin. I'll be in when we're done."

Violet hesitated. Her eyes searched Lily's and the concern lying there would only draw suspicion.

"*Go*, Violet." Lily gave her a gentle nudge, and her sweet sister ran from the field.

"Violet's too soft for hard work," their pa muttered. "Don't know why she got it in her head she could do this."

"She seen how tired I was last night, Pa. She only wanted to help. But I'm fine, so let's get back at it." Lily stepped away from him and sliced into the wheat. Another acre and they'd be done cutting.

Maybe Lily should've kept her secret a little longer. Violet's emotions often got the best of her, and her face revealed too much.

However, secrecy was wearing Lily down.

"This is borin'!" Lucas fussed, while tying another bundle of wheat. "I'd rather go huntin'."

"You'll do what I tell you," their pa said. "An' I don't wanna hear no more complainin'."

"Yessir."

"Pa?" Lily held out the scythe. "Reckon Lucas is big enough to cut?"

The boy eagerly gaped at the sharp instrument.

Her pa also eyed the thing and rubbed his chin. "Reckon so. Go on an' let him try." He faced her brother. "It's a *tool.* Not a weapon. Don't go hog crazy."

To Lily's surprise, Lucas mastered the scythe in no time at all. She took over the duty of bundling and tying the stems. Her ma managed the other scythe, along with Horace and Isaac, who scooped up the wheat and did what they could to bundle it. Their pa went behind them and helped best he could one-handed.

Thunder rumbled in the distance.

"We need to hurry," her pa said. "Rain's comin'. We gotta get this inside the barn to keep it dry."

Before the war, folks in the cove would help each other with threshing. Now, everyone had to fend for themselves. They'd get it done, but it would take time. Still, they had a healthy crop, bound to bring in plenty of money.

Lucas swung the scythe like he was at war with the field, cutting off heads of the enemy. If he hadn't been so good at it, the sight would be disturbing. At least he was using his destructive energy for something helpful.

Her ma's head lifted high and she stopped cutting. "Oh, dear."

Lily turned to see what troubled her.

Harriet Quincy headed their way with both grandsons on her heels. The woman briskly walked as if she were on a mission.

*This can't be good.*

Lucas kept slicing.

"Lucas." Lily placed her hand on his back, careful to avoid the swinging blade. "Stop for a spell."

His lip curled, then he spotted the Quincy boys and set the scythe down.

"Rain's comin'," Mrs. Quincy said as if they weren't aware. "My boys will help you finish up here."

Lily's mouth dropped open, but she quickly snapped it shut. This was the last thing she expected.

Her ma actually smiled. "That's mighty kind a you, Harriet."

"Just tryin' to be neighborly. However, I confess, you put a bur in my side. Why'd you lie to me 'bout your *niece*?" Mrs. Quincy fisted her hands on her huge hips. "That *Callie* girl. Them soldiers told me she was dangerous. Shot their captain in the back. Why'd you ever allow her in your home?"

The woman's *real* purpose for coming showed through loud and clear. Why she hadn't brought it up when her pa went to borrow the scythe was a mystery. Maybe she just wanted to challenge them when they were all together, tired, and unlikely to strike back. Lily struggled to keep her thoughts to herself, but held her tongue.

Her pa stepped beside her ma and stood tall. "We was actin' out a kindness. Did what the Good Book told us to do. I ain't happy 'bout what she done to the captain, but we couldn't a gotten our field planted 'thout her."

Mrs. Quincy tipped her head back and looked down her nose at him. "This field means more to you than an innocent life? There ain't nothin' *holy* 'bout that."

Fuming, Lily couldn't remain quiet. "That *innocent life* wanted to have his way with me! Callie stopped him!"

Mrs. Quincy's eyes popped wide, and she cupped her hands over Billy's ears. "You shouldn't speak a such things in front a my grandsons. Or your little brothers for that matter."

Lily took two long strides and faced the woman nose to nose. "They don't understand what I'm talkin' 'bout. But *you* do. Would you rather he'd done what he pleased with me? Would that a been *holy* enough for you?"

"Heavens, no!" She stepped away and squared her shoulders, then turned to Lily's ma. "I reckon we've both had our share of misunderstandin's. I assumed the letter you got from your sister had to do with *Callie*. Obviously not. So, why'd she write?"

Her ma crossed her arms and glared at the woman. "Not that it's any of your business . . . She wrote to flaunt her wealth an' say ugly things 'bout my husband."

"Oh." Mrs. Quincy's head drew back and she appeared speechless. Likely for the first time in her life. She took two slow steps backward. "Well, then. I reckon I'll leave my boys to help you an' be on my way. Come by sometime for coffee an' maybe we'll come to a *new* understandin'."

Expressionless, Lily's ma nodded. "I'll send your boys home with some apple butter to repay them for helpin'."

"That's kind a you." Mrs. Quincy bustled off, faster than she'd arrived.

Lucas waved the boys over. "You can help me. I'm real good at this. Watch an' see." He immediately returned to whacking down the wheat.

Their ma wasn't quite so eager. She paced in the field, mumbling, then marched over to their pa. "That woman sticks her nose so far into everyone's business, it's a miracle we can still see it on her face." She huffed out ragged breaths.

Her pa chuckled. "When you told her 'bout that letter, I thought I'd bust."

Her ma's face contorted, then she, too, burst into laughter. Lily couldn't help but join them. She was glad to have spoken her mind. Better yet, it felt incredibly good to laugh.

They finished the field with new determination. Their family would go on together, come hell or Mrs. Quincy's nosiness.

Lily couldn't wait till she could share the joy of a coming grandchild with her folks. They'd all get to hold a baby again.

Babies made everyone happier.

She rubbed her hand over her belly and smiled, then looked up into the sky.

*Please, God, make Caleb come back soon.*

* * *

Caleb walked and walked. He trudged slowly, taking every step with deliberation. Thoughts raced through his mind, moving much faster than his feet.

He'd not intended to go to his old house, yet ended up there regardless. A place far from Rebecca. He had to get his mind right and search his heart for answers.

*She loved us both?*

When he'd looked into her eyes, he'd seen it. The same expression he'd gotten many times from Lily.

*Love.*

The *other* things he swore he saw terrified him more. Longing and desire.

*She wanted me to kiss her.*

Worse yet, he'd considered it, only for a mere second.

He hated himself for it. He'd never believed he could be more disgusted with himself than when he'd pulled the trigger on his brother. No man should care for *two* women.

His ma always threw out Bible verses to guide their decisions. Oddly, the only ones he could think of now were all the passages that talked about how men took more than one wife. Verses his ma had never spoken aloud, but ones he'd read to himself. He'd thought the practice was horribly selfish. How could any man give enough of his time and love to multiple women? An even greater mystery was how those Bible women managed jealousy. No woman *he* knew was inclined to share her man. And if a man stepped out on his wife, he'd have hell to pay.

"Excuse me? Mister?"

Caleb stopped in the middle of the field and faced the small woman. The same one who'd come to the door when he'd first arrived in Waynesville. "Yes?"

"Why are you pacin' in our field?"

"Sorry. I used to come out here when I was a boy. Didn't know where else to go to gather my thoughts."

"Oh." She nervously looked around and clutched the front of her ragged dress.

Her children weren't with her, but she seemed scarcely more than a child herself. Tiny and short with stringy blonde hair. Her face was smudged with dirt and the pocket of her skirt had a tear and hung loose.

"I was wonderin'. . ." Caleb decided to be bold. "Could you use some help here? I know this ground well, an' I'm a good farmer."

She ground her foot into the dirt. "We *do* need help. I just ain't got much to pay."

"That's all right. For now, do what you can. Maybe we can work sumthin' out where I can share in the profit when it's time to harvest. How'd that be?"

"You'd do that?"

"Yep." He shrugged. "Odd as it may be, this place still feels like home. I know it belongs to you now, but . . ."

"You don't hafta explain." She eyed him up and down. "See you got some new clothes. I didn't recognize you at first." A slight blush reddened her cheeks. "You're a right handsome man. Not anythin' like the one who knocked on my door."

*I don't need this.*

He used to relish this kind of attention. Not anymore.

She worked her lower lip with her teeth, instantly reminding him of Lily. "My grandpa might have some things that would fit you a mite better. Them pants is too short. How 'bout for your first day's wages, I give you a new set a clothes? Well—not *new*—but better fittin'?"

"That sounds fine. I'll come t'morra mornin' bright an' early." The distant sky darkened. He needed to get back to the hotel before the rain came. "What do I call you?"

"I'm Mrs. Templeton, but I'd rather you call me *Laura*. What 'bout you?"

"Caleb. Caleb Henry."

"Nice to meet you, Caleb Henry." She smiled coyly, turned and walked away, then paused and glanced back. "Pace all you want. However, you better go soon, or you might get wet."

She acted completely different than when they'd first met. Similar to the way both Lily and Violet had changed after he'd cleaned up.

His looks were a blessing *and* a curse. More so the latter. Especially with all the widowed women left behind from the war. He could easily have his choice of any of them.

And up until two days ago, he only wanted one.

More importantly, he could only *marry* one.

Thunder rumbled.

He broke into a run and headed back to the hotel.

* * *

Caleb hadn't run fast enough. By the time he reached the hotel, he was drenched from head to foot. He should've been smart and asked Laura for the clothes before he left, but he didn't feel right taking something he hadn't yet earned.

"Mr. Henry!" Mrs. Iverson waved a key in the air. "Your ma asked me to give this to you."

He gladly took it, all the while dripping water on the floor. "Forgive the mess I'm makin'. Got caught in the downpour."

"I'll have the maid mop it right up. You get on to your room 'fore you catch a chill."

"Thank you, ma'am." He hurried down the hall.

It seemed a bit strange inserting the key into the lock and not knocking. He cautiously opened the door, fearing he might find one of the women undressed. Instead, he found the room empty. It both saddened and relieved him.

He shut the door and quickly removed his clothes. Even his underwear had gotten wet, so he stripped bare. Unfortunately, with only one set of trousers to his name, he'd have to wait for them to dry before leaving the room again.

He stoked the fire and threw on another log, then wrapped himself up in a blanket. After draping his clothes over the back of the rocking chair, he positioned it in front of the flames. Then he took a seat in the other chair and huddled close to the flickering fire.

Just in time.

The door opened and Rebecca walked in. When she saw him sitting there, she grinned, then turned and locked the door. "Can't risk the maid walkin' in an' findin' you like this. Her heart might fail her." She removed a white shawl from her shoulders and lay it on the bed.

It didn't seem right being in the room alone with her like this. He cinched the blanket snugly to his body. "I got caught in the rain." Though he stated the obvious, he didn't know what else to say.

"I can see that. Your hair's plastered to your head." She glanced at the rocker, then perched on the bed's edge. "Not enough places to sit in this room. We need to get another chair."

"Yep." He stared at the fire. The safest place to keep his eyes.

"I was afraid you might not come back."

The sadness in her voice turned his head. "Why?"

"Thought I scared you off. I understand why you wanted time to think. No man wants to be burdened with a woman *and* a child."

"What?" He stood, carefully holding the blanket, then sat on the corner of the bed and faced her. "You think you're a burden?"

Her eyes shifted to her bulge. She covered it with both hands as if trying to hide it. "I *know* I am. My parents coddled me. Never asked me to lift a finger. I'm lucky my ma saw fit to teach me to bake. Unfortunately, their pamperin' made me dependent. I'll love this baby an' raise it up proper, but I don't know what I'd do if sumthin' ever happened to your ma." She looked him in the eyes and his heart started to pound. "It was wrong of me to tell you how I feel 'bout you, so soon after you learned 'bout Abraham's death. You must think I'm dreadful."

"I ain't *never* thought that."

Her brows dipped low. "I loved Abraham. I swear it. I thought I'd die, too, when I lost him. Almost like my heart had been buried beside his. Then sumthin' inside me came back to life when your ma told me you were here. As if my heart started beatin' again. An' when I *saw* you . . ." She reached toward his shoulder, then searched his eyes, hovering her hand in midair. "Is that where you were shot?"

"Yes." The dryness in his mouth got worse the longer she spoke.

"Can I see it?"

He gulped and eased the blanket off his shoulder. "It's all healed up. But it left a bad scar. Ain't too pretty."

Her fingers inched closer to his skin.

He held his breath and closed his eyes. Her touch ignited a new kind of pain.

"All you poor, poor men. Havin' to fight an' kill."

He gasped when her lips touched the scar, and his body shook.

She rapidly sat up straight. "Forgive me. I shouldn't a done that."

"No. It was a kind gesture." *It was more than that.*

If the room got any warmer, he'd be tempted to throw off the blanket, which would further complicate matters. Something compelled him to hold her, but he didn't budge.

She pulled the blanket up and recovered his wound. "It's amazin' you're alive. A few inches over, an' the bullet would've struck your heart." She set her hand on his leg atop the quilt. "It's important you know, I don't hold your bein' a rebel against you. You an' Abraham both fought for what you thought was right." Her sad sigh increased the constricting pressure building in his chest. "It's honestly a miracle they brought him home to me. Did your ma tell you he'd been dressed in gray?"

"No." He stared downward.

"Seems some confederate soldier swapped uniforms to get away. I find it hard forgivin' that man. Not so much for killin' my husband. After all, they were at war. But dressin' him in the enemy colors could've put Abraham in an unmarked rebel grave. I'd a never known what happened to him. It's a cruel soul who'd do such a thing. Luckily, the federalist who found him recognized him."

Every word stabbed deep. A pain worse than what he'd felt having the bullet dug from his shoulder. Rebecca would never view him the same way if she found out the truth.

She cupped her hand to his face. "I'm sorry. I can see how much I'm upsettin' you."

"I'm . . . I'm glad they got him home." He choked out the words.

"My poor Caleb." Her fingers tenderly caressed his cheek.

Overwhelmed with emotions—guilt, regret, sorrow—he took hold of her hand and pressed his lips to her palm. "*I'm* sorry, Becca. For everythin'." He looked into her eyes, his own clouded with tears. She'd never fully know the extent of his apology. Somehow, he had to make it all up to her. And though he didn't want to accept it, he knew full well how he could atone for what he'd done.

"I'm sorry." He repeated the words, then brushed a strand of loose hair off her face.

Her eyes closed to his touch. When she reopened them, hers had also filled with tears. "Both our hearts have been broken." She moistened her perfectly formed lips. "I won't turn my head this time, Caleb."

Time stopped.

He didn't have to imagine Rebecca as she'd been all those years ago. The beautiful, warm woman facing him now pounded his heart. Whether from guilt, or maybe the undeniable desires of all men, he *needed* to kiss her. He had to try and honestly *love* her.

But his head ached, wrestling over Lily. Less than a week ago, he'd been in *her* arms. How could it be right to hold another so soon?

Yet, Rebecca was no stranger.

*Maybe I* did *care back then . . .*

Yes, he'd been arrogant. Consumed in himself. Even so, she'd always been *special* to him. If he shunned her now, he'd only harm her more.

*I ain't gonna hurt her again. Ever.*

Hadn't he internally pledged the same thing to *Lily*?

*I'm condemned no matter what I do.*

All the while thoughts raced through his mind, Rebecca's eyes hadn't left his. He encircled her with his arms and pressed his lips to hers. The blanket dropped to his waist, baring his upper body.

She trembled against him, but allowed him to deepen the kiss. And though she moved slowly at first, by the time their lips parted, her hands eagerly caressed his bare back.

"You feel right, Caleb," she whispered. "Maybe this is how it was always meant to be." She burrowed into him. Her fingers twirled through the hairs on his chest. *Exactly* the way Lily had touched him.

*Oh, Lord, help me.*

Though pierced and aching, his heart hadn't stopped pounding. If only he'd died in the forest, he wouldn't have to endure this pain. By living, he'd go on destroying lives. He had no choice but to lock away the portion of his heart that held Lily. He'd hold her there forever, yet he had to let her go. He'd crush her, but he could only hope one day she'd move on and forget him.

His long-ago lie to show up his brother had finally returned for judgment. His ma had said God brought him back home for a purpose. *This* reason. And horrifically, Lily had been the one who sent him here to set things right. Neither of them knew what he'd have to do to accomplish the task.

He'd take on the responsibility of his brother's widow and their child. A *punishment* that fit Caleb's crimes. He'd lied, pretending to care. He'd taken a life he *truly* loved. Wrongs that couldn't be undone, but he'd set aside his own desires to atone for taking away those of others.

His heart ached more than ever. Something he didn't think possible.

*I'm sorry, Lily.*

# CHAPTER 30

A rush of shame swept over Rebecca. This had happened too fast.

She separated herself from Caleb, cupped one hand under her belly, and pushed herself up from the bed with the other.

"Forgive me, Caleb." She took a step toward the door, but he reached for her arm and stopped her.

"Don't say that. Please?"

If she looked at him, she'd want to hold him again, so she kept her eyes on her stomach. All these months after burying Abraham, she'd ached for tenderness. More than anything, she'd longed to feel safe again and have security for her child. "I can't have you thinkin' poorly of me. In any way. But I can't imagine you havin' decent thoughts a me, when I invited your kiss after less than two days together."

He stood and lifted her chin with the tips of his fingers. "I told you before, I ain't never had a bad thought 'bout you, an' I don't *now.* We have a history together. I kissed you, only because I wanted to." He gulped hard, looking so much humbler than she recalled him being.

*He truly has changed.*

"So . . ." She kept her eyes on him and rubbed small circles over her child. "When you told me all those years ago you had feelin's for me, you weren't just playin' with my emotions? Seein' if you could steal me away from your brother?"

Again, he swallowed hard. "We was young, but even then I seen sumthin' special in you."

She hated pushing him, still, she needed to know. "In time, could you *love* me?"

His chest rose and fell so fast, it drew her attention. Not a good thing. Though in no condition to be considering any sort of physical gratification, she hated to admit that his bare skin had an effect on her.

"Becca . . ." He tightened the blanket and covered most of himself. *Thank goodness.* "I've always loved you."

She couldn't stop tears from forming. From the time she'd been old enough to see Abraham and Caleb through the eyes of a woman, rather than a girl, she'd wanted to hear the words. But Abraham had said them first, and she'd trusted him. So, she'd given him her heart *and* her hand. Yet, she'd never stopped wishing it had been Caleb she'd vowed herself to.

A key rattled in the keyhole.

She stepped away from Caleb and turned her back to him.

His ma walked in. When she met Rebecca's gaze, the dear woman looked both confused and elated. "Maybe I shoulda knocked first."

Rebecca crossed to her. "This is *your* room. There's no need." She glanced over at Caleb, then returned her focus to her mother-in-law. "Caleb an' I were just talkin'. An' I was fixin' to go for a walk. *If* the rain's let up. Has it?"

"Yes. However, are you sure you're up to it?"

"Course I am. I won't be gone long." She headed for the door, then paused before going out. "I'll be back in plenty a time for supper." She locked eyes with Caleb. The man had a way of making her tingle through and through simply by standing there. "I'd ask you to join me, but it'll be a while 'fore your clothes are dry."

He stared at her, without uttering a word.

As she shut the door, she swore his ma let out a happy cry.

The sound warmed Rebecca's heart. For months, they'd both been tearful and hopeless. Mrs. Henry had assured her God would see them through their hardships, but Rebecca had started to lose faith. Especially after they'd learned President Lincoln had been assassinated. She feared bringing her child into a country filled with so much hate.

*Our prayers were answered.*

Her faith had been restored. God had sent a blessed miracle in the form of the man who'd held a piece of her heart for a very long time.

*Is it right to feel happy?*

A genuine smile lifted her lips, then it broadened when she recalled *Caleb's* lips touching them.

She neared the front desk. "Good afternoon, Mrs. Iverson."

"Why, Miss Rebecca, I ain't seen you smile like that since . . . I can't remember when." She leaned across the desktop. "It's that Henry boy, ain't it?"

Rebecca held her head high. "My brother-in-law." Her cheeks started to hurt from smiling so big. "Yes'm. He's made his ma very happy. Sumthin' I'm glad to see."

The woman shook a finger, grinning. "That ain't all he done. I can tell. But I think it's mighty fine."

Rebecca placed her hands to her cheeks, feeling them heat. "Am I wrong for bein' happy 'bout a man? Mine's not been in the ground long."

"Don't matter." She stretched out her hand, and Rebecca took it. "Follow your heart. In these troubled times, you gotta latch onto *any* happiness you can find."

Rebecca squeezed, then let go. "Thank you. I'm headin' to the cemetery to make peace with Abraham. I feel talkin' to him might help."

"That's a fine thing to do." She waved her out the door. "Go on now, 'fore it starts rainin' again. But take care. Mind that child in you."

"Yes'm."

She wandered down the walkway in the direction of the cemetery. She'd not been there in more than a month. Going to Abraham's grave always brought tears, and in her condition, she believed getting so upset wasn't good for the baby.

*Latch onto happiness.*

She appreciated Mrs. Iverson's words. The woman had had her own share of grief, eased by an aging, wealthy hotel owner. She'd spoken from experience.

Though gray clouds covered the sky, the world seemed brighter.

She passed the mercantile, then turned on a side street and went several blocks to the old white-steepled church. The small cemetery lay behind it, surrounded by a thicket of trees.

No longer could she kneel beside his grave, so she hovered above. "Abraham, your brother came home." She nervously looked around, hoping no one was near.

*It's silly to feel this way.*

With so few people in Waynesville, why would anyone come here on a dreary day like today? And if they did, they certainly couldn't fault a widow for conversing with her late husband.

"Caleb was injured, but he's fine now. He's done with fightin', and we can only hope no one comes lookin' for him." She hugged her belly for security and strength. "I know you loved your brother, even while fightin' on opposite sides of this wretched war. My folks used to say, blood can overcome anythin', an' that there's no deeper bond than family. So, it feels only right to keep ours together. Our child needs a pa, an' Caleb needs a wife."

Dreaded tears started to form for a very different reason. "He said he loves me, an' I believe him. In all my days, I've never seen him so humble. An' I know he loves children. I still remember how he enjoyed playin' with the little ones at church. An' I can tell he cares by the way he looks at my belly."

She placed her hand atop the cold tombstone, needing to steady herself. "I wish you could speak to me an' tell me it's all right to love him. Because, I could use your blessin's. But since you can't, I'll listen to my heart."

A chill wind blew across her face. She closed her eyes and tipped her head back. "We'll see each other again someday, Abraham. Yet now, I have to go on livin' here. I swear I won't forget you." Her eyes inched open and she studied the grave. She shuddered, knowing Abraham's decaying body lay so near her feet. Thank goodness his spirit resided elsewhere. "I won't stop lovin' you. I can only pray you'll smile down on us an' accept what comes."

She lovingly ran her hand along his carved name. Small droplets of rain dotted her skin.

With a sigh, she turned and hastened home.

* * *

Caleb turned away from his ma and rolled his eyes. The woman's gleeful outburst didn't set right with his troubled heart, but he didn't want her to see into it.

"What happened here?" She practically sang the words.

He took a seat in the chair by the fire. "We talked."

"And . . ." Even with his damp clothes draped over the back of the rocker, his ma sat in it and scooted close to him.

"And . . . I kissed her." He stared at the flames, frowning. "She wanted me to, an' I couldn't deny her. It woulda hurt her."

His words sealed his betrayal of Lily.

"Oh, sweetheart." She grasped the arm of his chair. "Was it so *horrible* kissin' her?"

"No, but—"

"*Lily*?"

He turned his head and looked into her eyes. "Course, Lily. I shouldn't be kissin' no one. Not when Lily has my heart."

"Does Rebecca know?"

"Gosh sakes, *no*. If she found out, it'd be like stompin' her into the ground with my boot. I ain't gonna do that to her. I care too much. She's been hurt enough already."

His ma sat upright and folded her hands in her lap. "Did you tell Rebecca you care for her?"

He closed his eyes and nodded. "I said I *always* loved her."

"A *lie*?" Her joy vanished.

"Not exactly. I *do* love her. She's family. Has been forever in a roundabout sorta way. As much time as you an' Pa spent with her folks, it was like we was all akin to each other. I wanna do right by her." He rubbed his temples, but it did no good. His head relentlessly throbbed. "Did you tell her 'bout the blue trousers I was wearin' when I got here, an' how I got 'em?"

"*No*. That's one thing I don't want her knowin'. Rebecca has a gentle spirit. Until Abraham was brought home wearin' gray, I don't reckon I ever saw her angry. She despises the rebel who took his uniform. Hopefully, he's dead. A just punishment for what he done to your brother. I imagine that sort a thing happens a great deal. But I won't have her opinion of *you* tainted by tellin' her you used the same way to escape your situation. She might think less a you, an' I won't have that."

*How much worse can it get?*

His ma sighed, then faced the fire. "Rebecca needs hope. If my grandchild comes into this world to a heartsick woman, it'll be poor-spirited. I couldn't tolerate that. Every child needs joy—especially one who's my blood."

"*Our* blood." He covered his face with his hands, took a huge breath, and sat up straight. He had to start acting like a responsible man and stop wallowing in self-pity. "As I said, I'll do right by her. I'll treat her the best I can."

"Then you'd better be takin' her to the courthouse. Show her you mean what you say. Do it now 'fore the baby comes."

"What 'bout my waitin' till the war ends to make up my mind 'bout Lily?"

"Seems to me, your decision's already been made. To do right by Rebecca, you can't have Lily, too."

He doubled over and clutched his stomach, folding into himself. How long would it take for the pain to go away?

His ma tenderly rubbed his back. "As you told me, you only knew her a few months. That's a blink of an eye in a lifetime. Eventually, you'll forget her."

*No.*

Somehow, he had to regain his composure before Rebecca returned. But he felt numb—unable to move.

"Caleb." His ma continued rubbing slow methodic circles on his back. "Write Lily a letter. Tell her goodbye."

A sob erupted from deep inside him. He sucked in air and tried to stop more from coming.

"You'll be fine, sweetheart. You're doin' what's right. Sometimes it's hard. All you gotta do is think 'bout Rebecca an' the baby, an' you'll know you made the best choice."

"If it's right, it shouldn't hurt this bad." The sobs kept coming.

How could he write that kind of letter? Just imagining the pained look on Lily's face when she read it, sickened him.

*She's gonna hate me.*

And if Lily hated him, so would her family. Especially Violet, who knew the truth about them. She'd disliked him for a long time, and he'd finally won her over. He'd gained the trust of every single one of them, and now he'd hurt them all.

Worse yet, he'd taken Lily's innocence.

*I made her a promise.*

He twisted the edge of the blanket into a knot. Tighter and tighter.

"Caleb." His ma cupped her hand over his. "Stop this." She pressed his face in her hands and firmly held it. "Family is the most important bond there is. Lily is *not* a part of ours. Rebecca *is*." Her eyes pierced deep. "Go wash your face, get dressed, and go see Mrs. Iverson. Ask her for paper an' pen. You have a letter to write." She stood and fingered his clothes. "They're dry enough. Get goin' 'fore Rebecca returns."

"Yes'm." He sluggishly got up from the chair.

Still numb, he went through the motions. He washed his face, then grabbed his damp trousers and carried them into the bathing room. With the door shut, he pulled them on, not even bothering with underwear. And though it caused him more pain, he wore the shirt Mr. Larsen had given him. As much as it increased his agony, at least he had something dry to wear.

He opened the door and stared at his ma. "Why do I hafta write the letter *now*?"

"The sooner the better. Let her go, so you can rebuild your life here." She practically floated across the room to him. "You *want* to stay in Waynesville, don't you?"

What he *wanted* no longer mattered.

"Yes'm. I'm startin' a new job t'morra. I'll be workin' the farm at our old place."

"That's wonderful." She kissed his forehead, then ran her hand along his cheek. "I'm proud a you." She wandered back to the rocker and sat. "By the way, I spoke to Mrs. Iverson 'bout that other room. There's a vacancy across the hall. Because I'm such a good tenant, she's lettin' us have it 'fore the money comes from

Clara. When you get the things to write your letter, ask for the key. You'll sleep much better in a real bed. An' once you an' Rebecca are married, she'll join you." She looked over her shoulder. "Won't that be nice?"

He nodded, speechless.

She'd manipulated the situation, but he couldn't fault her. His ma had always been a good woman. Like Mrs. Larsen, she only sought the best for her children.

*Mrs. Larsen's gonna wish she'd let me die.*

He left his ma and headed for the front desk.

Though his insides felt raw and empty, he pushed a smile onto his face. "Hey, Mrs. Iverson."

"Hey, yourself." She grinned from ear to ear. "When you showed up here lookin' like a ragamuffin, I feared you were the worst kind a man. But I ain't never seen Miss Rebecca smilin' so bright." She grabbed his hand and gave it a pat. "God bless you, Caleb Henry. You best not break her heart. Hear me?"

"Yes'm. There ain't no need to worry 'bout that." He swallowed hard. "Ma said you have a key for me to the room across the hall."

"That I do." She turned around and lifted it from a peg on the wall, then set it down on the desk in front of him. "It don't have no bathin' room, but I'm sure you can use your ma's when necessary."

"Thank you. Ma also said you might have some things I can use to write a letter."

"Course. Got all you need." She yanked open a drawer and handed him several sheets of paper, as well as an envelope. Then she scooted over an ink bottle and pen. "When you're done, bring this back. I'll be happy to post the letter for you. Mail comes once a week. So happens, it's t'morra. It can go out then if you finish it in time."

"I appreciate it." He tucked the key into his pocket, then gathered up the other items. "Thank you again." Another forced smile.

She wiggled her fingers as he walked away.

He needed solitude, so he opened the door to his new room.

No fire had been lit, but the sole bed had been made up and the space was clean and tidy. It had a large wardrobe, a desk, and a stand with a water pitcher and bowl—similar to the one in his ma's room. As for sitting, aside from the chair at the desk, there was a large overstuffed one by the fireplace.

For now, he'd be comfortable in this small space, though he feared it might be too crowded once he added Rebecca and the baby.

He crumbled down into the cushioned chair and dropped the paper on the floor.

*What am I doin'?*

His life was no longer his own, but it was exactly what it had to be.

# CHAPTER 31

Fortunately for Rebecca, the rain had been merciful. Only a few drops had touched her clothes.

The farther she got from the cemetery, the more her heart lifted. It pattered harder as she neared the hotel.

Mrs. Iverson waved her over as soon as she entered the lobby. "Mr. Henry got a key to the room across the hall from yours." She grinned. "Reckon you'll be sharin' it one day."

"Mrs. Iverson!" Rebecca giggled. "*Hush.*" She quickly looked around to see if anyone had heard.

"Silly girl. There ain't no one here but us. Even the maid's gone for the day." Her expression softened. "You feel better now? After goin' to the cemetery an' all?"

"I do." Her heart did a little leap and she clutched her chest. "I've decided Abraham would want me to be happy. So, that's what I'm gonna do. An' I'm right *hungry*, so I best get to my room an' dress for supper."

"Eatin' for two." The woman winked. "I'll see you in the dinin' room."

Had Rebecca not been so large, she probably would've skipped down the hallway. When she reached the end of the corridor, she stood in the center of the floor between the two rooms, contemplating whether to knock on Caleb's door, or put the key in her own.

She lifted her hand, ready to rap, then pulled it back to herself. It wasn't wise to act so eager. She'd already initiated their first kiss. The next move was up to him.

*Let him* work *for my affections.*

She covered her mouth to stifle another giggle, then inserted her door key.

Mrs. Henry sat comfortably in the rocking chair, casually moving back and forth. "How was your walk?"

Rebecca shut the door and took the chair beside her. "Wonderful. I told Abraham 'bout Caleb."

"You went to the cemetery?"

"Yes'm. It seemed the right thing to do." She pointed over her shoulder. "Mrs. Iverson said Caleb got the key to that room across the hall. Do you know if he's in there?"

"Reckon so. He had a letter to write."

"Oh?"

"He wanted to thank the family who nursed him back to health, and he felt it was appropriate to let them know he'd arrived home safely." Her face brightened into an enormous smile. "I reckon he'll tell them 'bout *you*. Though I doubt he'll invite them to the weddin'."

"*Weddin*? Did he tell you he wants to marry me?"

"Not exactly. But he said he loves you, and he wants to treat you as good as he possibly can. What else could he mean?"

Rebecca let her laughter flow. She wanted to sing. Dance. Scream for joy. But her condition kept her seated. "Will he propose? Make it all formal?"

"That's up to him." She stopped rocking and took Rebecca's hand. "Are you sure it's what *you* want?"

"You of all people shouldn't have to ask. You know how I feel 'bout him. These past months have been a horrible nightmare. I feel as if I've finally woken up." She couldn't stop smiling and thought of a story her ma had read to her when she was a little girl. "He's my Prince Charmin', come to rescue me."

Her mother-in-law released her and placed her hand on Rebecca's belly. "Just in time."

Rebecca covered it with her own. "That's right. Nothin' can go wrong now." She leaned back in her chair and closed her eyes. The heat from the fire warmed her to the bone, and the love in her heart spread it further.

Her child would have a pa, and she'd have the man she'd always wanted.

* * *

Caleb's hand shook out of control. He couldn't get a decent grip on the pen.

Of course, Lily had never seen his handwriting. She'd have nothing to compare this to. But to *him*, the script was unrecognizable. Not only its form, but the words he'd put on the page were nowhere *close* to what he truly wanted to say.

He'd had to stop more than once to let the ink dry, as well as the tears that had mixed with it.

*No man should cry like this.*

He only allowed himself to weep with a promise never to do it again. He'd seal his heart and soul inside the envelope and mail every bit of himself to Lily. Then, when she tore it to shreds, he'd leave his brokenness with her.

Every day he'd wake with one purpose. To get through it.

He'd work, provide a home, and raise a child. In time, he hoped the emptiness inside him might be filled again. He had to try hard for Rebecca's sake.

*It shouldn't be difficult. She's a wonderful woman.*

He'd go insane if he kept wrestling with himself.

It would be best to just send the letter, then forget Lily. Exactly what his ma had told him to do. If he didn't wipe her from his memories, he'd never be whole again. And he wouldn't be any good to Rebecca or her child.

*MY child.*

If he married her, the child would be his.

"I'll be a pa," he whispered, and picked up the pen again.

Thinking about the life growing inside Rebecca lifted his spirits.

"I'll be a *pa*." This time he said it louder, with great conviction. He'd never wanted something more.

He sat taller at the desk, dipped the pen into the ink and wrote with confidence.

Lily would understand. She knew the truth about what he'd done to Abraham and would see he'd made the right choice. She'd overcome hurt with sensibility. A trait she wore well.

He signed his name, then sealed the letter and carried it to Mrs. Iverson, along with the pen and ink.

"Hmm." She read the address. "Cades Cove, huh?"

"Yes'm. Good folks there patched me up. Got me on my feet again."

"No return address?"

"No." He grinned and leaned close to her. "The woman who takes care a their mail is a meddler. Don't want her knowin' who wrote the letter, or for that matter where I am."

"What 'bout this Lily Larsen? She know where to find you if she needs to write back?"

"Yes, but I don't 'spect it. She's got plenty more to do on their farm, than worry 'bout me. I just wanted her to know I'm home, an' I'm here to stay."

The woman nodded and grinned. "Glad to hear it. How's that room? Suit ya?"

"Yes'm. It's fine. Thank you again for everythin'."

He walked away, but peered over his shoulder.

She put the letter into a bag, presumably with other mail. He couldn't turn back now. Soon, the letter would be on its way to Lily, and once she read it, she'd never want to see him again.

He stopped in the hallway, tempted to race to Mrs. Iverson and retrieve the letter.

*Lily will* never *wanna see me again.*

The thought haunted him. Whether she loved him or hated him, both brought pain. At least by hating him, she could move on with her life.

He filled his lungs with heavy air, then forced his feet to move again.

They took him to Rebecca's door.

* * *

Rebecca had nearly fallen asleep in the comfortable chair, when a loud knock stopped her from dozing. She'd already put on a clean dress and groomed herself for supper, and she and Mrs. Henry were waiting for Caleb.

She glanced at her mother-in-law, who merely grinned, then Rebecca eased onto her feet and shuffled to the door. "It must be him. Doesn't he still have a key to our room?"

"That he does. However, if it's Caleb, he's bein' respectful." She fluttered her fingers at the door. "Open it an' find out."

Rebecca's heart pattered simply from the thought of seeing him again. When she faced him, she saw something she never expected. "Caleb?" She closely studied his face. "Have you been cryin'?"

His ma jumped up from the rocker and rushed to her side. "Heaven's sake. Let him in." She grabbed his arm and brought him into the room. "You poor, boy. Been grievin' over your brother, haven't you?"

Rebecca placed a hand to her heart, touched by the thought. Caleb was so distraught, he hadn't said a word.

"*Haven't* you?" his ma repeated, then cast a concerned eye at Rebecca.

"Yes'm," Caleb finally said. "I feel right foolish. Thought I could hide it, but you know me too well."

Rebecca put an arm around his shoulder. "You loved him. There's nothin' foolish in that. I think it's beautiful when a man shows his heart."

He pulled her into his arms and laid his head on her shoulder. She looked beyond him to his ma and received a nod of approval.

"You never have to hide from me," Rebecca whispered, while rubbing his back. Her large belly kept them from being truly close, but she felt a bond with him they'd never had before.

"We best be gettin' to supper," his ma said. "Or the cook might decide not to feed us."

Rebecca stroked Caleb's cheek. More than anything she wanted to kiss away his pain—something inappropriate to do in front of his ma. "You up to eatin'?"

He stood upright and pulled his shoulders back. "Reckon so." His sad eyes searched hers, then he took a step back and spun on his heels. "I best wash my face 'fore we go."

Rebecca smiled, watching him try so hard to be strong. *Boys should never be told it's unmanly to cry.* At least she could attempt to take his mind off his grief. "How's the new room?"

He went to the wash basin and ran a damp cloth over his face, then dried off with a towel. "Small, but clean. I started a fire to warm it for t'night."

"Well," his ma said. "Eventually, we might hafta make some adjustments. I wouldn't mind a smaller room. Not if I'm by myself."

Caleb gaped at her, then uncomfortably smiled. "Let's go eat."

"That's a wonderful idea," Rebecca hurriedly said and headed for the door.

Caleb breezed by her and opened it, then extended his arm. She gladly took it.

His ma followed them down the hall.

Rebecca leaned close to Caleb as they walked. "I hope you don't feel pressured by what she said," she whispered.

"Ma has a way of pushin' for what she wants." He, too, kept his voice low.

"But what do *you* want?"

He rubbed across her fingers with his free hand. "To take care a you. *Both* a you."

Her smile broadened. "Can I assume you're not referrin' to your *ma* an' me?"

"You know who I mean." His hand moved from hers downward, and he gingerly reached toward her stomach. "Reckon I'll be his pa."

Her heart leapt. "*His*?"

"Or her. *Whichever* suits me just as well." He glanced back, then put his mouth close to her ear. "Walk with me after supper. I wanna talk to you alone."

*He's goin' to propose.*

She smiled and nodded. They didn't say another word all the way to the dining room.

Since he'd said he was going to be her child's pa, then he'd certainly decided he wanted to marry her. Even so, she needed him to *ask* her. From Caleb Henry, a proposal would answer all her prayers.

# CHAPTER 32

"If I never see another grain a wheat, it'll be too soon," Lily mumbled. She plopped down onto the sofa, exhausted. Though they'd finished threshing days ago, she'd spent all day replacing the bed ticks with new straw. They'd *all* sleep better tonight.

Violet sat beside her. "You won't be so irritable when Pa brings home the money. I hope he's able to buy some salt while he's in town. It would sure make our meat taste better."

"I hope he don't get ambushed on his way home." Lily grabbed a pillow and clutched it atop her belly. "I'm glad Mrs. Quincy loaned him her mule so he could take the wagon an' go sell the wheat, but I wish he woulda taken someone other than Lucas with him."

"Why? We both know Lucas can shoot. He'll defend Pa if it comes down to it."

"Or he'll shoot someone he ain't s'posed to, an' Pa'll be in a heap a trouble."

Violet pivoted on the seat and tucked a leg up underneath her. "You worry too much." Her eyes shifted toward the kitchen table, where their ma sat reading her Bible, then leaned closer to Lily. "You should tell 'em 'bout the baby."

Lily clamped a hand over Violet's mouth. Though she'd whispered, their ma had sharp ears. "Hush." She widened her eyes to drive her point, then moved her hand away.

Violet sat primly straight. "Well, you should. You're workin' too hard."

"Lily." Their ma bit off her name.

"Yes'm?" *If she'd heard what Violet had said . . .*

"Go outside an' check on your brothers. Make sure they ain't gettin' into sumthin' they shouldn't."

"Yes'm." Her heart rested. She stood and headed for the door.

Violet followed her. "I'm goin', too, Ma."

"Fine. I'm gonna sit here an' pray for your pa's safe return."

"That's good, Ma," Lily said. "We'll pray, too."

Lily hastened out the door with Violet on her heels.

"At least tell *Ma*," Violet pleaded the instant they stepped off the porch. "You're gonna need help."

"I ain't tellin' till Caleb comes back. If I say sumthin' now, they'll think poorly of him. Once they see he aims to marry me, everythin' will be fine."

Violet firmly folded her arms. "*When the war ends*. You've said it so many times, I can hear your words even when you don't utter them. But we don't know when that'll happen. It could be t'morra, an' it might very well be next year."

"I hafta give it more time. Don't you see?"

"Course I do. But you gotta stop workin' so hard. If you don't, you might lose the baby."

Lily peered around the property and couldn't see a trace of the boys. She headed for the creek—one of their favorite places to play.

"I ain't gonna lose this baby. Eatin' all that venison made me stronger. Ma always worked hard till her babies came."

"An' some of 'em died."

"*After* they were born. Only God knows why." She faced her sister. "I *can't* stop workin'. There's too much to be done."

Loud giggles erupted from a short distance away.

Lily took Violet's hand. "C'mon. Reckon they're in the creek again."

Sure enough, they found the boys wet to their midsections and covered in mud.

"Ma's gonna have a fit," Violet said.

Lily scooped Isaac up, then quickly set him down again. A sharp pain pierced her side. She grimaced and doubled over.

"What's wrong?" Horace said. "Lily don't look good."

Violet wrapped an arm around her. "You all right?"

The ache subsided and she eased upright. "I'm fine. Reckon I wrenched my back tryin' to lift Isaac." She patted his dirty head. "You're gettin' too big for me to carry."

"Yes, he is," Violet scolded. "Don't do it again, Lily. Hear me?"

Isaac giggled. "You sound like Ma."

Violet bent over and peered into his eyes, shaking her finger. "You shouldn't a gotten in the creek. Now both you boys need a bath."

"We just got one." Horace pointed at the trickling water. "We was huntin' for frogs."

"Well, you found *mud*. So, get inside." Violet patted his rump, only to get a confused frown.

Lily laughed. "Violet, you're even actin' like Ma. Seems you got a maternal instinct in you after all."

Isaac raced off, likely to avoid Violet's hand. Horace sped after him.

"You're the one who needs it," Violet said. She studied her hand, covered in dirt. "Look at this. All I did was spank his bottom an' he got me filthy."

"That's boys for you." Lily placed a hand to her belly. "Reckon I have that to look forward to. But I want it more than anythin'."

"More than *Caleb*?" Violet nudged her shoulder, grinning.

"Course not. The two go together." She linked her arm through her sisters and started walking back to the cabin. "I'm gonna have an amazin' family."

"I thought you already did." Violet gave her a squeeze, all the while holding her dirty hand in the air.

Though still far more dainty than Lily, her dear sister had displayed a bit of spunk that hadn't come out before. Lily was glad to see it. The girl needed some fire in her if she ever wanted to get herself a husband. From what Lily had learned about men, they liked bold women.

*Well, maybe not* all *men, but Caleb certainly did.*

She grinned at the thought and warmed through and through. April had nearly come to a close. Little time had passed since he left. Regardless, it had already been too long.

She ached for him.

Hard work kept her mind on other things. The very reason she pushed herself. She'd keep her hands busy till she could put them on him.

* * *

"Just sign right here." The court clerk pointed to an empty space on the document.

Caleb's hand shook as he took the pen and dipped it in the inkwell. Though he might look the part in the black suit his ma had bought him for the occasion, his heart wasn't in it.

"You don't have to be nervous," Rebecca said. "We're already married, this is for their records."

*Married.*

The past few days had been a blurred whirlwind. The only peace he'd had was at the farm, although Laura Templeton cried when he'd told her he was getting married. The *true* turbulence had started the second he'd gone down on one knee and asked for Rebecca's hand.

He bent down and scribbled his signature, then stood upright.

The clerk scooted the paper toward Rebecca. "Your turn."

Caleb handed her the pen. She dipped it, then proficiently scrolled her name. "Least I don't have a new last name. I'll proudly be a *Henry* till the day I die."

The clerk lifted the document and blew on the ink. "Congratulations, Mr. and Mrs. Henry."

"Thank you," Caleb said.

His ma stepped forward and examined the document. "Yes, thank you." She turned to the Iverson's who'd stood as their witnesses. "I'm glad you agreed to be here."

"We were honored to." Mrs. Iverson placed a hand to her breast. "You two make a lovely couple. I hope you'll be as happy as we are."

"Thank you," Rebecca said. "I know we will be." She met Caleb's gaze, smiling so bright it overshadowed the sunlight streaming through the courthouse windows. "We should go back to the hotel now an' have cake. I baked it special."

"No woman should hafta bake her own weddin' cake," Mrs. Iverson said. "But I'll enjoy eatin' it." She laughed and marched with her husband down the hall.

Caleb watched his ma read every word on the marriage certificate. It seemed odd for her to be so engrossed in it. Maybe she wanted to be sure it was real.

*I should be the one starin' at the thing.*

None of this felt like reality. It couldn't be his life.

He pushed a smile onto his face and extended an arm to his *wife*. "I agree with Mrs. Iverson. I'll gladly eat your cake."

Rebecca had never looked prettier, dressed in the same yellow floral print she'd worn the first time he'd seen her in the hotel room. She'd woven spring flowers into her dark hair and left it flowing free from the usual braid. Even *that* brought back memories of Lily, and how her silky hair had covered him as she lay against his chest after they'd made love.

"Caleb?" Rebecca stroked his face. "Are you all right? You seemed a little lost just then."

He took her hand and kissed it. "I ain't lost. I'm with you. Reckon I was gettin' all emotional again. I'll try an' do better."

She rose on her tiptoes and kissed his lips. "You're such a good-hearted man. I love you, Caleb Henry."

"An' I love *you*, Mrs. Henry." He touched one of the white trillium in her hair. Thank God the lilies hadn't bloomed yet or she might've put them there.

"Save your affections for later," his ma said. "Remember, you're still on public display."

Rebecca's cheeks turned crimson. "Sorry."

"Oh, my dear." His ma tipped her head to one side and smiled at her, then gestured down the hallway and started walking. "Don't apologize. I merely wanted to remind you where you are."

They followed her outside to a clear, cloudless day.

Rebecca cuddled his arm. "Everythin's perfect now." She giggled. "Even the weather."

He nodded and smiled. How could he not feel a tinge of joy while watching it radiate from Rebecca?

His mind flashed back to a long ago evening, when he and Abraham sat on their front porch and laughed as Rebecca raced around the yard trying to catch lightning bugs. She was only ten, but already beautiful. At eleven, Caleb hadn't seen her through a man's eyes. Not until his year-older brother pointed at her and told him he was going to marry her one day.

"Maybe *I* will," Caleb had said, just to see his reaction.

His brother just grinned and ruffled Caleb's hair.

No matter how many times Caleb had tried to show him up over the years, Abraham never once challenged him or raised his voice. Not until the war . . .

"Caleb?" Rebecca caressed him arm. "Where are you? I've been talkin' an' you haven't heard a word I said."

"Sorry. I'm a mite dazed. Hard to believe you're my wife."

"Well, I am. Today's just the start of our wonderful life together." She nestled closer as they walked.

One day at a time. That was all he could ask of himself.

* * *

A rush of emotion swept over Rebecca. She'd been moodier since the day she'd conceived, yet today she should only be happy. Any moment now the tears would come, which upset her further.

She opened the door of the bathing room and stepped out wearing a long white nightgown. She paused and fingered the beautiful cradle Mr. Iverson had crafted for the baby, then faced her husband.

Caleb stood in front of the fireplace, fully clothed and staring at the flames.

She pulled down the covers on the bed. "It was kind of your ma to move into the other room."

"She was happy to do it." He didn't move, or even look at her for that matter.

She lay back onto the pillows and rested her hands atop her enormous bulge. As suspected, her tears pooled, then trickled down her cheeks. "I ate too much cake," she mumbled, then sniffled.

Caleb slowly faced her. "Are you sick?" He crossed the room and stood beside the bed, gazing at her with such concern, it pushed her tears faster.

Her chin quivered and multiple droplets fell from her eyes. "Look at me. I'm useless to you. What kind a weddin' night is this? You deserve better."

He said nothing, but worked the buttons on his shirt, then took it off and tossed it on the chair. His trousers followed. He stood before her in nothing more than underwear. Not the full-bodied sort, rather the kind only covering his lower half.

Without hesitation, he lay beside her, propped himself on one elbow, and rested his hand on her stomach. "I don't want you to cry ever again. I knew who I was marryin' an' what tonight would be. I'm happy just layin' here next to you."

"Are you sure?" She turned her head to look at him straight on.

"Course I am." His hand tenderly rubbed over her belly, no longer showing any kind of trepidation.

Was it wrong to want so much more from him? Maybe he didn't understand what he was missing. "Have you ever had a woman, Caleb?"

His head drew back, and he swallowed hard.

*I shouldn't have asked.*

"N-No." He looked away, then returned his eyes to her. "Course not."

"I embarrassed you, didn't I?"

"Reckon so. A man my age—"

"Is good an' decent for waitin' till marriage." She ran her fingers over his chest. The feel of him ignited an even deeper longing. His perfectly formed body was more muscular than Abraham's and increased her desire. "Kiss me, Caleb."

His eyes searched her face.

*What are you lookin' for?*

She moistened her lips. "*Please?*"

He inched toward her.

She closed her eyes and waited for the contact she craved. His lips moved on hers with experience. Yes, he'd kissed her before, but not like this. Though he may never have bedded a woman, Rebecca had no doubt he'd had his share of kisses. But no matter how many there'd been, she wouldn't let it concern her. From this day on, he was hers.

"*Ouch*." A swift kick in her ribcage spoiled the moment.

He jerked away. "I hurt you?"

"Not you. Our baby." She took his hand and placed it on the spot. "Feel that?"

"Lawdy," he muttered. "Reckon he's bruisin' you from the inside out."

She giggled and all her tears dried. "*He* wants to be born."

Caleb pushed himself up higher and hovered close to her face. "I wanna see him. *Hold* him. Teach him all I can 'bout bein' a man."

She caressed his handsome face. "Let him be a little boy first."

"That I will." His eyes glistened in the lamplight.

*Tears?*

His beautiful, tender heart tugged at hers.

He threaded his fingers through her hair, then kissed her. Long and deep.

The feeling that transcended from his lips filled her heart with more love than she thought possible. One day, she'd give herself to him. Any man who'd waited this long deserved to have a woman who would complete him.

She kept on kissing him and caressed his bare back, bringing out sounds of pleasure from him that only increased her longing.

"One day," she whispered against his face. "You'll be able to love me."

"I already do."

"That's not what I mean." She held his face in her hands and penetrated his eyes with her own, searching and hoping he understood.

Breathing hard, he pulled away, then placed a quick peck to her forehead and lay back on his pillow. "There's plenty a time for that later. Don't seem right yet to even think 'bout it."

*He understood perfectly.*

"I did it again." She sighed. "I embarrassed you. I'm sorry. I just feel so comfortable with you. Like it's always been the two of us sharin' a bed."

"Give me time, Becca. Once the baby comes, we'll learn how to love each other."

She wanted to roll over and cuddle into him, but her body wouldn't let her. "It'll be wonderful."

He took her hand and kissed it. "You should sleep. It's been a long day."

"You're right. Promise me you'll stay close."

"I ain't goin' nowhere." He turned on his side and draped an arm around her.

Content, she closed her eyes.

# CHAPTER 33

Caleb sat up, his lower body covered in moisture.

"Oh . . ." Rebecca groaned.

He flipped the blankets off them. She'd completely soaked the sheet beneath her.

"Lawdy, Becca. I think your water done broke!"

"It hurts, Caleb." She clutched her belly and groaned again.

He hopped from the bed, raced out the door, and pounded on his ma's.

With eyes half shut, she opened the door and stared at him. Then, like a fire had been lit, her eyes popped wide. "Is it the baby?"

"Yep. Our bed's soaked, an' she's hurtin' sumthin' awful."

"Put some clothes on an' fetch Doc Garrison. Hurry!"

She spun around, grabbed a robe, and followed Caleb back to his room.

While his ma tried soothing Rebecca, he threw his clothes on, then sped from the hotel.

Seems he'd married her just in time.

The sun had started to peek out from behind the mountains. It gave Caleb plenty of light to see his way down the street. He ran hard and fast and was almost out of breath when he reached the doctor's house.

He banged on the door. "Open up, Doc!"

He'd not seen the man in many years, but his ma had assured him he still had his practice. Old as he was.

The door creaked open. The old gray-haired man fidgeted with his spectacles, then peered closely at Caleb. "You're that Henry boy, ain't you?"

"Yessir. My wife—Rebecca—she's havin' our baby."

"Your ma told me she was near her time. Come in while I dress." He jerked his head and motioned Caleb inside, then pointed at a chair. "Sit there. I'll be only a minute."

Caleb sat, all the while wringing his hands. Sweat formed on his face and his heart beat out of control. Not from having to run, but out of utter fear. Many women didn't survive birthing children.

Rebecca was so delicate. What would he do if she died?

The doctor returned carrying a black bag. "You all right, son?" He grinned and nodded toward the door.

Caleb stood, wiping the sweat from his brow. "Not sure. I just wanna know Rebecca's gonna be fine. You'll help her, right Doc?"

He opened the door. "Been doin' this longer than you've been alive. Stop frettin'."

It took a great deal longer to get back to the hotel. Though Caleb's feet wanted to move faster, Doc Garrison toddled along beside him, hunch-backed and feeble.

"It's her first child," the man said as they walked. "Takes a mite longer than others what'll come later. Your ma's with her, so take a breath or I may hafta revive *you*."

"Yessir."

The old man chuckled. "It's your brother's child, ain't it? The one what died in the war?"

"*Mine* now."

"You're a good man takin' on the responsibility. An' I can tell by lookin' at you how much you care."

*More than you realize.*

Caleb opened the door to the lobby and held it for the doctor. When they walked in, Mrs. Iverson was there at the desk waving her hands. "Your poundin' woke most everyone in the hotel." She grinned. "But I'm glad. Can't wait to see that baby!"

Too numb to say anything, Caleb merely smiled and hurried the doctor down the hallway. A nearly impossible task.

When they neared the room, Rebecca's loud moaning came through clearly.

He glanced wide-eyed at the doctor, who merely grinned. "As I told you, young man, I've been doin' this a long time. She sounds like every other woman I've cared for."

Caleb pushed the door open. Rebecca was more than some random woman. She was his *wife*.

She lay flat on her back, sweating worse than him.

The doctor faced him. "Go on out. This ain't no place for you right now. Your ma an' me will see to her."

"But—"

"*Go*, son. You can see her after she's delivered."

"Caleb . . ." Rebecca stretched out her hand.

He ignored the doctor's orders and went to her. He took her hand, kissed it, and knelt beside the bed. "I'm here."

"I'm scared."

"Shh." He leaned over and kissed her damp forehead. "You're gonna do fine. Nothin' to be afraid of. Doc Garrison will help."

"Tell me you love me."

He stroked her cheek, then kissed her lips. "I love you. *Both* a you."

His ma grasped his shoulders. "You gotta go. Like the doctor said, this ain't no place for you."

He begrudgingly nodded, then stood. "I'll be right outside that door."

Rebecca's face scrunched together, looking as if she'd cry. Then she rose slightly and clutched her belly. "Oh! It feels like it's comin'!"

"Course it is." The doctor calmly opened his bag. He drew out scissors and some other kind of metal instrument.

The sight knotted Caleb's stomach. His ma grabbed his arm and shuffled him out the door, then closed it behind them. "Go in the other room, sit by the fire, an' wait."

"How long does it take?"

"Every birth is different. Could be hours."

His insides churned and nausea dried his throat. "I don't feel too good."

His ma had the nerve to grin. "You care more than I ever thought you did. I'm glad. Rebecca's a fine woman who deserves *all* your heart." She laid her hand on his arm. "That other woman was never meant to be. You see that now, don't you?"

"Yes'm. I do."

"That's my boy." She patted his face, then pointed across the hall. "Go now. I'm sure you'll hear the baby cry an' know when it's time to come and see them." Smiling, she went back to Rebecca.

Caleb stood in the hallway utterly helpless. His weak knees nearly buckled, so he went into the small room and slumped down into the chair by the fire.

*Lily was never meant to be.*

He'd hated lying to Rebecca and wished she'd never asked whether or not he'd had a woman. There were only two people on the earth who knew the truth. He'd always keep it to himself, and if Lily understood what was best for her, she'd do the same. It would be their secret. Several moments of passion he'd cherish forever, but already, it felt like a lifetime ago.

His future lay in the other room.

Several times Rebecca cried out. Each instant punched deep into his gut. He couldn't shut out the sound or the fear of what was happening across the hall.

He tried to doze and went in and out of sleep, so he stood and paced.

Hours passed.

And then it happened—the blessed wee sound of a baby's cry.

He jerked his door open and rapped on the other. "Ma! Becca! Can I come in?"

His ma opened the door a crack. "Give us a few more minutes. We're cleanin' her up right now. The baby, too." She beamed. "You have a daughter."

"It's a girl?" Tears filled his eyes. "I got a little girl?"

"Yes. An' she's beautiful like her ma." She brushed his cheek. "Wait here." The door shut.

Caleb lifted his fists in the air and joyfully shook them. "It's a girl!" he yelled loud enough for the world to hear.

Mrs. Iverson bustled down the hallway. "A girl?"

"Yes'm. They're fixin' her up now." He hugged her. "I got a daughter!"

The woman tittered, then stepped away from him. "Land sakes. I ain't never seen a man so happy 'bout a new baby."

"*My* new baby, Mrs. Iverson. Mine an' Becca's."

"Well, you come fetch me when she's up to company. Hear?"

"Yes'm."

She chuckled all the way back down the hallway.

Caleb couldn't quite explain the elation he felt, but he wasn't about to deny it. The new life in that room meant a new beginning. A chance for him to start over and do things right this time. To make his brother proud of the pa he'd become.

The door creaked open, and the doctor came out. "You've got a strong wife, an' a healthy baby girl. My work's done here. But don't hesitate to come by if you need me."

He pumped the doctor's hand. "Thank you. Can I go in now?"

"Yep. She's askin' for you." The man slowly shuffled away, clutching his black bag.

Caleb took an enormous breath and went into the room.

His ma had scooted the rocking chair next to the bed and happily rocked. "I wanted to be near my granddaughter."

Rebecca lay in the bed, propped up partially on pillows. A tiny bundle rested in her arms.

Caleb crept toward them, almost afraid to breathe. The baby had stopped crying and he didn't want to frighten it. He got close enough to peer into the tightly wound blanket. A sweet tiny face greeted him.

Her eyes were closed, so he couldn't see their color, but the tufts of dark hair on her head were the same shade as her ma's.

He climbed atop the bed and sat as close as he could get to them. "She's beautiful, Becca."

"*Perfect*." Her voice sounded weak. She'd worked hard bringing their baby into the world.

He opened the blanket just enough to see her little hand, tinier than his smallest finger. "She's such a miracle."

"I thought it would be fittin' to name the baby Abraham, but I can't do that now, can I?"

"She wouldn't take kindly to it." He grinned and ran a finger over her precious head.

"My great-gramma was Avery. What do you think of that?"

"I like it. Avery *Madison* Henry?" He questioned her with his eyes.

"Yes." Rebecca's face brightened. "My folks would appreciate havin' their name carried on."

His ma stretched out her arms. "May I hold her?"

"Course you can." Rebecca passed her over.

Caleb had nearly taken her himself. He watched Avery being rocked by her gramma, aching to hold the child.

"You'll get your turn," his ma said, grinning. "I can tell you want *her*."

Rebecca pushed herself up higher on the pillows. She groaned, straining.

Caleb readjusted the bedding and helped her get comfortable. Her eyes met his, and he kissed her without giving it a second thought.

His ma stood. "You all need some time alone." She extended Avery to him. "Get to know each other."

He took his daughter and cuddled her close to his chest. His ma walked out of the room.

Rebecca's eyes hadn't moved from him. "Are you happy, Caleb?"

"I reckon this is the happiest day a my life. I don't quite understand it. I mean—I know she ain't really mine, but it *feels* like she is."

Rebecca cupped a trembling hand to his face. "You're the only pa she'll ever know."

He turned into her touch, then kissed her fingers. The truth in her words drove in the very reason he'd made the decision to marry her.

Avery whimpered and her little mouth puckered.

"I need to feed her." Rebecca loosened the strings at the front of her gown and exposed herself.

Though he'd become her husband, Caleb didn't feel right looking and quickly turned his head.

She took Avery from him, and when he felt comfortable enough to look at them again, he saw a precious sight he'd never forget. Mother and child bonded together. Beautiful. Perfect.

*Mine.*

He'd taken his wedding vows to heart.

Only death would part them.

# CHAPTER 34

"Ma!" Caleb beat on her door.

She flung it open, eyes filled with fear. "The baby?"

"No. I reckon they're fine. But I want you to go in our room an' stay with them. Keep the door locked till I tell you to come out. Hear me?"

Commotion filled the corridor. Doors slammed. Frightened folks cried.

His ma grasped his arm. "What's happenin'?"

"Colonel Bartlett's mounted infantry." He bustled her across the hall and went with her into the room.

Rebecca sat in the rocker with their daughter, scarcely a week old. She rocked rapidly, trying to soothe the crying child.

His ma took the chair beside her. "Why are soldiers here *now*?"

"Word is the federalists got this war won. Mr. Iverson said he got wind a them burnin' down homes and pillagin' over in White Sulphur Springs. Reckon they're tryin' to show how tough they are. The folks there called on the Thomas Legion to help 'em defend their homes. They fought hard an' drove them Union soldiers here. I seen 'em gatherin' when I was at the farm an' came right home. They've made the hotel their base. It was all I could do to sneak in. Mr. Iverson seen me comin' an' told me what happened."

"Oh, dear Lord." His ma buried her face in her hands.

"I'm goin' back out to see what more I can learn." He kissed Rebecca's forehead. "Stay here an' take care a Avery."

Rebecca's frightened eyes held tears, but she nodded.

"I'll return soon as I can." He went out the door and didn't look back.

Mr. Iverson latched onto Caleb's arm the second he entered the hallway. "Come with me."

Caleb followed him out the back door.

"You best keep yourself hid," the man said. His head darted without stopping, taking in everything around him. "I heard Lee already surrendered, but some a the rebels don't wanna accept that the war is over. They set fires in the hills. Reckon to show these Unionists they ain't scared."

"Ain't there sumthin' *I* can do?"

"Yes. Take care a them women and your child, and stay unseen. I'll have my wife bring food to your room. Keep the door locked and pray the soldiers leave you be. I have plenty of other rooms they're occupying. Them Cherokee soldiers put the fear a God in them."

"The Cherokee are fightin'?"

"Yep. War paint an' all. They're part a the legion. Most of 'em sided with the rebels. Not sure how this is gonna play out."

Footsteps neared them.

"Get in your room," Mr. Iverson firmly said. "I'll distract whoever's comin'."

Without waiting for a response, the man hurried off, waving his arms.

Caleb rushed back inside to his family.

"Well?" his ma said.

"Nothin' I can do. We just gotta pray this don't last long." He rubbed his temples and told them everything he knew.

"Lee surrendered?" Rebecca rocked faster. "Then it should all be over."

"It should. But it ain't."

Avery continued to cry. He took her from Rebecca and swayed with her in his arms. "Hush, now. Pa's here." He kissed her sweet cheek.

The day drug on.

As promised, Mrs. Iverson came with food, fussing about how the soldiers were eating most everything in sight.

She stayed just long enough to leave their supper, but they couldn't have been more grateful.

"Maybe if the soldiers knew I'm the widow of one of their own," Rebecca said, "they'd be kind to us. We wouldn't have to be so scared."

Caleb huffed a breath. "You're married to a rebel now. Sumthin' they don't need to know."

"I'm tired a this war!" His ma pounded her fist on the arm of her chair. The baby startled and fussed harder. "We're *one* country. We never shoulda divided to begin with."

"Ma," Caleb intensely whispered. "You're scarin' Avery."

"Let me take her." Rebecca lifted her arms. "She may be hungry."

Caleb eased her into her ma's arms, then crossed to the window and peered out through the slit in the curtain. Men dressed in Union blue surrounded the hotel.

He'd not been this close to a company of enemy soldiers since he'd shot his brother. Once again, he felt cowardly. Hiding to keep himself from being killed. When he looked at his wife and child, he had an even more important reason to keep himself alive. If that meant humbling himself and staying behind a locked door, then so be it.

Sleep didn't come easy that night. He and Rebecca kept Avery between them on the bed, instead of putting her in the cradle.

His ma slept in the bed beside them, as she'd done before his arrival.

The following day carried on much like the last.

Caleb had begun to feel like a caged animal and prayed they'd not have to live this way for long.

Someone banged on the door.

Rebecca gasped, clutching Avery close to her breast.

"It's all right." Caleb held up a hand and motioned calm, then went to find out who'd knocked.

When he opened the door, Mr. Iverson stood there, tall, proud, and beaming. "They done surrendered."

"Who?"

"The rebels. Some a their high-ranked commanders came in wavin' a white flag. Seems they got wind the fightin's *really* over. Decided they all wanted to go home. Soldiers on both sides are leavin'. Left us with one hell of a mess, but at least they're goin'."

"We'll help you clean up." Caleb looked over his shoulder at his ma and Rebecca. "Won't we?"

They burst into happy tears and nodded.

"Thank you," Mr. Iverson said. "And thank God this blasted war has finally come to an end. Maybe we can get Waynesville back on its feet."

"We will." Caleb shook the man's hand. "We'll be out shortly an' you can tell us what to do."

The man dipped his head and walked away.

Caleb stood in the doorway, vacantly staring into nothingness. He'd never had a prayer answered so quickly. Then a much deeper realization hit hard.

*The war's over.*

Lily would expect to see him, though more than likely she'd already received his letter.

"What are you lookin' at, Caleb?" Rebecca asked.

"Nothin'." He went into the room and shut the door. "Absolutely *nothin'*. An' right now, that's a very good thing."

* * *

The mail bugle blew. Lily kept working on the quilt she was repairing. She wanted more than anything to sew a blanket for the baby, but how would she ever explain it?

Lucas jumped to his feet. "I'll be back." He raced out the door.

"He gets so excited 'bout the mail," their ma said. She sat across from Lily at the table doing her own mending. "We ain't had any since that wretched letter from my sister. Nothin' worth gettin' all happy over."

"Lucas likes to listen to Mrs. Quincy's gossip," Violet said from the sofa, where she was helping Horace and Isaac with their slates.

Their pa casually rocked in his chair. "Maybe he'll share sumthin' interestin' with us when he gets back. I could use a good story 'bout now."

Their ma grunted and tugged the needle through the fabric. "We've made up enough a our own to last a lifetime."

Lily couldn't keep from smiling. "Yes, we have. It was all for the good, right Ma?"

"I ain't never liked to lie. But yes, sometimes we do it to protect folks we love."

"Or aggravate those we don't," her pa added.

Lily laughed. "Maybe Aunt Helen wrote again."

"Doubt it." Her ma grumbled. "I ain't answered her last letter. She's probably given up on me."

They went back to their sewing projects and the house quieted once again. Aside from the squeak of the rocker, and an occasional question raised by one of the boys, the cabin held a sense of calm.

Minutes later, the door burst open.

"It's over!" Lucas practically danced into the room. "Lee surrendered, an' the war's over! Mrs. Quincy got word from the postman. No more fightin'. The North won."

Lily sighed with relief and set the quilt on the table.

*Caleb.*

"Thank the Lord," her ma said.

Horace and Isaac jumped up and joined Lucas, frolicking around the room. Lily doubted her littlest brothers understood why they were celebrating. Still, it was a beautiful sight to see.

"Caleb can rest easy now," her pa said. "I pray his ma took him in."

"Why wouldn't she?" Lily asked. "Mas always love their children. Maybe now, he'll come back an' see us again."

"Why?" her ma asked. "He don't belong here. If his ma took him in, that's where he should stay."

Lucas wandered close and eyed Lily like he had something else on his mind.

*Don't you dare tell them I love him.*

"Ma's right," he said. "We don't need him here. We took care a the wheat field just fine 'thout him."

"Yes, we did." Violet rose from the sofa, then came into the kitchen and sat beside Lily. "But Caleb said he'd come to see us. I'm sure he will." She smiled at Lily, who knew exactly what her sister was thinking.

*He'll come. He* has *to come.*

Lucas kicked at the floor. "Lily? Would you mind showin' me the way you set them rabbit traps? I can't seem to do it right."

"*Now?*"

He rapidly nodded.

"Fine." She scooted her chair back and pointed at the quilt. "I'm just gonna leave this here. I won't be gone long."

"Can I come, too?" Horace asked.

"No," Lucas snapped. "Stay here an' work your letters."

His abruptness briefly lifted their ma's eyes, then she shook her head and kept sewing. They were all used to Lucas acting out. Lily only agreed to go with him because she knew it had nothing to do with rabbits. His eyes told her something else. Most likely, he wanted to tease her about Caleb.

She trudged up the hillside, all the while thinking about the first time she'd brought Caleb here and showed him how capably she could skin a rabbit.

Lucas stayed right on her heels. "You can stop any time."

She spun to face him. "You don't wanna look at rabbit traps, do you?"

"Nope."

"Then what's this all 'bout?"

"Your beau. Least I figger that's who this letter's from." He withdrew an envelope he'd tucked down into his pants and waved it in front of her face. "Ain't no return address, but it's postmarked Waynesville. Ain't that where he lives?"

Her heart raced. "Yes." She grabbed at the thing, and he yanked it further away.

"I hid this from our folks, cuz it's addressed to *you*. Mrs. Quincy 'bout had a fit wonderin' who it's from."

"Did she open it?"

"Don't look like she did." He held it close to his face and Lily jerked it from his hand. "Hey!" He tried to snatch it back from her.

"What? It's mine." She pressed it to her heart.

"A *love* letter?" His lip curled and he grunted. "You *owe* me. An' one day, I'll come collectin'." He headed down the hill.

"You're horrid, Lucas Larsen!"

She waited till he'd gone out of sight, then hurried further up the hill and went to the burrow. It seemed like the right place to read Caleb's letter. Surely, he'd tell her when he was coming back.

But they'd only just found out the war had ended. He'd written the letter long before then.

Though she didn't go inside the burrow, she sat comfortably on the ground and leaned against the hillside, then carefully opened the envelope and pulled out the contents. The love swelling inside her grew simply from touching the paper he'd had his hands on. She held it close and read . . .

*My dearest Lily,*

*I don't know where to begin. A lot has happened since I arrived in Waynesville.*

*My heart is aching and it's all I can do to keep this pen on the paper.*

Lily paused and smiled, gazing into the beautiful woods. She fully understood his feelings. Love kept her aching, too.

*You know more about me than most anyone. I don't have to tell you how hard it was for me to come here and face my ma. I'll never get over the guilt I feel for what I done to Abraham.*

*When I told you about it, you accepted me with all my flaws. That meant everything to me. I'll never forget what we shared, and the love I felt for you, but something happened here I didn't expect.*

She set the page aside and forced herself to breathe. Something had gone terribly wrong, and she feared reading more. Why did he write the love he *felt*?

*Don't he still love me?*

Her hand trembled as she lifted the paper again and found her place.

*I'm sure you recall me mentioning Rebecca, Abraham's wife.*

*I made her a widow, and facing her was the hardest thing I ever done. Till I found her with child. You know how much I love children, and I couldn't bear the thought of the baby being born without a pa.*

*My ma told me about some Bible stories where the brother-in-law of a widow took her to himself, married her, and raised her children as his own. God wanted that for them, and once I searched my heart, I knew He wants it for me, too.*

Tears clouded Lily's vision. She wiped them away, yet nothing could erase the ache in her heart. It constricted so tight, she feared it would take her breath. She placed her hand atop her belly and the child Caleb didn't know existed.

*I plan to make Rebecca my wife. I know you and me had our own plans, but her baby will come any day now. If you think on it, you'll understand it's best I go on and marry her, so I can legally be the child's pa. I can't never bring Abraham back to life, but I can make amends for what I done by caring for his family.*

*The only thing wrong in all this is that I'm hurting you. I told my ma about you, and she asked me to search my heart and decide what was best. It wasn't easy, but I made up my mind.*

*I'm writing to tell you goodbye. Maybe I'm a coward for doing it in a letter. I'm sure you can understand why I can't be there. You'll probably hate me once you read this. That makes me hurt even more, because I swear, I'll always love you.*

*There's no one like you, Lily. Rebecca is a good, gentle woman with a heart of gold. In that way, you're similar. But she's soft. She needs someone to take care of her. You're the strongest woman I've ever known, and I'm sure in time you'll move on with your life and forget about me. You have the strength to go on, without having me to complicate everything.*

*Please forgive me for breaking my promise. I'm doing what I have to do.*

*With Love,*

*Caleb*

Lily doubled over and fell sideways onto the hard ground.

*No.*

*No.*

*No.*

She sobbed and shed so many tears, she soaked the ground. Her sweet Caleb had done what he thought best, but wouldn't he have made another choice if he'd known about *their* child?

*It ain't fair!*

By now he and Rebecca were probably married.

*God, what do I do?*

If God willed Caleb to Rebecca, what about *her*? Why would He leave her to fend for herself?

"I ain't that strong!" Her tears streamed and she shook her fists in the air, unsure whether she was angrier at God or Caleb.

Maybe if she'd been meek and coy, he would've come back to her—the helpless girl who couldn't fend for herself. But she'd *always* taken care of herself and everyone else.

She curled into a ball and shut her puffy, aching eyes.

"Lily?" Violet rushed up the hillside and knelt beside her. "Lily what happened? We were all gettin' worried. Lucas said he left you here. It's been over an hour."

"I wanna die." She cried harder.

"What?" Violet pulled her into her arms. "Don't talk that way. What did Lucas do to you?"

"He gave me this." She pulled the crumpled paper from underneath her and handed it to her sister. "It's from Caleb."

Violet's eyes darted over the pages. As she read she breathed harder and faster. When she finished, she slammed the letter down to the ground. "I hate him! How could he do this to you?" She lifted the pages and shook them. "Did he kill his own *brother*?"

Lily grabbed the letter from her and hugged it to herself. "I shouldn't a had you read it. He confided in me. They fought on different sides, an' Caleb shot him. He didn't know it was his brother, till it was too late. He hates himself for killin' him."

"It's no excuse for turnin' his back on *you*! He *had* you. You're carryin' his child. How can he walk away an' not look back?"

"He doesn't know 'bout the baby. If he did—"

"He'd be in a real mess, wouldn't he?" Violet spit out the words, then stood and paced. "I hate him for what he done. I ain't never gonna forgive him."

"Don't say that. He's a good man. He's doin' what he feels is right. His penance."

"Don't defend him, Lily! He took your chastity and walked away. What are you gonna do 'bout the baby now? Bring a bastard into this world?"

"Don't call it that!"

"It *will* be. A child born to an *unmarried* woman. You'll shame the family."

"Then, I'll go away somewhere . . ."

"Where? How will you get by?"

Lily's mind spun. Her head ached, but not as much as her heart. "I don't know." She burst out crying again.

"What's goin' on here?"

Lily's head snapped around to face her pa. "Oh, Pa!" She lunged for him and held onto his solid frame. "I don't know what to do."

"Tell me why you're cryin'."

"Caleb," Violet mumbled. "He wrote her a letter."

"Violet!" Lily snapped, still holding onto her pa. "Hush!"

He pushed her away, then took her face in his hand. "You have sumthin' you need to tell me?"

Lily placed both hands over her stomach. "I . . ." She *had* to tell. "I'm with child."

His face lost all its color. He stumbled backward and nearly fell. "That man had you?"

"Yessir. But it wasn't his doin'. I—"

"Wasn't his *doin*?" Hatred filled his eyes. "No man takes a woman what doesn't mean to."

"Pa . . . we love each other."

Violet grunted and Lily glared at her. She whipped around and put her back to her.

"Then why are you cryin'?" Her pa's words couldn't sound any colder. "What did he say in his letter?"

"It's hard to explain." She swallowed hard, but it did no good. "He . . . he's marryin' his brother's widow. She's with child, an' he felt the need to help them."

"Help *them*?" He tightened his fist. "What 'bout *you*?" His chest heaved. "I trusted him! Took him into our home. *Cared* for him! He slapped me in the face an' made me a fool! An' you . . ." His finger shook, pointing in Lily's face. "I'm *ashamed* a you!"

"Don't say that, Pa."

"No decent girl opens her legs for a man who ain't her husband!" His hand shot into the air and hovered quivering above her.

She cowered, expecting the blow.

Air hissed from his nostrils, but he didn't strike. He wrenched onto her arm and pulled her rapidly down the hillside. She stumbled, trying to keep pace. Violet stayed right behind them.

When they reached the cabin, he opened the door and pushed Lily inside. "Violet. Take your brothers outside."

"Yessir." She bustled the three boys out the door.

Lucas glanced back, shaking his head. The other two didn't hesitate. They knew it was best to be far from their pa when his eyes shot fire.

Her ma got up from her chair. Understandable worry furrowed her brow. "What's wrong, Buck?"

He leaned against the table, then pounded it with his fist. "Lily's with child."

"What?" Her ma clutched her breast, and dropped back into her seat. "Can't be."

Lily stood tall, doing all she could to wash away the shame. "I am, Ma."

"No." She opened her Bible and flipped through several pages. "You ain't."

"Ma." Lily pulled out the chair beside her. "It's Caleb's. I know I shouldn't a done it, but I can't change things now."

Her head lifted. "He's comin' back for you. Ain't he?"

"No. He's marryin' someone else."

"Lily." Her pa's tone hadn't calmed. "Go to your room. Your ma an' me need to talk."

"Yessir." She slowly stood, trudged across the floor, and shut herself up in her bedroom.

Completely numb, she lay on the bed and clutched the down pillow to her chest.

Low mumbling came from the other side of her door. Worse yet, she could tell her ma was crying.

Lily had never seen Violet so angry. Nor her pa. And in all her life, she'd never believed he'd want to hit her, yet she knew he did. Maybe she deserved to be slapped. After all, he was right. She'd behaved indecently. If she'd done the proper thing, she wouldn't be in this mess.

Her pa opened her door. "Come out. We've decided what to do."

She eased into a chair and set her trembling hands on the tabletop.

"When did it happen?" her ma asked, stone-faced.

Lily gulped. "On my birthday."

The woman's eyes flew open wide. "While your sister was strugglin' for every breath?" She fanned her face and rested her other hand on the Bible.

Her pa gazed upward as if thinking hard. "Reckon it'll come in November."

"Yessir."

His eyes narrowed, penetrating deeply into hers. "We ain't gonna have you disgrace this family."

"Are you sendin' me away?"

"No. You'll have the baby here."

"But—"

He held up his hand and she snapped her mouth shut.

"No one is to know 'bout you," he went on. "I'll swear Violet to secrecy. As for your brothers, they ain't gonna know. You'll keep it hid. An' when you get too big to hide it, we'll tell 'em you're ill. You'll stay in your room till it comes."

"But I don't understand. When it's born, they'll know I had it."

"They'll think your *ma* birthed it."

Lily looked from her pa to her ma, utterly confused.

Her ma sat tall in her chair. "That's right. I'll tell the boys *I'm* with child. They'll believe it. Your pa hasn't stopped talkin' 'bout how much he wants another son."

"But . . . You won't *show.* This ain't gonna work. 'Sides, I *want* my baby. I can't pretend it's my siblin'. It'll be *my* child."

Her ma pointed a stiff finger. "What you want don't matter. This is the only way we'll keep decency in this family. You know full well, if Harriet Quincy gets word of your *condition*, everyone in the cove will know. We won't allow you to put us through that kind a shame."

"Ma, this ain't what I want."

"As I said . . ." Her ma pushed the Bible toward her. "Your wants ain't bein' considered no more. They got you into this. You should be thankin' us for comin' up with a way to get you out of it."

Tears streamed down Lily's cheeks.

"Go to your room an' rest," her pa said. "I aim to have a word with Violet. An' since Lucas brought you that letter, I'll tell the boys Caleb wrote an' said he won't be comin' back. They don't need to know nothin' more than that."

"They'll wanna know *why*," Lily whispered, unable to make her words any louder. "They loved him."

"He misled every one of us. All they need to know is that he's livin' his life back where he belongs. They'll get over it once your ma an' me give them our *happy* news. Now, get on to your room."

Lily's legs wouldn't work. She tried to stand, but couldn't.

Her pa came to her side and lifted her to her feet, then guided her to the bedroom. "Think on this." He lifted her chin. His eyes had softened, and she no longer feared he'd lash out. Still, it didn't ease her pain. "We're doin' what's best for *all* of us. You'll understand once you're calm."

She fell onto the bed and shut her eyes, praying once she opened them again, she'd discover this had all been a nightmare.

# Chapter 35

Caleb walked to the farm, feeling more hopeful than he had in months.

Now that the war had ended, folks could start piecing their lives back together. It would take time, but determination drove him.

Each day, he checked in with Laura before going to the fields. Though he never went inside the house, she'd meet him at the door with a jug of water and a cloth bag that held some kind of sandwich and something she'd baked. Nothing nearly as good as Rebecca could make, but he graciously accepted whatever Laura gave him.

He knocked on the door.

When it opened, the enticing scent of bacon greeted him.

"Hey, Caleb." Laura smiled broadly. "Hungry?"

She wasn't holding his usual provisions. "*Sorta.*" He always arrived for work at sunrise and never ate beforehand. He had an awkward feeling she intended to invite him in.

"C'mon in an' have some breakfast. Got eggs, bacon, an' fresh-baked biscuits."

*Yep. Just as he'd suspected.*

Oddly, Laura was already dressed in a decent-looking garment, and she'd even brushed her hair. Surely, she couldn't be coming onto him again, could she?

Though inclined to decline, Caleb's stomach won his internal argument. "Thank you. Smells mighty good."

He followed her to the kitchen table. Every step brought back memories. The furnishings had changed, but the essence of his life remained. Memories lurked around every corner.

Her grandpa and the two boys were already at the table. The toddler sat in a high chair—his faced covered in egg.

Once Laura took her seat, Caleb sat in the remaining empty chair.

She handed him a basket of biscuits. "I made plenty. Got some preserves in that there jar, too."

"Thank you." He filled his plate and dug in.

Silence hovered while everyone ate, till her grandpa loudly cleared his throat.

Caleb looked at him, expecting him to speak, but the man eyed Laura.

"I know," she said, then set her fork down. "I got sumthin' to say."

*Oh, no. I'm out of a job.*

Now he understood. She acted kind, merely to let him go.

He sat tall and put a smile on his face. "I'm listenin'."

"Well." She took a quick drink of water. "As you know, the war's over."

"*Yes . . .*"

"Grampa an' me been strugglin' to make ends meet. We appreciate all the help you've given, an' your low expectations on pay." Another quick drink. "We're sure that come fall, we'll have a good crop a corn, thanks to you. But . . ."

"You hafta let me go, right?"

"N-*No.*" Her brow dipped low. "*We* wanna go."

"What?"

"We can't pay the mortgage. We got family in Kentucky who'll take us in. An' now that the fightin's stopped, it's safe to travel. I know you ain't got much a anythin' neither, but I also know how much this place means to you. An' what with a new wife an' all, reckon you could find a way to buy us out?"

His mouth dropped open and he sat there, speechless.

The old man gnawed on a piece of bacon, and the two boys barely made a sound.

Laura nervously chewed her bottom lip. "Well?"

"I'll find a way," he whispered as the reality sunk in.

It hit like a jolt of glory. He jumped up from his seat, ran around the table, and hugged her, almost knocking over her glass of water. "Thank you!"

Her eyes came close to popping from their sockets. "You're welcome."

He rushed back to his plate, shoved the remaining food into his mouth, and headed for the door. "I'm goin' home to tell Ma!" he shouted over his shoulder, then sped away.

* * *

Rebecca loved this time with sweet little Avery. For once, someone was dependent on *her*. Only *she* could feed her child. It gave her a new sense of purpose.

Though she'd offered to let Mrs. Henry take the rocker to her room, her dear mother-in-law had declined, stating Rebecca needed it more.

She was glad. It was the perfect place to nurse.

Avery seemed to enjoy the gentle swaying of the rocker. It nearly always put her to sleep. Rebecca adored watching her; bonded with their tender connection.

The door inched open and Caleb tiptoed into the room.

Though happy to see him, she couldn't understand why he'd come home so early. At least he had a smile on his face.

He cupped his hand over Avery's head, then bent down and kissed Rebecca's lips. "How'd you like to live in a real house?" he whispered.

"What?"

"The Templetons are movin' to Kentucky. They're givin' us the chance to buy them out."

"Can we?"

He knelt beside her, took her hand, and kissed it. "Yep. I already talked to Ma. She's makin' all the arrangements."

"So, we'll all live there together?"

"No." He stared downward, then lifted his eyes to meet hers. "Ma wants to stay here. Says she's comfortable an' wants *us* to go. Thinks it'll be good for you an' me to have our own place so we can make a life for ourselves."

Rebecca wanted to grab onto him and hold him so tight he'd scream. All her dreams were coming true. She raked her fingers through his thick hair. "Do you know how happy I am?"

"Happy as me?" His smile reached his ears.

She rapidly nodded.

He kissed her deeply, then stroked her cheek. "I'm gonna get the farm runnin' the way it used to. We'll get us a milk cow, an' some horses, an'—"

"Stop." She pressed her fingers to his lips. "Let's take it slow. We'll start with cleanin' up the place. From what you told me, it needs it."

"Yep. But are you feelin' up to it?"

"It's been two weeks, Caleb. I'm doin' fine." She held up a hand. "I need to switch her."

"Huh?"

She gestured to Avery. Since she was trying hard not to further embarrass her husband, she draped a small blanket over herself and the baby, then gently pulled her from her breast and moved her to the other.

Caleb remained close, eyeing her actions. "Why'd you do that? She looked right happy where she was."

"If she doesn't drink from both, one side gets too full. It hurts when that happens."

His face flushed red.

Rebecca softly giggled. "Caleb Henry, I'm your wife. I should be able to talk to you 'bout such things without you gettin' all flustered."

"I ain't. But you talkin' 'bout them—"

"They're only breasts. A part of me our baby appreciates right now."

He nodded, then donned an awkward grin and the crimson in his cheeks deepened.

She placed a hand behind his head and drew him close. "It's fine for *you* to admire them, too." She kissed him, and he let out a tiny whimper. A sound that both tickled and warmed her. One day, he'd have to get over his nervousness around her.

He stood upright. "I best get back to the farm an' decide what all we gotta do to get it ready."

"Remind me . . . How many bedrooms does your old house have?"

"Four."

"Good. Plenty a room for all our children." She locked eyes with him.

"All our children," he mumbled and headed out the door.

Rebecca stroked Avery's soft head. Her sweet child, and the treasure Abraham had left behind.

It would be several more weeks before she could be intimate with Caleb, but she longed for that kind of closeness with him. She feared he might have difficulty with it, knowing his brother had shared her bed. But she had no doubt she loved Caleb. Hopefully, he'd want her.

She might have to muster up some of her womanly wiles to ease him into it.

* * *

"Lily, you gotta stop cryin'." Violet lay down beside her on the bed and rubbed her back.

"I can't. Every time I think 'bout Caleb . . ." She blubbered out more tears. "It hurts thinkin' of him with some other woman."

"He's a *wretched* man."

Lily rolled onto her back and looked up at her sister. "Don't say that. Please? No matter what he chose to do, I still love 'im. An' he'll always be my baby's pa."

Violet's sad eyes studied Lily's face. "No, Lily. *Our* pa will raise this baby. You gotta get Caleb off your mind. You hafta let him go."

"I can't."

The room had grown nearly pitch black, but Lily couldn't sleep.

Violet pulled the blankets up high. "You'll make yourself sick if you keep actin' this way."

Though she was right, Lily couldn't help it.

Weeks had passed since she'd gotten Caleb's letter. Her folks had put their plan in motion, and her little brothers hadn't stopped talking about the new baby their ma was going to have. Of course, they wanted it to be a boy.

They explained away Lily's mourning as illness, so she'd stayed locked up in her room most of the time. That made her even more miserable.

Lucas's suspicious eyes worsened matters. The boy had smarts. If he put two and two together, he'd figure it all out. And if he did, Lily would owe him more for his silence.

She sniffled and shut her eyes. Maybe sleep would help.

* * *

Lily gasped and sat upright, making Violet startle. "What's wrong?"

Morning had come, but Lily remained in a dreamy daze. "I had a strange dream."

Violet readjusted her pillow and sat up facing her. "Tell me."

Lily closed her eyes, trying to picture every detail. Even as much as it pained her. "I was in the woods, an' there was this cocoon hangin' from a tree. Much bigger than any ordinary cocoon. 'Bout the size of a melon." The image came back clearly. "I stood like I was froze to the ground, and the thing cracked open. A green an' yellow butterfly poked a wing out one side. I got all excited 'bout seein' it an' how beautiful it was. But then, it fell to the ground, unable to fly." Her eyes opened wide and she took Violet's hands. "It only had *one* wing. It flopped around in the dirt till it died."

"That's a *horrid* dream."

Lily clutched her stomach. "What if there's sumthin' wrong with my baby? If the dream was a sign?"

"That's silly. But . . ." Her eyes formed into slits and she leered at Lily. "If you don't start takin' better care a yourself, sumthin' could go wrong. When *you* don't eat, your *baby* don't neither."

Lily swallowed hard and pushed back the covers. "You're right. I've been hurtin' my child. It ain't this baby's fault his folks is a mess. He deserves to be strong an' healthy." She stood and grabbed her robe.

"You think it's a boy?"

"Yep. Don't know why, but I do."

"Pa will be happy. It's what he wants."

Lily chose to ignore her remark. Acknowledging it only confirmed the inevitable. Her pa wanted the boy as his own, and her son would never know her as his ma.

# CHAPTER 36

Lily wandered through the garden, plucking the ripened vegetables. For now, just enough to add to the stew. She'd already skinned the rabbit.

In her fourth month, her belly had a slight bulge. Nothing truly noticeable. Still, she knew it was there and had made up her mind to keep herself healthy for the baby's benefit.

She kept her mind off Caleb by keeping her hands busy. Not only in the garden, but now that the family expected a coming baby, Lily could knit baby sweaters and booties without questions.

"Oh, dear," she muttered.

Mrs. Quincy headed their way.

Lily hurried into the cabin and set the basket of vegetables on the counter. "Harriet Quincy's comin'."

Her ma huffed, then sat at the kitchen table, pretending to read her Bible.

Lucas and her pa were out in the field, along with Violet, who'd taken a new interest in the farm. Lily and her ma would have to deal with the nosy woman themselves.

Horace brought his slate to Lily. "Should I draw Mrs. Quincy a picture?"

"That would be nice. What would you draw?"

"My new brother." The boy grinned.

Lily swallowed the lump in her throat. "That'd be fine." She smoothed his hair and nudged him toward the living room. Isaac plopped down beside him on the sofa. In no time at all both boys were laughing over the drawings Horace sketched.

Even though Lily expected it, the rap on the door caused her to jump.

"Settle down, girl," her ma mumbled. "An' keep your mind right."

"Yes'm." She opened the door.

Mrs. Quincy marched in. "Shame to see you all cooped up inside on such a glorious day. I simply *had* to come by." She looked down her nose at Lily's ma. "How are you feelin'?"

"Fine." Her ma casually shut the Bible. "Well as can be."

"I heard your news. Your boy told Jeremy you're expectin'." Mrs. Quincy crossed her arms. "Land sakes, Rose, haven't you lost enough babies already?"

*When will Lucas learn to keep his mouth shut?*

Her ma caressed the leather binding on the Good Book. "I ain't losin' this baby. I feel better than I did with the last few."

"Well, I pray for your sake you're right." She unfolded her arms, then clapped her hands together. "That's not the only reason I came by."

"Oh?" Her ma's head lifted higher.

"Services are startin' again this Sunday. Since the war's over, the preacher's returned to the cove." She glanced at Lily, then back at her ma. "Can I expect to see you all there?"

"Reckon so. It's high time we start comin' together again as a faithful congregation."

Mrs. Quincy folded her hands and smiled, then turned to Lily. "My dear, I've been right curious 'bout the letter you received. I should've come by sooner to ask, but didn't wanna be intrusive. Who do you know in Waynesville?"

Lily's mouth opened, but not a word came out. What could she say? She gaped at the woman like a struggling fish out of water.

"The letter came from Callie," her ma said in a tone completely undaunted.

Mrs. Quincy whipped back around the other direction. "Callie? I wouldn't think a girl like her could read let alone *write*."

"She can't. Somehow she found someone else to pen the letter."

"No wonder there was no return address. The girl's obviously still in hiding. But why write specifically to Lily?"

"Harriet." Lily's ma stood and fisted her hands on her hips. "Why you're so insistent on knowin' everythin' that goes on here is beyond me, but I'll tell you. Callie *bonded* with Lily. We thought Lily had made progress with that poor girl. In the end, we was wrong. Even so, Callie feels a kinship with her. She wanted Lily to know she was safe, but wouldn't be comin' back here again."

"Well, that's a blessin'. Reckon we shoulda notified the authorities the girl was in Waynesville. Why didn't you say sumthin'?"

"Cuz we'll never condemn Callie for defendin' Lily's purity." Her ma cleared her throat, then stood even taller.

Isaac tugged at Mrs. Quincy's skirt. "My ma is makin' me a baby brother."

The woman patted his head. "What 'bout a sister? Wouldn't that be nice?"

"Uh-uh. Girls ain't as much fun. They don't like frogs."

"Then I hope you get your brother." Mrs. Quincy walked toward the door. "I'll see you Sunday."

The instant she left the room, Lily finally breathed. "Everyone in the county will know 'bout your baby now, Ma."

"That they will." She dimly smiled, then went to the counter and started cleaning the vegetables.

Their house had always centered around the teachings of the Good Book, but the lies inside their small cabin could easily blow the roof off.

* * *

Every day the house looked better and better.

Caleb stood back and admired the curtains Rebecca had sewn. "I thought you said you couldn't do nothin' but bake?"

Rebecca circled him with her arms and cuddled against him. "I wasn't fully honest 'bout that. I have other talents." She tipped her head back and puckered for a kiss.

He happily obliged her.

They'd been in the house a little over a month, and it already felt like home again. Living with Rebecca seemed natural. Like something he'd done forever. Yet, he had one thing left to do. He doubted he'd ever be ready for it, but every night she'd become needier.

Her fingers danced across his chest. "Avery's sleepin'." Her touch grew more intense, as did the beat of his heart.

He ran his hand down her long silky hair and breathed her in. He swore she bathed in roses. She always smelled so good. "What do you want, Becca?"

She blinked slowly, then locked her eyes with his. "You know."

"I don't wanna hurt you." It'd been a good excuse for weeks, but he couldn't use it forever.

"You won't. I'm fine, an' our proper weddin' night is long overdue." She grasped his hand and led him to their bedroom.

His heart drummed harder with every step.

They'd managed to accumulate a decent amount of furnishings and were given the fine bed as a gift from the Iversons. Caleb had slept beside Rebecca every night since their wedding, but had scarcely laid a hand on her.

Every time he'd come close, an image of Lily came to mind, and he stopped. If he took Rebecca to himself, it would be his final betrayal of the woman he swore to love forever.

*But she's my wife.*

How could they carry on with a marriage without intimacy?

Though he loved Lily, as a man, he had *needs*. And the way Rebecca had been behaving lately showed she did, too. She deserved a complete husband. She'd done nothing but love him. Didn't he owe her the same respect?

They stood beside the bed saying nothing.

Rebecca stepped closer and tenderly rubbed his arm. "You're shakin' like a leaf. You don't have to be afraid. We'll just love on each other an' go slow."

She loosened the ties at the top of her gown and let it drop to the floor. With her eyes affixed to his, she removed her undergarments.

Barely a trace of her baby bulge remained. Her perfect curves only magnified her beautiful face. She climbed atop their bed and lay back.

The warmth of a late June evening kept away the need of blankets. Her body beckoned him, and his own reacted.

"It'll be fine, Caleb." She searched his face, then covered herself with a thin sheet.

Heat coursed through his veins. His hands shook all the while he undid his buttons. He'd never fully bared himself in front of her, but the longing in her eyes kept him going.

He dropped his drawers, then used his hands to cover himself.

She softly giggled. "I'm your wife. You don't have to be shy." She bade him to her with the bend of a single finger.

*The burrow.*

He lifted the sheet and climbed in beside her.

"That's better," she whispered, then cuddled into his shoulder. Her fingers strolled back and forth across his chest, and her black hair draped over both of them.

He tentatively put an arm around her.

She lifted her head. "Do you want me, Caleb?"

He swallowed hard. Would it be a lie? "Course I do."

"Then there's no need to be scared. I won't break, an' I promise, once we get started, it'll be beautiful."

That's what he was afraid of.

He couldn't do it. "Rebecca . . . what 'bout Abraham?"

"I had a feelin' that's what's been holdin' you back." She raked her fingers into his hair, soothing him with each gentle touch. "It's just you an' me now. You're not betrayin' your brother. I love *you*, Caleb, an' I want you so bad it hurts."

Her eyes locked with his, then she took hold of his hand and eased it onto her breast. So much larger than Lily's, but he attributed it to Avery. Even so, he couldn't deny he enjoyed the feel of it.

He tenderly caressed her, moving his hand from breast to breast.

"I love you," she whispered again and dotted his neck with kisses.

*Lily.*

He rolled her onto her back and kissed her with love and tenderness. He joined with her as if they'd always been one body. And maybe they had.

Her hands roamed over him with genuine, heart-felt affection. He let his own love flow free. Maybe his ma had been right. True love came with time. Gentle and pure, like Rebecca herself.

So why couldn't he erase Lily's image?

He kept his lips sealed, fearing he'd call out her name. Was he truly making love to Lily? His eyes remained closed and he could see her clearly. Her shimmering blonde hair on the pillow, and her large brown eyes begging him to love her.

"I love you," he muttered and kept moving.

He grasped onto Rebecca like his life's blood, he feared might trickle away. Her sensual sounds of pleasure hammered on his guilt. "I love you," she rasped and drew her nails lightly up his back.

He shivered. The sensation she created intensified every other feeling, until he couldn't hold back. He thrust harder and in a heated rush, released. His body shuddered and he rolled onto his back, breathing hard and hating himself at the same time.

Who had he betrayed more? His wife or Lily?

Rebecca let out a long, contented sigh and once again cuddled against him. "That was wonderful, Caleb." She smiled and caressed his chest, then rose up and kissed his lips. "You'll never have to be afraid to do this again." Her brows dipped low. "Did I feel good to you?"

He ran a single finger down the bridge of her nose. "Silly question."

Her beautiful smile elevated his guilt. "All I've ever wanted was to please you. I never dreamed I'd get the chance. Life has a funny way of workin' itself out."

"Yes, it does."

He drew her close and kissed the top of her head.

*She deserves better than me.*

If this was how he'd atone for his sins, then why did he still feel so ashamed?

*I won't never be able to let Lily go, that's why.*

He'd put on a false front. Like those silly buildings in every small town that tried to make themselves look bigger and better to every passerby.

All he could do was puff himself up, love his wife and daughter, and work the farm.

Maybe time would set him straight.

# CHAPTER 37

Lily had been locked away in her ma's bedroom for more than a month. Just like when Violet had been sick, their pa had been sent upstairs with the boys. They'd been told Lily suffered from complications of something *womanly.* And because they were used to their ma locking herself away weeks at a time for similar reasons, the boys merely shrugged and went on with their lives.

Lucas had fussed when Lily couldn't help harvest the corn, and complained more when she wasn't able to help sow the wheat. But their pa had purchased a horse and a mule to pull the plow, so her obnoxious brother learned how to manage it.

Violet helped with the other new livestock. It had become her responsibility to milk the cow and feed the chickens. They'd even gotten a rooster, and her pa promised Isaac a puppy in a few weeks from the litter of a neighbor's dog. It would be his Christmas present.

Life was looking up for everyone but Lily.

November had arrived and soon her baby would, too. She'd been having on and off pains all night.

Her ma entered the room, moaning and holding a hand against her lower back. When she shut the door, she stood upright and withdrew the large pillow from beneath her dress.

The woman had become an exceptional actress.

"I'll be glad when this baby comes," she grumbled.

"You? What 'bout me?" Lily tossed the blankets aside and exposed her enormous stomach. "How's it ever come out, Ma?"

"Painfully."

"Wonderful." She pulled the covers back up again. "What if there's complications? We can't get no one to help. Then everyone would know our secret."

"That's right. So you best be prayin' your delivery goes well."

"Oh!" A sharp pain shot through Lily's body like a knife.

"Hush. You want your brothers to hear?"

"I don't care." She pinched her eyes tight. "Oh, Ma, I think it might be time. That pain was much worse than others."

Her ma stuffed the pillow back in place and waddled out of the room. In mere moments, she returned with Violet.

"Oh!" Lily cried again. "It hurts."

"Hush!" Both women fussed.

"Violet." Their ma grasped her arm. "I want you to boil water. Gather plenty a rags an' get my sewin' scissors. Then, tell your pa an' your brothers I'm fixin' to have this baby."

"Yes'm." She turned to Lily. "You all right?"

"No." Lily clamped onto the edge of the quilt. "Do as Ma says."

Violet rapidly nodded, then hurried from the room.

The rocking chair had been brought into the bedroom in anticipation of the coming baby. Her ma pulled it up beside the bed. "Try to keep your yellin' down. I done my fair share when I birthed all a you, but—"

"Then let 'em think it's *you* yellin'." Lily panted out heavy breaths.

"Fine." She stood and pushed the blankets off Lily's legs. "I need to see how you're progressin'."

"You ever helped birth a baby before?"

"No. But I've had plenty." She gestured to Lily's gown. "Pull it up so I can see."

Her ma had seen her through every illness. Wiped her tears. Cleaned her cuts.

This was different. Embarrassment set in, and it was all she could do to abide by the woman's wishes.

The door creaked open and Lily quickly covered herself.

Violet came in with a handful of rags and shut the door behind her. "I'm heatin' the water."

"Good," their ma said. "Now come over here an' watch."

Violet's eyes widened. "Why?"

"So you'll know what happens if you get yourself tangled up with a man. You best learn from this."

Lily shook her head in disbelief, but her frustration was overshadowed by another pain. "Ugh." She clamped her mouth shut and scrunched her eyes together.

Her ma pushed aside the blankets once again. "Bend your knees an' open your legs."

"Oh, Ma." Her bluntness stung.

"Lily. This ain't no time for shyness." She took it upon herself to readjust Lily's legs, only to be met with a gush of water.

"Oh, lawdy," Violet muttered. "Ma, I can't . . ."

"You *will*." Every word came out in a raspy whisper. Their ma seemed to be doing all she could to keep up their ruse. She repositioned Violet at the foot of the bed. "Her water done broke."

Lily closed her eyes, panting hard. The pains came faster.

"Is that . . ." Violet's horrified-sounding voice reopened Lily's lids. She found her sweet sister pointing.

"Yep," their ma said. "The top a the baby's head."

"I don't feel so well." Violet dropped down onto the edge of the bed.

Lily shut out all that was happening around her and concentrated on what she needed to do.

*I'm havin' your baby, Caleb.*

She pictured his smile. His gorgeous brown eyes. His firm, strong body.

*That's what got me into all this.*

"Lily." Her ma's harsh whisper rasped loudly. "Next time you get a pain, *push*."

Lily bobbed her head.

The pain struck like lightning. Lily bore down with all her might.

*Caleb, it hurts!*

"Good girl. The head's through." Even whispering, her ma sounded almost giddy.

*She wants my baby.*

"Oh, Ma." Violet's interest had renewed. She stood and bent over, watching. "Look at all that hair."

Another pain, and another large push. Lily groaned and kept pushing through the contraction.

"Oh, my, my." Her ma had a smile like Lily hadn't seen in a great while, as she expelled the baby. "Your pa has the son he's been waitin' for."

"A boy?" Lily craned her neck to see.

Her ma wiped off the child with a cloth, then turned him over her arm and swatted his behind. He let out a squall.

The wee cry tugged at Lily's heart. She desperately wanted to hold him.

"Hand me the scissors, Violet." Their ma reached for them, then cut the cord and tied it off. "Go get the water. I need to clean up my baby."

"Yes'm."

"Ma?" Lily's heart wrenched tighter. "He's *my* baby."

"No, he ain't. We been over this, Lily. I've been struttin' around this cove the last four months wearin' a ridiculous pillow under my dress. This is your *brother*, Noah."

"*Noah*? You already named him?"

Her ma wiped at his face with the cloth. He continued to bawl. "That's right. Your pa an' me decided what to call our son."

"But *I* shoulda. Ma, he's my boy."

"No, he ain't!" Her eyes shot fire. "The sooner you let him go, the better."

Lily sunk back into the pillows. Tears instantly formed.

*I can't do this.*

Violet came in with a pan of water. "I told 'em it's a boy, Ma. Pa wants to see him."

"In a minute. Bring that pan over here."

Violet set it on the nightstand. Their ma dipped the rag, then wrung it out and ran it across Lily's crying baby.

Lily tried to sit upright. "Are you sure that water ain't too hot?"

"I know what I'm doin'." She wiped him down completely, then wrapped him in a blanket. "Violet, take Noah out to meet the rest a the family, then bring him back here so I can feed him."

"But Ma, *you* can't feed him."

"No, but they need to *think* I'm doin' it. Lily will feed him." She turned to Lily. "An' that's *all* you'll do for him. Once we can get him on cow's milk, your work will be done."

*My work?*

Violet looked at Lily with so much pity, her tears flowed faster. She took Noah into her arms and walked out of the room.

"Don't cry, Lily," her ma said. "One day you'll see that we done what was right for this family. Remember what I told you 'bout lies?"

"Yes'm. You tell them to protect those you love."

"That's right. An' you know your pa an' me will love that baby. Like we've loved all a you. An' you'll be able to go on with your life. Maybe even get married one day."

Lily's belly cramped. "It still hurts, Ma."

"It will. For a time." She dipped the rag again, and this time washed Lily.

* * *

"I love you," Lily whispered and kissed Noah's cheek. He had Caleb's dark hair and brown eyes. The most beautiful baby she'd ever seen.

He eagerly suckled. This was the only time she had with him. And sadly, she had to share it with her ma. Whenever he needed to nurse, her ma would ask her to join her in the bedroom. Fortunately, her brothers never questioned why she had to help their ma. They attributed her odd behavior as one of those *strange womanly things*.

The nighttime feedings were a little more complicated. When Noah cried from his cradle in her folks' bedroom, Lily would get out of bed and go to him. She'd change him, then sit in the rocker and feed him. The boys were none-the-wiser. During those feedings, her ma wouldn't bother to get out of bed. But Lily didn't mind. She wanted all the time in the world with her son.

The most painful moments were when Noah cried and either her pa or ma would rock him to sleep. If Lily tried to take him, she'd be shooed away.

The winter drug on. They tried all they could to break Lily's bond with Noah, never allowing her to touch him aside from the feedings. But he was in her heart, right beside his pa.

Day after day, Lily lost more of herself. Her spirit had been snuffed out. Her heart crushed with it.

Spring turned to summer, and her ma decided it was time to put Noah on cow's milk. She bound Lily's breasts to help dry up hers.

Lily's appetite plummeted—her will to live along with it.

They never even let her hold him anymore. And when they went to Sunday services, she had to stand idly by while her folks paraded her son around like a prize. She felt forgotten, and so alone.

How could this be best for her? By doing all they could to break a motherly bond, she wasn't even allowed to get close as a sister.

Lily sat on the sofa, clutching a pillow to herself and swaying back and forth. She stared at the cradle in the corner of the room where Noah lay sleeping.

"Violet," their pa said. "Take your brothers outside. Your ma an' me need to talk to Lily privately."

"Yessir." She shuffled the boys out the door.

This couldn't be good. The last time they'd had this kind of talk, they'd decided Lily's future and it had nearly broken her.

"Lily." Her pa pulled out a chair at the kitchen table. "Come over here an' sit."

She slowly stood and plodded over to the chair. Once she sat, she gazed blankly at the wood surface as they took their places beside her.

"What now?" she whispered. "I ain't got nothin' more to give."

"Sweetheart." Her pa lifted her chin. "You're shrivelin' away to nothin'. You'll die if you don't start eatin'."

"I can't eat. I feel dead inside."

Her ma drummed her fingers atop the Bible. "We're makin' a change. Sumthin' best for all concerned."

Lily glared at her. "You're always decidin' what's best, but you never ask how *I* feel. It's like you stopped carin' 'bout *me*. All you think 'bout is my baby."

Her ma ran her hand along Lily's hair. "It's because we *care* that we're helpin' you."

"How? Are you gonna give me Noah?"

Emotionless, the woman shook her head. "We're sendin' you away. So you can detach yourself an' start livin' your life."

"No." Tears bubbled up from deep inside her. "I don't wanna leave him."

"It's decided," her pa said. "I'm takin' you as far as Sevierville, then we'll be meetin' up with a man who's gonna take you the rest a the way."

"Rest a the way where?" She sniffled and kept crying. How could her heart shatter any further?

Her ma grasped her hand. "We're sendin' you to live with your Aunt Helen in St. Louis. I wrote an' told her you've been havin' some difficulties. Depression brought on by this ugly war. She's agreed to take you in."

"No!" Lily's anger replaced her tears. She jerked her hand away. "I won't go! I can't stand her." She looked to her pa for help. "You know what she's like. She's hateful an' mean. Don't send me there. Please, Pa?"

"You're goin'. Helen ain't so bad. She's family, an' she has the means to care for you. She'll see to it you learn how to be a proper young lady."

"*Proper*? You're punishin' me, ain't you?"

"No." Her ma spoke without feeling. "We're helpin' you, an' we're helpin' Noah, too."

"Only cuz you want me outta his life!" She hugged herself and rocked back and forth. "Why'd Aunt Helen even agree to this? She's ain't never lifted a finger for us!"

"Well, as she wrote in that letter last year, she'd do whatever she could for us, long as it wasn't givin' us money. I reckon she sees this as an opportunity to make good on her offer."

Lily stood and stared numbly at the table. Her life had stopped being her own the day she fell in love with Caleb Henry. She doubted she'd ever smile again. "When do I leave?"

"T'morra," her pa said.

She nodded, trudged to her room, and shut the door.

* * *

Lily hadn't slept at all. How could she when she had to leave everything and everyone she loved behind?

She packed all her clothes into a cloth knapsack along with her hairbrush and a few other personal items. Nothing that really mattered.

She hadn't cried since she'd shut the door on her folks. Her heart had gone cold. All she could do now was go through the motions. Part of her wished she could shrivel up and die and not have to face any of it anymore.

Caleb had felt that way, and she'd pushed him to grab onto life and stop feeling sorry for himself. She finally understood brokenness.

"Lily?" Violet came into the room and wrapped her arms around her, then started to cry. "I hate this. All of it. It just ain't right."

"Don't cry, Violet. Please?" Lily stepped away from her, then took hold of her hands. "You hafta promise me you'll watch over Noah. And you've gotta write me an' let me know everythin'. All right?"

"I will. But things ain't gonna be the same here with you gone. Can't you just get over your feelin's an' stay? Learn how to be his sister?"

"No. I can't." Lily sat down on the bed, and Violet took the place next to her. "Every time I look at him, I see my son, an' Caleb, too. It hurts sumthin' awful. Much as I hate to admit it, Ma an' Pa are right. I'll die if I stay here. Reckon I might even die by leavin'. But if that happens, least y'all won't hafta see it."

Violet's eyes drew open wide. "Don't say that. You gotta get yourself well an' come back home."

"It won't be anytime soon."

"I hate that Caleb Henry! It's all his fault this happened."

Lily took a tight hold of Violet's hand. "I've told you before, you *can't* hate him. He'll always be Noah's pa no matter what our folks say. And . . . don't be mad at me, but I'm never gonna stop lovin' him. I understand what he done, an' why he did it. But that don't make any a this simpler."

"Well, I'll *never* understand."

Lily peered deeply into her sister's eyes. "Try an' trust me 'bout all this. An' Violet . . . watch out for Lucas, too. I worry 'bout him, an' I'm afraid he's gonna be jealous a Noah. Jealousy can do ugly things."

Violet silently nodded.

Someone rapped on the door, then opened it a crack. "Time to go."

*Pa.*

Tears trickled down Violet's cheeks.

Lily stood and grabbed her bag, then walked toward the door. Violet followed.

When they got to the living room, their ma handed Lily her coat. "It ain't cold enough to wear it now, but it will be soon enough."

Horace and Isaac raced across the floor and latched onto Lily. Both were crying.

Lucas stood far away, hovering above the cradle. The sour look on his face roiled Lily's belly.

Violet walked over and scooped Noah into her arms, receiving a scowl from Lucas. She joined the rest of the family, close to Lily.

Having Noah so near brought a renewed ache to Lily's heart. "I'd like to hold him."

Her ma's eyes narrowed. "Fine. Take him to the front porch. You can hold him till your pa has everythin' loaded in the wagon."

"Yes'm."

The two boys stepped back as Violet passed Noah into Lily's arms. She held him close and carried him outside.

Birds chirped around them. The sun glistened overhead and warmed her, but not as much as the precious child near her breast. Her heart beat harder with each passing second.

"I'll always love you," she whispered and kissed his sweet cheek. "Someday, maybe you'll be old enough to know you're mine."

His beautiful brown eyes blinked and met hers. Her heart burst with so much love, it split in two. Nothing could ever stop this pain.

She wished time would stand still, but it seemed as if her pa loaded the wagon faster than ever. Even with only one hand.

Other than Lucas, the whole family gathered around her.

Isaac tugged at her skirt. "Do you like Noah more than me?"

She bent down to his level. "Course not. I love you all the same. I'm just sad I won't be able to see Noah grow up an' do things like take his first step, an' learn to talk. I watched you boys do all that an' more." It hurt saying every word.

"Why can't you stay?"

Lily glanced at her ma. "Cuz, I gotta go somewhere, so *I* can learn not to be so sad all the time. Aunt Helen said she'd help." She stroked Isaac's cheek. "Will you promise to teach Noah how to play marbles?"

"You gonna be gone that long?"

"I don't know."

Her ma laid a hand on her shoulder. "Don't be talkin' 'bout playin' marbles. You should have more sense, Lily. If that baby got hold a one now, he'd swallow it an' choke."

Lily slowly stood upright. "Yes'm. You're right."

Her ma stretched out her hands. "Give him to me."

The tightness in Lily's chest grew, and she nearly crumbled to the ground. With trembling arms, she passed over her son.

Her ma drew him in close and smiled. "That's my boy." She kissed his forehead. "Lily, say goodbye to your brothers."

She hugged Isaac and Horace a final time, but couldn't utter a word.

Her ma motioned to the front door. "You boys go inside with Lucas. Lily hasta leave."

They hesitated, but when their ma gave them a stern gaze, they went in.

"I guess Lucas didn't wanna tell me goodbye," Lily said. "I reckon he's mad cuz I won't be helpin' with the farm anymore."

"Reckon so," her ma said. "But he's gotta learn how to take on the responsibilities of a man someday, an' he might as well start now."

They headed for the wagon. Her pa was already up in the seat holding the reins. "Best be goin'. We got a ways to travel."

Violet latched onto Lily. "I'll write, like I promised. But please, swear to me you'll take care a yourself."

"I'll try." Lily climbed up onto the seat. Her ma wandered close enough that Lily was able to reach out and touch Noah a final time.

But she'd barely laid a hand on him when her ma took hold of it and stopped her. "This is for the best. One day, you'll realize it. We only done it cuz we love you. Remember that."

*Love should never hurt like this.*

Her pa popped the reins and the wagon jerked. The capable mule would take them to Sevierville, then someone unknown would be waiting to take her further.

Lily had never been out of the state before. It had always been Violet who wanted to leave Cades Cove and see what lay beyond. Lily had been content to live out her life in her beautiful cove.

Yet life had turned out to be something other than she'd ever envisioned. She'd thought when the war ended, all would be well.

She couldn't have been more wrong.

# ACKNOWLEDGMENTS


For more than twenty years, my husband and I have spent our wedding anniversaries in the Smoky Mountains. We love to stay in Gatlinburg and Pigeon Forge, but no matter where we spend our nights, we always journey into the mountains to visit Cades Cove.

If you've never been there, I highly recommend that you put it on your list of places to go. I fell in love with the cove and its rich history. There's a one-way road that loops through it, dotted with many of the original homestead cabins. You'll even find a mill, several churches, and other interesting buildings to explore. You're sure to see deer and maybe even a bear or two. Now that Cades Cove is a national park, the animals are protected and roam freely.

When I learned about the difficulties the people in the cove experienced during the Civil War, I was drawn to write about it. I hope I captured the essence of the lives of the families who inhabited the land, before selling it to the state to become the park it is today.

When you go there, you'll step back in time and get a feel for what it was like living off the land. More than that, you'll appreciate the incredible beauty of the valley and the mountains surrounding it. It's truly breathtaking.

I enjoyed starting this new saga and hope you'll fall in love with the characters as much as I have. Though the people in this book are fictitious, their experiences are similar to what folks of the cove went through. Their lives weren't easy by any means, but they worked hard and did all they could to make the best of things.

Thank you to my editor, Cindy Brannam, for working with me on this new project! I'd also like to thank the other members of my creative team; Rae Monet for the beautiful cover design, Karen Duvall for the back-cover setup, and Jesse Gordon for formatting. They're all amazing and wonderful to work with!

I'd like to thank my three Beta readers for this project—Joy Dent, Fred Frazier, and Diane Gardner. Joy and Diane gave me some helpful input and suggestions, as well as encouragement and interest in the storyline that definitely helped, too. Fred was my Civil War expert, who kept me on track with war-related details. I highly appreciate his invaluable knowledge.

A special thank you goes out to my dad, Bob Launhardt. He grew up on a farm in Illinois, and I picked his brain over everything that had to do with crops. He has many interesting stories to tell, and I hope one day, he'll write his memoirs.

Thank YOU for reading this book! I appreciate your feedback and reviews, and I'd love to hear from you. It's so much fun to share these historical journeys. As my website states: In the footsteps of the past, we, too, shall walk.

God bless!

# Coming Soon!

## *Hushed into Silence, Smoky Mountain Secrets Saga, Book 2*

Lily Larsen is given no choice but to leave her beloved home in Cades Cove, Tennessee. She's sent to St. Louis to live with her uppity aunt, who's determined to turn Lily into a *proper* young woman.

Brokenhearted, Lily succumbs to her aunt and uncle's odd ways, though she can't understand why her estranged relatives suddenly care about her. She's schooled in etiquette and groomed for the purpose of marrying into wealth. However, she remains guarded, fearing that her secrets will be discovered and ruin any chance for happiness.

Violet Larsen desperately misses her beloved sister. She carries the burden of family secrets and wishes that *she'd* been the one sent away. Her feelings change when a childhood friend returns from war. His battle scars are evident, but she's determined to help him mend his body and more importantly, his heart.

Caleb and Rebecca Henry struggle with a marriage that should be happy. They love each other and enjoy raising their beautiful baby girl, yet something's missing. Caleb knows exactly why they're having difficulties, but if he tells his wife the truth, it could ruin everything.

Secrets abound. Fear keeps everyone hushed into silence.

If you enjoyed *Whispers from the Cove,* you may want to read Jeanne Hardt's other historical saga, the *Southern Secrets Saga!* Here's a bit about book one . . .

# *Deceptions*

A little more than six years have passed since the end of the War Between the States, and life in Mobile, Alabama isn't easy.

Claire Montgomery is twenty-five and unmarried. After years of listening to her mama's caution about men, she's determined to stay single. Until Dr. Andrew Fletcher arrives in her little town on the bay and she's irresistibly smitten.

Andrew tends to the elite at Mobile City Hospital, but also cares for the poor Negroes in a less desirable part of the city. Despite criticism from the hospital administrator, he's determined to stand by his principles and help anyone in need. Regardless of the color of their skin.

Their whirlwind romance is quickly followed by a wedding proposal. But Claire's world crashes around her when she discovers a painful truth. With no choice but to run away, she leaves Mobile and soon realizes she's carrying his child.

Every decision Claire makes changes the lives of those she loves. The secrets and deceptions she creates blur the line between lies and truth, until she can't discern one from the other.

https://www.amazon.com/dp/B0139LASFS

Other titles in the SOUTHERN SECRETS SAGA:

*Consequences*
*Desires*
*Incivilities*
*Revelations*
*Misconceptions*
*Redemption*

Step back in time even further and travel by steamboat on the Mississippi River, in the *River Romance* series by Jeanne Hardt!

## *Marked*
## *River Romance, Book 1*

Cora Craighead wants more than anything to leave Plum Point, Arkansas, aboard one of the fantastic steamboats that pass by her rundown home on the Mississippi River. She's certain there's more to life out there...*somewhere.* Besides, anything has to be better than living with her pa, who spends his days and nights drinking and gambling.

Douglas Denton grew up on one of the wealthiest estates in Memphis, Tennessee. Life filled with parties, expensive clothing, and proper English never suited him. He longs for simplicity and a woman with a pure heart—not one who craves his money. Cora is that and more, but she belongs to someone else.

Cora finally gets her wish, only to be taken down a road of strife, uncertainty, and mysterious prophecies. When she's finally discovered again by Douglas, she's a widow, fearing for her life and that of her newborn child and blind companion.

Full of emotions, family secrets, and the search for true love, you'll find it's not just the cards that are marked.



Other books in the *River Romance* series:

*Tainted*

*Forgotten*

# Another Southern Historical by Jeanne Hardt!

## *From the Ashes of Atlanta*

After losing his Atlanta home and family to the war, Confederate soldier, Jeb Carter, somehow wakes up in a Boston hospital. Alone, desperate, and with a badly broken leg, he pretends to be mute to save himself from those he hates—Yankees.

Gwen Abbott, a student at Boston Women's Medical College, is elated when she's allowed to study under the guidance of a prominent doctor at Massachusetts General. While forced into a courtship with a man she can scarcely tolerate, her thoughts are consumed with their mysterious new patient. If only he could talk.

Two strangers from different worlds, joined by fate. Perhaps love can speak without words and win a war without a single shot being fired.

http://www.amazon.com/dp/B00PB84TTO

# Contemporary Novels by Jeanne Hardt

## *A Golden Life*

In the beautiful mountain setting of Gatlinburg, Tennessee, something unusual is about to happen…

Traci Oliver may be a best-selling romance author, but for the first time in her writing career, she can't type a word on the blank page. Book number fifty is supposed to be her best ever—her *golden* book—but inspiration joined her husband in the grave. How can she write about love with a shattered heart?

At the precise moment of the anniversary of his death, a knock on her door changes everything.

Characters from her books take on human form and tell her they've come to help her. Of course, she doubts her sanity. Are they real, or has she lost her mind? When she lands smack dab in the middle of one of her own love scenes, she assumes the latter.

Her doctor says grieving is a process, but she never dreamed that part of the process would bring her heroes to life. She wonders if all people experience this kind of thing, or is it a weird phenomenon reserved solely for romance writers? Truthfully, the only hero she wants is her husband, and she can never be with him again.

Or maybe she can…

http://www.amazon.com/dp/B017Z6CREI

## *He's in My Dreams*

Amber's just seventeen, but *wants* to die. With no chance of remission, she's tired of pain.

Regret makes her even more miserable. She's never been in love. Never had that first kiss. She can't even imagine what it would feel like.

Her mom is so bitter about her own past, she refuses to answer Amber's questions. About men. About sex. And most importantly, about what it's like to fall in love.

Then Amber meets Ryder, and everything changes. He's exactly what she'd hoped for in a guy. Not only is he funny, smart, and kind, he's better looking than any actor she's seen on TV. When she's with him, she forgets her pain. He makes her want to live again.

There's just one problem with her newfound love. He exists only in her dreams.

For more information about Jeanne's books,
check out the links below:

www.facebook.com/JEANNEHARDTAUTHOR
www.jeannehardt.com
www.amazon.com/author/jeannehardt
www.goodreads.com/jeannehardt

Made in the USA
Lexington, KY
09 May 2017